Waiting for Tonight
a novel

Darren Tomalty

DEDICATION

For Brian

ACKNOWLEDGMENTS

This is a work of fiction. Names, characters, photographs, places, events and incidents are either the products of the author's wild imagination or used in a fictitious manner.

Thank you to
Brian Sastry, Melanie Harris,
Bramwell Pemberton, Erin McLaughlin,
Richard Pinnock, Marjorie Wilby
Alannah Myles, Pauline Nottingham,
Thomas Haivarlis, Rychard Bannerman
Martina Vuksinic, Laura Kennedy
for Judy and Dennis Sheppard

Cover design; Darren Tomalty
Photographs by Brian Sastry
Author photograph by Heidi Zeiger Photography

4

CONTENTS

Darren Tomalty

PROLOGUE

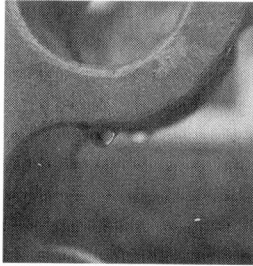

Montage of Sick

[A robotic voice emitted from *shit* speakers]

"If there are any White Supremacists reading this, I have a message for you: You will find no fulfillment in your ideology. Your hate will never be satisfied and your anger will never subside. I encourage you to find peace and mercy in the only place where it is authentic and unending. That is in our Lord and..."

Fr. William Aitcheson [2]

[I'm sorry, your call has been disconnected; please press *6 AT&T wireless for assistance]

In grade nine math, Eunice Johnston's teacher Mr. Osborne kept an aqua-blue budgie in a cage near the front window. While Mr. Osborne wrote formulas on the board, his back to class, Terrence Battle one of the slick boys took the bird from its cage and effortlessly broke its neck. He tossed it to the floor and stepped on it, forcing out bloody goo like toothpaste from its tube. It smeared Terrence's nice white Nike treads.

The students watched in silence.

The ginger haired forty-something teacher perhaps sensing a disturbance turned to scan the room with his ice cold stare. He marched over and stood before Terrence.

Terrence looked at Mr. Osborne with a *whatcha gonna do about it* smirk, his metallic grill showing from inside his mouth.

Mr. Osborne placed his two large hands around Terrence's African American neck and sealed his windpipe closed forever.

The students remained silent with their mouths agape.

Terrence's metallic grill was no longer visible as he slumped to the ground. He was deader than a doornail.

Moments later the door opened. A Black Panther in full regalia sporting a dark beret, a leather trench coat and kickass boots entered the classroom. He cocked his .38 shotgun and aimed it at Mr. Osborne. Then fired enough shots to blow Mr. Osborne to smithereens.

"I cannot make myself believe that God wanted me to hate. I've seen such hate on the faces of too many sheriffs in the South. Our oppressors have used violence. Our oppressors have used hatred. Our oppressors have used rifles and guns. I'm not going to stoop to their level. We have a power that can't be found in Molotov cocktails."

Martin Luther King Jr.

[In robotic voice]

"Almighty God created the races white, black, yellow and red placing them on separate continents. Except with man's interference with his arrangement there would be no cause for such marriages. The fact he separated the races shows he did not intend for races to mix."

Chief Justice Warren [3]

Eunice prayed on her hands and knees while rocking back and forth. Tears seared her cheeks, "Forgive them for they know not what they do... but you know what YOU did. YOU changed our lives FOREVER! As long as I live I vow to never rest while the weak suffers."
[Crackling noise blared from the too-loud P.A.]

"The images from Birmingham embarrass America! But for those who have repented from their destructive past, these images should bring us to our knees in prayer. Racists have polluted minds, twisted by an ideology that reinforces the false belief that they are superior to others."

Fr. William Aitcheson [2]

Eunice woke in the middle of the night to the sound of *snap, crackle and pop* from a bonfire just outside her bedroom window. She got out of bed to take a look. From her second floor window she saw a ten-foot cross burning on her Columbia Street lawn. She heard her parents, Martha and Curtis none-the-wiser snoring in their master bedroom.

Earlier Eunice had witnessed the murder of a black boy in her math class by a White Supremacist. She was still numb wondering how the Black Panther had been so swiftly detained for murder and how the *klan* knew she'd witnessed it.

In her black slip dress and ballet slippers Martha ran downstairs and out the front door. She tripped to the ground falling on her stomach. The heat of the cross burned behind her back. She picked herself up and made a bee-line toward the First Street Baptist Church.

She would hide there until she mustered enough courage to file a police report. She prayed Aunt Angela would be there when she arrived.

"Eunice Johnston is obsessive, bordering on psychopathy. She demonstrates a complete inability to maintain human relationships due to her passion for assisting the maligned and in turn jeopardizing any human relationship she has ever had."

Dr. Lynch [top-notch headshrinker]

BOOK I

1990-1995

Montgomery, Alabama

Alabama was known for many things but not many outside the realm of the racial divide between blacks and whites. The capital city of Montgomery had been best known as the *cradle of the confederacy* and home to the first US White House.

Montgomery was the birthplace of Civil Rights, the march on Selma with Martin Luther King Jr. and the place Rosa Parks stood up for herself on that infamous bus ride.

Now *that* was a history to be proud of.

Not so amazing were the grim reminders of the painful past. Practically every street in Montgomery, every church and every historic landmark held nostalgic tales of infamy. For townsfolk there were many lesser-known horrific facts;

You see, that there's the tree where they lynched Gator in '58. That's the house where one of the seven men who raped Recy Taylor lived. I'm not saying we don't have crazy whites and blacks saying racist stuff but they usually live deep in the forest.

Montgomery's historic downtown had become run down and less than appealing with storefronts now decorated with desperate and hungry people, many altered by the effects of invisible crack-pipe smoke. No right-minded tourist had browsed this part of the *Deep South* in years and years.

The general consensus of upstanding Alabamians was; if you were white, the west and south side were to be avoided at all cost and if you were black, good luck finding a job or place to live. "Most of the whites have moved out to Pike Road where they paid a pretty penny for them houses," a store clerk said.

Some thought it was due to a bad attitude that black folks still blamed white folks for slavery 'when no black or white person alive today had owned or been a slave.'

"It's juvenile and ludicrous I say! My family goes back 150 years and we never owned a slave. I don't know why *they* are so hung up on it!" said a white Anglo-Saxon, as he spit his Shoals tobacco across the porch floor.

Rarely was it mentioned that the output of slavery was far beyond the human to human business deal. That all systems, policies and laws had been implemented with a *slavery-is-okay* mindset. That racism was the firm bedrock of America. The culture functioning on the belief that one beating human heart was superior to another. For so long the US façade had been pretty on the outside yet was being destroyed by termites on the inside.

It was America's precarious house of cards.

Eunice Johnston lived with her parents in a bungalow [some called it a shack] on low-income Columbia Street. Her mother Martha was an elegant but frail white woman, while her father Curtis was a hardworking barrel-chested black man.

Eunice guessed her neighborhood would have been called a suburb if it were outside the city like Pike Road was with its cookie-cutter likeness. Yet, she'd never seen her type of house with its crooked window shutters and leaking roof, on TV except maybe surrounded by red and blue police lights on *COPS.*

After WWII American real estate zones had been established across the country assigning ratings based on a home's proximity to trains, roads and schools. The output was captured on a special red lined map which translated to property value. If an area went from unlined to red lined its worth sank like a stone to the bottom of a sewer.

Three guesses as to who the predominant populations of red lined areas belonged to?

The black communities of major U.S. cities, thus giving birth to the ghettos known today. Concentrated areas of poor racially segregated people had not been lumped together before the red lining business.

When a black family came house hunting the white folks got nervous. If they succeeded in their purchase it was inevitable the neighborhood would be red lined. *They won't be happy until they turn this into a ghetto.* Red lined maps propelled terror and drove fire sale prices in what real estate experts called block busting.

Montgomery had many red lines on its map.

The Johnston's weren't wealthy by any stretch but their modest home sat amongst some of the richest history in the South. Nearby stood the long abandoned Holt Street Baptist Church, the meeting place for the community during the Bus Riders Boycott and the first mass meetings to protest the arrest of Rosa Parks.

Eunice's parents had been well connected to Civil Rights up North and had affiliations to the Black Panther Party. Curtis had been involved in organizing breakfasts for underprivileged school children.

Eunice had grown up hearing all kinds of neat stories. For years she'd heard her father recite stories word-for-word adding charming pauses and sly winks in her direction. She loved his stories but as she got older she'd only smile and nod as he read them to the famous movement friends who would drop in to socialize.

With her parents being interracial in the South, Eunice was accustomed to a certain amount of attention paid to them. It was rare they would go unnoticed at a shopping mall or family restaurant.

Alabama had a nasty penchant for racism to say the least. It would become the last state in the country to overturn the ban on interracial marriage.

In the 1990s, polls in Old South states showed a quarter of people were opposed to marriage between blacks and whites. Later still, when a poll asked if interracial marriage should be illegal, 46% thought so and 14% weren't sure. (1)

An amazing number of Alabamians felt this way.

In the late 1950s, a seventeen year old Mildred and her childhood sweetheart, Richard 23, drove 90 miles north to marry in Washington, D.C. because interracial marriage was illegal in Virginia.

Upon return they were promptly arrested and charged with unlawful cohabitation because their marriage certificate was not recognized as valid.

They plead guilty. The judge sentenced them to one year in prison or the choice to leave the state for the next 25 years. Living together unmarried in a 'loving' relationship was still illegal in some states. This was in America. [4]

Eunice imagined the Loving's were her parents. She knew Martha and Curtis had gone through *stuff* back in their day but hadn't paid much attention to detail until she learned the Loving story in school.

Alabama was all Eunice knew so when she saw evidence of progress on TV she took it with a grain of salt. She guessed the best was yet to come for Montgomery!

It was a well-known fact; *Alabama don't take kindly to criticism from outsiders.* Even songs had been written about it. After *Neil Young* wrote about slavery and segregation on the songs *Alabama* and *Southern Man;* Southern rock band *Lynyrd Skynyrd* responded in kind with the more upbeat and radio friendly *Sweet Home Alabama.*

Alabamians official motto was *we dare defend our rights* but for those who had lived their whole lives there, the real motto was something like w*e shall not be told what to do.* That suited Eunice just fine because she didn't like being told what to do either!

Her first calling had been a fashion stylist and makeup artist. She spent hours working on her blond-haired Mattel bust of Barbie. She perfected fluorescent hair color techniques and elaborate braid work. However, her dream had dwindled recently, since she thought women of color should be encouraged to wear their hair natural.

"Sure, that's easy for you to say Eunice. You've got good hair. It's loose and wavy, especially when it's all grown out like that," the ladies at mother's choir practice had said.

Eunice inherited her father's brown hair and curls mixed with her mother's fine hair giving her looser ringlet curls. Martha said her own hair was so fine she feared losing it altogether. Sometimes mother straightened her hair and sometimes Eunice wore it like *Orphan Annie* by adding a colorful bandana.

Her aspirations evolved as she got older with the inclination to be a singer. Ever since that day she recorded her voice singing in the shower she knew she was way better than those contestants on idol shows.

When she was about 7 years old she felt compelled to articulate her thoughts about life to someone. She tried with Martha but could never muster the exact words to convey the feeling of not fitting in, "Mummy, I'm not the right something... I don't know,' then she would just stop.

Her apprehension stemmed from rarely feeling secure in herself. She had only felt peaceful when she had a quiet place alone. The exact childhood timing was a blur as logical thinking took center stage and emotion took the back burner. There was no rational time to think about feelings and she wasn't convinced feelings were a real *thing* anyhow.

Eunice intuitively saw the world as a Tetris game where people's moods touched down in front of her. After a while, she realized it was best not to assume the rest of the world thought like her. To assume was to imply she'd had the foresight but she hadn't. She had a knack for working through plausibility in her mind before making decisions.

Therefore, it was easy to see problems in other people's arguments. Most people who knew her didn't want to hear her opinions.

She never felt cheated though. It was fine vicariously absorbing peoples pitiful emotions. She'd size them up, draw a conclusion and secretly hold onto their pain making her feel superior.

She had grown so accustomed to seeing things through everyone else's perspective, she lacked the confidence to reveal her own unique view. She'd be taken aback if people reacted negatively about her findings.

Didn't everyone think of every fucking angle too? And why the fuck do I have to wait around for them to catch up? Out of pity or sheer exhaustion, by the time she started school she had accepted dumbing herself down to fit in.

Eunice identified with her black heritage most circumstances but gave up when it came to her father's family in Georgia. They loved her dearly but were hung up on percentages. Daddy's family thought she was far too pale to be considered black, "Oh no dear, you're our special princess," Grandma Cora said.

When she was with them she was free to embrace her real self in a way that wasn't always possible anywhere else. They expressed opinions all day but practiced *live and let live.*

The most important thing being biracial taught her was she had no right to question the identity of other people and wished everyone else had lived by that standard.

Her mother's family in Montreal didn't count as she didn't remember ever meeting them, although mother insisted that she had once. In the context of white people, Eunice's curly hair, darker skin and freckled nose stuck out among the blond, blue eyed set.

Whatever her racial specifications were, being a unique and attractive girl may well have carried her through many storms.

Martha and Curtis Johnston

The history of the Johnston household was patchy at best. Martha and Curtis could manage a long while without disturbance but Eunice would never say her family had been close knit growing up.

When Martha and Curtis arrived in Montgomery circa 1970, they had been selective about what church they would belong to, given their mixed race. Churches were suspicious of the connections shown on Curtis' credentials from New York, Atlanta and Kansas City all the way down highway 61 to New Orleans. He had known some of the liveliest characters.

Church officials had questions on why he, with his U.S. Navy success up north, would choose to move his white wife and no children south. The South was MLK land, *Gone With The Wind,* antebellum pillars, segregation, peach cobbler, rednecks, Christians and the *klan.*

One could reason he was simply up to no good.

Once accepted by First Baptist the Johnston's were loyal ever since. "It was a good thing too! We were shown the ropes on dealing with *dumbass* country boy antics, rednecks, neo Nazis and *klan* enamored by exciting self-promotion rallies. We learned white folk didn't mess with the black folk of First Baptist, no Sir-ee, Bob!" mother had said.

The so-called supremacists and *klan* hobbyists were ignorant to progress and kept oblivious on purpose. For decades Montgomery had enjoyed relative harmony with unofficial laws like *don't ask, don't tell* and *stick to your own kind* which only kept people apart.

It was called voluntary segregation to scholars but to Eunice it was called *the way things were.* How could she stick to her own kind? How could she trust anyone's opinion or advice? It left her in a conundrum of which side of the fence she should lay down roots.

Curtis a former Navy Ensign now worked at Berry Plastics a factory known for making freezer bags, ice cube trays, brooms and other cleaning equipment. He would bring home wonderful multi-colored plastic brushes and other goodies Eunice could add to her trunk of science experiments.

He didn't complain about work except he despised carpooling to Gunter Park with a few other fellows. He left mornings to avoid traffic on the single lane highway out of town. He said he fantasized about honking a foghorn at the slow *idiot* drivers who tailgated but wouldn't pass. She would giggle at how he could spin gripes into entertainment.

Eventually he became plant manager and she only saw him on weekends except one time he took her to work with him. She watched while he tested the boiler water by reading how the little vials changed color. She imagined him as the actual wizard in *Wizard of Oz*! He had an office overlooking plant operations below. On the wall was a girly calendar and locomotive train poster, his desk covered in paperwork and plastic brush prototypes. His colleague Nelson stopped in to shoot the breeze. Eunice thought he sounded like he was a character from *Mary Poppins* but later discovering he was South African.

On lucid days Martha told stories of her old life which gave Eunice a glimpse of how her skin had toughened up after moving south.

Martha was no longer the arrogant girl too good to work in factories like her alcoholic mother. Instead she'd developed quick thinking and practicality in life's challenges. After meeting Curtis she left Montreal and set up their home in Harlem almost overnight. Martha said if she had learned anything in the South, it was that heat slowed down the pace of life to a crawl.

After a decade or so in New York they left in a beaten up Dodge. Martha wasn't exactly welcomed by Curtis' folks in Georgia. "His momma was fit to be tied. She'd tell us point blank, 'You'se kids better think about moving on from here lickety split!' And you know what Eunice? She had fear in her voice. Afraid of what people would think. Although your father claimed she was a loving woman, my first impression was she was rude and irrational. She didn't want any trouble," Martha said.

"It was because you were white, right mother?" Eunice asked dryly unable to imagine why her grandmother would be so frightened.

"Yes of course it was because I was white Eunice! You really are a distant little thing sometimes," she laughed.

"Grandma Cora treated me better once her health returned. I had no idea one day I'd have a beautiful baby girl to show her. You were stunning and she adored you Eunice," she said.

Martha wasn't always well enough to tell stories. It was difficult to say if the various anti-depressants prescribed by multiple doctors were friends or foe but recently Eunice noticed she seemed more confused. One time she asked, "What do the meds actually do? What do they feel like?"

"I used to feel so many emotions all at once. At least your father always said so. Now I don't get upset or angry at all which is good I suppose. I don't get into a tizzy over silly things or overly excited or happy for that matter. I am alive Eunice. Sometimes I think I am only *just* living," Martha said.

Eunice didn't think it sounded all that bad.

"I remember rolling myself off the bed crashing to the floor hoping to shock my body into getting up and making tea," Martha said.

Martha lived a quiet humble existence in her bedroom, knitting baby clothes for the church bazaar or doing crosswords while simultaneously staring at the television.

Eunice sensed a calm aura around her. Perhaps her mother was a real life angel and had mastered the art of accepting her *lot in life*. It wasn't necessarily a bad thing.

Eunice could relate to her mother's trauma. Her peers mocked her in class if she mentioned Civil Rights referring to her parent's involvement. They'd look confused when she got upset at their racist jokes and say, "but Eunice it's okay, you're not really black."

"I'll have to carry around a picture of my parents in my wallet as proof!" she remembered saying to trusted friends.

While she constantly defended herself, peers with deeper complexions were defending their right to live with racism she was largely oblivious to.

Her quickness in defending her heritage wasn't just pride in her roots but the embarrassment of being associated with whites.

Nixon Elementary

Eunice attended Nixon Elementary not far from home on Goode Street. The class photo of pretty white girls in uniforms showed her standing there third from the left next to Rachel Whitaker. It was curious how a picture could make everything seem perfect. She almost passed for white in photographs; she was a cute girl with a caramel sun kissed glow. Her reality was different.

She'd notice students or teachers staring trying to figure her out. Being mixed, her hue was darker than Caucasian, sometimes more black than white in certain light. She laughed her head off when she passed for Spanish, Brazilian or one time, olive skinned Italian.

She remembered asking Sam Hood, her neighbor two doors down, as they skipped rocks at the pond, "Do folks look at you funny?"

Sam had the darkest skin in the neighborhood.

"Sure. It's funny when they look away when I catch em. It only happens when I'm somewhere I shouldn't be," he said sheepishly.

"Shouldn't be? What do you mean?" she asked, honestly not knowing.

"Let's just say I stay outta trouble," he said.

"I see," she said, not knowing if she had stayed out of trouble.

CSCSCS

Eunice realized she was a curiosity due to her parents' friendships with movement folks. Everyone around town knew Curtis was a former Black Panther, the dormant political party from the 1960's. Panther pals dropped by from time to time inspiring school kids to tease *your daddy's a panther lover!*

Given the family houseguests, Eunice's passion lay on the Negro side of her birthright, she barely paid attention to Martha's Irish Canadian heritage. It wasn't nearly as interesting to be half Canadian except on those days she wished she could disappear up north and never to be found.

Curtis' story was much more interesting too. He'd had enough degrees of affiliation with the Panthers to be defined as an enemy to southern harmony but in reality he never was a member and had no direct connection to the party unless you counted Angela.

To Eunice she was wise Aunt Angela but to the public she was Angela Davis, the political activist and academic. Among the multitude of fascinating events in her life she had grown up in Birmingham and had been friends with two of the girls killed in the terrible bombing at the 16th street Baptist church.

It was Nixon elementary Eunice first learned to trust her instinct by listening to the itchy twitch of her nose just like *Sabrina the Teenage Witch*. Intuitively she saw a clear line between right and wrong, almost as if an allergic reaction would strike to tickle her nose when someone was lying. The girls at school pretended to be friendly but later deceived her, often too late for her to clue in to the twitch.

As a child who saw herself as black, vibrant and connected to the African American community, Eunice was deeply pained by the lack of acceptance of white girls in school.

She was asked regularly, "Which one of your parents is white, your mom or your dad?" they'd ask, her boundaries inconsequential to them. Eunice was appalled by the question and grew increasingly fatigued by it.

Public consensus said she was supposed to choose a race and stick with it. If she didn't the girls assumed they had every right to ask whatever questions they wanted.

Even if she had followed societal norms at Nixon there was a catch. If she leaned white she might get, "You're tryin' to act better and smarter than everybody!" Conversely leaning black would get her, "Listen Oreo, you ain't even black!" both black and white girls used that line on her. Nobody else was supposed to define her. *Dumb bitches!*

In shopping malls or on buses she seemed to bump into archetypical underdogs at every turn. She'd feel a trigger tripped by how itchy her fingers got and a burning up the back of her neck. One time during English class she slipped out to the washroom only to find Brittany Carlisle being accosted by tormentors. Britney was confined in a back brace which was meant to straighten the S shaped spine she was born with. Brittany was locked in a stall crying after an alleged deluge of taunts by Jenna Neal and Melanie Harris, two entitled white girls. Jenna's father was a *big wheel* judge in town.

"What in tarnation is going on in here y'all?" Eunice asked confused. The foggy moisture of the washroom squeezing her brain like a tight bandanna didn't help.

"Brit-Brit here won't keep her word on the geometry tutoring I paid her good money for!" Melanie said, as she kicked the door again to scare Brittany.

"She wanted me to let her cheat off my exam!" Brittany shouted from inside choking back her next round of snotty tears.

"Hells bells girls, cut it out!" Eunice commanded.

Jenna shoved Eunice against the adjacent stall knocking her backward. Without hesitation Eunice did a karate side-kick plunging her sneaker into Jenna's stomach. It bent her in half like a soft-shelled taco and sent her to the floor. Her eyeballs looked berserk in a hissy fit not seen since *Who Let the Dogs Out* won a Grammy for best song.

"Oh wait! *Jesus* Eunice never mind! We were just settling a score on Brittany's broken promise," Melanie said, defending Jenna while helping her up.

"You're gonna get it *bitch*!" Jenna said in a winded whisper. Her eyes looking as if she held back a conniption fit.

Jenna and Melanie slowly hobbled out.

Eunice let rosy-cheeked Brittany out of the stall, a number eleven of mucus dripped from her nostril to her mouth, her back brace a tangled mess around her waist.

"Darlin' you can't play games with rich girls. They are complete *assholes?*"

"Well I just hope Jenna's face freezes like that!" Brittany said, as if it were the wittiest thing.

"Just lay low with those cows. Mark my words karma will get them," Eunice said.

Back in class Eunice thought about her lightning speed reaction to protect Brittany. She had no remorse or fear of consequence which could bite her one day. It should have scared her but memory gaps like this had happened to her before.

She forgot about the incident until a few hours later heading to Principal Skinner's office. Jenna Neal, Justice Neal and her mother sat in the waiting area glaring.

"Eunice as per the district and school board guidelines, I have no choice but to suspend you for three days," Skinner said, with authoritarian dryness. His tired eyes lacking compassion.

Eunice was quiet. She wished she had a great comeback line to defend herself but she didn't understand what all the fuss was about. In fact, she had zero recollection of ever leaving English class.

"Judge Neal, Jenna, please excuse me. I need to discuss next steps and protocol with Mrs. Johnston," Skinner stood up to direct the Neal's out. Jenna gave Eunice a customary *fuck you* look.

Skinner turned back to them with a concerned frown. "Mrs. Johnston, in light of the recent violent episodes, that's two this month," Skinner said. "We've contacted Booker T. High School and they've agreed to take Eunice one year early providing she doesn't get into any further incidents," Skinner said. He winked faintly at Eunice. *Was he doing her a favor by getting her out of Nixon and into Washington?* She wanted to think so but Booker T. was known for being a tough school so perhaps it was a punishment.

Not light enough, not dark enough. Why me?

"But, that's a high sch..." Eunice said, as Martha interrupted.

"Mr. Skinner I'm forever grateful for your intervention but does Eunice have enough credit under her belt to skip a grade?" she asked.

"As you well know Eunice is smart and if I may be frank Mrs. Johnston, that high school will put Eunice where she belongs. The student body is mainly African American. This will be much healthier for all involved," he said. The all black high school excited her. *Enough with this trying to pass for half-white bullshit!*

"I see. You have my word that after suspension Eunice will be bright eyed and bushy tailed. You will notice a huge difference. Eunice let's go please," Martha said, yanking her daughter's arm.

One of the few things her folks agreed upon was being *pissed off* she'd squandered the opportunity at *white bread* Nixon Elementary, "Young lady I had to pull a few favors to get you in there! Oh well. *C'est la vie!*" Martha said.

Booker T. High School

Martha gave her a pep talk the night before her first day of high school, "Eunice I've been called every name in the book. I remember being your age in Montreal. They called me a *chiqué* for being stuck-up just because I knew how to dress nice. My mother had been a professional seamstress so I came by it honestly. In New York there were cat calls or curses due to your father and I being sinners but it's lucky your father is a large man so it was not a big deal. Small town Georgia was bad. Let's just say by the time we got to Montgomery, I'd heard it all. I felt disturbed up until we were accepted at First Baptist and then I didn't notice anymore. As long as people know your story Montgomery folks tend to *mind their beeswax* or keep their comments to themselves," Martha said, fiddling with Eunice's hair.

"I think you were maybe three when I heard the funniest one. You were sweet in your stroller with your head a bobbin,' plumb tuckered. I'd refused to bargain with a farmer selling ears of corn but I knew my prices. I swore he doubled his price because I had on my Sunday best clothes but it was a Tuesday. He said, well *la dee da* this girl sees herself as *high cotton*. It was my cue to go to Ernie's stall for corn so I wished this character good riddance," Martha said.

"Ha ha! Mummy, they say way worse nowadays," Eunice laughed as her mother's eyebrows complimented her words meaning she was in good mental condition today.

"But mother *high cotton* is hardly name calling," Eunice said, rolling her eyes.

"That's what I said when I got to church that evening for choir with the ladies! They laughed their heads off saying I was madder than a wet hen. Their words. Celia cackled, 'If only he knew you lived on Columbia street!' The ladies laughed even more. It's not because it was such an insult. The funny part was he was calling me the Southern version of *stuck up* all these years later," Martha laughed reliving the moment.

"Cute mother. When the girls are mouthy with me I just stare them down and they back off," Eunice said.

"Good to hear. Don't you ever let them ruffle your feathers," Martha said.

Her first day of school was one where she could have just as easily gone to the pond and lolled around listening to headphones.

Booker T. Washington High School was on Union in Centennial Hill. It was true the student population was black with a sprinkling of others and an even lesser number of impoverished or special need white students. Perhaps they didn't *make the grade* at all-white schools.

Booker T was named after a black educator who subscribed that black people *postpone any attempt to gain political power until they achieved economic equality with whites.* Eunice wondered when it would come true because that speech was from long ago.

She walked up the entrance path of school to the tune of *Gangsta's Paradise* playing in her head. *...why are we...so blind to see...* She imagined musical notes and a bouncing ball hovering over lyrics like karaoke. As her eyes passed over vignettes of students she thought of the opening sequence of a teenage movie. She wasn't sure what angst riddled drama would play out but was sure she would learn a few lessons.

At her last school she'd strategically gravitated toward popular kids but this place was unknown. The groupings of students all looked out of her league. Since she skipped a grade some of them looked like adults. She'd need to change tactics to fit in with this crowd, maybe she'd get a tattoo to show look street smart.

The student cliques were wrapped in important conversations she didn't dare interrupt. Most students were black and the ones who weren't didn't give off a *come sit with us vibe.*

It didn't help she was self-conscious of her light skin so she concocted a story in her head about being sent undercover to investigate the school for a *20/20* expose! The last thing she needed was to be labeled borderland on her first day.

She noticed there were other minorities in high school who weren't interrogated. They weren't black and some of them had lighter skin than Eunice, yet they seemed accepted; 'I'm Arisbel Latina from Puerto Rico,' 'Hey, Nelson here Chinese,' or 'My name is Ravi, my parents are from India.'

People got nervous when they couldn't define things. *How could Nelson born in Guangzhou, China blend in better than her?*

Eunice guessed she wasn't dark enough for black cliques or not weird enough for the freaky whites. Perhaps the Latino girls didn't want her either.

She took a deep breath and introduced herself, "Hi I'm Eunice. It's my first day," she exhaled.

"Wait a minute, I know you," the familiar voice said and magically a door was opened. Arisbel had been her pal in Sunday school when they were about 8 years old. Without missing a beat Eunice went along with Arisbel's vibe as if they'd been best friends ever since.

"How did you end up in my grade? I remember in Sunday school you were younger," Eunice said.

"I don't brag but I've skipped two grades and English is my second language!" Arisbel said.

"Wow. I got bumped a grade too but I swear the principal wanted me out of that school for causing trouble," Eunice said. "I never asked you where you were from."

"I'm Puerto Rican. Born in a town called Ponce," she said. Eunice sensed she was wanting to tell her more.

"Have you been back there since?" Eunice asked.

"No. I wish. My father is still there somewhere. My mother doesn't make enough money at Comfort Lodge to send me," Arisbel said.

They were interrupted by two skater boys.

"Hey you a *mutt?*" a pimply black boy asked, as he made a circle around them on his skateboard.

"You boys behave. This is my good friend Eunice," Arisbel said. "and Henry you don't even know what you're talking about!" Arisbel screamed in Eunice's defense. "He's from my math class. Pay no mind," she told Eunice.

"Nope, I'm a fine blend of not one but two purebreds!" Eunice called after him thinking twice about her parents own racial purity. Who knew about anyone's true lineage unless you studying ancestry.

"Good one Eunice!" she praised. Then turned to the boys, "Her nose is the only way to even tell she's black. Otherwise she has such fine features," Arisbel said. Her description implied her white features made her prettier.

"Do you know you're dissing me right now?" Eunice poked her gently on her arm. She gave Arisbel a pass with an English as a second language card.

"Come on Eunice, if you blew your hair out you'd be my Mexican sister!" Arisbel said.

"Good idea but she'll never be ghetto fabulous like me!" Arisbel's friend Gabrielle said. She was classic urban chic.

"Or she can be like Mariah who cranked up her ghetto cred after her first album dropped and failed to sell to white radio!" Arisbel said.

"Whatever! The record companies made her do it!" Eunice said.

"That's because her producer was her husband!" Lindsay said.

The good thing about high school was the kids weren't exactly shy about getting personal. However shocking it first seemed, Eunice got the feeling she'd be desensitized pretty quick. Some were bold like another skater boy, "What is your background? You white?" cool dude asks, smacking his gum.

"I'm black and white," Eunice answered to curious beady eyes or confused smirks.

"What do you mean? You can't be black and white," he said.

"It's exactly as it sounds man. I have a black father and a white mother!" she said.

"Which race do you relate to more?" he asked.

Nothing was more jarring than having people stand there, blinking and clearing their throat with *ahems* as if expecting an explanation. Later she learned to toy with them, especially if they were cute.

She wanted nothing more than to be black only because calling herself white felt deceptive and saying black got her reactions like Uncle Leo's angry eyebrows on *Seinfeld*.

"If you must know I identify as black," Eunice said, feeling liberated.

What a relief. She could decide for herself. Otherwise how else would she have functioned without a meltdown!

Well fuck me! I'm tired of this shit! Why the fuck do I need to explain myself to every asshole who asks!

That night alone in her room her mind ran the gamut of emotion; anger at the constant intrusion of questions and relief at the new freedom to use her voice if she was pigeon holed. When her heartbeat calmed she let herself be excited about fitting in. She remembered all those times she ran to her room when her house was chaotic. With headphones she could leave present worries behind and thrash around to grunge music like *Nirvana* or *Pearl Jam*.

Eunice looked at her reflection in the vanity mirror happy for having survived the day. She was ready to take it on academics with a questioning attitude.

She would analyze various scenarios and their outcomes to devise strategies on how to *play* high school. She surmised the best **PR** tactic would be to become the ultimate high school bad girl and keep her cards close to her chest. Not even telling Arisbel.

She didn't think it bothered her until conversations amongst schoolmates turned to race and oppression. It was good that students were more aware of police brutality, racial profiling and the idea of privilege but she hadn't signed up to be a spokesperson or mascot for anything.

Her experience at home had been mother's church visitors or Daddy's pals passing through from up north. Most were black, some were white and many shades in between but her racial identity had never been questioned because they knew her parents story.

High school culture was obsessed with designer labels race, sexual orientation and cliques she didn't identify with. *Oh well!* She was doomed to be an outsider.

It was here she was first accused of having *white privilege* due to being half white. She was confused when she heard the term. How could she have white privilege if she weren't white? After that she was uncomfortable in racial discussions because the spotlight inevitably pointed to her, "Given your background what do you think *half-breed?*" she imagined the teachers question.

She'd cop a sarcastic attitude and push back on interrogators but it proved tiring. She didn't remember the exact day but eventually it stopped bothering her. Everyone knew high school was the most cruel phase of life but wasn't it the most dramatic?

ෲෲෲ

One time Eunice and Arisbel were at the back of the grounds near a thatch of sycamore trees smoking when she saw Terrence for the first time.

"Arisbel check out the guy with the chains!" Eunice said, nudging her now-best-friend. She was delighted to see a gorgeous black boy with stunning eyes and aquiline nose.

"His name is Terrence. Now *he* could be mixed but I'm not sure. A black boy mixed with Japanese or maybe Mexican which makes him so cute," Arisbel joked.

Eunice clued in they were sizing him up just like she was tired of being victim of. Hopefully he was used to it like she now was.

Terrence clearly embraced his gangsta side dressed in a white quilted track suit and large gold dollar sign chain on his neck. He was new but already well connected smoking with some senior guys.

"My cousin was in a gang that worshipped *Pablo Escobar*," Arisbel said, without taking her eyes off of Terrence.

Eunice figured she was watching Arisbel experience love at first sight.

"Did you know mixed race teens experience trouble in school, repeating grades, getting kicked out, smoking, drinking, feeling depressed, having access to guns and having sex, woo hoo! So good luck with that Eunice!" she teased.

Was she saying Eunice would turn out to be a troublemaker because she grew up mixed and confused. Arisbel enjoyed being a walking public service announcement. Perhaps her double grade skip was the result of teachers bumping her ahead traumatized by her overwhelming knowledge.

"Honestly I never had too much trouble. At Nixon I got suspended for sticking up for a girl against some snobby white girls though," Eunice said.

"I know. Being mixed is not a stressful experience," she said. "It's the *idiot* reactions that can stress me out. Society creates the stress then people go and shoot up a place! Scary," Arisbel said.

Her parents had never discussed dual identities or feelings. She'd only known the value of open mindedness.

Eunice daydreamed about Terrence while Arisbel shared her PHD level knowledge on several topics. She was the girl you wanted on your Trivial Pursuit team but could exhaust you with a constant inundation of facts. Eunice tolerated it; she was grateful Arisbel had been there on her first day.

"People think racism has been dismantled but it's still very much alive in our education system!" Arisbel said, looking as if awaiting confirmation.

Eunice sometimes thought Arisbel was hiding how damaged she was by her experiences as a Latino. Eunice drew on one of her father's stories which often worked in a pinch.

"My father told me about the Little Rock Nine over in Arkansas. They called segregation a thing of the past but the kids there went through hell in high school. It makes this place a walk in the park! He said Little Rock had to demonstrate and protest; *2-4-6-8 we are going to integrate*! Even the teachers would say, I'm just sick to my stomach we are going to let those people in here,[5]" Eunice said, in a prudish librarian's voice.

"Eunice you are such a good storyteller," Arisbel said.

"It reminds me of LA. It was worse for Mexicans there. Latinos are considered servants in the eyes of whites," Arisbel said.

"Really? Those Little Rock students didn't even want to integrate but it was the 50s so they had to do what their parents told them. It was all over the news and the president at the time sent in *Stormtroopers*. Can you imagine how exciting it would be having *Emperor Palpatine's* men protect us from white people. Ha ha!" Eunice exaggerated.

"Whoa, that's quite the imagination," Arisbel said, somewhat less animated.

Eunice was pleased.

"Actually that would be really hot!" Arisbel added, throwing her hair back with a laugh. Eunice was amused by her being an *agent provocateur* in a cute girl's body.

"My Aunt Sybil was the first student to finish the year in that integrated school," Eunice said, imagining Sybil's voice, *Oh no dear; it was never intended to be integrated. It was never the intention we'd be treated equal.*

"Eunice people used to think the earth was flat, isn't that ridiculous? And that Jesus was a real man and not a fable," Arisbel said.

"Arisbel! People still believe in Jesus!" Eunice said, surprised she was not Christian being Mexican.

Arisbel could easily make conversation with her trivia knowledge. Bantering facts back and forth with her gave Eunice the idea to ante up her black history. It wouldn't be difficult considering the tall tales she got at home and she could listen to more rap and hip hop. Being the bad girl would counteract her perfectionist pride but also be a surefire way to blend in. Who didn't want to be a *badass* anyway?

That first year of high school was her education in more ways than one. Eunice decided to stay away from being too popular. *Who wanted to burn out too fast or too soon!* She found her niche by staying just under the radar.

She figured excelling in study's, even working ahead of the teacher's curriculum by handing in assignments early would keep her in good standing. A *Super-good girl* archetype balanced with *crafty-bad girl* became her modus operandi. She suspected the purebreds never had to fathom such duality.

They simply were one or the other. Inside she knew she was still Eunice though. *What did all this have to do with anything?*

Being hyper aware of her evolving persona left her spent. Most evenings she could do little else but hide out in her bedroom with headphones.

In Literature class her second year girls she didn't recognize gave her death locked stares so the boys, jocks and nerds in class avoided eye contact with her. Most just following the nasty girls' lead not wanting trouble.

For African American literature like *Uncle Tom's Cabin*, Mrs. Sanford played snippets from movies, probably so the boys like Terrence and his lot had a snowballs chance of passing because they never completed the readings.

"They hate me Terrence," she whispered. He'd arrived late so took the seat next to hers.

"Ach. They are only envious of your looks and brains ya goofball," he said, poking her arm with his pencil and smiling sunshine. "Hang in there."

She didn't believe him but it made her feel special.

"Folks next we are doing Alex Haley's Roots so I need you to start reading," Mrs. Sanford said.

The guys in back groaned.

"Have you seen how many pages are in that book?" Terrence said to her.

"Hopefully she'll play the entire miniseries!" Eunice said.

Mrs. Sanford played excerpts from Roots.

The girls started teasing her daily, "That looks like you Eunice, child of rape!" Francine said.

Eunice couldn't identify with any character and tried to ignore they were equating her with mixed race characters sired by the master.

"She's so pretty I love her," Eunice said, then froze the *bitches* out. Eunice didn't take any more offence. What did she care, Terrence Battle was friends with her.

"Hey Eunice, aren't you glad you know where you come from? Mulatto-land!" Francine said.

Ironically, learning racially offensive words was the start of her being called out as *mixed, multiethnic, double-raced* and even that slave word *mulatto* was making a comeback.

Eunice thought *Kunta Kinte / Toby /Levar Burton* was cute. She knew him from the *Star Trek* TV show. He reminded her of her neighbor Sam Hood. If she didn't identify with characters in the movie she wondered if Sam would identify with Toby. He had always been easy on her eyes.

Angela

Eunice grew up with all types of visitors in her living room, overheard and been a part of discussions well beyond her years.

"Angela and Reginald are coming for dinner," Curtis said, "Best we be get for an education!" Eunice thought it was hysterical when he used that line. It always meant there would be lots of swearing or discussions of sex and violence. He meant she would be educated on what not to do.

"Fabulous! I'll get Aunt Angela's opinion on my composition! Or maybe she'll do it for me!" Eunice said.

"She'll like have an opinion or two for sure!" Curtis said.

Aunt Angela felt like blood kin. The way she and Daddy carried on teasing or arguing she might as well have been his sister. Eunice thought it was beautiful that long time friendships could turn into family. Maybe one day that would happen for her.

Eunice probably learned her kinship to the dark horse from Angela. Often those struggling to fit in would look at her confused wondering how she recognized them. They came in all shapes and forms so she believed she was exempt from prejudice.

When she saw someone in need her protective side was stronger which made her less of an isolated loner. Fueled by the camaraderie she could became charming and even exude sparkling wit. She also liked when the one in need thought highly of her.

Aunt Angela had opinions about everything race related as it was part of her profession. She was a famous public speaker but Eunice saw her as a lifelong freedom fighter. Angela said the biracial movement in the last decade was designed to target and undermine the black community. It fuelled anti-blackness sentiment resulting in racism internalized by black teenagers. "I'm not putting the onus on the mixed race but simply stating facts. It's important for you to always recognize the status quo uses mixed people to their advantage. No amount of sugar-coating can ward off the fact that lighter skinned people often feel better than those who aren't," Angela said. Eunice loved how opinionated she was. No woman could compare to her education and distinctly velvet voice.

"You mean light or dark skin makes a difference in civil rights?" Eunice asked.

"Are you kidding me darlin, it set us four steps back to plantation mentality. It was called *colorism* then. That's one great thing about California, the West Coast is newer, the old ways aren't set in as deep but many intellectuals I've worked with in Oakland, happily turn a blind eye," Aunt Angela said.

She was always aglow when she got fired up, almost as if her superpowers were activated.

"What I'm saying in some sense is you are part of the hope and change," Angela said.

Eunice blinked at her, probably looking clueless.

"For the love of God, don't fall into victim mentality. I know you won't babydoll," Angela said, hugging her.

"Some see race diluting as wrong but in terms of evolution it's harder to argue," Eunice said.

"Don't you see it every day? Society treats the light skinned under a guise of inclusion. The status quo throws a bone to us so we're supposed to forgive and forget. Look at movies and music. Actors and models succeed when they are light. Can you name me one dark one?" Angela asked.

"*Miles Davis, Louis Armstrong, Nina Simone*," Eunice said, nervously.

"Genius musicians. I'll give you that for sure. God has granted us to break the barrier with musical talent," Angela said.

Eunice got inspired with brand new ideas when Angela was over. She would literally need note paper to jot down things she wanted to look up later.

Angela thought the hope of equality was coming as if evolution was about to be turned on its head after centuries of sameness. It had more silent victims for mixed race kids who couldn't find a place in society but, *you are the race Eunice.* Just as every human originated from Africa, we will end up a unified oneness in the end," Angela said with authority.

"I remember my older cousin Ellen, who was mixed from back in slavery times which was rarely consensual, was very active in the campus at her University. In her senior year, she was elected president of the African American Student Union. I remember celebrating the news with her mother and mine in their kitchen. My mother congratulated Ellen with a big hug and offered a wry smile, 'Ellen, just don't tell anyone you're only one quarter black,' my mother said,' do you see?" Angela asked, taking a sip of her tea checking to see if Eunice understood.

Eunice waited patiently through her effective pauses.

"At this we all burst out laughing, laughter that expressed as much relief as it did humor because mother had exposed an open secret by pointing out the irony we'd all been thinking. How was it ironic that a woman who was of only partial African descent could be a leader? Angela said.

"Why?" Eunice asked.

"Multiracial in the black community was something to be tolerated, not celebrated. It left us vulnerable to accusations of divided allegiance. We knew that although people could be tolerant of a biracial in the black community, we weren't about to celebrate one fourth black," Angela said.

"When whites know I'm half black they apply a stereotype. You're saying the same is true if you don't have enough black like your cousin Ellen?" Eunice asked.

"I know. Eunice I've spent a lifetime in this stuff. Don't let me bring you down. It won't help us now but there'll come a generation where the world will be mixed enough for biases to melt away. I believe that is where the Promised Land is. No race or religion wars. Until then we've got to walk our walk. We've got our work cut out for us," Angela said.

It was true, American culture gave *carte blanche* to those considered appealing and sexy. Beauty Queen *Vanessa Williams* was living proof. Amid her pageant controversy circa 1982 no one seemed to give two *shits* about what color she was. The public was more interested in the scandalous nature of nude photos and the morality of a slutty sex kitten. The big story only underlined how *friggin'* beautiful she was. *Voila* her racial identity was eclipsed. Ever since then there's been countless beauties accepted on looks alone.

"But for regular brothers and sisters skin shades completely make a difference. Just like shade levels on window blinds. I just got new ones in my apartment. You can choose between level 1 which lets in the most light and level 10 which lets in the least. Level 1 revealing what's inside while level 10 hides you and makes you less likely to let people in," Angela said.

To be less ashamed or more ashamed based on the level of light and dark was a terrible thing. Eunice decided that day her ambition in life was to fight for freedom and social justice.

ᴄ₃ᴄ₃ᴄ₃

In grade 10 Sociology with Mrs. Gates they learned racism from an intellectual perspective removing some of the fiery emotion they experienced on the street.

Gates lectured in an old fashioned professor's style, "Experts saw racism as socially constructed, which meant they knew race wasn't *real* biologically. They couldn't simply change what they wanted race to mean or ignore it," she said, referring to a binder bursting with articles which she passed around.

"Take a look at the classic stereotype of *mulatto* where a *deeply troubled characters stumbled through life in racially tortured turmoil.* Were they black? Were they white? Why weren't they accepted?" she asked the class.

Hands went up.

"Maybe they weren't trusted."

"There minority was visibly obvious."

"They had no self-esteem becoming self-fulfilling prophecies. Or okay, punching bags!"

"They were martyrs all because Mommy and Daddy didn't stick to their own kind."

"Although these characters lived tragic lives, they were praised as an *exotic* mix and somehow revered as being better than *plain ole black*," Mrs. Gates said, knowledgably modern which contradicted her eccentric old time cat glasses with neck chain.

Eunice put her hand up.

"You know I read somewhere there were labels for the levels of concentration of African blood! Is that true?" Eunice asked.

"It must have been a slow news day when scholars and scientists spent time on nomenclature. The words mixed and biracial were remixed versions of terms like: *mulatto, quadroon, quadricepts, octoroon, meameloucs.* All words to classify amounts of blackness," Gates said.

Drops of blood! Eunice boiled at the fact there were labels for the number of drops of blackness in her body.

"Okay folks I need you to brace yourself for the origin of the word *mulatto.* It was derived from the mating of a donkey and a horse, which created a mule and mules were sterile," Mrs. Gates said.

This dropped a bomb on the class who burst into uproarious side discussions.

Mrs. Gates liked to get the class active, "You all will get sick of my voice and I need a rest for talking!" she assigned a weekly oral presentation. The boys thought she was lazy and cruel but Eunice didn't mind after the first one. The first one was personal!

Eunice had to think about what she would discuss for the presentation. She spent her early school years hiding her white mother. She carried guilt in her heart for being often relieved when Martha was hidden away with symptoms of her illness so she didn't need to make excuses for her. The truth was she didn't want her friends reminded or focused on her white roots.

Eunice had prepared her first high school oral speech with care, "My father is black American and my mother, a white Canadian. I never identified as biracial, which is a term that didn't exist when I was born. Even today, *biracial* is not a legal racial identity; it's a pop-culture identification. It's a way for people to separate themselves from African Americans, a way of saying, 'I'm better than that,'" Eunice said.

"Thank you Eunice. Class I want to point out that Eunice's life experience has given her a natural expertise from a blended race perspective. It's important that we keep connected to our experiences to see where we can use them positively.

A few weeks later Eunice wanted Angela's opinion on her next assignment, "Auntie, here's a fabulous excerpt from my essay for Sociology class," Eunice read her latest work.

I'm Eunice Johnston, My father is black and my mother is white. I identify as African American. I have experienced being biracial in Montgomery. As someone who has endured persistent racism via name calling, threatening and even spitting.

I don't believe I have ever been considered half white. I personally do not think about my lineage and have never had racial-identity issues myself. It is only placed on me in social situations, school, the mall, restaurants.

Historically, there was tragedy in the lives of light skinned black women as well as dark skinned black women. The tragedy was not that they were black or had "Negro blood," although whites saw that as a tragedy. Rather, the way race was used to limit their opportunities. There is more tolerance of interracial marriage pop culture but here on the frontlines in Montgomery, as a mixed daughter, I see people's reactions nearly every day, positive and negative.

And that's where I got to. What do you think?" Eunice asked.

"You're one *helluva* girl you know that? I swear in my day we had to fight for all that you wrote there. It makes me feel good knowing that fighting for the right thing is always worth it," Angela said, her eyes welled up. "It gives me chills to hear you've captured an aspect of race that was also true when I was a girl."

"Thank you. I feel like asking them if they think I woke up saying, 'do I want to be black or white today?'" Eunice said.

Eunice could sometimes pass whiter without trying to. Purposely pass if she changed her speech affectations using a quasi-brit accent. She turned it into a game.

"I wonder what white privileged kids my age think about?" Eunice laughed.

Eunice thought of how she could use this knowledge with her parent's friends. She could turn up the dial on urban black detection by matching a visitor's linguistic style. When she failed at matching their style, she could tell by the look on their face they was perturbed. Then they would ask the prying questions Eunice was tired of answering. If Martha was present all bets were off because they would figure her out. They smiled with a twinkle in the eye, *oh I get it,* relieved they could classify her as mixed.

"Just like in *To Sir with Love* we all bleed red child. It's the idea that the self is not a possession of the actor but what the audience places upon the actor. Angela said.

"I can see that," Eunice said.

"It's impression management," looking at her over reading glasses. "From the colored actor's perspective ethnicity is both a physical and mental state. Thus mixed-race folks can think they are black racially but depending on how they were raised, might not fit in socially anywhere.

"You have learned this young Eunice. Not like me. I was naïve at first; I thought it couldn't possibly be like this given my Frankfurt education. But I see what all the protesting was for. I had purpose and faith and I still do," Angela said.

With racial fatigue, Eunice wondered when Mrs. Gates would cover topics about love, marriage and sex education.

೮೮೮

Eunice's beliefs were challenged by film history and how movies reflected a society's perspective at a specific time. Miss Jones was young, hip and one of the most beloved teachers at school. She was *avant garde*, artsy and activist-minded plus she herself was intrigued by the subject matter. She gave passionate critiques of race films like *Within our Gates*. Eunice was surprised a black produced silent movie existed from 1920.

They learned how the burning cross imagery wasn't actually an original idea of those sheet wearing fools' but a product of Hollywood. It was life imitating art.

"The first epic movie *Birth of a Nation* in 1915," Miss Jones said, "it was arguably the most racist movie ever produced in the United States. Originally called *The Clansmen* it's a 3-hour plus Civil War epic that glorifies the *klan* and promotes every black stereotype as caricatured *mammies, sambos, darkies and brutes*. The villain is a black power hungry sex-obsessed criminal who lusts after white women," Miss Jones' arms waved passionately as she spoke.

With mainly black classmates, Eunice feared jumping into discussions, self-conscious others saw her lightness countering her opinion and dismiss her.

She might catch someone jerking their eyes away or glaring, *Puleeeeze, you're the sorriest looking black girl I ever saw!* She wanted to blurt out, "My daddy's 100% African American.

I'm not stealing your experience! Besides, she thought stating her race, religion or orientation was ludicrous.

Perhaps they didn't know if it was safe to make fun of whites in front of her. While she knew complexion made it unlikely she'd be unjustly targeted by police, who's to say her Georgia cousins weren't? The day to day race experience probably made her commitment to injustice even stronger.

"Miss Jones, why didn't the government pull the movie?" Eunice asked.

"Great question Eunice. The stock answer is we live in a country and world that perceives dark skin as evil, threatening, foreign, *exotified*, and objectified. With so many answers I could tell you, I'll boil it down to just one. The film was screened at the White House by the sitting president so you can draw your own conclusions," Miss Jones said.

Whites would welcome her with trepidation as they'd be afraid they'd need to filter themselves. All in all it made her feel as if she lived in a plastic world.

At least violence had truth in it.

Street Cred

The day Eunice finally embraced black culture, other things changed too. There had been a resurgence of interest in Malcolm X among youth, fueled by the use of his iconic image by hip-hop acts like *Public Enemy, Wu-Tang* and *Jay Z*. Malcolm X's image hung in student lockers and adorned T-shirts and jean jackets of hip students.

Eunice was unapologetic about sun tanning as much as the pop culture obsessed beach bunnies did. With a dark tan her father's Johnston heritage came in more prominently reminiscent of *Halle Berry* from *Jungle Fever*.

To get the popular vote at school she got mileage from stories of her parents' well-known visitors like Aunt Elaine [Brown] and Aunt Kathy [Cleaver] each of Panther notoriety. Or Eunice would embellish some of her own, "Martin Luther King Jr. has been to our house on Columbia Street," she'd brag. "Okay, so it was before my folks lived there but he's been there!"

"You're Daddy knew MLK? Did you ever get to meet him?" Terrence asked, he was even cuter with bright eyed earnestness.

"Well no Terrence, I wasn't born yet," she said deadpan. "Daddy worked a bunch of gigs as a security guard in Harlem just before Malcolm X was killed. I never met him either," she also figured he'd mixed Malcolm with MLK.

"Duh I knew that!" he said.

Unbeknownst to Curtis, his popularity was on the rise. She had found an untapped niche with boys from different grades wanting to hear stories about her father. Maybe she'd ask him to do a guest spot at the school's general assembly!

Gaining acceptance from someone like Terrence and his crew was huge and eventually brought the trendy *fly girls* around too. Gabrielle stood out as having the most spunk. She remembered her as untouchable back on the first day of high school.

Gabrielle was a hip hop princess every guy wanted hanging on the back of his moped. She charmed her way through life as a vixen rebel with her leather hat and a revealing camisole tops. She was living proof beauty broke through the race barrier.

"Girl don't listen to Terrence, he failed history!" Gabrielle said to Eunice, "He's probably sweet on you because you're easy on the eyes like a pale Bambi girl and I don't mean a deer caught in headlights!" she looked back at her girlfriends who laughed and averted Eunice's eyes.

Eunice suspected ridicule.

"I'll have to take that as a compliment!" Eunice exaggerated. She thought of her mother as a Harlem fish out of water. *Why not just speak the truth!*

"I like how you sassed Miss Jones. She looked *pissed!*" Gabrielle smiled. "Eunice girl, you can't play a player. You know full well you're a *hot tomale,* right Arisbel?" Gabrielle said.

Eunice was used to hiding inside her tomboy phase and had never embraced her looks. Her goal was always invisible camouflage. She never thought any clique would want her membership.

"Stop it. I'm plain and free of zits so I look clean is all but okay I'll take it! Thanks," Eunice said. She felt a jolt of excitement rushing up her spine as if someone had remembered her birthday.

"Gabby's pretty good at cartwheel's. I seen her in gymnastics," Arisbel said, acting completely different around probably the most popular girl in their grade.

"Are you taking gym this term? I hate it on Mondays. I can't do a cartwheel to save my life. I used to. I think I pulled my pelvis or something," Gabrielle said.

"I still do em pretty easy but I imagine all girls stop doing cartwheels after their period. Womanhood doesn't include flipping your head upside down," Eunice said.

The girls all laughed.

"I did gymnastics in grade 6. Springboard first then aced that double bar *thingymajig,*" Juliet said.

"You went to Nixon right? Now that's *Wonder bread!*" Gabrielle said, sarcastically.

"I played down my acrobatic talents there. Those girls didn't understand me. They thought I was Latin. When I told them my father was black they stopped talking to me. That's when things got wicked," Eunice said.

"HAHA. Well that's child's play. They probably were jealous of course. It always boils down to envy and jealousy right girls?" Gabrielle said.

"You said it, Gab!" Sheena, a quieter girl said.

Eunice laughed. She didn't want talking to Gabrielle and the girls to end. Her head felt like she had sipped Daddy's beer.

"I'm cutting gym today!" Gabrielle said.

"How do you cut?" Eunice asked.

"It's a *cakewalk,* you bring on your girly girl act," Gabrielle said. She started re-enacting in a *Jessica Rabbit* voice presumably used to cut class, "Carl, my calves are still killing me from the hay bailing my daddy had me doing. I sure wish I had two brothers instead of sisters," she said.

They all burst out laughing.

"You don't really do that, do you?" Eunice asked.

"Naw. I call home and get my mother to call the school secretary. Totally legit!" Gabrielle said, unclear whether it was true or all talk.

"It's funny you said *cake walk*. My aunt told me cake walk was a secret word used when slaves performed at plantation masters parties. They would dress fancy, sing and strut but all the while compete with each other to see who was the best master mimic! Imagine like us doing Mr. Osborne impressions then voting on the best one? Afterwards the winner got cake, thus it's a cake walk," Eunice said.

"Oh my God that's hilarious! It's like the origin of disrespecting someone!" Juliet said.

"…the best part was white folks didn't have a clue," Eunice said.

"I betcha some of them figured it out. I bet the smart mixed women figured it out," Gabrielle said, playing to her audience of friends who all laughed.

Eunice was embarrassed. It felt like she and Gabrielle had been sparring. She visualized Angela's face. What would she do? She'd ignore it completely.

"Yeah, what exactly did those ladies do? I'm sure some of them were none too pleased to own slaves," Sheena said.

"Those poor women. They had to keep their figures then have babies. Once they were done with that it didn't matter if they got fat and ugly. No one cared. You're not obsessed with your weight are you Eunice?" Gabrielle asked, rhetorically. "Wendy Jackson is the biggest flip flopper! She starves herself to keep Lance interested. Last month I asked her, 'how's the diet going Wendy?' as emergency personnel wheeled her by on a stretcher," Gabrielle smacked her gum as she spoke.

"You're awful!" Eunice said. Whether she believed in her point of view or not, Gabrielle was charismatic and not afraid of anything.

"Is Wendy okay?" Arisbel asked.

"I'm fine. I just eat my feelings!" Sheena said, who was likely not humoring them as she took a bite from her bagel cream cheese.

"You are a good person Eunice," Gabrielle said, cupping a hand over hers. She held an intense Cleopatra stare.

Perhaps since Eunice didn't question her dis she'd got respect and earned her stripes in Gabrielle's circle.

Before Eunice ever heard the phrase *purple black*, *blue black*, *midnight*, *ape* or *monkey*, spewed from the mouths of brats at the mall, she had already heard them from the kids on her street. Most of the boys had names bred into them by older siblings. They used the venomous adjectives on each other frequently to remove their power and thicken their skin to face the outside world.

Eunice dreamed of being called those names all her life. Since forever she wished she was as dark as Daddy or Angela or Gabrielle. She was often delighted when privy to the subtle racist comments said around her, proving she was accepted on some level.

Whenever a white person said something derogatory to her, intentionally or not, Eunice wanted to smash their face in. Then she wanted to deal out an 8x10 glossy picture of her father. Why did people think they could get away with their racist *bullshit*? Was her lighter skin an excuse for bigots to investigate her roots and be idiots in the process? Why was it an excuse? Why couldn't she fit in? Why couldn't it be like *Tolkien's* middle *fucking* earth where nobody understood or cared to ask.

Gabrielle, the girl who had everything envied her free ride, "You're so lucky Eunice! You get to be mysterious. You can do anything and go anywhere! No one is questioning my ethnicity. I'm clearly a black woman. Of course I will doing anything and go anywhere anyways," she stared with hands on hips.

Later at home in her bedroom, Eunice was riding high on acceptance as she examined her face in the mirror. She found herself plain compared to other girls but Gabrielle had said she was a *hot tomale*. She'd never been called that before.

She guessed her facial symmetry was alright; her eyes, nose and mouth seemed to be in the right places. If she focused specifically on mother's thinner European nose she could see the white side of her family, then if she squinted, she saw Daddy's chocolate eyes and full lips from her black side. She touched the freckles on her upper cheek and realized they probably threw people off. Her final appraisal was she *was* a pretty girl. Gabrielle was right. She was blessed in uniqueness!

Why did that thought make her feel sick in her belly?

Something about blending into crowds with decent looks was a gift to keep her out of trouble. The flip side was in her chameleon state she was a key eyewitness to the pain of watching others treated badly. She would never ever consciously try to pass for white like she'd seen on *Oprah*.

Algebra

By grade 11 she was confident in her abilities with numbers and formulas. She had an adequate reputation for being the best female in mathematics, a skill that came naturally or was inherited from her father.

Gabrielle and others were freaking out about stiff-lipped Mr. Osborne's dramatic announcement of an oral math exam. He'd recently stated how discouraged he was by kids today and their lack of concern for his beloved mathematics.

Rumors swirled Mr. Osborne had hit a mid-life crisis and was sick of teaching. He was crusty and some said had become a secret alcoholic. The fact that he'd assigned the final as an oral math exam was his cruel revenge against the students.

The hard truth was Mr. Osborne had been correct in the first place. No one aspired to use math in their future. They planned for enough wealth to employ a computer calculator for every mathematical requirement. *Why would anyone need algebra in the real world?*

Eunice found playing a *smart ass* in class, especially at the risk of punishment kept her in good standing with Terrence and Gabrielle's respective cliques. Secretly she was delighted the final math exam was oral. With her competitive nature she seriously aimed for the top score.

Osborne's previous take-home had been a *no brainer!* Once she saw his formula patterns she'd whipped through it in seconds flat.

ϐϐϐ

On the day of the exam students were clamoring and erratically gabbing about everything except algebra.

"Terrence is doing a sit in protest up in Birmingham commemorating the church bombing Saturday, are you interested Eunice?" Josh asked.

"Definitely! What time and where?" she asked.

"A field near Lizard Loop at Ruffner Mountain. Three o'clock and don't tell a soul. Last time, the prep spot was discovered and the cops called it off before it began," Josh said, not looking very nervous about the algebra exam.

Eunice hadn't told her parents about Saturday. She'd need a reason that wasn't a protest. She could say she was taking the girls to Cedar Point to check on mothers old friend Aunt Cathy. Martha or Angela usually visited her but mother wasn't travelling these days and Angela was back in Oakland.

Eunice spun around to Gabrielle seated behind her, "Listen you guys wanna go to Cedar Point beforehand? I need to visit one of my mom's friends. She was a Freedom Rider from Nashville. I promise you'll love her. If anyone can get you fired up about injustice, it's Cathy [Brooks-Burks]."

"Yea, sure, as long as we get to the Loop in time," Gabrielle said.

"Aunt Cathy told us they were scared when rocks got hurled through the church windows...okay it's starting tell you later."

"Alright, everyone, take your seats. If you're not ready for the exam you will never be ready," Osborne said. Eunice smiled at Josh then motioned thumbs up to Gabrielle.

"Here we go. I don't need math do I?" Gabrielle made a sucked-in cheek fish face.

Eunice was perfectly calm. She had an ace up her sleeve. She'd rely on her knack for seeing formulas take shape in front of her eyes like dancing holograms. It didn't matter what variables Mr. Osborne threw up she was confident she would see the formula.

Lindsey went first. She was related to Sam Hood somehow. She had turned up at one of their Columbia street barbecues. Lindsey stood at the board shiny from perspiration.

As Osborne spoke in a dull voice, Lindsay scribbled along the whiteboard in green marker her bracelets made clicking sounds as they went. Right away Eunice could see Lindsay's hologram formulas in the air.

When she was done Lindsay stopped to look for Osborne's approval. He was first neutral then said, "Good job. Clearly Lindsay has practicing her exercises. Remember, algebra is like music, the more you practice the more it becomes a talent," Osborne said.

The boys snickered from the back. They constantly made fun of his passion for math, "Oz probably gets a semi as in semi-erection with his passion for math. "Yea! Watching us squirm for orals is gonna make Oz blow his mind!"

The boys laughed nervously.

By the time two thirds of the class had gone, Eunice's holograms stopped dancing. The live action animation had turned into plain old classroom. She wasn't familiar with what Sam was writing. There weren't too many ways to do algebra and he wasn't doing it her way. They were mostly simpleton calcs! So simple she couldn't see a logical pattern. *Hell on wheels!* There must be some tricky mistake on the assignment but no one else noticed it either. Osborne was really screwing with them.

Sam got his marked correct.

Josh went up next. He was probably the brightest of them all.

"That's right Josh, I was completely betting against you at mid-term but you squeaked it out. Fine job," Osborne said.

The class groaned.

"Who's next?" Osborne looked at his sheet, "Eunice Johnston!"

"Wait Mr. Osborne," Gabrielle said in a weak voice, "I can't take the pressure anymore. I'm gonna barf. Let me go next please?" Gabrielle asked.

What the hell?

It was an alternate universe if Gabrielle was volunteering for anything.

"Gabrielle let's do this!" Osborne said.

As Gabrielle wrote out formulas, she exaggerated her handwriting and added extra zeros for the classes entertainment. Osborne was quiet looking disheartened they weren't passionate about math. Gabrielle was moderately successful in other subjects but it was only mildly shocking she bombed the exam.

"Okay Ms. Johnston. You're up," Osborne said.

He recited the equation. Thank God! The variables danced in the air above his opalescent skin and red hair which did not make for an attractive man. She'd often thought of style alternatives to make him remotely date-worthy. A haircut and maybe some base foundation to even out those blotches. Some ugly just couldn't be fixed.

She scribbled out the formula in blue marker with gusto. *No brainer! Her goose wasn't cooked after all!*

Her marker moved across the board like mother knitting a baby jumper for the church bazaar. She was a math genius like *Jeff Goldblum* in *Jurrassic Park* until there was a snag.

Eunice foresaw two steps ahead that her solution would fail. It just wouldn't add up.

How rude? There was no hologram.

What happened to her perfect confidence?

Perspiration broke through at her forehead. She had cultivated an analytical persona to combat being thought of as a *stupid mulatto* laughingstock. The class was quiet except for Osborne's gloating grunt but she could tell the back row was dying to razz her.

"Uh, uh, uh, no, no, no Eunice. That'll never work out. What are you playing at? Making drama for your classmates?" Oz said, with a laugh indicating even he didn't expect her to fail.

She was frozen stiff. The energy had drained from her fingers as she couldn't think of any mathematical recovery. Moments passed. She stood dumbfounded the blue marker dangling from her hand.

"Ms. Johnston are you quite alright. Do you need a moment?" he asked.

She knew a moment would just prolong the agony. She was completely blank. She dropped the marker to the floor.

"Unbelievable! Even your best girl Gabrielle got closer than that. It's unprecedented," he was gleeful. He had a reputation for destroying his students so it was her turn.

She wanted to disappear as the class erupted in chatter, followed by peals of laughter that deafened her ears. She could hear Terrence and the boys in back, noisy like crows on a wire.

Eunice turned to the unruly class, curtsied and sat in her seat. She immediately escaped to the safe spot inside herself, barely hearing Osborne's Shakespearean soliloquy of doom, "Let this be a lesson to you all. You need to keep on top of mathematics. Each lesson builds upon the last. You can't skate through math! No sir. Look at Eunice. Isn't it shocking what happens when you stop trying," he paused and looked at Terrence, "staying out late instead of keeping up with your exercises will result in failure, just as I was certain it would."

As she ruminated on Osborne and the others reveling in her demise she thought of ways she could avenge herself from utter humiliation. *Who did this pasty cracker think he was making an example of her? She was absolutely sure what he did was wrong. The motherfucker would get his!*

The period end bell sounded.

By the time the bell stopped ringing she had buried her resentment as if none of it had ever happened. *All's well that ends well.* In the coming weeks she successfully retook the exam in Osborne's office with a good old fashioned pen and paper. *There's always a silver lining.*

At Lizard Loop, Eunice found girl power in the form of *compadre's* Gabrielle, Juliet, Patty and Arisbel. The ladies would eventually become the first members of her girl posse.

The boys were forgiven. Terrence and his chums made fun of everyone and had never given a *flying squirrel fuck* about Eunice's analytical talent. It would end up an anecdote, 'remember those grade 11 exam orals?' and simply go down in the lexicon of high school memories.

Eunice was more concerned about losing all she had gained in popularity during the school year. Mother had told her she was going to a music camp summer as a semi-punishment for letting her grades slip. It was a punishment that would change her life's path.

Musicology

"Why am I really going to music camp Mother?" Eunice shouted, from her seat at the kitchen table.

"Marjorie pulled a favor with her brother in law!" Martha said.

"Are you trying to straighten me out since I've been running wild with my friends? I know that's what you're doing mother," Eunice said.

Or punishment for wisecracking at home?

"I honestly thought you'd embrace it Eunice," Martha said.

It was true she loved getting lost in her music. It took her outside herself. Music crossed boundaries and overrode life's problems. It was glorious.

"It sounds like you'll get to sing in a real studio," Martha said, as she read from the brochure, "*Musicology songwriting and recording experience camp. This summer give your aspiring young musician an opportunity of a lifetime.* Well Eunice you're my aspiring young musician," she said.

"Mother! Please don't gloss over the fact you're forcing me to go away for six weeks!" Eunice said. Being away from home was fine; being away from her own bed wasn't.

"I'm sorry Eunice," Martha said, ruefully.

"It's fine mother, I'll believe it when I see it is all!" she said. Her mother seemed to have made a miraculous recovery with the news Eunice would be away.

"Well bless your heart," Martha said, sarcastically. "Are you teasing me girl. Can't you make an effort? I didn't have to get you into camp!" she said.

"Ya but Arisbel got a job at Vespa's Diner downtown. She was going to get me in. I won't see the girls for soooo long!" Eunice said. Musicology camp actually sounded cool. It also sounded too good to be true like how glitzy amusement park TV commercials make them look so incredible.

"What's going on in here?" Curtis came in with weekly Pabt's Blue Ribbon empties already looking to reverse out of the room. "I'm fixin' to go to Wallymart. Do y'all need anything?" he asked.

"Daddy we were just discussing your sending me away," Eunice said, with pleading eyes.

"Now what's with the face? You gotta start somewhere!" he said.

She softened slightly. Perhaps he was disappointed he never pursued his own jazz and blues dreams. All she knew was she'd miss the action around here.

"Wait a sec, you figured out your mothers plan to tuck you away and keep you outta trouble!" he teased.

Alright enough trying to wriggle out of it! Eunice decided to embrace music camp. Even lighthearted pop songs could feed her ego and make her feel important. Especially sung along with her faux mic on the set of the big budget video she imagined in her bedroom.

She could easily slide into a *kickass* dominatrix, mermaid or bullfighter persona. Singing was all about being full of yourself, flaunting your body and a free license to be envied. Music didn't have taboo racial divides like movies did. No matter what your sex or skin color, if you could belt out *Chili Peppers, Hole* or *Whitney* you were applauded.

Gabrielle, Arisbel and Patty came by the house the night before Eunice left.

"I can't believe you're getting shipped off," Gabrielle said. "I'll be working my *ass* off at Cottonwood golf course for all those *ritz crackers* so I won't even miss you."

"I'm not going that far! Don't worry we'll talk on the phone." Eunice said.

She must not have slept much that night as she dreamt of international stardom. *Very funny!* It wasn't as if she'd be discovered at a soda fountain on Sunset and Vine in LA while she lived in Alabama.

CBCBCB

The Musicology Program was on Mimosa Road near the waterfront of Gun Island Chute. The focus was songwriting and elements of composing original songs. Students would collaborate in a series of songwriting drills.

Aside from the recording studio, the compound included lodging in cute red cabins with white flowers cascading from window boxes. Each had two bedrooms, a bathroom and sitting room. Eunice would share accommodation with a quiet blond woman named Cecile who had a classical background. Nearby was horseback riding and paddle boat rentals for some fun in between making hit records!

On the first week students met a musician guy named Mike Watts who spoke in technical terms she didn't understand, "I'll guide you through the recording process. You will record your written material in a state-of-the-art studio where bands like *Skid Row* and *The Pixies* have recorded," Mike said, pointing down the hall.

At first she thought he was bragging but the place seemed like the real deal. The group of ten students in their late 20s early 30s, mostly rich looking and white. They all looked ultra-serious as if it was going to be cut throat like on a reality show.

Instead of feeling weird being the youngest she was relieved she wouldn't think of competing with anyone except herself. Eunice still wondered what she was doing there.

"This is a unique opportunity for aspiring musicians such as yourselves to get a sense of how music is made. You will leave here with a professionally recorded CD of your songs." Mike Watts' confidence and resume inspired her.

She felt spoiled by listening to the other artists and musicians *chit chat* about scales, sharps and flats. *My darling mother this is not what I expected at all!*

Later at the cabin while Cecile was still at mess hall, Eunice called home, "I've got a bone to pick with you Mother! Did you spend your life savings for this camp? It's very nice. Too nice. Marjorie's connection? I don't know what to say. Thank you?" she said.

"I'll only say Angela had a part in it and I'm not to tell you anything more," Martha said.

Later Eunice would find out it was a three thousand dollar course someone Angela knew couldn't attend.

The days were filled with classes called sessions in the music business. In music theory they studied the jazz hit parade which meant jazz with vocals, "If y'all are into hard-core jazz that'll both jangle your nerves and relax you I got *Coltrane* and *Miles Davis* for you," Mike said.

To learn proper musical notes and scales they were tutored by crusty Bernadette, an elderly church lady who'd once been a successful gospel singer in Atlanta. She relished in giving *nobody's* like them lessons on rhythm, harmony and melody.

"Is it me or are we in a movie where Bernadette is really a nun with a large ruler?" Eunice joked with the man named Dennis beside her.

He smiled sheepishly.

Sam Hood

Out of all her friends back home, Eunice was surprised it was Sam Hood who turned up at her cabin door on the Tuesday evening of her second week. She had just returned from dinner at the mess hall.

"What on earth are you doing here Sam?" she asked, opening the door.

"Hey Eunice! I was running an errand," he said, looking awkward.

"Well you're a sight for sore eyes," she smiled.

"I thought I'd swing by to see if you wanted to take a walk before it gets dark. It's pretty by the water," he said.

She was just about to make her round of evening phone calls to Gabrielle and Arisbel but they could wait. She was delighted to see a familiar face.

"Okay, sure. Cecile don't you worry, I'm just going out with a childhood friend," she smiled at Sam, calling over her shoulder.

She had known Sam her entire life as her neighbor but hadn't noticed him much over the past few grades of high school. Her popularity put her in different friend bracket. Sam was more of a loner sidelines type of guy.

The Hoods were neighbors a few doors down on Columbia. There were three Hood boys; Otis the oldest who had married and moved to north, Sam in the middle and the youngest was Rory whom she didn't know much except he had left a few years ago. Sam's father worked for city maintenance as a garbage collector and his mother was a midwife.

A grownup Sam stood before her a tall thick and fit man in an army green golf shirt, khaki shorts and espadrilles. He was smart and mild mannered. Some called him overly passive but hearing him speak reminded her how he was the most authentic person she had ever known.

Sam said he'd just got his driver's license and wanted to take the family car out for a spin. She thought it was sweet but wondered if there was another reason. She had adapted to independence at camp quite easily and seeing Sam made her realize she wasn't home sick.

She vaguely remembered them playing *house,* sneaking into abandoned houses and construction sites as twelve year olds, "Okay Sam you are now officially the daddy. I'm the mommy. Okay?" Eunice said, asserting her most natural tomboy bossiness.

"Yes okay so now how do we play house?" Sam said.

"Well I don't know. Either we have a fight or we make up," she said. She didn't remember her goal being to kiss him but that's what happened.

Until now she hadn't thought about that moment. How scary and indescribably exciting it had been in her loins maybe not then but she certainly felt it now. She wasn't supposed to think frisky with Sam Hood. He was supposed to be like a cousin.

CRCRCR

By Sam's second visit on Thursday of the same week, he brought her favorite Moon Pie's, Zapp's Chips and Goo Goo's. They walked by the water's edge then watched horseback riders in the distance as they drank canned sodas.

She was open to seeing him differently. All she knew was something had changed about her feeling toward him, he was comfortable and safe as if he were kin. She didn't need to sport a mask to fit into his clique expectations like she did with her real friends. She wondered what it would be like to have him kiss her on the mouth again.

CRCRCR

Sam came to see her twice a week for a month. She'd tell him about what she'd accomplished in her music sessions. They'd get into long talks about life, dream trips and reminisce about the neighborhood.

Her stomach panged with a crush. She had never fallen for guys who chased her like the other girls did. Even that charismatic Terrence. Sam made her feel a bit sick to her stomach. She actually missed him minutes after he left.

Eunice looked at him, "You seem to dig me. You want to take care of me. I love how curious you are and like to try new things. You see the positive beyond the negatives. You are handsome and stylish," she hugged him tight.

He adjusted her shoulders with his large hands so he could look into her eyes properly, "Eunice, I like how you don't really care what people think of you. You never get bored and you try to help people without knowing the consequence. That one I find a little kooky!" he laughed.

"I guess I had to get over myself. I was the lightest girl on our street. I don't care about that as much now," she said.

"Maybe I always thought I was the darkest guy in Montgomery," Sam said.

"Oh Sam. Think about it. The lightest and darkest kids on Columbia! I didn't think that mattered to boys. They're not superficial like girls. Wicked *bitches!*" she laughed.

"Funny. Guys see girls as scary and difficult. My brothers had the good looks while I had to grow into mine," he said, making his eyes wide in exclamation. She laughed.

"We must remember even black people judge beauty based on white features. We've been hypnotized over hundreds of years," Eunice said.

"You're a wise girl," he said.

"Naw, I take what I've heard and share. That one is my Aunt Angela's," she said.

"You sly thing," he said.

She thought of a brazen idea.

"Say, Cecile is going away this weekend. Maybe if you could come Saturday morning instead of Thursday. Maybe stay over on the sofa. Are you working?" she asked, casually as if she didn't care what his answer would be.

"Mmmh. I might well do that," he said.

Kryptonite

In Friday's music session, Eunice and Dennis struggled through trumpet scale drills neither of them knowing how to play. The larger group had been partnered up to spend one hour practicing before coming back together to *perform* scales as a group. The objective was to understand the value of notes and the difficulty in hitting the right ones.

The only time Eunice had seen brass instruments up close was when she'd dropped into Arisbel's marching band practice after school one time, "What's this *dohickey* for?" she asked, pointing at the spit valve on the trumpet.

"That's no *dohickey*, I believe it's called a *thingamajig*," Arisbel said, laughing. Her Mexican face was bright red from blowing so hard just to get the slightest bleat out of the damned instrument. "This is *friggin'* impossible!" she said.

Eunice wondered how songwriting and trumpet scales even went together. Dennis seemed to hit the right notes.

"I get it now. It's the muscles in your lips," Dennis said.

"Huh! I didn't realize my lips had musculature," she said.

She took the trumpet mouthpiece to her lips. For some reason she imagined Sam's face in her mind as if he were a musician which he wasn't and blew into the trumpet. She knew she had hit the right note by the look on Dennis' face.

"Mike says it's the way you pucker your lips," Eunice said, as she made a high-pitched squeal from her instrument.

Later Mike Watts led a discussion that likely gave his students zero hope of making it. "Musicians are peace and love. That's why they end up prey to vultures who want to 'manage' their money and take control," he said.

Aside from the business part of music, Eunice found a sense of equality and camaraderie amongst her musicology mates. Perhaps working creatively lowered her inhibitions and prejudice. She had never felt as much a part of something as she did at Musicology Camp.

She came away feeling confident. She learned that musicians seemed an ideal set for her. They didn't give a second thought to her identity. Hopefully over time she would stop thinking about being the right type of white girl or the right type of black girl!

Her sense of harmony also opened her up to Sam's obvious interest in her.

Sam arrived for his invitation by 9:00 a.m. as planned. Cecile had gone for the weekend. Eunice didn't have a strict agenda for his visit so they took a walk along the water's edge of the Shute parklands.

"What's your sign?" she asked. She had thought up a few things to ask in case of dead silence.

"Taurus, what's yours?" he asked.

"Scorpio. What's your Achilles heel?" she asked.

"I don't even know what that is," he said.

"It's this long part of the back of my heel, see?" she said, showing him hers.

"Yeah, Isaiah Thomas tore his Achilles tendon and ended up retiring," he said.

"I bet it hurt something fierce. Just the thought of it makes me wanna barf," she said.

"It's basically an expression for your most debilitating weakness. Some call it vulnerability. I hate that word," she said.

"Sounds like church talk or the deadly sin stuff like don't lie, steal or kill your neighbor," he said.

"There's a neat story about the Trojans, the war not condoms! Ha! Remember the story where people hid inside a fake horse to enter a walled city? One guy was killed in the end by an arrow shot from a bow severed this part of his heel. Guess what his name was?" she asked.

"Eunice that's terrible! I don't get it. Let's sit here," he said.

"It was Achilles silly! Achilles heel," she said, laughing.

They found a bench. She curled up like a cat and wedged in the crook of his arm. She imagined herself a beautiful black woman with her basketball player husband.

"What I'm trying to say is I don't let anyone inside. I do have feelings. I just don't think I feel them half the time. I act tough. You know. Well imagine my toughness and think of what my sore spot is," she said.

"That's dangerous territory for me. I'd be walking right into it answering you. Okay, you have such pride you can't admit when you're wrong," he said.

"Yes. That's right. Try another one but think positive and stop being silly, Silly!" she said.

He thought about it for several seconds.

"Come on Sam. Or else I'll chicken out telling you," she said.

"This is hard. Let me guess. You love me so much it pains you and near kills you but your Achilles heel is you're too proud to show me or tell me," he said.

Eunice got a bit misty eyed.

"Okay I'll stop playing. Why do I find it so difficult to discuss my feelings? Sam it's as powerful a fear as parachuting out of an airplane, which I'd never do either," she said.

She decided to open up to him. She told him about her folks and all the chaos at family gatherings growing up. How her parents' visitors probably saw her as some *tragic mulatto* girl who didn't matter. How she felt abandoned by her mother who was often medicated and resting due to health problems. Sam seemed like a thoughtful listener so she continued.

"There was one episode I don't fully remember. I know Aunt Angela intervened and ended up slamming an iron skillet over a man's head," Eunice slumped into him crying softly trying her best to hide her face with her hands. At the same time she'd never been so relieved.

"You poor thing," Sam said, "but guess what Eunice? I think Kryptonite is green," he pat her head gently.

"Huh?" she said. She started to laugh from somewhere in her crying mess.

"Kryptonite weakens Superman so badly he can't move. It's to the point of not only losing his superpowers but the complete physical shut down of his body. It will kill him with long-term exposure. Eunice your pain is my Kryptonite. All I want is for you to be happy. I want you in my life," Sam said.

Eunice smiled secure in his strong arms. She looked up at his face following the line of his nose to his lips, down to his cleft-chin below a square jaw, then to his throat and Adam's apple.

Don't ever leave me Sam.

One day he would and she'd be alone. She would always be alone. The summer breeze blew up off the water giving her the kind of chills she feared would never go away.

He was smiling at her, "There's nothing you need to worry about. I got you," Sam said, cradling her ever so gently.

Back at her place, Eunice wanted to spend quality time and hibernate with him like in *The Blue Lagoon* where the couple were stranded alone on a deserted island. She had thoughts of going all the way with him that night. *Summer Lovin,' it happened so fast!*

They spoke of running away to Europe, fantasizing how they could blend into a provincial village, run a vineyard, or make designer cheese. "Sam, you might be the one for me. I know you can take care of us. My strong solid man, I want you to *protect me from the hooded claw and keep the vampires from my door.* Yes I'm quoting song lyrics but I mean it!" she said.

"I feel different here. I'm not shy. I don't stammer with you. I feel like I'm the real me right now," his voice was husky.

She noticed his chest and biceps. Was he secretly flexing for her? Was her childhood neighbor showboating for her? She hoped so.

When did he become a player and why hadn't she ever noticed him? He could see the part of her no one else saw but also show her his foolish vulnerability. Their sense of ease together coupled with his *Michael Jordan* cologne unlocked her synapses.

The thrill of being loved was intoxicating. Their mutual affection really did happen as clear and simple like in a movie. Telling each other truths about each other. It was an entire courtship in one long day.

Sunday when he got up to leave, she had forecast the attention he would shower on her. Soon he'd be gone and she'd be alone in her room waiting for Cecile to return.

"You're off then, okay mister!" she looked him up and down, "Make sure you're wearing your ball cap straight. No close calls," Eunice said.

"Yes ma'am," he kissed her forehead.

"If you see a police officer, you call him 'Sir' okay? Tell him where you live right away. Remember what happened to Charlie from school?" she asked. She knew how police would respond to Sam. The cops would think he'd been out looking for trouble. Charlie was stopped for no reason aside from his complexion and questioned with his back against the wall and his hands up. He ended up in jail overnight for no reason.

As a female whose complexion was associated with whiteness she didn't need the same warnings so she guessed that qualified as having *white privilege*. It made sense to her. Although young pretty girls had to abide by their own warning checklist of questions.

"I'll do my best to stay out of trouble. Thank you for inviting me for a beautiful weekend Eunice," Sam said.

"It was nice to feel no pressure Sam. You had no expectation. I adored it," she hinted for him to kiss her.

He did.

Heart Shaped

Sam didn't know what had gotten into him. He would never act on something as bold as pursuing a girl. Even one he'd known all his life like Eunice. *To boldly go where he had never gone before* just wasn't his style. He was shy and rather square.

If it wasn't for Pa asking him, "Son, run over to the air force base and pick up a part for me will you?" Sam would never have thought of going to the Mimosa Road area.

The street signs spoke to him, gently directing him toward the music camp as if Eunice had left a breadcrumb trail. Or maybe he was lead there by something else.

Directed by one of Grandma Hood's 'meant to be' things. She said you had to slow down and listen before you sped up. *Don't be afraid of the bogeyman Sam. It might just be fear talking. Follow your destiny.*

As hokey as it sounded something led him to Eunice.

His feelings had developed over time. As children he'd been protective of her. Was it shady to take advantage of her being away perhaps missing home? He would never lay a hand on her if she didn't allow it first.

Where were her girlfriends? Where were Jaxon and Terrence? Who was taking care of her? His opinion had definitely changed in his opinion of her. He had no doubt he was smitten with Eunice Johnston in the man woman sense.

His drives home were laced with imaginings of spending his life with her and waking up beside her. It was like a hole in his chest only she could fill. At home he stood in front of his open fridge, only to realize it wasn't food he needed. Those hours spent with her filled him with enough he couldn't eat.

Aside from his older brother Otis up and moving to Atlanta ostracizing himself from the family or Rory gone a few years probably high as a kite, Sam had grown up ordinary. The family had maintained reliably modest since he could remember. There was never a spike in spending on check day for the Hoods. Sam was never the kid to say, 'remember that Christmas when I got everything I wanted?'

At 12 Sam was able bodied enough to work. Harpo would harass him to get a job, "Sam, ya lazy good for nothing *shit*! What's that job paying? With all that public schooling, why can't you invent something useful. No one's thought up everything yet! I seen this guy on TV who invented a new kinda car wax that takes away imperfections. That clown is rich!" Harpo said.

Sam thought him a harmless bitter *asshole* much of the time. "Pa it's not like I'm going to NASA. I'll try my best," Sam said, without fanfare.

"You soft in the head boy? You queer?" Harpo antagonized.

Sam thought the idea of inventing a gimmick for a quick buck was cheap and classless, "Sure Pop let me pull an idea outta nowhere. I'll get a better job after high school," Sam said, to pacify him.

Sofia and Harpo Hood

Sofia and Harpo Hood lived through such oppression Sam swore it was the reason they were such defeatists. Some said they lacked ambition or they were *good for nothin' and lazy*.

They freely admitted to not being driven by ambition. Their dour sensibility and defeatist attitude may have been connected to two of their three sons abandoning them but Sam wasn't sure what went on in their heads.

He thought it was as if they lived in a self-imposed slave code dating back to the last dark days of Jim Crow or when it was illegal to read and write. Once, he read an excerpt that knocked the wind out of his sails and Sam was able to stop judging his parents.

> It was unlawful to operate a restaurant or other place for serving of food in the city, at which white and colored people are served in the same room, unless such white and colored persons are effectually

separated by a solid partition extending from the floor upward to a distance of seven feet or higher and unless a separate entrance from the street is provided for each compartment. [6]

Any thought that the aftereffects Jim Crow could be gone in a generation would have to expect a child not to inherit mannerisms, speech patterns and gestures from his parents. Effects of Jim Crow would take centuries to eliminate. It wasn't something his folks were going to shake off.

At five years old he'd been confused and embarrassed when an old timer would correct his subservience, *"yessir, nossir, yessir,* You better be careful you be sounding like your Uncle Tom *boy, boy, boy!"* he'd be told with a menacing look. Sam figured it was something he'd understand when he got older. All he knew was they didn't have an Uncle Tom in the family.

He learned to read minds and body language by predicting his parents behavior. Unconsciously he must have known what made them happy and what got him into trouble so he acted accordingly. His ability to read people was strong enough he could probably open a fortune telling shop. When he saw characteristics in others he lacked the guts to tell them for fear of conflict. *You think you know me Sam!* Getting involved made mischief and generated into worrisome night sweats so he kept his mouth shut.

Harpo's views were often pro status quo and against his own people. He thought the so called *southern strategy* was a reality where Republicans created a fear of black people so the general public blamed them for economic troubles, believing it gave him an excuse to be a constant downer.

"Perhaps the government is afraid of a revolution after all they done to us," Sofia said, toggling between what people wanted to hear and her own hidden agenda.

"The whites in power are afraid we'll retaliate. I don't blame them but how can they not expect it. They'd retaliate all the same if the tables were turned. It's easy for them to stay two steps ahead by framing us," Harpo said.

"Dunno how anyone's ever gonna change that!" Harpo said.

"I swear to God if we just teamed up with those *honkey trash fools*, we'd be some powerful enough to overthrow things!" Sofia said. A natural ally to the black community would have been impoverished whites but politicians painted them as bitter adversaries.

"Can't trust the *yahoo rednecks* to keep allegiance. Especially the way the *blue eyed devils* stare at you. It's the way it is and the way it's always been," Harpo said, skepticism was an understatement.

Sam's folks mentality was so *old school* they didn't want to hear about anything else. They kept close to others they'd grown up with so lived in a fishbowl. Like many of their contemporaries they lacked trust in government, law and society overall, leaving trust to *swap dog kin*, an expression used to describe love and friendship amongst those with like experiences. Harpo had many *aunts* and *uncles* who'd taken him under their wing as comrades in mutual oppression.

When they covered Martin Luther King Jr. in class some boys groaned but Sam perked up. They were assigned essays based on listening to audio recordings of his speeches. One example King noted was when the Alabama governor stood in the schoolhouse door blocking entrance and preventing two African American students from enrolling.

It was nasty no matter how you sliced it!

Sam dreamt of getting the hell out of Alabama, maybe even venturing as far north as New York or Boston. The trouble was he lacked the backbone to forecast beyond his dreams.

With parents like his, it wasn't a huge surprise he'd put his woman first. Sofia had always demanded it and acted of her own free will not in accordance with men or with what the public expected of her. It didn't take much for her stoicism to give way to sanctimony. To put it simply, she wore the pants in the family!

Sofia was a strong woman who could have fixed a roof if she'd wanted to and she might have preferred if Harpo had raised the boys. Her assertiveness wasn't limited to her husband or townsfolk as she often got into trouble saying the wrong thing. It wasn't an admirable quality in a woman so there'd been many a detractor. Her pent up anger was ever simmering beneath the surface so Sam was careful in making decisions for fear of reprisal.

As was passed down from her mother, Sofia was a masterful chef who could have run her own restaurant. She specialized in distinctly Southern dishes like fried chicken, okra, green beans and mashed taters with pan gravy. She could turn corn into any kind of meal, from hoecakes, to hominy and grits. Sam's favorite was spicy deep fried balls called Hush Puppies named for treats to keep the dogs quiet and prevent them from begging at the table.

On Sundays before Easter every year, Sofia had the homemade fudge pans and paraphernalia set out so invited guests could partake in fudge making after church. "Who else remembers eating the test fudge? Where you pour a tablespoon of boiling fudge into a cup of cold water to see if it makes a ball. We kids fought for those bits of chocolate that weren't quite ready," she said.

She had taught Sam how to make flour biscuits, "God willing you'll have a wife cooking for you but nowadays you need to know your way around the kitchen. Can't have my boy eating out of tins! When I was a young girl, being able to make biscuits and homemade gravy was a rite of passage. Us women would be in the kitchen watching, talking and laughing at the old stories. Your grand mamma was so high-strung; she'd *whup* us if we didn't follow her recipe to a T. Oh them were the good ole days," Sofia said, reveling in Sam's undivided attention.

Sofia had worked hard being a son to her father, perhaps it was why she used aggression as a defense mechanism. Plus she was raised in a home where she had to fend off sexual advances of fathers, uncles and cousins.

"Oh Sam, you shoulda seen the jaws drop when I appeared as pallbearer your grand mamma's funeral. She must've been laughing down from heaven that day," she said.

Sofia was aligned to the black community and unimpressed by Sam's choice in a light skinned flower named Eunice. Her tactic was to generate doubt in his mind regarding his own deep espresso skin. She was doing him a favor by teaching him to manage any lofty expectations.

Harpo's belief was there was nothing Sam could do about it, "Your lot in life is predetermined. The darker you are, the less equal you are. Simple as that!" he said.

Sofia survived immeasurable racism in her life so doubted her sensitive son would carry her ballsy torch. She would live to regret not having told him everything.

During harmonious times Sam greatly admired his mother's upright self-respect. Later he learned submission and passivity were not the only responses to a patriarchy.

Harpo on the other hand was smaller and much less assertive for a typical southern man. He was unable to control his wife and was lovingly teased by his pals at the local bar. "Now Harpo why ain't ya doing somethin' about the missus. *Shits* only gonna get worse the more you play punching bag!" They egged him on but whenever he attempted to subdue her with physical violence, he got a good licking.

"You know how many times I warded off them men Harpo?" She said, her face twisted and intimidating. He gave up soon after the millionth time she described staving them off.

"Ma, stop worrying so much. I don't need you defending me and getting yourself into trouble!" he said, alarmed by her interference.

"But Sam I do worry. You're a black man ain't cha? Black men get killed every day. Black men go to jail no matter how sweet and polite they are. Back in my day there'd be things written about us square in the newspaper. We had nothing to hold onto but now there is a little bit of hope. If you need to *kowtow,* just do it," Sofia advised.

"Yes Mama," he said.

"Who knows what scientists are cooking up behind the curtain. I remember this *godammed varmint* doctor, invented a disease called *drapetomania*, sayin' it caused slaves to run away. That they had a *morbid desire to be free, by which the only cure was whipping.* You need to pray boy," Harpo said.

Praying didn't do *shit* but he tried.

"Hush now. Enough of that Harpo. You still need to pick up the batch of hog jowls I ordered from Hank. I don't want him selling 'em to someone else." She turned back to Sam, "I know it's wrong Sam but you gotta do everything possible to stay away from the law. They used to say, 'by any means necessary' well I say, 'stay under the radar by any means necessary.' Please Son?" she hugged him tight.

One time he overheard his parents talking in muffled voices from behind their bedroom door. The discussion turned to Sofia screaming at Harpo.

"What you telling him to bow down to whites for? You want him to appear lazy and simple like I done?" Harpo said.

"You sure don't want him gettin' picked up? They don't ask questions first Harpo! You remember what the Donald's went through in Mobile? Jayzus Beulah wadn't ever the same after that!" Sofia hollered.

Sam was sickened. Somehow he had caused them to argue over Michael Donald again. The Donald's were folks they knew whose son was innocently lured to a car, nabbed at gunpoint and lynched on a tree on the front lawn of a high ranking *klansman.*

Sam got overwhelmed thinking how everything was his fault. Otis and Rory leaving him and now his parents possibly splitting.

CRCRCR

After their weekend together, Sam couldn't get Eunice off his mind. It was foreign for him to feel so good but it also felt too good to be true so he was tempted to end things first.

He was on the bus to Willie's World Flea Market, famous for its jingle that was forever stuck in your head, *"We got it, you need it, it's just like, it's just like a, it's just like a mini mall, you heard me, come shop, living rooms…"*

The song was just as bad as having thoughts of Eunice stuck in his all day. Too bad he didn't have a song to get her off his mind. He was losing his mind. He was addicted to love.

What would happen next? When she returned she'd be surrounded by her friends and other guys.

On drives back from camp he'd convince himself he could muster up the courage to be cocky and step out of his own shadow to become a man. By the time he reached home he'd talked himself out of it. He didn't deserve her. *That's just my lot in life, right Pop?*

The reality was, Sam choked.

On the bus he felt eyes on him. A small dog sitting at a white dudes feet a few seats ahead was looking at him. When Sam looked back the dog's eyes darted away then back. Sam was spooked enough to feel his nerves run sending tingles to his fingers. *Holy cow! What kind of frigging dog is this?*

The dog had a wolf or coyote quality to him but was a proportionate miniature like windowsill figurines shrunk by magic wand. Sam wasn't thinking about Eunice anymore but fixated on the wolf's steady eyes, now scanning passengers one by one. He was Frank from when Sam was a boy.

It was Sunday Church service when one of the old-timers gave him advice, "Boy, you look bored outta your tree. You got imagination don'tcha?" he asked.

Sam nodded.

"This place, this church is only in the world. These people think it's real but you don't gotta be here. You can go anyplace, see anything using your mind. I'll give you an example. What's your favorite animal Son?" he asked.

"A dog," he said, although he was afraid of some dogs.

"Well what if you had a dog or let's say a powerful wolf who was your guide. Who got between you and harm. Say you could sorta talk to him in your mind," he smiled.

Sam took him up on it. From then on Sam thought of the wolf he'd named Frank at Sunday Service. He'd use Frank in his mind's eye to get through sermons. He always knew Frank's messages weren't coming from the preacher's mouth, but from elsewhere like maybe the stained glass windows. Some messages gave way to Sam's church giggles where Sofia would turn and give him an evil eye.

Sam realized the dog on the bus was Frank. His deep stare became communication. Sam thought of Pinocchio. *Why think of Pinocchio now?* All Sam knew was he was safe with Frank around. He had to trust everything would be okay.

What's troubling you Sam?

He spoke to Frank in his mind, *Frank I get upset when people try to screw with me or pull wool over my eyes. It seems like the world is against me. Like I have an invisible magnet pulling negativity toward me. I have vengeful thoughts and urges. I want to wreak havoc on those who treat me bad.*

Sam felt lighter and better as he got things off his chest. He continued, *there are mutherfuckers out there ripping each other off. Preying on each other. If I can make an offering of substance. Help me not feel cheated. If I keep quiet, can you promise to take away this awful hole.*

Sam wasn't sure if he was praying but knew he wasn't praying to the same bearded white man at Sunday service.

Terrence's Boys

When Sam arrived at Willie's World he was riding high on some kind of spirituality, until he saw Jaxon leaning up against a wall smoking a cigarette. When Jaxon spotted him, Sam could tell by the hate in his eyes he had fallen a few notches in Terrence's Boys club standing.

It had been a long haul but in grade 11 Sam had finally been accepted as one of Terrence's crew. He'd been lured by the vain *prick* who fathomed himself the all powerful leader.

The thing was, the crew were made up of many of the natural born bullies who'd tackled, teased and cursed Sam all through grade school. Even though he was above average height and solidly built, he didn't fight back. His being the dark boy with a stammer had earned him a bull's-eye that haunted him since childhood. Bullies and *assholes* sense weakness like a mirror onto themselves.

Newer hooligan boys in the crew didn't get how Sam got in and were oblivious to the fact he and Eunice had grown up building forts and sandcastles by the creek together. The new boys had only heard Sam was interfering with the pretty girl Eunice at her summer school.

"Yo Sam! You got some nerve getting close to foxy Eunice! Who do you think you are chum?" Jaxon asked, exhaling from his cigarette.

"Mind your business," Sam said, feeling cold tingles from Frank on the bus but half believing Jaxon was right. What did he think he *was* he doing?

It was wacky to think he and Jaxon had actually been buddies growing up playing sports at church barbecues. *What now you don't know me?* His precious allegiance to Terrence had him pretend he never knew him. Jaxon had also laid off Sam since his initiation and since discovering girls and weed.

"What'cha gonna do about it?" Jaxon said, blowing smoke burning Sam's eyes. *Jax it's me, you dumbass! Terrence ain't around for you to impress.*

Sam wanted to believe he'd risk fisticuffs fighting for Eunice's honor but he was afraid of what his rage might do to Jaxon. Being the larger stronger one, Sam could easily bust his jaw.

"Shut yar pie hole Jax!" Sam said.

He gave Jaxon a pass for being a *dickhead* and showed mercy knowing the guy was white-knuckling to fit in himself.

Given the chance Jaxon was the first one the other guys ridiculed behind his back.

Terrence showed up wondering why they were sparring. He looked as high as a kite, "You're an alright fellow Sam but let's face it, you are what you are," he said, regressing back to his former bullying voice. "It's a joke you should even try with her and you know it!"

"And if you don't leave her alone Sam, you best be watching your back," Jaxon added.

Sam wanted to break the guys *fucking* neck.

Soul Mate

Everyone at school knew Eunice was out of Sam's league and prior their summer interlude he wouldn't have disagreed. Most thought Sam's dream girl should have been someone simple like Stacey Rogers.

Stacey was the girl who made funny eyes at him ever since grade three. The same girl who had always vied to beat him at the milk bubble blowing contest in homeroom. The crowned winner was the first kid to blow enough foamed milk to flow over the desks edge. Stacey was the only girl who could compete with the boys.

By grade six she was gone. Her family had been run out of a home purchase on a *white bread* street for fear it'd be red-lined. They gave up on the South and moved to Vermont where her father became mayor, them becoming the first family in the mayor's residence in Montpelier.

Sam and Eunice had enough in common they could spend hours discussing current events, or hurricanes and fantasize about chasing twisters. Had he imagined their chemistry?

He tried to stay logical but the thought of her presence eclipsed his reality turning it fantastic. He knew she was different by how his pulsating heart calmed when she was around. She could stop heart palpitations. It had seemed like she only had eyes for him. He ached when she looked in his eyes for long spells and ached more when she didn't. How could he ever fulfill the needs of a girl like that?

They had laid on her bunk cot fully clothed. In fact he made sure to be overly clothed for fear their mutual attraction would take things too far. He was new to all that sex business. They stared at each other nose to nose for at least an hour without speaking in words as if they were mind melding respective DNA like on *Star Trek*.

Now thoughts of Eunice were spoiled by Terrence and Jax's ugly voice in his head. They were right he wasn't worthy. If they made his life hell at school it would only be an embarrassment reflecting on her. He'd be doing her a favor by ending things.

He had Harpo's voice of reason in his head too. It was critical Sam kept up with his studies and graduate so he could start bringing home real bacon. "Whatchu playin' at boy? You're gonna move on and get a real job that pays. Three sons and all I got is you? An offspring is supposed to take care of his old Pappy," Harpo said.

It wasn't so hard to let go of the fantasy of living happily ever after with Eunice. The sheen of cordiality of first love had stripped away boundaries so the killer pain point was knowing their childhood friendship wouldn't survive either. He wished they could simply be back like before when they were neighborly and familial friends. If there were tiers, levels and castes Sam was out of her league on all counts, he was in a sub class even for the Columbia street set.

"Listen Eunice. The summer was perfect but I gotta tell you we're from the same world in one way but different worlds altogether. We are 17. When we are back in school I'll be sticking to my own kind. It's just cleaner. I know you probably f-f-feel the s-s-same," he said. In his mind he added, *I want you to know that no one will ever take your spot in my heart. This summer has shown me that it has always been you. I lo-love you and would die for you Eunice.*

Sam's stammer had returned.

CRCRCR

For the first weeks when Sam saw Eunice at school he wasn't ashamed if dismay showed upon his face or hold back and hide his feelings. *See what you've done to me? You have killed me.* What a shitty feeling lovesickness was! It was worse than his worst cold with chills and a fever. Eunice was a professional icy purveyor so he wasn't sure she had noticed him anyway. *Sam you don't know what people are feeling on the inside. Don't be afraid, the truth only stings for a second!*

Sam's long face was inconsequential to rumor mongers. *Can you believe she went out with him? That was like crossbreeding a poodle and a Doberman! What do you expect him to say? He must be biiiittt-er!* [Warning: Any thoughts or opinions expressed by Sam Hood are equivalent to the concerns of a disgruntled former employee].

Sam remembered being in the woods with her, they were maybe ten, searching types of bark for their respective science projects. He needed birch, the coveted white paper bark with dark random blotches. The trees life sustaining sap flowed like blood through veins circulating up and down. Teachers warned not to strip the birch bark away or else kill the tree.

Sam had been obsessed with finding the right example to make his project the best to win the top prize of a one minute shop which granted you a free-for-all in the school supply cupboard. He was dying to get his hands on a stapler.

A distraction over near the creek took Eunice off her search. Three white boys were *frog gigging*. They had cornered a huge frog and were taunting it. Hunting frogs for eating was one thing but to gleefully torture and kill one was wrong.

Eunice noticed the boys first. He saw her eyes squint turning bionic as she honed in on the threat to the frog. *She could smell trouble a mile away!*

She flew off the handle and dashed over twig and stone to where they stood. Sam called after her but she was deaf except for her mission.

From a distance he saw her hands moving wildly. The white dudes were in deep *shit!* She was crazy and fearless but the dudes lacked respect.

Things took a turn as one boy had her by the wrists while another looked over at Sam on route, shrugged then hunched down to grab Eunice by the ankles.

Sam an underweight bean pole, picked up a palm sized rock and headed after her. By the time he caught up the gangly dudes had her held down. One guy waved a large dead frog in her face. He targeted the one holding her by the shoulders, faking him out by pretending to karate kick his face instead surprising him with a rock-fisted gut punch. It sent him backward into the mud. The diversion gave Eunice a chance to grab the other two boys by the backs of their necks and knock their heads together.

"Whoa, what are you doing you uppity *bitch!* We was just messing around," one hollered.

"You had best skedaddle back to where you came from," she said, fuelled by adrenalin.

Her tomboy determination scared Sam while he also admired her drive to action. Tough guys would've only talked about doing what she acted on. He figured they had bonded and she'd appreciate his being her accomplice.

The commitments they'd made while at music camp were fantastic memories now. Maybe he was exhausted by her or too lazy to make a move but frightened of being alone.

He reverted back to a dopey romantic, imagining them as two oak trees with roots entangled beneath the soil and out of sight. The taller and older they grew the deeper and wider their roots would flourish; connecting them to other tree roots under the forest floor. *We will never stand alone; even if above ground they see us separate. We will have a deep connection beneath the earth's surface forever.*

Real Life

After Musicology Eunice was back for grade 12, her final year of high school. Music Camp had been utopian and civilized compared to regular life in Montgomery.

She was known as the mixed girl who ran with the black girls. You couldn't just refer to Gabrielle's squad as a bunch of black girls without saying 'and Eunice.' They knew she used to be a *brainiac* who had skipped a grade in elementary school.

Eunice had a handle on the whole popularity thing but it mattered less now. She had spent the few weeks before school started catching up with Gabrielle, Arisbel and Patty whom she considered her circle of friends.

Sam had been on her mind but she promised herself not to think about him. He was the only person she ever told stories of her childhood to. She almost thought she'd been under a summertime spell. Never would she have opened up to him had she not been away. Eunice had trusted him more than anyone but now was afraid he would hold her softer side against her but she already had prepped her denial scripts.

When things went well she never thought they would go bad again. When they sucked she never thought they could get better. As it stood being without Sam sucked. *What was it about sweet Sam that stuck with her?*

He was a comfort without pretense and wore his heart on his sleeve. He was beautifully dark like an Ethiopian runner. It crossed her mind that deliberations on dating would have been shorter if he had been lighter. *Do you want life to be harder on you?* She heard her mother's bias. Martha would want her to marry white based on the struggles she had lived. She had her own reasons.

Walking home from school she thought about how far she had come this year. She had gotten over Sam by filling her life with people who satisfied her ego. She'd become a champ at swapping one persona for another, bobbing and weaving to make connection. Rather than feel rejected she bragged about her oddities and tried to embrace them.

The output of her music CD ended up laughable with her sounding like she'd inhaled helium on most of the songs but it had been fun. Except for the bump in the road with Sam Hood she was feeling like the king of the world!

Excitement and adrenalin drove her endorphins feeding her brain as she played the tapes of ten lives already lived since the beginning of high school. She was keen on getting her knowledge up on social justice and civil rights.

Exchanges between her and Terrence, Gabrielle, Patty, Miss Jones, Martha, Curtis, Angela and Sam made for a chorus of voices inside her head perhaps reminiscent of her mother's mental illness. It was a matter of deciding which voices to listen to.

After school she walked past the Y then cut over on Jeff Davis Street where her feline instinct picked up the oncoming figure. A small desperate voice hovered in the air, "Please HELP me." Before her stood a shell of a woman in rags with dusty chalk bleached skin.

"Sorry Dear," Eunice said, missing the millisecond she'd had to avoid her eye contact. Poverty stricken or crack addled or both were daily occurrences on her walks to and from school. The rule had always been 'no eye contact.'

Her guard was usually strong but this woman's desperate eyes and toothless mouth put Eunice back in her mother's womb.

She remembered sidling up close to the coin Laundromat washing machine to listen to the cushioned hum of the motor moving through its predictable cycles. Imagining it was the same sound she would have heard in her mother's womb she knew nothing would harm her floating inside of that rhythm.

"You *fuckin bitch*. I said I need help!!! I HAVE to go see a DOCTOR," the woman's metal on metal shriek cut through Eunice's spin-cycle of disassociation. The woman paused,

"Wait a second, you got any sugar? Sugar," her raspy screech coming from her sunk in tear stained face.

Eunice crossed Court Street and wasn't about to break her stride. She knew from previous episodes the scene would either go simply, like helping an old lady across the street or turn ugly with the beggar morphing into a lying demon.

"You're a pretty thing but don't you GET it, I need to get to a doctor or I'll die. You got any Krypto?" the woman sounded sweet and sour at the same time. Eunice figured her out pretty quick, the woman needed her fix.

As Eunice got farther, the woman's screech was more animal than human, so she widened the gap between them. Even if she had been designated the woman's guardian angel, Eunice decided not to help her. She fought off the guilt which created a war in her mind between being humane and urban reality. Tears welled in Eunice's eyes. *I can't stop to take her to a clinic.*

"Why can't you help me little *Miss Prissy,*" her voice was defeated. A sad animal licking its wounds and slowly winding down, "You *cunt...*" her voice that of a little girl.

Eunice continued walking but it got quiet. She took one last peak behind her to see a man fitting a burnt-yellow glass tube into the woman's slash-for-a-mouth, as if an electrical plug into a socket. The woman inhaled deeply raising her arms in alleluia, then clamped hands around the pipe to prevent any precious smoke from escaping. Her mouth was a siphon. Her cheek flesh adhering to her skull as the smoke shot like a bobsled down the tube and into her needy mouth. There should have been a celebratory *ding, ding, ding* as the strongman's sledge hammer hit its mark, on a fairground midway.

From a safe distance Eunice had no quantifiable feelings. *She's an addict. Lost cause, too far gone, tax write off and as good as dead. There are shelters. It's Montgomery's problem not mine. I can't help everyone. My oxygen before my child's. I am awful!*

She felt an insatiable itch all over. She couldn't help this woman but why was the power stronger in other situations?

It reminded her of the dog in the car at the north end Home Depot. The day hadn't been a complete scorcher but hot enough for the Cocker Spaniel to plead when he saw her through the glass, its owners presumably shopping inside.

She marched into the store, stormed the service counter giving the pimple faced clerk a fright and yanked the microphone stem to her lips, "Attention shoppers. There is a vandalized green Cavalier license plate 88-0522 in the parking lot. Please come to the service desk immediately!" her voice echoed through the huge store.

Within minutes a large frantic man with a long beard and overall's came to the desk. Eunice watched beady-eyed as the culprit followed the clerk outside, "Heavens ta Betsy. It's my car that got broken into!" he said, sounding utterly victimized.

Later Eunice woke from a fugue state in a nearby park with only a mild recollection of a panting blond Cocker Spaniel. She knew in her soul the dog was safe but remembered little else.

The memory loss had given her a scare.

Eunice could spot injustice and had boundless energy to protect those in need but couldn't seem to put up with the fakers and whiners. She had a zero tolerance policy for entitled *assholes*!

Posse Girls

Everyone and everything orbited around planet Eunice. Even though people didn't know how to read or understand her, they knew to adore her. With an often absent mother and a father she could wrap around her finger, Eunice had managed to spin a sleek force field around herself. She didn't care what the naysayers thought! Her ability to self-absorb and block out negativity made her fearless. Plus she reveled in the admiration knowing the younger students wanted to BE like her.

Enough listening to ignorance. How could she not be black enough or white enough? It didn't even make sense. She hadn't been able to articulate the obvious, *How about you be you and I be me, bitches!* She was done being stuck in some invisible chasm. Instead she was thankful to her driving ambition.

She turned bitterness into power like lemons were turned into lemonade. *Fuck em!* At some point, probably influenced by MTV she realized how the Western world worked. *If you wanted something, you took it. If you were denied, you found another way!*

When doubt crept in she promised herself she could move to Europe or Canada where they didn't focus on hierarchies as much. Aunt Angela had said, "You can either tell yourself you're good or you're not good. The ball is in your court. To listen to the media telling you you're not skinny enough, not pretty enough, your hairstyle is out, not smart or not black enough, is all up to you. We are free to decide what happens in our minds!"

She loved how people feared Angela's super militant side. A strong beautiful, confident black woman who commanded respect for her brain despite race or gender and could sometimes be a bit of a nut bar. Eunice wanted to be just like her.

Eunice resolved self-pity was a trap. Nobody said being born any different would have been easier. She felt evidence she'd grown when leafing through her old grief laden journal or when favorite songs and poems she used to sulk to no longer registered.

Lately she couldn't help notice the chemistry between her and Terrence. He had become one of her inner circle confidantes even though he was a walking cliché of swagger, good looks and arrogance yet somehow trustworthy. She wasn't blind to his being a two-faced self-promoter, who used intimidation tactics and favoritism to crush people but he was always good with her. It was fun to visualize Terrence as arm candy. She noticed she acted different around him, she snickered about misfits and made fun of people. They had a like-minded sense of humor.

For the first time, she veered away from kindness and began speaking disparagingly of Sam, "He liked to stay home and read books on weekends nights. What a bore!" She had twitches of guilt knowing Sam wouldn't approve of their friendship. He'd be jealous of their rapport but it wasn't enough to distance herself from Terrence. *Why was she thinking about what Sam would think?*

Eunice had become proudly bold and powerful, fueled by the excitement of hanging out with Terrence and finally starting to follow her own path. In associating with the *wrong crowd* she ended up the leader of the *wrong crowd,* adopting arrogance, thinking highly of herself and using false sincerity by embracing on a diva persona.

Terrence's boys were far too amateur so her plan was to recruit her own girl gang.

೮೮೮

The original posse girls were Patty, Lil Red and Gabrielle. They all knew Gabrielle as a mostly useless member of the group but she was a lot of fun, outspoken, popular and a damned good sport so no one complained. Eunice thought of her as that value added guest like when *Brad Pitt* showed up on *Friends.*

Eunice didn't need posse girls to be best friends, she just wanted girls who wouldn't balk or run away the first chance they got!

Patty was a loyal follower unless she felt ignored, in which case her self-preservation kicked in and paranoid gossip would start. She could suck the life force out of the room pitting people against each other if she had a bee in her bonnet! At least they always knew who the toxic source was.

Lil Red was a vixen obsessed with Lil Kim and known for fire engine hair extensions. She was under five foot and super feminine but could go tough as nails on command. She was a shape shifter, loner and squabble fixer. Men and women alike were attracted to her mysterious ways.

"Don't you find it funny how you can buy a gun so easily in Alabama but selling sex toys is illegal?" Gabrielle asked.

"Dildos will never be legal although they're really just nasty plastic objects!" Lil Red said.

"Things don't change too fast around here. That's why we need to be a part of the change," Eunice said.

"Montgomery had the most sexual diseases in all the US last year? I'd say we are repressed," Patty said.

"I guess repressed folks get angry and buy guns!" Lil Red said.

"I saw some story about a store selling guns to kids and was fined $500, while selling sex toys gets you a year in jail," Patty said.

"Sex toys are perverted," Lil Red said.

"My ex, the guy who doesn't know how to live used to say that. I just ignored him," Gabrielle said. She liked to give people long nicknames. Eunice had already heard about *the dead person* and *the person who doesn't know how to laugh!*

"Ha! Nothing wrong with vibrators," Patty said, sheepishly.

The girls were quiet.

"Yeah, that's some kind of backwards!" Eunice said.

"How come you broke up with your ex?" Patty asked.

"He said to me one night after dinner, 'I was planning on going Dutch, I guess I wasn't quick enough to pay half! He said, 'Boys have feelings too, they are not pay checks,'" Gabrielle said.

"What did you say?" Patty asked.

"I didn't have a witty reply. Maybe they he was right Boys aren't paychecks," Gabrielle said, sounding sad.

Eunice got the girl posse idea from a story on WSFA-12 News. The news had reported:

Reducing gangs and gang violence couldn't be achieved by law enforcement alone. A community response was necessary. All partners needed to be involved; parents, transit authorities, Retail store and restaurant management community members, and schools. Inner city desperation has forced groups to start harming their own brothers and sisters. [7]

She wanted the girl posse's good deeds to be a news story. Their first mission as a team would be to patrol troubled areas of Montgomery. They would look for women and girls in peril and assist them to safety. It was Gabrielle's idea since many of her kin had been through sexual harassment and rape. Most of her family lived in conservative Edgemont Heights so they would start there.

They targeted a bus route notorious for late night attacks on women. Often there were witnesses but since prostitutes also rode the same bus route, folks didn't defend and protect them.

The girls even got prepared with Lil Red giving them self-defense classes. When they discussed sexual violence they found out each had stories of being in danger by the hand of passengers or bus drivers.

The night they executed the plan the posse met at 11:00 p.m. for their late night ride. The plan was to taunt potential and known offenders.

It must have been the most peace-loving ridership in history. They ended up playing friendly Walmart greeters for passengers getting on and off the bus. Eunice still backed the idea but decided to put more thought into the plans feasibility.

ಐಐಐ

In May, just five weeks before graduation and the end of the high school era the talk around was about the influx of drugs. Recreational drugs had changed the landscape of youth culture at school and around town. These weren't the previous generations unwind after work scotch or drink a six pack of beer by the river.

Meth and crack thrust you into a virtual reality of synthetic feeling. It was like laying on a shopping mall massage recliner with goggles that sent you on a hazy mission to Mars. Upon your return to earth all you wanted was get back in line for your next trip.

It was Josh who first heard Juliet was missing, "Her Ma ain't seen her for three days now," he said.

"*Holy shit!* Eunice we need to get on it. Juliet wanted to be us and join the posse," Patty said.

"The poor girl. Anyone know if her biological father is still in the picture?" Eunice asked. Juliet had never gotten into trouble when her father was around but he wasn't always around.

"All we know is she has a new 'step daddy,'" Joshua used air quotes. She had a new step father every time her mother hooked up again.

The posse voted to search for Juliet. They agreed saving her was also a way to honor Sara Brown, a former Booker T student who had been murdered six years before. It was before their time but a memorial plaque of Sara was on display in the front lobby near the staircase.

Sara Brown had been an athlete with potential, whose tragic life took a turn for the worse after dropping out and becoming pregnant. Once the bad boy baby's daddy ditched her, she got deeper into crystal meth and crack, turned to prostitution on I-99 and was later found dead. Her body was discovered badly beaten at the side of a service road near the truck stop.

Juliet also had a tough go of it at home and her issues were talked about all over town but Eunice knew she was a good girl. Her single mom had been known to date *assholes* who treated women badly. The most recent being an alleged drug dealer. The gossip started when he got picked up for pimping girls.

Eunice was especially concerned since Juliet had recently discussed an interest in joining the posse, "You can't join us just yet. You're too little young and a good student. You don't need to jeopardize your grades. Us bad *bitches* kind of messed that school thing!" Eunice joked but was honest. She kept her own decent grades quiet. Juliet was such an innocent.

"Oh come on Eunice, I'm younger than you all but only by sixteen months," Juliet said, making the gap inconsequential.

"Sweetie you can come out Saturday with us if you're not minding Alex," Eunice said, referring to Juliet's baby brother.

"You'll be an honorary posse girl, "Gabrielle said. "We're TLC. Eunice here is *Left Eye*, I'm *Chilli* because I think she's prettier, so you can be *T-Boz*, no offence Jules!" Gabrielle said.

"All about the external stuff ain't ya Gab? But my question is, what's going on in here?" Lil Red said, patting her own heart.

"Yup! What about it? If you got it flaunt it *bitches*!!!" Gabrielle said, bending forward and squeezing her cleavage together, "learned this move at weight training."

They girls all laughed.

The girls split up to spend time asking around their social networks around town for any information on Juliet's whereabouts. Word of mouth was she was last spotted with a guy in a sketchy park at a pawn shop in Arlington.

"That's right beside the Vineyard. The cops are always there but who knows in what priority a hood girl from state housing goes missing in a crack house? They'll think she was out looking for crack," Patty said.

"Imagine if a white girl from Idlewild was doing that. They'd have a city wide hunt started by now!" Eunice said.

"What are we going to do? We're just high school students!" Gabrielle said.

The Vineyard

Eunice also learned about vigilante's on WSFA-12 News. The FBI's Safe Streets Task Force and Montgomery Police had begun cooperating to investigate neighborhood gangs.

"Many young people are lost to gangs. There is simply nothing else for them to do. It's time for us to get our head out of the sand. We have to compete with gang money to stop gang violence. We can't fix it without the proper resources for our police departments. This has to be a situation where the community comes together and solves its own problems. [8]

Eunice figured the posse girls could go above the law since they might know things the cops didn't. The actual law didn't seem to protect their neighborhood demographic, since police seemed to have an accusatory attitude rather than protect the community.

When she looked up the definition for vigilante she found the *eye for an eye* interesting. Wasn't it justified in the Holy Bible? Vigilante was defined using words like intimidation, extortion, vandalism, drug trafficking, stabbing, shooting and sometimes murder. *It basically described gangland corruption in Montgomery!*

Rumor had it police were so overflowing with calls they would turn a blind eye to vigilantism and guardian angels even though they were illegal.

Didn't joining a gang feed the thrill seeker's ego? That exhilaration of being a hero could mentally give one a heightened sense of importance.

"Guys, we need to learn how to read graffiti. The markings look artsy but there are words and symbols on buildings, walls and random places that mark the gang territories signify warning messages to intimidate their rivals," Eunice said.

"I think some graffiti is beautiful but it just trashes up the city!" Gabrielle said.

"Did you know gangs actually go out and recruit members. They look for impressionable young people in malls or where kids hang out," Eunice said.

"I've seen some shady cats at the bus station. I wonder how they recruit," Patty said.

"What are you doing at the bus station?" Lil Red asked.

"No surprise there with hip hop videos. Why d'ya think I joined you gals?" Gabrielle said.

"Girls are often attracted to gangs without knowing how violent they are," Lil Red said.

"Oh my God. Do you think Juliet is less a missing person and more of a gang banger?" Lil Red asked?

"It's possible. We better go check out the Vineyard," Eunice said.

"Wait! On our own? Shouldn't we wait for Terrence at least?" Gabrielle asked.

"I knew those guys wouldn't show!" Patty said, referring to the fact Terrence and Jaxon had been asked several times to join them.

"That's because they're all talk. Out smoking weed no doubt!" Eunice said.

Hours later Patty looked at Eunice then Lil Red and Gabrielle and nodded in direction of the Vineyard. The area was in Montgomery's south end where two streets, John Morris and Martin Patton join to form a U. Violent crime in the Vineyard ran the gamut from drugs to murder. It was not your typical expected description of southern hospitality unless you were looking for your next fix.

At dusk it was eerily quiet except for a few strange moans and curses. This place was on WSFA-12 News a few times a week most recently with reports of two separate stabbings and an untethered *Cujo* terrorizing the community. The humidity from the day hung in the air leaving a layer of margarine-like sweat on Eunice's skin.

Residents on better surrounding streets had reported trouble to the Safe Streets Task Force. They had become so jaded that if a gunshot went off during a backyard BBQ they would pause mid-sentence, roll their eyes in disdain then continue talking.

With Patty in lead and Gabrielle trailing with her eyes on the street, the posse moved in formation stealthily as if on assignment in Afghanistan. They had practiced hand signals based on a show called *Bones* but it was easier to just watch butch Patty lead.

Behind Patty, Eunice scanned the surroundings. She was taken aback by the realities of strung out junkies. Men, mostly black, some white and a handful of women. She saw a tragic looking woman with severely pipe burned lips.

Junkies cried without shame, seeking invisible euphoria. Some wandered near oblivious to the fact the posse were passing a mere six inches before them. The scene made Eunice increasingly concerned for Juliet's safety.

"Onward brigade," Patty commanded. 'Brigade' reminded Eunice of the big squabble they had picking a gang name.

"Why haven't we chosen a name?" Patty had asked. She had been adamant they be called the *Pussy Tongue Gang* but the other girls reacted with Garfield's blasé stare.

"No Patty! Giving us a name will seal our fate as bad guys, like all the other gangs and we'll be targeted by police surveillance in no time!" Eunice said. By the looks of distorted faces, she assumed the addicts didn't care whether they had a gang name or not.

"This way!" Patty said, leading them to a busted up walkway to the entrance of a bungalow.

"How do we know this is it?" Gabrielle asked, sounding nervous but looking sharp, dressed all in black with heavy eye shadow. She was the image of confidence, as if she'd been in SWAT teams all her life.

"The dealers mess around with new girls. There's a short shelf life for girls before they turn into the walking dead *fuckers* we saw back there," tougher talking Patty said.

They crossed paths with a disoriented skeletal man with a pointed Billy-goat tuft growing from his chin. He scratched and picked at his skin and his pant fly was undone. He was oblivious to their existence.

The addicts were restless and seemed to risk everything for a specific paradise not found on earth. They surrendered their personal safety and physical appearance for the unimaginable bliss. Their wild eyes seemed to yearn for more elusive crack. Eunice shuddered at how powerful the addiction was. It seemed whatever voyage they went on, they weren't concerned about brain wave functionality or conscious of health dangers.

Eunice enjoyed Alabama slammers at the club like every other hot blooded American and even enjoyed alcohols sedative effect. Yet the idea of losing all self-control was beyond comprehension. They were fish to bait without the will to escape. They could only be rescued from this hell or die!

The aluminum screen door opened and there stood an angry *crack head,* spewing incomprehensible obscenities, "What the *fuck* do you want up in here?" he asked, with spittle flying off his lips. He looked crazy but less strung out then the others. Perhaps fewer hits on the crack pipe allowed him to retain a few wits.

"Trust me buddy, we don't want to be here! We need to pull a girl out. You got any girls down there?" Patty spoke over him.

Eunice was impressed by Patty's assertiveness.

"Ain't any girl here. Get on with it. Go on, git!" his voice sputtered out like a dying lawnmower. He worked for just enough crack to keep him angry and dutifully on guard.

Patty pushed forward. The bouncer stepped aside sulking instead of stopping her so she soldiered them through the front vestibule. They entered the open layout of a typical bungalow. Walls were vandalized down to the joists and spray painted with graffiti. End to end work benches lined one wall, debris and other rubbish along the other. *If these crack house walls could talk there would be nightmares!*

The place reeked of decay, urine and old hair. Moist moldy air struck Eunice's nostrils. In darkness she heard a flock of jittery nomads whispering for more crack.

"Get out of here!" the bouncer was agitated.

"Don'tcha worry 'bout anything! I aim to see Manny," Eunice barked back at the bouncer. The jittery nomads were momentarily awed by her authority, then forgot just as quickly. The bouncer looked at Eunice then looked away.

As her eyes adjusted to the darkness, figures were huddled in shadowed corners whispering incomprehensibly. She stepped over someone laying on their stomach who seemed to frantically search the floorboards for crack crumbs. A beat up picture book of children's bible stories lay opened beside him.

"The stairs are in the kitchen," Lil Red said, to Patty. Perhaps it wasn't her first time there.

Down the creaky wood stairs they went single file to the basement. The throb of heavy bass electronic music grew louder along with a collection of chanting voices sounding like a bone chilling version of the Atlanta Chorus she'd seen at Christmas. Was she about to witness a cult ritual that would send her into a nuthouse?

At the far end of the long basement were silhouettes of people huddled together looking downward at something. Murky light streamed through the seams in plywood boarded up windows. The group surrounded what looked like a game of dice or a cock fight. Perhaps bets had been waged and they routed for a winner. Were these simply blind followers who would do anything asked of them? What could possible happen in a crack house? It couldn't be that bad.

They followed Patty toward the action.

Eunice's eyes landed on a naked woman on her back laying on a low level wooden table. She started to scream urgently, "Come on, who's next? Who's hard enough? Please! Do it again! Somebody help me! Do me again!" she begged the group of a dozen or so junkies. Eunice's brain took moments to catch up with her eyes.

They had found Juliet.

Gabrielle caught up to Eunice from her position of rear watch, "Oh My God, Eunice!! That's too much! I'm outta here!" she cried. She turned away. The basement steps cracked as she banged Doc Marten's up the stairs screaming wildly.

Eunice was crushed at her analytical miscalculation. They were too late. The sight of Juliet begging for anyone to fill the void of pain inside her was beyond comprehension. She must have gotten so messed up she orchestrated her own role in a *gang bang*. How could the girl come back from this?

Patty and Lil Red were tough. They each grabbed an arm of the robotically gyrating male who seemed under the devils possession. Zombies waiting their turn were fickle and nonplussed by being shooed away from the huddle scene. They had been indifferent to her begging for it anyhow.

Juliet was not present and if she survived would not remember what the posse would never forget.

These addicts were at the dope fiend stage; absolutely no hungers or desires outside of dope. Crack addiction fed the ego, by using the host up until it was nothing at all.

Eunice later learned Juliet's crack addled brain told her *tweaker* zombies were the only things the drug enslavement required. That the drug affected some users with an uninhibited sex compulsion, coupled with a fierce need for punishment. Early phase crack addicts like Juliet had human physicality to appeal to the uncontrollable sex compulsion in others. Foregoing logic good vs. evil played out within the addicts mind. All this unfathomable to the addicts sober loved ones.

In the post nymphomaniac phase, the addict lived for the permanent high to purposely relinquish the physical world. Thus resulting in the appearance of a human carcass, teetering between life and death and engaging in penetration solely for the drug.

Addicts avoided interaction with the final stage addict as they represented horrific windows into their future selves.

BOOK II

1960-1970

Mother and Daughter

It didn't help that Martha had always had a microscope up Eunice's *ass* growing up! As soon as she'd get in the door Martha's questions would start, "How was class? Where did you get that blouse? How much was it?

It gave Eunice a good reason to back off and keep personal things to herself, "My day was great mother. Pretty much like every other day," Eunice answered with a snotty attitude.

Looking back, she hadn't intended to be so insolent to her mother and blamed it on teenage trials and tribulations of fitting in at high school.

"You don't need take that tone with me!" Martha said.

Eunice rolled her eyes. The dynamic was awkward and she was convinced Martha watched and waited for her to mess up. She could always find fault with her. *Why was she suspicious of her own daughter?*

Eventually Eunice clued in her mother might have been lonely cooped up all day so she would try and get her telling stories to allow her to focus on something else.

"How did you meet Daddy anyway?" Eunice asked.

"Good question. I don't know *what* I was thinking," she laughed. "Ever since I was ten years old I had colored friends. Montreal was more multi-cultural than other places in Canada. I guess the French language attracted immigrants. I wasn't allowed to have a boyfriend until I was sixteen and when I did, I made *damn* sure he was white on account of my father's attitude toward colored immigrants stealing jobs. I stand corrected, my mother only *saw* me with white boyfriends," Martha said.

"Where did you and Daddy get married?" Eunice asked.

"The Macedonia Church. It was in the Spanish area in East Harlem. You would have adored it Eunice. Mixed marriages weren't such a big deal there. I had to let go of worrying about my family in Montreal and embrace my risqué marriage. It was the flower power 1960s after all. My big romantic notion was to marry Curtis and get a secretarial job until we had a family of our own. Nobody's life turns out how they plan it though. Have I ever told you I had several miscarriages?" Martha said.

"Yes of course mother. It's so sad," Eunice said. She never asked directly about those stories as they sometimes set her off for days. Mother had two maybe even three miscarriages.

"It is sad. Thank God you came along. Even more cherished than you can imagine," Martha said.

Eunice's annoyance melted away upon seeing her mother turn into an enigmatic storyteller. Her mood switched from bitter to content right before her eyes.

Verdun

Martha Regan was raised to be a sweet, well-mannered Canadian girl so [Who did she think she was?] destroying it all by taking up with an espresso skinned sailor? *It was worth every minute.*

One night at the Regan apartment in Verdun, an area in Montreal, her mother Dot had a bunch of people in to celebrate Martha's birthday. Guests were mainly barflies from the tavern, some lesser known cousin's and Auntie Ethel. She couldn't remember if her father had been home so it was more than likely he was on a bender, passed out due to excessive drinking.

Martha's best friend Teresa was there too. She was a beautiful Jamaican girl who lived around the corner and knew all Martha's secrets.

When it was time to open presents, Dot with a curious smile handed her one. Teresa sat next to Martha, gleefully tipsy. She was eager to get Martha out to Rockhead's Paradise an R&B club, where they would meet up with Curtis.

Martha carefully opened the blue autumn leafed paper, revealing a lovely wristwatch. She recognized the watch as the same one Curtis gave her a day earlier. The same one she had shown Teresa that very afternoon.

Oh no Teresa don't tell!

Martha's first thought was to warn Teresa from riling her mother up about the duplicate gift and Curtis' existence but it was already too late!

Without a chance to think Teresa shrieked, "Oh my God Martha it's lovely! What good taste Mrs. Regan. Martha's fiancé gave her the exact same watch for her birthday! He's a negro too!" Teresa said, referring more to her own Jamaican heritage but that wasn't how Dot heard it.

"Mmmh, what was that dear?" her inebriated facial expression told everyone in the room the question was rhetorical. Dot rose from the table without regard for the ten or so intoxicated guests and all hell broke loose! She was all of 98 pounds but larger than life.

"Why you little *tart*! How could you do this to me? I thought you said he was gone. You're lucky your Pa ain't home!" Dot bellowed like a lunatic. Conversations ceased as all ears turned to the excitement and the real reason they came.

Dot chased Martha around the living room aiming to smack her, "What will people think? I'm gonna drive the devil out of you girl!" she scoffed.

"Dottie we spoke about this!" Aunt Ethel said, frowning.

"Geez Martha, your mother. I forgot she didn't know about Curtis. I'm sorry. Come over later okay?" Teresa jumped up and headed for the exit. "Thank you Mrs. Regan," she said, as she high-tailed it out of the apartment.

"That will be the *Christ-ing* end of you. I'm going to be on you like *white on rice*. Escort you to work and pick you up too. You'll see!" Dot was blitzed but she was also at the peak of alcoholic pleasure. In recent years her temperament and alcoholism had joined forces and become inseparable.

"You won't have to escort me Mother! I've been working, paying the rent on this dump far too long. I'm getting the hell out of here and away from you!" Martha seethed.

"*Okeee Dokeee* Martha! I'll pack those bags for you. How could you think of doing such a thing to me? It's not okay," Dot feigned defeat. She would likely get an avalanche of sympathy from her drunken friends afterward.

It would be the last time Martha fantasized about planning to leave, instead of *frigging* acting on it. She fled to her bedroom. She didn't deserve such uncivilized treatment anymore now that she had Curtis to cling to.

She cleared off her bedside table, which was a travel case covered with a silky table cloth. Her hands shook with anxiety. From the armoire she gathered her smartest outfit combinations and lay them out on a flat bed sheet. She filled two pillowcases with other things she might need.

Anywhere but here.

Curtis would have to make their plan work sooner was all. He was still waiting for US Navy orders that would allow him to leave Montreal. *It's okay Martha don't panic! He's sure to get word this week.*

She opted for an overnight bag to Teresa's instead. She'd have to figure out how to get her things another day.

She headed out through the living room while Dot's barflies carried on, celebrating her birthday all but ignoring her. They didn't need a reason to celebrate anyway.

Martha stopped at the front closet to grab her favorite umbrella then went out the door and closed that chapter of her life. *You're gonna get it old woman!*

At Teresa's place she called Curtis, "That's cool baby, maybe it's time to make our move," his voice was empathetic, "but listen Martha, I need you to hang in there a few more weeks okay? Maybe we can get your things…" he said.

"Curtis I can't go back there again. When Daddy gets back, I'm finished. He'll kill me," Martha said.

"Martha, Martha you can stay here…" Teresa whispered, while looking her in the eye.

"Okay Curtis, I'll stay here with Teresa," Martha said.

C3C3CS

Days later it was time for Martha to go back home to pick up her case and things to keep at Teresa's until she went to New York.

"Listen. Me and a few boys will be down to help you with your belongings tomorrow at noon," Curtis said, the sound of his relaxed southern drawl hypnotized her. She was grateful he would come in case her father was home.

She figured they would need official back up. Half expecting she'd get the *run-around* at Verdun Police Station she was lucky with an understanding officer, "No trouble at all ma'am. We will send officers to meet you there," he said.

"Thank you so much," Martha said, second guessing the an instigation police involvement could be.

An hour later a cruiser showed up at the Regan apartment with two large black cops! *Oh God! This will send her into a frenzy!* Martha's stomach was in knots. It was not at all what she'd envisioned.

"Now don't you fret. There won't be a problem or else she will be arrested," the officer said, assuring Martha as if her escape was completely routine.

"Martha your mother will implode!" Teresa said, watching from a safe distance on the sidewalk.

That's when Curtis and a couple of Navy buddies pulled up in a Cutlass Supreme. She thought she might drop dead at the scare her mother was about to receive. *Too much?*

"Here we go!" the officer said.

Dot opened the door.

The policemen explained politely why they were there and what they were taking. As Martha passed through the front vestibule Dot took a swing aimed at her jaw. The officer gently blocked Dot's arm, "Mrs. Regan there'll be none of that. Martha might not press charges but we will arrest you for disturbing the peace!" he said.

Dot's eyes narrowed as she glared at Martha.

Martha and her fellas proceeded on through the apartment to fetch the last of her belongings.

Goodbye Mother.

Many years later, after Eunice was born Martha sent Dot the hospital picture, *Meet your granddaughter Eunice Elena Johnston. She's blood whether you like it or not!*

There was no immediate reply.

"A long time later your grandmother wrote back saying how truly sorry she was. That her reactions were extreme due to medications and panic because her friend had married a black man and she had seen them discriminated against. *They were shunned away and had to sit far away from Canada Day festivities on account of their union.* Dot was afraid they'd be stoned to death and didn't want Martha to live a life of misery. She wanted me to bring you up to visit her in Montreal," Martha said.

"I don't remember that. How did you respond?" Eunice asked.

"I wrote, *no, not happening. You may not see her until you've first accepted her father.* I told her we couldn't travel due to low income and taking care of you, which was true. And that she'd need to meet Curtis over the phone. I guess I was a little harsh. Your grandmother ended up sending baskets by Elizabeth Arden and baby stuff by post every other month for about a year. We did end up visiting one time but it was at the end of her life. I don't like telling that story so much," Martha said.

Eunice listened quietly. She had no recollection of meeting that grandmother or travelling to Canada.

"Our intention was to go up and stay a few weeks before moving south but we got so wrapped up in your dad's work and movement stuff. Then we moved and you came along soon after! It was a whirlwind," Martha said.

"It's interesting how Grandma's views aren't that different than today's views in Alabama. Does that mean it's always been this way and it'll never change?" Eunice asked, feeling sadder than she let on.

Eunice was fascinated to the stories before she was born and wished she'd been born and raised in Harlem instead of

Montgomery. Las Vegas had showgirls and gambling; New Orleans Euro flare and creole cuisine and Los Angeles glitzy movie stars; everybody knew Harlem represented what it meant to be black in America.

Mental Case

"Don't get me wrong Eunice, we all struggle with stereotypes. Even our own. A culture that seems to oppose your very existence can wear you down. I realized my own prejudice after we got together. I often wondered if I had backed myself into a corner," Martha said. She was pensive with her eyes turned downward.

Eunice gave her mother undivided attention. For once she didn't have anywhere to rush off to.

"We realized we'd been hiding our individual race perspectives for fear of hurting each other. I was raised it was rude to point out differences. It kept me from acknowledging some things I should have been more open about. I couldn't tell him, 'these poor black men look at me like they despise me,' or the like. I understand what it's like to be the only white girl in the room. It made me tougher. Upstanding white women didn't respect me, said I couldn't find a man of my own kind. I disgusted some of them for letting him touch me but I'm sure some envied my boldness. They called me a *slut* or said I had a fetish. A fetish! Eunice can you imagine your mother with a fetish?" Martha said, in a shrill laugh.

"Where did you get such nerve Mother?" Eunice asked.

Martha looked at her daughter incredulous. She took a sip of water, cleared her throat and began her story in an almost audiobook narration.

That Saturday November 1959 was one of those occasions I got the gumption. My mother was hard on me but she herself didn't take shit from anyone, so was my protector. I had seen a lot I guess. Especially when those men tried to take me down. I never wanted to be put in that situation again, so I'd fight off anyone to make up for what my brother did for me.

Back home, I was attacked once. Two men came into my bedroom, "What a pretty velvet dress you have Martha," Ralf said. His eyes on me as I sat at my makeup vanity mirror. He stood behind me and put his fingers on the nape of my neck.

That was Ralf. Always the charming man, "Where are you off to tonight?" He was eastern European with a Dracula accent, which made everything he said sound soothing and exotic.

I didn't take notice but Ralf's friend Gus had closed the door behind him, drowning out the party out in the living room. Top 40 music blared from the turntable. Your grandparents had guests, or whatever cronies they could dredge from the tavern. I remember it was intermission on a hockey game night.

Pa was often a hog for attention so would play big spender treating his buddies to a night of food and drink. This was much to Ma's dismay but she was too far into the sauced to effectively protest.

"You know you're Ma is very concerned about you Martha. Going with that darkie. She needs you to be a good girl. Make good grades in school and stay put like a lady," Ralf said. His fingers sunk deeper into my skin sending my alarm bells off. How he knew about Curtis I didn't know! I wondered if mother told them my business.

"I'm not sure what you mean Ralf," I said. I went to stand up but his caress turned into a grip on my shoulder. His hand slid swiftly down to my wrist. His trouser belt came unloose as quick as anything. He pulled me up from the chair. His bricklayer arms were iron strong and he was stealth. I yelped but he clamped my mouth shut with his other hand.

Gus had duct tape. I remember the sound of it ripping off the roll. He taped my mouth, suffocating me until I adjusted to breathing through my nose. Another strip ripped. I clued in, that they were prepared with readily available tools and this was pre-planned! I thought of my mother immediately.

"Sit tight you schwarzer-loving bitch," Ralf threw me on the bed.

I tried to scream from behind my taped mouth.

"You let that animal touch you. Rip open your top like this? Suckle your titties!" He was rough as he tore at my chest exposing my camisole and bra.

His hand let go of my wrist, for a second so I swat at him. I knew no one would hear my muffled screams, through the jangle of music and drunks out front.

Ralf slapped me with his open hand as I heard the sound of more tape ripping off the roll. Gus fastened my wrist to the bedpost. Then the other wrist.

I tried to kick at Ralf but his massive stalky legs were quickly on either side of my waist, with him sitting on me. I hung half off the bed trying my best not to cooperate. A bed spring or something pinched into my back.

I was dizzy from the acrid sweat of Gus' street odor, mixed with Ralf's sweet after-shave.

There was another scent, like a pot burning on the stove. I looked up backwards over my left shoulder, to see my bedside lamp. I had laid a scarf over the lamp to give the room a moody red glow. Teresa had said, "you can make any dump look enchanting with the right lighting."

I prayed the scarf would touch down on the hot light bulb and burst into flames, so I could wriggle free. Ralf pulled the bottom of my dress up.

Hot wetness moving down my face from a cut. I kept my eyes on the lamplight praying for a miracle.

My prayers were answered when the bedroom door opened and I made out the top of my brother Russell's wavy hair.

Ralf still struggled with my dress. "You should have taken my dress off before tying my hands you fucking piece of shit!" I remember thinking.

My brother dove towards Ralf's back but I could tell he hadn't seen Gus crouched behind the door. Gus grabbed Russell from the ankles and pulled hard so he crashed to the floor. Gus's face was a rabid animal drooling and foaming at the mouth.

Ralf's hands were off me as he turned his attention to Russell, the real threat who looked like a grown man with brawn and muscle.

"He he, Ralf we got a live one. This is the shithead who got his first knockout boxing me!" Gus said.

"Why don't you teach him a lesson then," Ralf turned all his power, holding Russell's upper body down.

"I been looking for you. You fucking cunt," Gus said to Russell.

All I could do was watch them overpower my little brother.

I left for Montreal soon after the incident. My father tried to stop me but quickly gave up, preferring his drink instead.

The pain and guilt of leaving Russell was so intense I focused only on my new life with your father and getting myself to New York. I didn't have a choice.

Eunice was still as she took in the story. She cupped her hands over her mother's hands. Martha smiled back looking sleepy but also relieved. Eunice suspected she appreciated being heard.

Penn Station

The first time Curtis brought Martha to Harlem it was 1962, during one of New York City's famous heat waves. At a whopping 96 degrees he didn't think the temperature could get any hotter in Yankee country. He was set out to pick her up at Penn Station on 31st Street between 8th and 9th at noon. The plan was they would apply for a marriage license, settle into the apartment his pal Dougie Barnes helped them find and be married within a few days.

At the station entrance, he marveled at the vaulted ceiling adorned with steel and glass. The arches resembled an umbrella mosaic of colorful light, that streamed down from its dome like veins. Such an outstanding masterpiece of Beaux-Arts style and an architectural jewel of Manhattan. The fact Penn station would be demolished in less than two years was akin to a Greek tragedy.

Curtis held a single red rose as he watched for Martha at the busy arrivals gate. He stood over six feet with a solid torso and tough demeanor. He'd always been active working the family farm in Georgia, then a master of menial tasks aboard the SS Valley Forge.

He hadn't seen Martha since the day he helped her retrieve her belongings and take them to Teresa's place. A frightful thought crossed his mind. He pondered telling her gently they should forget the whole thing, as soon as she arrived. Not because his heart didn't want her but practicality and feasibility. *What the hell was he doing messing around with a white Canadian woman?*

His cold feet eased up, as travelers flooded in through arrivals with luggage and parcels in hand. He was eager to see her on U.S. soil without her family drama to worry about. If it was going to work, they needed a blank slate to build a future and New York would be neutral ground, for them to start.

He tried to spot her amongst the passenger heads and hats bobbing down the gangway. Behind a woman in a wide brimmed hat scolding a pair of teenaged sons, Martha Regan popped out of the darkened passageway and into view.

The raven-haired beauty, looked a bit frazzled but was the vision of an angel nonetheless. She wore a light pink skirt and white blouse. She tugged at a heavy worn-out red plaid case on caster wheels.

She looked from left to right, up and down the grand hall until her eyes landed squarely on his. When she smiled in his direction, the doubt he'd had pre-arrival washed away. Penn station was the exact place, she was supposed to be.

"Oh Curtis look at this place. I've never seen such a beast. I watched the skyscrapers get bigger and bigger, until we passed into the tunnel. It's a wonder how the trains go underneath all this," she halted her rolling valise and jumped into his arms.

"Welcome to New *Yawk* baby," he said, attempting a native accent. He couldn't believe he was saying New York out loud. *How dare he even be here?* All he knew of the world so far was his stint on the Navy ship. Farming seemed like ages ago.

He took over her luggage.

"It's like a house for gods," she pointed to a stone angel looking down at them from above.

"Don't say it too loud but folks are sore, this place is set for demolishment and replaced by a shiny new arena called Madison Square. I guess it'll be a venue for Mohammed Ali," he said.

"I can't believe you're right here in front of me. It's time for our lives to begin. Free at last," Curtis said.

He hugged her again. She was boiling. "Damn woman. You're hotter than Savannah. You got any lighter clothes to wear in there?" he pointed to her suitcase. "This here's a record heat wave."

"You nearly squeezed the perspiration out of me!" she laughed. "I wore this outfit for you Curtis. Do you like it?" she looked up at him.

"I sure do," he nodded and smiled.

"Great! Now that you've seen it, let me find somewhere to change," she asked.

She emerged from the ladies room in a white tennis skirt and light blue t-shirt, sunhat and ponytail dangling. She carried her large bag with one arm with determination on her face.

He felt he'd known her all his life and was impressed by her gumption to leave her home.

"From the sounds of what you told me over the phone, we've got many tasks to accomplish today. I hope you won't miss your army barracks too much," she said.

"Naw, I've been counting the days to get out of there," he said.

"I'm no princess. That's why I changed my clothes. Let's get a move on!" she laughed, curling her arm under his as they walked.

"We've got to get up to Harlem, to the flat I arranged for us. After our marriage license I'll introduce you to Dougie and get the keys before he goes. He plays sax at the Lenox Lounge, *John Coltrane* and *Billie Holiday* have played there," Curtis said.

Curtis tried to play cool but he could barely hide how awestruck he was, at navigating through New York. The sun and sky was challenged by skyscrapers, piercing so high into them, he strained his neck if he looked too high. The enormity of the city was a giant organism, operating all around them.

He walked proudly guiding them through the streets. His confidence, must have exuded from him as they were granted a marriage license without as much as a blink. Perhaps they looked so smitten and hopeful. Curtis felt like a proud rooster.

"My God Curtis, you mean it's true? New York recognized our love! Who would believe it back home!" she hugged and kissed him lightly on the cheek.

"Yeah baby! Once you've made it here, you've made it anywhere. Come on let's go. We've got to pick up a parcel and then get to Harlem, before Dougie gives our place to someone else," he said.

Dougie was a friend of a friend of a second cousin from Atlanta, who knew the ropes in the North. He'd promised Curtis four walls, a toilet and a kitchen instead of the usual bunk at Navy headquarters at the port authority base.

After the subway to city hall near Chinatown, they zigzagged their way through scores of business men, hippies and beggars with guitars. Through the underground across City Hall Park, the busy weekday hustle was in full swing.

Curtis led them through the underground, so they could take the C train uptown. He saw the odd look of concern on commuter faces, perhaps wondering if this white girl was being held captive. Then he looked at how happy she looked, hanging off his arm and extinguished the thought.

Harlem

They emerged from the subway and walked from 116th Street at Riverside Drive near Columbia University, the top Ivy League school. He admired how Martha kept pace. It was true, Martha was no shrinking violet. She was a gal who knew how to hustle.

They would find the address for a care package, sent to Curtis from Georgia. He left her waiting outside, while he ran up two flights of stairs.

There was no one around but he heard a throbbing bass beat and voices coming from inside. He saw the package sitting on the floor. It had a crinkled note roughly taped, in child's handwriting from his mother Cora. He looked around, snatched the parcel and barreled back down the stairs. He didn't want to be accused of theft.

"Okay got it. Come baby doll. We'll cut up to Harlem through a park," Curtis said, tugging her case and holding the small package under his arm.

"Curtis, let's take a break in the park. Aren't you curious to see what your mother sent you?" she asked.

"Okay let's do that," he smiled.

They sat at a picnic table, on the north end of Morningside Park. He was excited. In the Navy he didn't trust his mail hadn't been tampered with, by prankster bunkmates.

"I love seeing you so excited," she said.

His sweat showed through his military pocket breasted blue shirt. He wore light slacks and aviator sunglasses. His shoulder badges had little white stars, sparkling in the sun.

He took a breath and savored, the hint of a cool breeze shimmering through the trees. He unstuck the rectangle shaped brown paper, affixed with colorful stamps. Martha reached out to help him tear it open but he brushed her fingers away playfully.

He couldn't imagine what was inside. He pulled out a framed family photograph, of them sitting at the coast and a letter. "Would you look at that. This here's Ma and Pa, my brother Will and sister Louise. Would you mind reading the letter to me?" he held it up for her. Give him a stack of numbers and he could add them easily in his head but reading out loud embarrassed him.

Martha obliged, smiling warmly, "Sure. What a lovely family photo Curtis."

It was a good thing Mama had learned to read and write.

Dear Curtis,

I do hope you are healthy and eating well, on those Navy ships only God knows where. We appreciate the help you've been sending home. Your brother has opened a general store and sweet Louise is taking a class, thanks to some of the money you wired over. She also says there's a nurse you might like!

There was a helluva flood on the Savannah last week. The river swole and flooded all the way up to Telfair Street in Augusta. Your Gramps is getting old and frail too. It's day by day.

I saved the best for last. The biggest news is Ole Man Johnston passed on. Didn't he go and leave us a plot of land. The one our house sits on and the lower field too. We had to go to town to hear the will read to us. Said it was for gratitude, for generations of service. Can you believe it? No more monthlies for us. We is like that TV show Beverly Hillbillies! Mabel says it was like Jesus saved us in this life, instead of making us wait for the next one.

Please think on settling down back home.

We miss you something terrible.

Love, Mama

Curtis choked up thinking she probably neglected her housework, collecting farm eggs and feeding hired hands to write the letter, "I'll be damned. They've inherited the house!" he said, looking at Martha.

"The house you grew up in? Who's Old Man Johnston? Is he related?" she asked.

"A relative you could say. For five generations my family has lived on or within 5 miles of the same tract of land. At one time it was a booming cotton plantation. Those relatives weren't there by choice. When cotton moved to mass production, the tract became a grain and vegetable farm.

"Well your momma sounds happy. What is her name?" Martha asked.

"Cora" he said. The letter raised his dread of breaking the news to them, about Martha being a white girl. They would steer clear of Georgia indefinitely.

"Maybe we should settle in the South!" she said.

He started to laugh, thinking of tough Cora, 'you boys get on in the house or I'm gonna jerk a knot in your tail.'

Mama was sweet in the letter but one look at Martha's pale skin, would send her over the edge. She'd be worried sick. *Why d'ya have to make things so hard on yourself Curtis?* He imagined Mama's face and felt a pang of loneliness in his heart.

"The South is tricky Martha. I'll tell you all about it one day. I promise. For now let's think of ourselves!" he said.

"But surely times have changed. Do you think the South has gotten more tolerant since you left?" she asked.

God love her. Only an innocent white woman could ask that!

"Nope. The news channels may say a lot of good things up here but you can bet the local stations, are reporting at least one negro man, wreaking havoc each and every night," he said.

The thought of going south made him tense. At least in Harlem black people, could willfully rebel in a defiance they couldn't in the South. It was dangerous and exciting in one way but looking around Harlem's poverty and chaos, he wasn't a 100 percent sure this would be any better. He was less likely to be embroiled in mischief and there was financial opportunity in New York.

In the past few weeks he'd noticed people of color in Harlem, following their own rules. They were second and third generation city people, instead of subservient farmers. Their relatives had come up from the South, slowly discarding the *massa* and *yessir* attitude.

He was a country boy at heart so nervous about adopting urban life and protecting her. The 60s were amazing, riotous and groovy but Martha stuck out like a sore thumb. If he hadn't met her he could easily have gone back home to work at his brother's store. There was a rich history with black people pioneering trade schools in nearby Augusta, infirmaries for decent education and plenty of trade jobs. You could live your whole life in Georgia, without interacting with white folk, if you kept to the right areas.

What right did he have to ruin her life? He could spare her future grief and send her back to Montreal. She'd get over it in time.

Then he became thirsty realizing, he'd wilt and die without his spunky Martha. He felt sick in his throat just thinking of her in Montreal, happily married and raising children without him.

He'd find a way to protect her, from the brunt of stares and comments. He'd love her till death do them part.

"Cora has been through a lot but she's an old softie. There ain't much for us down there. I'll make enough dough, to take care of my woman," he said.

He lifted her lithe hand and caressed it to his beard giving himself sparks of excitement. Her hands on his face, could have him in a heap of trouble back home. He felt stiff passion at the excitement and sin the of it. *What could be better than forbidden fruit?*

She was in danger for defying not only her family but every white person, who would be offended by their union. He wondered if the defiance was a thrill for her. The fact that he was the cause of her defiance, made his stomach leap.

Martha stood up enthusiastically, "Alright enough resting. Rest is for the wicked and the lazy and that ain't us! Lead the way my prince," she said, with newfound energy, as she slid the frame and letter into her valise.

He smiled at her spunk.

"I got out of there so I could make a living. We'll try our best here in the big apple and if we can't we'll move into a shoebox, as long as we're together," he said. Even though the stinking breeze blowing through reminded him *baby shit* the sailors would call smelly grease on the ship.

He hoped Dougie meant what he wrote in his letter, "If you're ever up in Harlem, just let me know…" Of course this was the same Dougie who used to get by on *pommie baths,* only changing his clothes instead of bathing for days at a time. Curtis had been partial to the long hot *Hollywood showers* himself.

CRCRCR

Before coming to New York, Curtis didn't know a lot about Harlem. He'd heard of Sugar Hill, just to the north known as a mecca for musicians and writers. Movement authors Thurston Hughes, *Here on the edge of hell;* and Richard Wright, *Native Son* hung out in bars and cafes there.

People of all backgrounds, headed to Harlem for the music, fun and racy frivolity. The *Cotton Club* was one of the more famous places but there were many others.

He found out being black in Harlem, made it tough to get a job. Harlem couldn't support itself because business owners, were racketeers and police were mainly white. You needed a network or connections.

Harlem had once been a proud black capital until it was devastated by depression and ghettos. It turned into a slum without opportunity, had substandard amenities, squalor and tuberculosis.

It had seen the *New York Slum Clearance Program,* where slums were turned into high-rise project buildings.

A Robert Moses city committee had uprooted more than a hundred thousand black New Yorkers and forced them into Bedford-Stuyvesant and Harlem. The people affected most were those with the least voice. (15)

Blocks of historic brownstones, were demolished and replaced by high-rise apartments. Many of those who lost their homes to demolition, were not re-housed. Those who were relocated, found themselves in large apartment *projects,* in towers segregated from the community.

Dougie got them a flat at the St. Nick, a decade old super-block apartment built on a large swathe of land that had displaced hundreds of residents. Curtis thought it macabre, like living on sacred burial ground.

The St. Nick was the only building black people didn't need to pay more rent than white people because white folk refused to live there. On the street it was known as *A sparkling complex of buildings with an entrance but no exit.* The city didn't think it was worth creating parks, or anything beautiful in the poor areas.

Curtis saved telling her too much about the flat and the fact he only had four days, before heading up and down the Eastern seaboard again, unless he could get his U.S. Navy orders changed.

Ghettos and Slums

Culture shock had Martha's mouth jaw tense up from maintaining a pleasant smile on her face. Looking happy required extra muscle effort; perhaps akin to the model who sat for *Mona Lisa*.

Despite the wicked heat she kept her grip on his hand. They came to the north end of Morningside Park, where walls of brownstones could be seen just above the trees. The further they walked the more she noticed the park deteriorate before her eyes. She could gauge by how the children's playground amenities had got worse and worse.

She knew Harlem was infamous for destitution, burned out cars, condemned buildings and graffiti. She wished she could go back home and hang out with Teresa.

On the streets above the park they walked along sidewalks marred by cigarette-butts, chewing gum, litter and burnt weeds growing, through broken cement cracks. They passed brownstones and walk-ups with chunky stoops and staircases. Harlem was a shock.

She tried to be okay with the devastation, juxtaposed against the glorious summer weather but her survival instinct told her, this would be *kill or be killed*. Panic had her scanning for a way out; an escape hatch, a teleportation device or a telephone booth, where she could turn into a flying superhero.

What if Curtis can't protect you?

He was the only one she knew. What if he became annoyed with her ignorance or racist fears?

The simmering poverty accumulated the farther they went. She'd seen her share of dumps in Montreal but this was over the top. She saw boys having fun under a sprinkler hose, beside piled up stinking trash in the hot sun.

At 121st and 8th Avenue people sat around looking down, from windows and balconies.

How could they stand being inside, given the sweltering heat? After the park she only saw the deepest darkest skin color. She saw young, old, thin and destitute all unkempt with dark faces.

Oh my god, I'm the only white person!

Optics plagued her mind so it was all she focused on. What exactly was she afraid of? Skin color? She'd never been afraid of differences before. Hasidic Jewish men with ringlets; busy Asians in Chinatown, Middle Eastern, Indians or other visible minorities, living harmoniously in Montreal.

Her coping mechanism was to avoid eye contact, for fear *they'd* speak to her but she also couldn't help but gawk. It was natural for humans to be amazed by each other.

Too many thoughts took the air out of her lungs and made her heartbeat vibrate in her ears.

They were surrounding her. *How could everyone be black?*

Martha felt vulnerable and physically weak. If anyone messed with her she would cave in. She was done.

The most horrifying thing was she couldn't reveal anything to Curtis, so she was alone.

I'm terrified because your people are black and I am white.

Why was she so stupid? Her father might say after a couple of Canadian Club whiskeys, 'Go to your jungle zoo!'

One false move and Curtis would be gone, leaving her eaten alive. Her need for him became survival.

She shivered in the heat and wished she could snap back to reality. *Wisen up Martha!*

The spell was broken by Curtis' familiar voice, "Martha the apartment is coming up at 129th, just eight more blocks. You're looking a bit peaked," he said.

She gave him a weak smile and burst into tears. *No one could hurt her with this man on her side.* "I'm so sorry Curtis. It's just so different here," she sobbed uncontrollably.

He pulled her into his arms, choking back his own tears. "Baby, baby. I'm scared too. This ain't home. We're in this together and I got you," he whispered.

They remained locked together until she began to laugh softly. She would never in her lifetime, feel more connected to a person.

"It's what they call culture shock. If it's any help, I have plenty culture shock myself! I've never seen such poverty, trash and druggies in my life. It seems we've passed the worst ghetto blocks. Do you feel better Martha?" he asked.

"Yes. Better thank you," she inhaled and realized, she was breathless from heat stroke.

They reached a busy intersection at 125th and 7th. It bustled with street vendors, musicians, and fruit stands. It looked normal like Montreal. She breathed relief.

The lively street buskers and aroma of roasted chestnuts and other delicacies calmed her. She saw smiles and heard laughter, of people enjoying themselves.

Women and girls with colorful Caribbean style kaftans, braids, pigtails, Afros, ruby red lips, large and small. Men and boys in summer shorts: sandals, bald headed, some conked smooth or dyed red.

Throngs of people but her panic was gone. Harlem wasn't so scary. She burst into fresh tears of relief and started to laugh at how madcap it was.

People on 125th Street looked at her out of curiosity. First at her then at Curtis and then her again. *It's fine.* She would have stared too.

"Let's get something to wet our whistle. Maybe a popsicle," he pointed at a small supermarket across the street. Darling why don't you wait in the shade. I'll get us something cold," Curtis said.

Leave me on the street?

"Of course, there's a bench in the shade," she pointed to a lady selling pineapples. He jay walked across and entered the shop.

She sat down.

Their love had to be strong. Society would tempt them to go 'back to their own kind.' Being biracial meant bucking up and fighting for their love. Nobody told her it would be this tough.

Curtis would need to be on guard. One false move might give ignorant folk cause to see him as a criminal. Upsetting a neighbor or making a shopkeeper suspicious of him could mean trouble. He could get held up in that very store and no one would know she was sitting on a bench waiting for him.

"Chile, those are pretty earrings, where did you get them?" a lady asked. She wore a bright yellow kaftan and purple headscarf piled high. She motioned Martha closer to her merchandise where other ladies browsed jewelry.

"Thank you, I…"

One girl poked at her sun hat with curiosity. Another woman honed in too close. Martha felt smothered until a deep voice cut through the ruckus. "Now what are you girls doing to this poor gal minding her own business," a jovial gentleman said, seemed protective.

After the women left, Mr. Jovial changed his tune. His kindness was replaced with looking her up and down.

She crossed her arms over her breasts. What had she been thinking wearing a tight blue T-shirt. Where the hell was Curtis?

Another man stopped, "Hey Mackie who's your friend?" he asked.

Martha glared.

"Now you fellows run along, unless you are interested in these fine earrings for your momma," the purple lady said.

Martha had seen this kind of smooth operator in Verdun, hanging around the hot dog place. *Wait a second.* It dawned on her that back home, she would have sassed this jerk right back. *Why wasn't she protecting herself?* Men were pigs everywhere.

"Well Doug this little lady is clearly lost. I was just helping her out," the man smiled at Martha, as he licked his lips.

117

"Don't you worry about me. It's broad daylight and I know exactly where I am. My man will be along soon," Martha said, hoping her quivering voice wasn't noticeable.

The men looked at each other, then at her.

It's good to see a gal who knows where she's at," Dougie said, putting his spindly arm on her shoulder. He smelled of Irish Spring.

"Martha!" she heard Curtis calling, "That's Dougie! Up to your old tricks, you son of a gun!" Curtis said, trotting toward them, from across the street.

"Hehe Curtis *dawg*, how long's it been?" Dougie said.

So this was Dougie Barnes.

"You caught me. How's I supposed to know your lady was so fine and light on the eyes," Dougie said.

Martha was disappointed Curtis' friend, was a shady character. She knew Harlem was going to change her. What was she going to do, if not follow her instincts?

God only gives you what you can handle!

In the Navy

The next morning Curtis woke up eager to get his Navy business done, at the base while Martha slept off her journey. He needed to clear things up about a transfer. There had been prospects in Connecticut, New Jersey and somewhere called Nantucket.

He looked around the apartment. Thankfully Martha had been too tired to have a good look, at the degraded state of the flat. It was a *shithole*. The previous tenant had left junk and drug paraphernalia all over.

Martha could wake up to regret her decision, since there was only so much he could clear away. He was banking on her vibrant spirit to carry them forward and he'd come home with bagels and coffee, to make up for leaving so early.

Walking he thought of how lucky he was, to U.S. Naval Headquarters at West 125th Street. The Navy had been good to him. What other employer could get you a distinguished resume as cook, orderly and manager of ship services, all in a few short years?

When they were married he planned to continue, Navy duty based out of New York but something was nagging at him. He was disturbed how Martha was such an attention magnet. How could he leave his new bride, to fend for herself?

Harlem's racial ghetto of black and Hispanic, was different than where they met in multicultural Montreal. You could see the danger and desperation in how people scoped each other out, as if they were assessing who would be the most lucrative person to mug.

Curtis had joined the service nearly four years ago in Charleston, the city famous for Civil War memorials, lighthouses and forts. He had never been outside of Georgia before that. He had been intrigued by the U.S. Navy poster slogan, "Join the Navy, See the World," posted around town. *See the world and get a free education.*

His heart skipped at the thought, of bypassing a predestined Johnston career that evolved, from former slave to former servant, to independent farmer.

The second son didn't reap the same rewards, as the first-born, "There's only enough to go around to get Will up and running at the store! You know I need you in the field," his father had said.

In the end Cora may have intervened because Ben changed his mind, "You boys have been hard working hands. I'll manage with you'se gone. Your Ma would rather get you into something, you will be successful at, 'Sides having a service man in the Johnston family, my god wouldn't that be something,'" he said. Ben had always said the service offered a disciplined structure, that a black man could *perform* in his sleep so why not do, whilst watching *crackers* in service.

Curtis signed up.

Leaving his family and friends had been tough but he'd heard the Navy kept their colored boys together, so he'd get himself a network. His experience growing up had been whites were mostly *assholes* until he got to the Navy, where he learned entitled white boys made Georgia *rednecks,* seem tame by comparison.

He bunked with Norman, a slow learning, heavy-set white man with a big heart who'd lived with his mother before enlisting. Norman surprised Curtis in his childlike simplicity, perhaps due to some accident or condition. He wondered how Norman made it this far in life.

Norman had fearsome spells where he completely froze, unable to make up his bunk some mornings for Sarge inspection, "Come on snap out of it Norm!" Curtis would plead. He'd try to mitigate trouble on behalf of the squad, who end up taking the punishment. Curtis wound up cleaning toilets or doing their laundry, if Norman messed up.

Norman had terrible nightmares often waking up screaming, for his mother or long deceased father. Curtis would console him with pats on the knee, or by reading to him until he fall back asleep, "You good now Norm? You're momma is sitting back home, proud as a peach for your service to America. You are U.S. Navy," Curtis said. Norman was from Savannah, so reference to the Georgia Peach State cheered him up.

Of course he knew Norman would betray him one day. That was how things worked with white folks. As soon as it made sense, *white man logic* had Norman pulling out an accusatory finger.

Norman accused Curtis of keeping him up with nightly harassment, for months making it impossible for him to continue in the service. He was charged for the incident but the betrayal was significant, since Curtis had been the only one to stick up for Norman.

"Curtis, what would Jesus do?" he heard his mother's words.

"I know Momma. Turn the other cheek," Curtis would answer. That answer just didn't fly anymore.

Curtis questioned Jesus. *What about this lifetime?* Couldn't this life be fair instead of having to wait for the next one?

After much consideration of Norman's moral fortitude and possible mental illness, Curtis took the blame in stride stating, "It's quite possible my nightly sleep patterns, have interrupted my bunkmate over the months and for that I apologize."

When Norman declined alternative accommodation, he was honorably discharged.

Curtis learned most whites liked and accepted him just fine. At the same time he grew weary, continuing levels of *sugar coated subservience* and began to feel deep resentment, where he'd previously been easygoing. Flare ups resulted in a couple of serious altercations.

On the day after a payday Curtis and a few fellows were having pints in the canteen. He was in a *shitty* mood fed up with the needling, not in right frame of mind to tolerate the ignorant captain.

"Would you look at that, your palms are pink like mine while the rest of you is so dark!" he said incredulous. The captain kept turning Curtis' hand upwards, then downwards then up... while others watched. Curtis wasn't shocked by the comment but his reaction made the captain angry.

"You best be watching your P's and Q's! [pints and quarts]. I ain't never seen a *colored arse bandit!*" the captain sneered at Curtis.

"That's due to you *ship honkeys,* working us until my color clean worn off," Curtis had said.

A bar brawl ensued and Curtis was charged.

In the end Curtis was lucky the incident, was chalked up to drunkenness all sides and the charge got dropped.

Soon after that, circa 1958 Curtis was lucky to be chosen along with five other mates, to transfer up to Montreal. They would share best-practice with the Canadian naval division and be housed in shared accommodation, at the city's old port area.

"Sir, my home base is currently Charleston. I need to put in a transfer request to district 3, as soon as I can. You see my wife is from up here," Curtis said, to the red-haired coordination officer.

The only way he was going to keep his employ with the U.S. Navy having a white wife, was to have put down roots in liberal minded New York.

"Listen Ensign, it's not as simple as that. You wanna think about the consequences of your actions here. There's the request, approvals and then the availability of course. Do you understand?" he asked.

"Yes Sir," Curtis said. He was panicked again almost like a hamster in his head took breaks of calm but then jumped back on it's crazy wheel. *What would Martha do in Harlem if he was out to sea, except be harassed…*

For him the leers were different. Martha was ogled as prey for money and otherwise. When they walked to Harlem from 116th subway his muscles had tensed up, knowing he'd be required to defend if she were attacked. Upping the risk of him being misunderstood or framed, then jailed as a troublemaking Neanderthal.

He had pulled her tight and hated whispering, "don't look them in the eyes." The attention might be tough to live through.

"Who's the man now? Married? Good for you Son," the officer said grinning.

Curtis was surprised. These superior officer types usually wanted to dissect decisions of subordinates as if they were children.

This man was different, "Is she a pretty young thing with some curve appeal?" he waved his hand in an hourglass shape.

Curtis didn't let the locker room talk irk him. All he needed were some nice clean transfer papers.

"Alright Johnston, you're in luck! Here are the openings in district 3. Oh well wait, not those," he scanned his eyes down the sheet of paper. "The North is open-minded but your best bet is this galley cook assignment," he said, pointing to the line item on the sheet, "Don't worry Son, even a *dumbass* can learn to cook this caliber of mess hall slop," he said. The officer thought himself a comedian.

"I'll take it. Thank you." Cooking was way better than latrine officer or ship custodian.

"Good on you. Can I tell you somethin'? It won't be no better up north," he said, staring peculiarly. The thing about advice from white folk was you never knew which part was sincere and which part wasn't. It was hard to keep up the *Yes Massa* act.

"I appreciate that Sir. As soon as you sign me outta here, you won't need to concern yourself about me," Curtis said, wincing at the insolence he heard in his own tone. Intentional disrespect had nearly cost him his career, many times before. He couldn't afford to mess it up this time.

Curtis retained eye-contact with the coordinator but held his tongue. *Just keep it together a few more seconds, without clocking this mutherfucker 5-4-3-2-…*

"Here you go Ensign you're all set. Good luck to you," he sounded civil as he handed over the documents.

The truth was, Curtis couldn't tell if these young *fucks* were prejudiced, or wielding superiority due to higher rank. *Forgive them Curtis for they know not what they do.*

It was the first official process related to having a fiancé, depend on him. No longer was he the suave ladies' man making regular stops in ports of Wilmington, Hilton Head or as far south as Jacksonville. At ports of call sailors were bigger than *Elvis Presley*. Even the dark handsome ones like himself, *Come over her you Foxy Thing, Easy Mama, Hey Brown Sugar.*

Curtis probably used that foolish *shit* on Martha, when they first met. All he knew was the lingo didn't make sense anymore.

He loved Martha's spirit and sense of humor; her tight little waist, the way her breasts sat high and statuesque and her curvy bottom. Maybe he loved her shape because she was a white version, of a girl he had a crush on in Georgia. It never mattered what color she was.

He hadn't been purposely seeking out a white woman, although he did enjoy running his fingers through her silky raven hair.

125ᵗʰ and 7ᵗʰ

Martha squinted at herself in the mirror above the kitchen sink as she slowly took tiny rollers, out of her hair one by one. She had chosen the smallest rollers from the drug store in Penn Station.

Curtis had gone out to his Navy base. She *dilly-dallied* lazily in bed not knowing what to do. Was she supposed to go outside on her own? The one-room apartment was sweltering.

She pulled the last roller out with one hand and grabbed a towel from the refrigerator door handle, with the other. With an urgent two-handed rustle she shook her newly *permed* 'afro' free. *Voila!*

She tied a pink and blue paisley scarf around her head and checked herself in the front mirror. She was pleased. Very current. *Age of Aquarius,* circa 1960! Maybe she'd find some orange hoop earrings, to go with her yellow dress. She'd joked to Curtis that when they got to Harlem, she'd get "a *godamned afro* and rub brown shoe polish all over her face," to stop people from staring, knowing full well how racist it was.

"People! Haven't you ever seen a gorgeous mixed couple before?" *Clearly they hadn't.* Strangers ogled them for their exotic mystique and perhaps they'd never witnessed, true love in the flesh before. All she knew was they didn't stop staring!

She needed the incognito cover, to muster the courage to leave the apartment, hence the tight-curled hairstyle. She had a summer caramel glow, so hoped she looked dark. She threw on sunglasses and hummed *Sinatra's Stormy Weather* back at the mirror.

Ever since she laid eyes on Curtis at Brandy's cocktail lounge, she knew it was destiny. His elegant white uniform and consoling eyes, had been irresistible. At first, the race difference had been admittedly erotic and she could *stick it* to

Daddy, who'd made her life a hell! If padlocked chastity belts were sold at the hardware, she would have been forced to wear one.

Mother was no help. The more Dot drank, the less inclined she was to advocate on Martha's behalf. Mother became a jukebox of repeated anecdotes and warnings

Never trust a man in uniform!

Fantasy is the most dangerous kind of escape.

Your heart was always too soon made glad.

Martha swatted negative thoughts away and replaced them with marrying Curtis. That's when real life could begin for them and they would find better accommodation. Curtis thought she would have been more upset, by the state of the apartment but she'd seen her share of dumps back home.

In the main room was a bed with its brown quilt, yellowed to beige by the sun, a scratched up armoire with faulty door hinges and a lamp with a naked bulb sans shade. Peeled paint and a dried rust stains on the wall, looked like a tattoo artist had inked a spiders web, all the way to rotten linoleum.

With nervous procrastination she stood, peering from the window down onto the lawn. She hoped there was a cool breeze. She saw a frail balding woman in a floral print dress sitting, in her wheelchair smoking. She sat awkward and twisted as if her limbs were misaligned. Next to her on guard was a large dark poodle, with a blasé sense of entitlement written on his face. Martha thought the dogs purple vest with its Red Cross emblem screamed, "Don't touch me I'm working!"

Okay dog let's do this.

She got the nerve to venture out alone.

Martha wheeled a rickety metal shopping cart, through the dank sulfur-stench of the ground floor. She opened a large steel door which must have sent sneaky rodents, scampering away by the sound of their little toe nails on the concrete. *The bastards are quick here!*

Her cart clanked along behind her as she walked.

She passed a woman lacking a few front teeth, minding toddlers playing marbles on the damp floor, "Girl what's going on with you?" she said staring, "You some kind of 'spic or something? You got any money to help a gal out?" she asked.

Nodding no, Martha wondered what a 'spic was.

Outside was humid and must've been what tropical felt like. She adjusted her satin scarf and smoothed down her dress hem. The apartments were towering plus signs, that rose up into clear blue sky. She would send a postcard to Teresa, describing her new modern sleek Manhattan highrise, which was impressive compared to some of the tenement dumps in Verdun.

She walked to 129th towards Lenox Avenue, passing three black boys frolicking under a garden hose, reminding her of the joyous effervescence of youth. Curtis had gone into a small grocery on their arrival, so she set it as her target destination. *We must have goals.*

She thought of the catalyst that got her to New York and her younger brother, Russell still stuck there. Daddy's boozing was epic but it worsened, when Mother caught up, outshining him with her cursing dementia and self-absorption. She could hear her mother's voice, "Your father was too good to *them*. He let *them* all in the house. I always knew you's kids were ungrateful *cunts!*"

Thanks for letting me know in advance Mumzie!

Her mother had sealed Martha's decision to leave and accept, Curtis' marriage proposal. Then the Amtrak train to Penn Station brought her to the most famous city in the world. It would be her history but right now it was her terrifying present.

She was still sickened thinking how Russell, must've taken a severe beating trying to protect her. *Martha you don't need to protect Russell anymore.*

She'd grown up in a rough area at home but it was familiar, people staring at her wasn't. Was it her ravishing beauty and style? Or was it her inauthentic farcical afro-styled hairdo. Did homage miss the mark and verge into blackface racism? All she ever wanted was to fit in.

Martha it's just paranoia. Put one foot in front of the other.

As she got farther away, her senses heightened. She kept looking back to make sure the St. Nick towers were still there. Two good things about her solo trek so far were visibility of the St. Nick and the fact New York streets were a numbered grid. The sheer number of people was new to her. Five people waiting at a bus stop at home, looked like fifteen in Harlem.

At Lenox she looked south toward lower Manhattan. She thought the grocery store was down that way, so crossed onto the Malcolm X side. It was the epicenter of Harlem's hustle and bustle. Intense heat mirages emanated, off sweaty asphalt making things ripple in slow motion.

Chaos sparked at the pedestrian crosswalk with crowds six people deep, crossing both directions all at once. She blindly followed the person in front of her, so didn't at first see the skeletal figure slumped over the sidewalk subway grate at her feet.

Martha was awestruck but couldn't look away from the shriveled woman's creased forehead and sweat-sheened face. She had never before seen a person looking so close to death, perhaps kept alive by the cool air blasts coming out of the subway grate.

"*Jay-sus!*" Martha shrieked. She coughed and gasped all at once. Her jaw jerked away as if unseen forces, shielded her from anymore horror. She was numb all over. Her body sank as if molten lead had pulled her down. She felt as if she were on that grate.

Martha you drama queen.

She felt as if invisible King Kong had gently cupped her in his palm, lifted her out of the intersection and set her down safely, beneath the ivory spire of a red church. She felt his giant hand around her waist like cedar bushes wrapped in winter burlap. Martha burst out crying, pitying the woman

Yet, she was relieved and grateful to be away from the crowd. *Talk about a hell on earth.*

Shell-shocked, Martha got herself up and pressed on to the Green Garden Deli at 128th. With her heart rate stabilized she pushed her cart down one aisle and up the other intrigued, by the different brands. She snuck peaks into other passing buggies, to see what women bought for groceries. She selected canned peas and corn, catsup, kidney beans, macaroni and potato chips among other ingredients. She welcomed the normalcy of women with lists in hand shopping for dinner fixings.

With the grocery mission accomplished she walked two blocks south. Martha's attention was caught by Sylvia's Soul Food purple signage, the large steel gray stonework stood out.

Curtis had said food there reminded him of his youth. She stopped in for a coffee and perhaps get something sweet for him.

A man in a tan safari suit, overdressed for the heat moved from table to table wearily asking for change, "I've been trying really hard to get into the city program. I haven't seen my girls in two years. Please help me," he said, his voice sincere.

Her opinion was he hadn't always been a beggar. His motivation was hunger and desperation instead of dollars, for booze or narcotics. She watched as he was repeatedly declined. *Were the clientele onto his scheme?* For all she knew he made a decent living with his earnest voice and engaging story. She averted eye contact when he looked over but her fingers twitched toward her change purse.

A well-dressed woman entered in a red dress and large sun hat, the brim shading her face. Her elegant wrist dipped and dove as she pointed out items to order, in the glass display case.

The safari suited man saw her too. Martha was relieved he hadn't gotten to her change purse. He made his move on the woman, "Would you be so kind as to get me some macaroni?" he asked, in a whisper. His eyes trained on the delights behind the display glass.

Martha anticipated a negative reaction from patrons lined up behind the woman but without fanfare or a pause in her order, she said, "Sure sweetie," as if this happens every day.

"Thank you kindly," he humbly bowed to her.

The lady paid for both orders and sashayed out the door like a fashion model. Martha admired her poise.

The din of conversation and clinking silverware made for a peaceful soundtrack. Her world was starting to make sense. In a big overwhelming city there were angels, taking care of things.

She headed to 7th along 126th, toward home toting the wheelie cart with the newly purchased peach cobbler teetering on top. Feeling changed by the solo outing she wept joyous tears behind her sunglasses.

She had fallen for the same fearful exaggerations of 'poor inner city black folk, the she despised hearing from others back home. This wasn't any different.

In Montreal she was in the majority, while in Harlem she wasn't. The more of *them* there were, the more dangerous it was for *us*! Her mind was foggy with the concept but she knew there was something important in there. *Yes, but Martha girl, you could have raped and left for dead!* Martha giggled thinking how judgmental her parents were, except with drinks in their bellies. Her mind was elsewhere until noticing the sound of shoe treads beside her.

"Hey pretty lady," a man said. His voice was amiable as if they'd been old classmates, "let me help you out with that cart..." he was well-spoken and gallant.

Straight home now, Martha. How many times do I gotta tell you, No dilly-dallying!

She stopped and turned to face him. He was tall and slender in pajama bottoms and a white tank top, so overstretched it looped low revealing far too much of his bare concaved chest, armpits and spindle-arms. She was more horrified by his outfit than her safety.

His eyes willfully locked onto hers. She recognized the power was in his abrupt ability, to catch her off guard. *Alright listen buddy, I'm a naïve Canadian gal conducting an undercover experiment, to see if I can pass for black in Harlem without getting robbed! Go ahead, rob me now!* Honesty felt so good in her mind but instead she wondered what the fancy lady would have done. "Thanks darlin,' I might've taken you up on that offer but I've got just the right balance here!" Martha said, nodding at her cart.

Her heart skipped a beat sensing this the moment control would be taken from her, "I'm perfectly fine. You'd be amazed how much I can tote in this thing. These rubber wheels are a godsend and I'm convinced this cart has paid for itself several times over!" She wasn't sure if her fast talking came across as fear but as she spoke she felt more connected to him and more in control of herself.

Time stood still while stood assessing her. His moldy odor caught her nostrils. Greying dreadlocks and a long goatee were too close to her face. How much more could her senses take? Her hand closed into a fist with fingernails stabbing her palm, to absorb the hysteria inside.

"Okay pretty lady," he said.

"You go ahead and have a good day now! I'm sure I'll be seeing you around town," she said, with a casual hand wave. She started walking. Her muscled calves energized to propel her forward, with the stride of a gazelle.

"*Alrightee* then... I look forward to it ma'am..."

Within minutes she was out of urban mischief, looking onto a manicured park near the St. Nick. Heart-palpitations were replaced by calm. It was funny how adrenalin felt so good almost like a drug.

What if he'd just wanted company? What if we were all starving for connection? She replayed the scene. A simple and firm "no thank you," would have sufficed, instead of all this fear.

At the St. Nick Martha entered through the ground level entranceway. She paused at the stoop where the woman still sat. She gave her the brown paper bag of peach cobbler.

"Oh chicca, you are angel, the boys will be over the moon!" she said.

Martha was back safely tucked into the apartment, which didn't look so bad after all. She unpacked the cart and smiled wondering, how the women whose grocery ideas she'd copied, would prepare their meals tonight.

She sautéed cabbage, onion and kidney beans together in a saucepan. Then opened a can of beef stew and poured it over top, adding collard greens and chili paste from a jar. The cornucopia of color and aroma smelled just like Harlem. Curtis was bound to love it.

BOOK III

1995-1998

Life after High School

The year after high school had gone by so quickly. Many of Eunice's friends had gone their separate ways looking for jobs, so the group dynamic was gone. Eunice was working at Vespa's Diner downtown on Madison.

Civil unrest in one neighborhood or another was pretty normal in Montgomery but overall the city wasn't as dangerous as Talladega or Atmore, with racial violence and crime. She imagined Angela's famous interview voice in her head, "...ever since the time the first black person was kidnapped from the shores of Africa."

After the drama of rescuing Juliet from the Vineyard crack house a year before, her posse girls had laid low. She'd only kept up with Gabrielle. Besides, it wasn't like she needed anyone.

Eunice had been occupied with domesticity since she and Sam had shacked up together against her parents' wishes. They moved into the RV trailer out behind the Hood house. Sam's father had modified it into a winterized guest house.

It was her idea to postpone marriage, "We're eighteen Sam. Let's try this first and get married when it feels right," she said, leery of committing.

"Alrightee then," he sounded disappointed. "We can set a plan for next year. We are lucky to have found each other. What more could I ask for," he said, giving her a hug.

"Look on the bright side, we can actually save up for a real wedding and maybe go on a proper honeymoon to New York or someplace," she was interested in walking her parents footsteps in their early days. "I don't want to work in that *god-awful* diner forever! I'd rather focus on getting a better job," Eunice said.

"Sure thing," he said, looking bored.

The months following the Vineyard had gotten her depressed, perhaps it was a letdown after such high octane drama. She compared it to how a hangover made you pay the price for drunken fun the night before.

Maybe Eunice hadn't played out the living together story to the end. If she were honest she could admit she shacked up with him for the wrong reasons. She brushed the thought away. All she knew now was Sam had his snout into every move she made.

Before moving in together, things had been stressful at home with her parents. Not only had Martha isolated from the world in a private shell, when she did come out of it she was bitter and cynical toward Curtis. It made for a strained household so Eunice jumped at the opportunity to leave them in their own misery.

She had kept her promise to go over every day and make sure they were eating properly. Martha was endearing in her simplicity satisfied with soup and crackers; and Daddy was even easier, having whatever Eunice brought.

Sam had been a reliable rock but lately he seemed testy, protesting the things that interested her. *What do you want to get involved in activism for Eunice?*

She couldn't figure out if he was jealous of her ambition or over protective. It never crossed her mind he might have the foresight into danger that she lacked. He had always been a little clingy about her comings and goings, paranoid she'd be maimed or killed whenever she stayed out past 9:00 p.m.

She couldn't imagine how Sam got through a day with all his watching and worrying. Life didn't need to be so dramatic and all he did was stress out. She was overwhelmed by his demands and admittedly more comfortable being with her friends.

It wasn't as if she wanted Terrence for life but they were friends and he was a good laugh. Being with him allowed her to let her hair down, so what was the big deal? It didn't hurt he had a motorcycle and was slyly captivating but Sam never wanted to hear that. She'd need to get Sam a copy of *Don't sweat the small stuff!*

His overbearing grated on her nerves. She guessed it was payback for moving in to escape her parents!

CB CB CB

On a beautiful afternoon, Eunice languished in front of *The Real World: New Orleans* on pirated cable when she realized she had turned into an ambitionless loser. *Holy fuck!*

She needed to make a change instead of eating junk food in bed, watching *Shorty* and *Mercy*. It was time to get out and reconnect instead of thinking of herself a prisoner.

The thought of her being poor white trash made her laugh hysterically, relieved as if she'd just won the state lottery, even though Alabama didn't have one. Admitting to becoming lazy was oddly exhilarating, "Eunice *fucking* Johnston lives in a trailer [some call it a shack]. All she was missing was a bun in the oven!" She looked in the mirror and slapped her own face, "now snap out of it!"

She had seen an MTV show about *Marrying up and out,* which gave her another reason to be apprehensive about marrying Sam. Wouldn't it be wise to hook up with a lighter man? She was light enough to pass for white or at least be accepted in white society.

She fanaticized of moving away, marrying white and having a white child so all the race stuff would simply go away. If genetics favored her mother's pallor, it was plausible she'd have a fair-skinned child. Having a son with Mike Watts for example, would be a gift to her unborn son. Perhaps being born mixed meant she was supposed to choose who she wanted to be.

Eunice had been living with Sam for just over a year by the time she decided to reconnect with her girls, Terrence and others. She felt some of that spitfire motivation coming back.

She rarely revealed private thoughts but may have come across as cynical in her relationship with Sam and the girls didn't hold back letting her know staying with him was a serious mistake. *You can have any man, what are you doing with Sam?*

Reconnecting with friends wasn't without a few awkward moments with Patty and Lil Red wondering why she'd dropped off the map. They wanted to know she was serious about renewed friendships. Eunice was committed, she wanted to recreate the magic and good intentions they had started around the time of the Vineyard.

"Listen, I'm sorry guys. Maybe it was the shock of Juliet or my mental health. I don't know. It was wise to take care of myself and rest but I let it go on too long," Eunice said.

Eunice could tell Patty had no use for Sam and often made sly comments about him. He was wise to her though. At home he liked to guess what bad things she had said about him, "I bet dear old Patty had me on the very top of her hate list. Such lovely companions you keep!" he said, sarcastic making snide remarks about Patty and Terrence. She guessed he was jealous she was getting motivated again.

He didn't like Lil Red either. "I don't see the magic in that girl. Is she actually a rapper on the side? I thought her name was Vanessa," Sam said, the first time he met her.

"Maybe she's shy about being gay or something. I don't know. Wouldn't that make you prejudiced!" Eunice said.

"For a brother he's a bit of a dud don't you think? He's definitely *rhythmless nation*. Have you seen him dance?" Terrence said. He still seemed to wait for Eunice's reaction to his flirtation. It made Eunice feel special.

"Come on guys, Sam ain't the wildest guy but we love and respect Eunice all the same," Gabrielle said, giving her a pass with the backhanded compliment.

"Well if he was a snake he'd a bitten you by now, so he must be alright Eunice!" Patty said.

"Eunice how are you coping with 'married' life?" Arisbel asked. She was the only naturally kind one in the bunch.

"Alright I guess," Eunice said, but offered no more.

"This will cheer you up. The place I'm tutoring at is so wacked, they had us doing a musical variety show singing show tunes! I'm on a mixed team, the other team is all black. For rehearsals my team went first but as soon as the other team sang *Hello Dolly* for the white teachers, we all burst out laughing, teachers included. It looked like we were putting on a minstrel show. All that was missing was the white face makeup. Isn't that hilarious? The beauty was everybody noticed the gaff," Arisbel said.

Eunice laughed but was barely listening, too distracted by the argument she had with Sam last night.

"Please don't tell me what I did wrong. You telling me what I should have done upsets me. I'm just being honest Sam," she had said. It was nearly impossible for her to listen to him without judgment anymore.

"Eunice it's like you can't listen to my ideas without making them your ideas," Sam said.

"No, I was just giving you my perspective. My mind plays out the scenario so my unwillingness is because I've already played out the possibilities in my head and formulated my opinion. Don't you trust me?" she said, feeling guilty her intelligence was getting in the way of their closeness.

"Fair enough but when you're two steps ahead of me and cut my ideas down I feel like a dope. It's like you have a sensor predicting what I'm going to say next and a rebuttal waiting on why I suck. Have you ever thought you could be wrong?" he asked.

She looked at him skeptically. *No not really Sam!*

"Okay. I hear you. Maybe we're in a rut. Don't hold things I tell you against me later. Like how I might treat my folks or my independent nature," she said, thinking she'd made an indisputable point.

"I think I'm being misunderstood here. I'm not trying to diminish you Eunice. I'm just trying to be heard," he said.

"Well it feels like you're analyzing me. It's one thing to discuss disagreements but quite another to throw subtle insults my way," she said, bored with the same old argument.

"Yes but wait a minute…" Sam said.

"I want someone who tells me I've crossed the line without being aggressive. Anger is okay but rage isn't," she said, biting her lip.

She was well aware of her natural evasiveness with close encounters of the emotional kind. She couldn't help herself from shifting the blame to him. What *pissed* her off was she had broken a personal promise by opening up to him in the first place and now regret it. She needed to get this puppy off her scent. Maybe she'd be able to open up to him one day but she needed more time.

Relationship friction paralyzed her where words didn't come so she kept conversations simple, "What did you have for lunch Sam?" she would change the subject.

"What a weird question. What did you have for lunch with Terrence? Was it his birthday? I saw it on your calendar. Where did you go?" he asked.

She was afraid he would flip out at any second. She had enough smarts to know he liked reassurances but her minds search for empathy always came up empty. Instead she said, "Terrence and I tried a new Chinese place at the strip mall. You know, where Denny's used to be," she said, calmly as if it weren't out of the ordinary.

"Any good?" he asked, surprisingly civil.

"Yeah, we were saying how surprising the selection was," she was trapped.

"What else did you do?" he asked.

"Oh uh, we went to a movie!" she said. *Best to keep talking Eunice*, "I checked in on *mumzy* too. She was in a *helleva* mood," she said. She could see the detective's wheels turning in his eyes.

"Oh good. How's she doing? The last time I was over she looked a little weak," he was sincere. He was fond of her parents.

"Well I worry about her of course. I need to spend more time with her. I don't know if she'll ever get her spark back. Maybe I'll take her to the Y. I read swimming was the best exercise because you don't know you're sweating in the water. Come to think of it, that's really gross! I hope chlorine sterilizes the pool. Imagine all those old people sweating in a big pot of soup!" her voice was high pitched, with anticipation of moving past feelings talk.

"Yuck! Your basically in someone else's bath," he said, then was quiet. He probably was thinking negative thoughts about her and Terrence but the worst was over.

"Come now Sam, let's watch a movie. Didn't you want to see the *Foxy Cleopatra Tarentino* one?" she tried her best to appease him.

"Okay that sounds good. Are you hungry? I'll make us nachos later. Max adds blobs of cream cheese, says it gives your mouth a surprise," Sam said.

"Ha ha! Max, Todd's partner right. He sounds funny. I'd love it if you cooked. If you call nachos cooking!" she joked. *Phew!* Completely out of the woods. Maybe she'd even put out for him. He never wanted to discuss deep stuff after sex.

Sam pulled her close wrapping his arms around her waist. He was buff now, probably in the best condition ever. She'd known him ever since he was a green Gumby.

"You know what *Babycakes*. I can handle Terrence, I just want to know you still dig me. Our sexy time helps me feel closer to you. I love you, you know," he said.

"Okay, come on kiss me. Just don't be mad at me. I'm a delicate flower," she stared into his eyes like she'd rehearsed in the mirror.

"I like you frisky like this!" he said, "Eunice you know I'll never intentionally hurt you. I might make dumb comments but when I cross the line I need you to help me understand," he said.

"As long as I'm your princess and feel protected. I had an uncle with anger issues who used to yell at me, then shower me with affection. He was unpredictable and it kept me off balance. Whenever he came to the house I would hide in my room but he would always find me," she said.

"I wish I'd been there to protect you from him but I don't think anyone sees you as delicate," he said.

She believed him.

"I need someone I can trust, have fun with and is easy to be around," she said.

"I can be that. I'll try harder. Things will come up that create tension between us but nothing should ever be long lasting. We need to be more open. Please understand I can't always read what's going on in there," Sam said, tapping her temple softly.

"I want someone who loves me for my positives despite my flaws," she hugged him.

"I hear you. Seriously I am listening," he said.

She pulled him closer so he would stop talking so much. She noticed he and Terrence were starting to make the same comments about her. They each saw something familiar. It frightened her to think they could see the motor under her hood.

"Eunice!...Minstrels. Isn't that crazy?" Arisbel said. "Maybe we should bring white face back and own it. You know like taking back a curse word."

"So true," Eunice said, back from deep thought. She refocused herself, "Guys, my buddy Mike Watts has a cabin we can borrow. He's got some ideas to run by us," Eunice said.

"Isn't he like 40?" Gabrielle jeered.

"Who cares how old he is and I'd say he's 30 max!" Eunice had grown up with adults confiding in her, which probably made her wise beyond her years. She gravitated to adult wisdom and life experience so was surprised by Gabrielle's immaturity.

She hadn't shared her activist planning with Sam so felt a twinge of guilt for starting arguments just so she could sneak out. Either he wouldn't understand or he'd be overly worried and try to stop her.

So what if she was addicted to the dangers of stirring the pot! If they pulled it off they'd have WSFA-12 News on scene in no time. She would be credited with getting much needed attention on the school's drug problem. Sam would understand it was all for the greater good.

Serious Business

After high school Sam landed a full-time job at an employee relations help center which came with benefit coverage, which had been a contributing factor in getting Eunice to move in.

"It's over in Forrest Park," Sam explained, "We handle IBEW union worker disputes and get this Eunice, it's an adult job. We are now covered for dental appointments and other stuff I haven't looked into yet," he beamed with pride.

"That's so great Sam! What do people call about?" she asked.

"If you ask my colleague Todd, he would say, 'every caller is crustier than the one before.' Todd says it's the crappiest job he's ever had but I don't think so!" he said.

Finding a job outside of fast food or janitorial work was a leapfrog over his parents' expectations. They didn't dare show pride lest jinx his good fortune. He knew they were proud though. Whenever he mentioned the job, he could tell they held their breath knowing with their pedigree he didn't deserve it. Sam felt like he had struck gold.

Todd Sheppard was his cubicle mate, a white middle class prep school guy from the edge of town. He got the impression Todd thought the job was beneath his intelligence and expected the company owed him. As a new recruit Sam had become his sounding board but Todd was comical so he didn't mind. They became fast friends.

"I don't want to spoil the fun but I had way better benefits at my last job," Todd said.

That's probably because your white Todd! Sam half listened when Todd complained. Not many guys around his hood had perks like these. *White people were so endearing when they moaned about money!*

Todd had grown up well off. His father had invested in a few dilapidated houses on Pike Road, before the enclave got popular. Just like *Flip This House,* his father renovated then lucked out by selling properties at a profit. That coupled with a bonanza of expansion with middle class whites moving in. Meanwhile most of downtown Montgomery's neighborhoods were dilapidated.

When Todd confided he was gay, Sam's first reaction was of disgust. His thought was Todd was going to try and *get it on* with him. The fear subsided as they got to know each other and eventually Sam met his partner Max.

Friday nights after work they'd go to Zaxby's Chicken Fingers & Buffalo Wings on Zelda Road, a local of the after work crowd. They'd chat about work drama then once the social lubrication took effect they'd get into deeper topics.

"Alright Sammy boy. Now that I'm good and toasted let me ask you inappropriate questions," Todd said.

"Alright, go for it!" Sam said, happy to be out on the town.

"What the *fuck* is a *cracker* anyway?" Todd asked sounding buzzed.

Sam burst out laughing, "What is it with you guys. You sound like one of the guys from *Queer Eye*. Eunice loves that show. Not me! After they get the guest looking halfway decent they tease how bad he looked before, 'I barely even recognized you without your nose hairs!' It is a pretty funny show!" Sam said.

"What on earth do you meeeeeean?" Todd purposely lisped, making them both laugh. "Go on now, what's a *cracker*?" he asked.

"I get it you want racial slur lessons. Being southern I can't believe you don't already know what a *cracker* is!" Sam said.

"I went to St. Jude's. I figured cracker was like saying *white bread* or *Wonder bread*," Todd said.

"Say no more, you went to St. Jude's. You're forgiven," Sam said. "Try 'crack a whip.' Although I don't know if anyone thinks of that literally now," Sam said.

"Whoa really?" Todd looked shocked. "Okay I'm not laughing anymore. That's heavy duty."

"My Mom says it's a corn-cracker like in the nursery rhyme, *Jimmy cracked corn but I don't care.* I see a *cracker* as a rich, big mouthed buffoon who cracks dumb jokes. A loud bragging fat guy. Not you, don't worry. You're thin!" Sam laughed, "You could also use *ritz cracker* for that same guy if he's rich," Sam said.

"Like the Ritz-Carlton hotel I suppose. You are expanding my horizon. Sometimes I hear things I'm not sure are racist slurs," Todd said.

"Well you called me Sammy Boy earlier? That could've been a slur if I chose to be offended by the Boy. You *dumbass honkey*! I won't even tell you about *Mungie Cake* or *Memphis*," Sam said.

"WHAT? You must..." Todd pretended to beg.

"Or how white folks stink like wet dogs so we call them Lassie," Sam choked on his beer swig as he said it.

"Stop! Okay frank talk Sam. What's the most offensive word to you? Is it the obvious N word? Just so you know, I don't use the N word even though I do listen to some danc-y hip hop," Todd said.

"It's hilarious how all these white boys like hip hop, even hardcore rap. Spitting rhymes in their showers," Sam said.

"Do you use that word?" Todd asked.

"Sure sometimes but I have a membership so I'm allowed. I heard *n***** at least 50 times a day back in school. It's different though. Probably best you don't start using it *white bread*," Sam said, with a grin.

"White slurs are totally warranted. I guess I'm privileged but I can relate to some of it. *Wonder bread* makes perfect sense. As a gay man, I'm more offended by *faggot*. I even hate the word gay though it's acceptable. It means happy. Who says I'm *fuckin'* happy! And *queer* means weird. *Fuck* words! The world needs love and tolerance..." Todd trailed off.

Sam thought it was hilarious how mild mannered and professional he was at the office, then a trash talker at the bar.

"Max is away at his mom's. What's your excuse for hanging out here on a Friday night? Where's your girlfriend? Eunice right?" Todd asked.

"Yeah. I dunno what she's doing tonight. It's a long story…" Sam said.

"So you guys ever go out on dates?" he asked.

"We live together, what do you mean dates? Not really," Sam had enough beer to confess, "Okay since you asked. I don't think she's into other guys but lately it's like she doesn't dig me. She can't sit still and watch a movie with me anymore. She always has something on the go like she's on a mission."

"Mmmmh, that sucks. Any idea why?" Todd asked.

"I stopped asking her. I stopped being interested as revenge. Then she stopped telling me anything. I guess I had it coming," Sam felt relieved to release what he'd never said out loud before. "Todd, imagine I liked football and you didn't. You'd be bored with my talking about football all the time, right? So in consideration for you, I wouldn't constantly talk football. I'd try to talk about stuff we both liked," Sam said.

"Max and I have things we do apart but we've learned to schedule the common stuff. We figured it out after many fights, believe me. Now if I say as a joke, 'Max you can put the needlepoint down dear!' He clues in and stops what he's doing to give me some time. He doesn't actually do needlepoint," Todd joked.

"Yeah. We're missing that part. That's where we argue. She doesn't care what I do and I don't show interest in her ridiculous stuff," Sam said.

"In my experience, it'll never work out if you stay quiet. How would she know? How would you know? We used to use, 'I can't read your mind *asshole*' on each other but it didn't get us anywhere. Then we stopped. When you think about it most humans are selfish and don't feel like reading minds," Todd said.

"To some Max and I are a boring married couple but we're okay with that. I'll have you guys over sometime. Max set up a home theater sound system he's proud of," Todd said.

"Cool. That'd be awesome," Sam felt gooey inside. Having a friend outside of his usual neighborhood felt kind of exciting.

"You've given me some good ideas. Thank you," Sam said. He was sick of reaching out to her though.

Sam hung out with Todd or would go to their place to play video games. How could gay Todd turn out to be the most enviable *normal* person Sam had ever met? He found it funny that whether Max was present or not, Todd acted exactly the same. *Were gay guys different than straightees?*

Eunice had an entirely different persona when they were out in public together. It was like she needed to impress everyone with her boasting or be the center of attention. It often came off as phony and sometimes embarrassed him.

Then there was the added pressure for him to play along with it. God forbid if he did something outside of the *shtick*. One time at a BBQ he joked, how Harpo would knock on their door Saturday mornings asking if he could renovate the trailer. Eunice glared and changed the subject. Perhaps his use of the word trailer instead of R.V. was distasteful. She'd ignore him the entire way home.

"Maybe she needs time to open up to you. You might have known her since you were kids but you don't know her as a woman. Living together is a huge change," Todd said.

"What if it's like this forever?" Sam felt the familiar nervous belly.

"She might not want to look bad in front of anyone. Could be insecurity. You need to build trust. Make her understand the two of you are a team and she doesn't need to hide anything from you," Todd said.

"I understand what you're saying but I'm talking about regular things. We bicker over garbage collection, house chores and deciding which movie to watch. I even went to the library to look stuff up on the internet. It's called *emotionally unavailable*. She wasn't like that before," Sam said.

Sam was proud to be an early adopter of the internet. He'd become a regular at the library on High Street and took his online searches seriously. "It says she rarely admits to her mistakes," Sam said.

"The trouble with online research is it's so *godamned* believable," Todd said.

"I've become an expert at spotting tell-tale signs before they happen. The internet helped me develop a radar to spot symptoms," he said. Maybe it was the exact reason she said he had a microscope on her.

"Oh my God. You're funny! What sites are you visiting my man? No, don't tell me. Maybe she's actually the macho man in the relationship and you're the sensitive one. Or she has no idea and no control over it. It's just one of her beautiful flaws, Todd said.

"That's what I don't get. How do I convince her I'm an understanding guy?" Sam asked.

"Accepting her unconditionally assures her you love her. Max and I had a cold spell once, so I went to a psychologist. She said some of us have gone through childhood traumatic experiences that have left scars. Something big may have impacted us and we don't know how to feel. Max was terrified I'd find out he had the emotions of a tin can! Ha! Just kidding but don't tell him I said that. Things got better when we looked at it together," Todd said.

"Maybe she's afraid of rejection. Maybe letting go of her tough exterior will make her feel naked," Sam said.

"Didn't you like her tough exterior when you fell for her?" Todd asked.

"Yes. It made her unique," Sam said.

"My shrink used to say, 'Todd you can't afford to bottle your emotions.' Max was a tough cookie. I found out his childhood conditioning was set in stone. It's just a part of him. Ask yourself if you really want to be the cause of pain to someone you love, by not accepting them," Todd said.

"Wow. That's deep. It does help to share these things, like with you here now," Sam said.

"Sorry. Don't let me preach," Todd said.

"Is it normal she ignores me while she seems to idolize certain friends?" Sam asked. He was too embarrassed to tell Todd how jealous he was of Terrence. How he felt cheated by her attraction to him.

"Here is the tough talk. You only have two choices. You either accept unconditionally or you let her be herself. It's really your issue to figure out," Todd said.

"What? You mean accept Terrence?" Sam was angered at the thought. It was perverted for him to accept Terrence. She was always nice and in a better mood after seeing him. *Come home whistling Dixie.*

"Ah, when there's another person involved the game changes. Who is Terrence?" Todd asked.

How could he accept Terrence as a part of her life. The thought of Terrence and his *homies* made Sam feel inadequate. Some of those guys were his childhood bullies.

"A dude from high school. You know the popular leather jacket kind," Sam said.

"Mostly we form connections with people who present themselves transparently and similar to us," Todd said. He helped Sam see a new perspective.

"Yes. I hate when people hide who they are. Even if I come off as nitpicky, I don't accept fakeness," Sam said.

"Feeler types like us, understand that unhappy people have themselves to blame. *Lack of self-reflection is one of the main causes of unhappiness.* Okay those are my shrinks exact words. Have you thought of seeing a psychologist? The company pays for half a dozen sessions," Todd said.

Sam was less anxious. It really did feel better getting things off his chest. Both he and Eunice were perfectionists but everyone makes mistakes.

Sam's refusal to admit he contributed to their conflict was a serious flaw. If only he could catch himself in the moment, before things went wrong. He wished he could have a cartoon frying pan slammed over his head, as a signal like on Saturday morning cartoons.

Spoiled Brat

Eunice wondered why growing up she had wanted buckteeth, eye glasses and a back brace. Okay maybe not the back brace like poor Brittany Carlisle, who ended up quite beautiful.

For some reason she wanted a handicap, so others would know she understood their pain. She didn't understand why she was attracted to their weakness but it gave her a powerful urge to save them. It never crossed her mind they might not need saving.

Was the same true in her relationship with Sam? *Did she pity Sam as a misfit and resent him for not needing her?*

He was her ultimate underdog. A diamond covered in mud needing a good polish. He couldn't see his own worth but she saw his potential to be her ultimate soul mate. She had been excited to mold him.

She couldn't stop percolating on improvement ideas for him. What was wrong with wanting her man to live his best life? It never crossed her mind, she might be smothering him like a puppy or treating him as damaged goods.

Some people did well with confronting their issues, while others seemed to let them go *like she did*. Her letting go was to lock bad things away in a safety deposit box in her brain and lose the key. Sam was different. He seemed to remember everything and let things fester getting very upset when she sidestepped issues.

In childhood she went through the insolent phase of refusing defeat, which was unique and admirable for a female. She was pre-wired to never back down. She had grown up hearing her parents blame each other, instead of owning their mistakes.

When she was wrong she denied it. The shame of having made a mistake felt yuckier. It was the lesser of two evils, admit and feel shame or deny and cover your tracks. She used *little white lies* like a glossy coating.

She learned the symptoms of mental illness from Martha's agoraphobia and paranoia. It was as if their roles had reversed and Eunice had been the caregiver. She read her mother's mood swings which ran the gamut, from self-pity to defiance and all the quirks in between.

She was inspired by her mother's brave stories that seemed to leap from the pages of her albums. Instead of the incapacitated invalid mother, Martha was full of life in those stories, "Mother think about it, you were so brave to leave Canada for the U.S. That took such guts. Now eat your apple sauce, we've got to get your strength back," Eunice said.

"It was a different time back then. I was boundless," she said, sounding hollow and struggling with her speech.

"Now I feel lost and alone. I wake up filled with anxiety without any idea how to get through the day. Some days all I want to do is stay under the covers," she said.

Eunice doted on her mother but Sam needed something else. He wasn't looking for a caregiver, he wanted her by his side 24/7. It was intense like the skunk, *Pepe le Pew* chasing the black cat, who in every episode got an accidental white stripe down her back. Like the cat, Eunice couldn't help meet him with cold distance when he overdid it.

"I'm afraid I'll never rid myself of this independent trait that makes you feel unwanted Sam," she said, "I want to make you happy but I don't know how. I seem to eventually do or say all the wrong things," she said.

"If you let me know when you're feeling distant and forgive my right to ask. Last night for example, I was telling you about the new parking garage down near the courts and you got quiet. It was like invisible dismissal. I want us to look forward to being together, rather than dreading it," he wrung his hands, as if he was agitated.

"I don't know what you mean by dismissal. I was listening," she said, wishing she were somewhere else.

"Do you notice yourself checking out?" he asked.

His eye contact made her uneasy.

"No! You are very descriptive. I don't know when you will get to the point. Why does everything turn into a fight?" she was annoyed.

"How can you ask that? I don't know when you'll zone out, so I'm not sure where the issue started. Are you being honest with me? You can't have it both ways," he said, in a tone that would lead to silence.

"You get angry if I zone out, then you give up on me. I've got things on my mind you know," Eunice said, dying to go do her own thing.

"Like saving the world?" Sam said, sarcastically.

"It's good to know you don't understand. I guess I don't want to discuss feelings now, or ever. So how do we turn it around Sam?" Eunice asked, but was only vaguely interested. She was bored with his long *assed* stories and lost focus on his words.

He gazed at her, speechless.

"Okay Sam," she reset her tone, "You misinterpreted my calm demeanor. I'm not devoid of feeling and I'm sorry it bothers you," she held her breath for fear of laughing in his face.

She thought it was cute how the mention of hurt feelings, jerked him away from an argument. He'd become remorseful for hurting her. She knew it was manipulative but it got him off her back every time.

She thought about the next plan for her posse and wondered if Terrence would crash their meeting like he did last time. Her spine tingled at the thought of his sensuous mouth.

"You take my asking questions as interrogation. There's no sense in asking for my opinion, when you only expect a *Yes Dear*," Sam said.

She envisioned Terrence's cleft chin and how he bit his lower lip to accentuate a point.

"If I make you happy through my words and actions, you will make me happy through yours," he said.

"Do you ever feel sorry?" he asked, with hopeful eyes.

"Sure. I'm sorry for being in a foul mood last night. I was stressed out so I was looking for calm at home. Then date night dissolved when Todd dropped by, so I detached myself and went to my quiet place," she said.

"I find whenever I comment or have a viewpoint you dismiss me and go to your headphones," he said.

"I went to bed wondering how to resolve our issues and fulfill each other," Eunice tried channel Arisbel's kindness but couldn't find the words. She didn't have a script and was bad at improvising!

"You're telling me when you have phones on you are not upset with me?" he asked. His blinking eyes looking hopeful again.

This fucker was right up her ass! If only he had another outlet, he'd be less likely to pick on her.

"I guess I have work to do on myself," Eunice said, lying.

Now she was fucked. The fuck she'd work on herself!

She thought of Terrence showing up on his motorcycle and whisking her away.

"We should have our own lives too. Not be chained up and get sick of each other. I was home a lot. Now I've got the diner job and friends," she grew more uncomfortable the longer he watched her. She couldn't hold her tongue forever and began to recognize the body tingles she got before zoning out.

"In the morning you act like nothing's wrong, like we didn't argue. You don't own it," he was upset and panting as if after a jog.

It didn't sound like something she would do. She didn't think his description was accurate so felt nothing.

"Okay Sam. I don't own it. What do you want me to say?" she said.

She couldn't tell him about her memory gaps. She felt sick not remembering. Sometimes she thought it could be Alzheimer's but she was only 18. Then she would forget she had worried about it. The recurrence was not a joke, she was afraid of it getting worse.

"The easiest way to explain is I'm not at ease with you Sam. I feel constantly on edge. You are unpredictable and I'm never sure which Sam I'm going to get. Right or wrong, I like calm and peace so I have learned to avoid your mood swings," Eunice said, employing her shameless method of blaming him. *This poor guy is so in love!* She admired herself in her compact mirror.

"So now you run to TERRENCE?" he shouted, "Do you think it helps us get closer?" he asked.

Fuck! She didn't expect him to be so quick.

"What do you mean?" she asked. He was right she *would* turn to Terrence. Why couldn't she just play nice for a couple of days, instead of antagonizing him for sport.

"Sam I'm sensitive to being picked on. You're sensitive to being picked on. We're the same," she said, batting her eyelashes.

"So if we're so similar, why can't we agree on anything?" he asked.

Sam was a beautiful soul, an amazing guy; intelligent, caring, dependable and forever reliable. He was the moth to her flame. She wanted him in her corner. *Why did she try to destroy him?*

She thought about resolving things but it wasn't her fault he kept pushing her into Terrence's arms?

"Fine Sam! If you're going to be like that, I'm going to follow my own path. The heck with you!" she said, throwing the first pitch.

A shadow fell across his eyes.

She alone could not remove the pained expression on his face but she was too proud to save him.

Why did it feel as if they were still children skipping rocks at the pond? Why didn't she remember she regret it every time she started this?

"I've got to work now. Maybe we'll talk about this later," she said, although she hoped not.

"Fuck this!" she said.

Surely Terrence wouldn't be such a motor mouth.

Stuck on Repeat

Todd invited Sam and Eunice over, since Max was headed for a convention in Las Vegas. Eunice was busy so Sam gladly went on his own.

"She's out with her posse of militants tonight but like I told you, Terrence and his crew never fail to show up. Whatever! I swear that *asshole* wants to get in her pants so bad. I'd like to take a spade shovel to the back of his head!" Sam said.

"That's extremely macabre Sam. No violence please!" he laughed. "What sort of activist is she?" Todd asked.

"Ever since they saved this girl from the Vineyard, they've been looking at ways to foil drug profits, or at least lead police to them," Sam said.

"Pretty noble stuff," Todd said.

"Okay you're right but it *is* annoying I never know where I stand," Sam said.

"To me you either want to be together or not. What do you want Sam? What expectations do you have in your life?" he asked.

"I guess I want her to participate!" he said.

"Okay, let's switch to you. What career do you want?" Todd asked.

"I want to be the governor I dunno," Sam said.

"No seriously, when you were a kid, what did you want to be?" Todd asked.

"As a kid. Easy! An astronaut or fighter pilot like *Luke Skywalker*. No, I actually wanted to be *Lando Carlissian*," Sam stood up to recite his best *Billy D. Williams*. "Todd, you slimy, double-crossing, swindler..."

Todd laughed, "Who's that? Oh, wait the black guy from Star Wars? That's pretty good! Seriously Sam look at me. What do you want to be when you grow up?" he asked, staring intently Barbara Walters style.

Todd got philosophical and turned into a life coach. Sam didn't mind, no one had cared to ask him before.

"I want to make my old high school a better place for the kids coming up. My school got zero funding. You should see how its falling apart. I bet your school isn't falling apart *ritz cracker!* Where did you go again?" Sam asked.

"Not a fair question. You know I went to school on Fairview. And you're right, it wasn't shabby or falling down. It was all *white bread* except for a Chinese guy, one Mexican girl and a few African Diplomat kids," Todd said.

Sam liked how Todd wasn't ashamed or careful about his white privilege which in itself defined white privilege.

"Uh-huh, no surprise there. There's a lot of commotion about grades these days. There was a news report about how America was failing in low income schools. Black schools mainly. My high school was in the worst category," Sam said.

"Have you ever thought maybe Eunice is following her path and you need to find yours? Put your passion into action. That's why dad's get hobbies. My father took his hobby seriously. His business was all he cared about. I never saw him but it was better than a deadbeat dad," Todd said.

Sam relaxed. Things weren't so terrible.

"I don't know if my thinking is right. Does everyone worry about this kind of stuff? I wonder if I'm having anxiety or depression. How does someone know when they are clinically depressed?" Sam asked.

"It could be your just one crazy *mutherfucker!* The only thing we can depend on is change. The minute we get used to something it ups and changes! I notice you aren't satisfied now and you want to do something about it. Knowing you need to change is a good thing. Better than not knowing. Cheers to that!" Todd said.

Sam did have a calling. High school stats for black boys showed they ended up in pro sports, as dope dealers or school drop outs at risk of incarceration or death. There weren't too many playing sports.

Principal Butler and the school council seemed out of touch with reality. They didn't notice the facilities were decrepit. So where was the government funding going? It was a problem that no one talked about solving.

At work a few days later, Sam caught up with Todd, "I've been doing some digging. There *have* been successful improvements to urban schools in other states. There's this guy in Little Rock for example. I sent him an email," he said.

Sam had done hours of research on school board issues at Morgan Library. Government spending was based on district votes across southern states, which impacted Booker T. City reporting. It didn't specify which schools got funded and which didn't so voters didn't know how funds were distributed. They had no insight to inner-city budget operations.

"What did you find out?" Todd asked.

"The bottom line is funds don't go to the schools that need them most," Sam was dour.

"I guess no one looks at the numbers state by state," Todd said.

"It's no surprise living in a country that segments society into black, Hispanic, LGBT, even wealthy and poor ghettos," Sam said.

"It seems no different than a caste system. The Statue of Liberty's serious face should have a smiley face sticker slapped overtop," Todd said.

"Ha! It reminds me of the expression, 'if you put lipstick on a pig, it's still a pig!'" Sam said.

"Ouch, poor pig. Do they think we're stupid? I guess when you think about it, we *are* stupid. Everyone knows money makes the world go round. The ones reaping turn a blind eye to what's going on," Todd said.

"It's like saying I see the problem but I didn't create it so why do anything about it," Sam said.

"That would mean taking a financial hit. No thanks. I have my kids university to think about. *I would do something but my son Timmy is number one.* At a family level is it so wrong to look out for #1?" Todd asked.

"No. If Timmy is your son it's not wrong. So the less thans are right and the middle class are right," Sam said.

"Only there's a piece missing. The root of *the thing* is missing. It's obvious but invisible. The taker takes. The unspoken rule says *go for it.* It neither encourages nor discourages us from cheating. When I take or do whatever I want, no one stops me because they're doing it too. The actual root of the problem is the secret pact that's never verbalized, just influenced. Elites witness other elites take, take, taking so they copycat and discover they aren't getting caught," Todd said.

"What about the honor system?" Sam said.

"Right. The unchecked honor system. It's like the urban legend of the illuminati, a elite meeting in secret. It's a free country with great opportunity on the surface. I'll tell you a secret, the rules of the game are there are no rules, but there is a game. Maybe nobody verbally dictates it and the wealthy figure it out," Todd said.

"So when they're caught they seem like total crooks. Meanwhile they want to say, 'but that guy is doing it too!'" Sam said.

"We know there are rules but we don't try to find out what they are. We don't have time or reason to. We wait to get our hand slapped," Todd said.

"Then we pivot away and try something else. If I don't see a law I'll just implement my idea. It might be well intentioned and I might not see the consequence but I still won't ask permission," Sam said.

"Yeah, asking for permission is degrading. By the time I think I should ask, I'm making so much money because it's America. If I'm wrong, I'm innocent until proven guilty. If I have means and friends with interest in my *idea,* I'll just get a good lawyer.

"Once I'm free and clear the law protects me under the constitution," Sam said.

"How on earth is it my fault Sam?" Todd asked.

"There are powerful people and the secret is a lie by omission. Why would you mention the elephant in the room, if the elephant was your American Dream? I guess it's better to know than not to," Sam said, with an awkward smile.

Blue Ridge Cabin

Eunice pulled onto Jasmine Hill Road in Blue Ridge around 9:00. She had checked on her parents at dinner, then drove in Harpo's old Plymouth, the car she shared with Sam.

Mike Watts the musicology camp musician Eunice admired, had become a close friend of the posse. He offered up his folks' cabin for them to use for meetings. The posse and a few of Terrence's guys would converge there to analyze facts and discuss demonstration ideas.

"I'm finally here!" Eunice said, without vigor.

"Things okay with you?" Gabrielle asked, meeting her at the door.

"I'm still with Sam, if that's what you mean. I've been going nuts. I swear I'm not even trying anymore. I tried to be his girl and do everything dutifully but it just made me low. I guess I lost my sense of adventure for a while. It doesn't mean I don't love him but I was bored without you guys. You are my true friends anyway. I feel guilty sneaking away but he'd try to stop me. Right now he thinks I'm at my folks' place. Wink, wink. Clearly I'm not!" Eunice said.

"I think there's more to life than boys!" Gabrielle said. "What are we doing letting boys control our destinies anyhow? Did you know that *bromances* are more important to them than girlfriends? After sex you're in third or fourth position, depending how many bro's he has. Ladies need to get wise. There's no such thing as romance!" Gabrielle said.

Eunice dropped her duffle bag and gave Mike a friendly hug, "Thanks for letting us use your place Mike!"

Mike's teaser line enticing them to meet up was he had information they would find intriguing. He had spies within Montgomery's Business Association and City Hall.

"Some of them might be third hand information but I consider them solid leads," he said. Being a session musician he was also well connected to a diverse mixture of people. Plus he'd previously been involved in activism for music and artists rights.

"Guys, think about it. We need to strike a chord now before another big story like Rodney King breaks," Eunice said.

Mike, Gabrielle, Jaxon and Patty were present so far. A few more including Terrence were on their way.

"Come on Eunice, don't you think it's a waste of time? No one's even thinking about how we saved Juliet anymore," Gabrielle said. She was sitting near Jaxon on the sofa.

"At least she's still clean," Eunice said.

"… and locked away in a sober living house," Patty said.

A year ago they'd been known as a vigilante girl posse who weren't taking it anymore. They still teased Gabrielle for her sound bite on the newscast.

"OMG look Gabrielle's on TV," Jaxon had screamed.

"Well I knew Juliet was going down a bad path big time! She failed her algebra finals because of that awful boyfriend. What was his name…I guess she would do anything for love. I'm just glad we could help," said Gabrielle's TV talking head. The boys peeled with laughter.

"We all had our time off to do other things. I was one lazy *bitch* sitting in my trailer. My man off working a real job with benefits! What can I say, I was a kept woman," Eunice said, with a curtsy.

Eunice pulled out a folder with photocopies and passed them around. One document showed a city council request for Alabama to legalize a state lottery so each jurisdiction could share in the generated cash flow.

Another was proof of a meeting about council's budget allotment for a river walk casino.

"Geez, this one looks legit!" Patty said, referring to meeting minutes with attendee member signatures.

"You guys have no idea how many private establishment dinners there are. These elected officials play chess with citizen's lives. My source says corruption happens in every city," Mike said.

"I guess the way to go in government is to get *loser* gamblers and alcoholics to pay your debts. My Uncle Sonny lost a whack of cash last year. Now my aunt is divorcing him," Patty's serious tone sounded as if she had parachuted into a spy movie.

Mike talked them through each document.

"My buddy works with a guy who brags about cooking the books to make it look like schools are adequately funded but as you see here the money goes to these other schools. You see how only the lowest ones on the list have a Sundry items entry with a zero next to it," Mike interrupted.

"Terrence says the sheriff is doing *diddly squat* about drugs in the black areas of course. That's what Terrence said," Eunice said. She hoped they could beef up their game. Get things done faster and be impactful.

"Where is Terrence anyway?" Mike asked.

"Whoa! I bet you got together with him, huh Eunice? Didya?" Patty asked, feigning shock.

"Lady P you are ridiculous! He and Lil Red are helping a girl move out of her parents apartment at Parks Place," Eunice said.

"Naw, she's gonna give up Sam for Oreo Jax here! Ha-ha!" Gabrielle said, poking Jaxon. They called him Oreo sometimes because he was less urban and more stiff on the inside.

"There is a correlation between this information which hopefully Terrence can confirm. Something gang related..." Mike said.

Terrence and Lil Red arrived looking beat.

"Speak of the devil," Patty said.

There were nods all around but no one interrupted the intriguing discussion.

Eunice watched excitedly. WSFA-12 News had been focused on daily reports about the *war on drugs* so this information might very well get them a splash of air time.

"My informant Jack says conspiracy theories about government involvement and denial that black youth are failing in school, hide the fact they are hooked on drugs," Mike said.

Decades old rumors fed the urban myth that the introduction of crack in black ghettos was by design.

"Are they knowingly letting us die off. Addicted on purpose to squeeze us out?" Patty asked.

"They don't care if blacks are killing blacks! Police don't even patrol for drugs, break ins or shootings in these marked areas," Terrence said, holding a map.

"Okay, first of all addicts aren't all black just most of them we see around here. You're saying the gangs know the police don't care and the police know the gangs know? That's lawless!" Eunice said.

"You mean no one knows about this?" Jaxon asked.

"Course not. No city official wants us to know they've turned a blind eye to black schools and are letting drug overdoses do the clean-up for them," Mike said.

"You mean they *don't* want to know how many are dying of drug overdoses?" Eunice said.

"My sources say it's a classic case of turning a blind eye to the drug problem," Mike said.

"We definitely need to do something about it!" Terrence said.

Eunice looked at Terrence, then Mike and the rest of their faces. She threw her first fist in the air like the quintessential rebel rouser, "One team!"

"One Team!" everyone shouted. The posse was now a diverse mix of a dozen or so unofficial members.

She was used to manipulating to a goal. The best way she knew how to control a situation was to be one step ahead of it. She had always been able to steer her father toward the new outfit she wanted. She didn't think all manipulation was bad. Persuasive facts weren't manipulative.

She thought of how she and Sam had grown completely apart. "You were right. We need to get parts of us satisfied in other people. When I chatted with Terrence at the barbecue we talked about stuff I wasn't interested in anyway. I wasn't jealous or envious of him," Sam said.

"I don't always whisper *lovey-dovey* stuff to you but it doesn't mean I don't love you Sam. I didn't realize how deep your mistrust was," she said. It was easier to apologize, "I'm sorry for ignoring your calls yesterday. I don't want to argue."

All she could think about was how to get out of the schmaltzy conversation and up to the cabin where her friends were meeting.

"You told me it was my job to tell you when I have a problem. I wasn't saying it in a mean way. You said we could discuss things calmly," Sam said looking disoriented.

She kept still not knowing how to handle his gushing emotions. Didn't he feel like a weakling? It was bizarre and foreign to her.

"Ignoring me and dismissing my feelings won't make me forget you hurt me. Ignoring me is a different kind of fighting. I don't know what to do with it because sometimes I haven't done anything wrong, then all of a sudden you're distant," he said.

"You're trying to make me feel guilty," she said. It was working. She'd been open to talking if he was calm but she felt accused so she let nature take its course.

"Okay I'm sorry. I told you I don't like being called names," she said.

"I know but is everything a name to you? Seriously, is calling you selfish or self-centered like calling you names? I was pointing out that I find it selfish when you go out with your friends, have discreet birthday lunches and see movies without me. Have you considered I might want to spend time with you, on a date or something. All the while you act like nothing's wrong," he said.

"You have to admit you get angry for no reason. You called me a *bitch* a few weeks ago," she said. It was a long shot but she might sway his pendulum away from Terrence and back to his own guilt.

"Oh my God! Insults were hurled from both sides Eunice! Didn't I apologize on one knee and make you dinner after? I'm sorry again. I get infuriated repeating the same conversations. It makes me feel crazy. No wonder I'm blamed for having mood swings, I guess I really do have them," Sam said.

Eunice asked herself what was wrong but in order to dig deeper she'd have to ask herself why she had animosity. She gave up. *Did she even want to be with him?* He was dull and she preferred the excitement of her friends. There was a big difference between ignoring him due to self-absorption and staying away from him to avoid conflict.

Tom Horsley

Sam had been inspired to write a letter to Tom Horsley, the 27 year old youngest African American teacher promoted to principal. He had made news with his novel approach to inner city education in Little Rock, Arkansas.

To his surprise Horsley didn't respond to his email letter but called Sam up one day saying he was touched to see someone fresh out of high school, interested in doing such work.

"Sam, it's immoral to not send the best educators to low income schools," Tom explained. "A principal needs a sense of urgency and actually care about what's going on in his surroundings. The difference here is to provide professional development for teachers to help them support students. There are homeless and domestic issues, drug issues, guns and gangs. God only knows what else. As I'm sure you have seen in Montgomery, underprivileged kids need to know teachers care and can spare that extra time or even give them a few dollars for the book fair. Our students hadn't eaten or didn't have money for school supplies or *whathaveyou*. It's difficult to learn when your basic needs aren't being met. Their family and communities have given up on them but if we push and motivate them, they will succeed. It is startling how the same crazy *shit* our parents' generation went through continues today!" Horsley said.

After several phone discussions and emails Sam convinced Horsley to come down to Montgomery to be a guest speaker, "It's a peaceful awareness rally I was working on with Principal Butler, aimed at garnering support and funding from City Council. Something along the lines of an information session and to show how far your school program has come," Sam said, to Horsley over telephone.

Along with Horsley, Sam would be delivering his first awareness speech.

Sam hadn't shared the news with Eunice as yet. She had been secretive and away from house a lot so he kept the rally from her. He didn't think she'd taken more shifts at Vespa's but to comply with her request of silence in place of harmony, he didn't ask her whereabouts.

The morning of Horsley's visit he mentioned the rally to her, "Today's a big day for me," he said, matter of fact.

"Oh yeah, why's that Sam?" she asked.

"This principal from an Arkansas school is attending a rally I've organized. It's affiliated with Principal Butler," he said. The words hung in silence making him regret he had said them. It made him open to criticism and he felt childish for keeping it quiet.

"Oh *damn*. I would have come if you told me sooner. I'm heading to a movie," she said.

"That's cool. We need people so if you're around city hall after 1:00 swing by," he said. He felt sick satisfaction that her posse wouldn't be upstaging his event. It would also prevent his embarrassment over her phony persona in front of Horsley.

Sam introduced Tom Horsley via bullhorn to the sparse crowd of twenty or so. At least a few of Sam's invitations were honored by Todd and Curtis attending. He was even glad when Eunice arrived with Terrence.

Principal Butler, the school secretary and Vice Principal as well as a handful of Booker T. High teachers showed up filling some gaps in the crowd.

"*...Desperate but equal never came true. Divided we failed. Through history there has always been a black and white achievement gap. We stay segregated by choice or force of habit. School budget spending is not distributed to reflect individual school's needs. Many of you were appalled at what happened in South Central L.A. I myself could not believe the excessive force seeing Rodney King beat 56 times with batons. We hoped we were past such displays of white supremacy but living in the South we know racism has never really gone away. It has just changed forms.*

"I'm here today to share that our banding together for the sake of education is our best option. As Martin Luther King Jr. said, 'because it doesn't affect you, don't think you're not part of the whole. Our lives begin to end the day we become silent about things that matter.'

"Within our constitutional right we can earnestly demand Montgomery city council take heed in the equitable funding of our inner city schools. Writing our government officials and school boards will make a difference. Together we are stronger!" Horsley finished his speech.

There was mild applause and a few cheers from the crowd, which had increased to fifty strong since the brown bag lunch set had trickled in.

"I wonder why the cops haven't busted us yet," Sam said, to Curtis.

There were a few watchful police in cruisers but no sign of halting the assembly.

"Usually when Dr. King quotations start the cops get agitated," Curtis said.

"I wonder if it's jealousy over not having the same affinity with white heroes as we have with ours," Eunice said. Sam was always touched when she made mention of her beliefs.

"I hear we are a good distraction from another bill council is eager to pass," Principal Butler said.

"Let's take advantage of them leaving us alone," Sam said.

With Tom Horsley's semi-rousing opener Sam was up next. He didn't want to blow his speech in front of distinguished guests so imagined MLKs voice.

"Ladies and gentlemen. My name is Sam Hood. We're here today to communicate awareness on a serious issue with our government funding. Historically, black people have had to rally for their rights through demonstration and that's pretty much what's happening here in Montgomery," Sam aid. With some courteous claps, Sam's quivering voice grew stronger.

"A lot of people want to say racism is over but we know that's simply not true. Until we as a city accept the fact there are a multitude of identities and perspectives. Some are more discriminated against than others, we will not be able to move to a post-racial society. This begins at the top with equal funding," Sam was invigorated. He actually did it!

The brown bag lunch workers had dwindled but the crowd sounded livelier. Principal Butler, Eunice and others crowded around him in congratulations.

"Awesome!" Terrence said.

"You're a natural," Curtis said.

"I'm so proud of you," Eunice said.

"Thank you," Sam responded to them all. He was touched. Maybe he misjudged her recent independence.

Tom Horsley leaned in and handed him an itinerary, "Fine job Sam. This here is a two-week curriculum. I want you to come out to Little Rock for a few days to see for yourself. Sit in classes, talk to the teachers and students."

Sam was choked up and had a lump in his throat. "I'd really like that. Principal Butler?" he motioned for approval with wide-eyed enthusiasm.

"Let's not get ahead of ourselves Sam. My leadership team will consider it and come back to us. Let's see if council approves our funding," Butler said.

Sam had never admired a mentor more than Tom Horsley. He was stimulated with fresh ideas. Maybe they could reinvent the breakfast program for a new generation. He would make a point of speaking to Curtis.

Anything to help the school.

Several weeks after the courthouse speech, there was still no news regarding school funding. Sam was told it was still being looked at. Principal Butler did have good news, "While council takes their sweet time, we are still considering sending you to Little Rock Sam. I'll let you know in a few days."

Horsley and others advised him that regardless of positive feedback, activism was a thankless job that required a *shitload* of patience. To keep up the momentum he began working on a follow-up demonstration agenda.

Sam felt more alive than ever. He had a clear sense of calling. A month ago he would never have imagined being fulfilled by something outside of his relationships with Eunice. He was encouraged by the pending Little Rock invitation.

Perhaps he and Eunice could align their activist efforts and come together with a common goal. If not intimacy, at least they could share in something together.

Eunice remained the same *Stepford* girlfriend where everything was hunky dory. They rarely spoke of anything except news reports but to outsiders they appeared to get along better.

Skulls

Sam figured eventually his work activities would intersect with Eunice and her posse crew goals. He wasn't privy to what they were planning. He knew it was something related to Booker T where they had graduated from a year and half ago.

Drugs and crime in Montgomery had increased month over month at alarming levels. For six months straight the situation had grown more dire with a series of unfortunate events.

The Skull gang had put a stake in the ground in setting up operation in three abandoned houses on Grove Street. The gang was affiliated with Manny's Vineyard dealers, so much of Montgomery was now being run by drug lords.

A host of narcotic and opioids, were being sold openly on or near school property. Addicts from all over got wind of a cheap, easy fix and lax police scrutiny so showed up in droves.

Worse still, they tripped out on school grounds and spent nights around bonfires destroying adjacent property. The disheveled junkies lingered into daytime hours begging school students for cash and cigarettes.

At the back of the school near a thatch of trees closest to South Street, a blue tarp prompted concern that *they* were building a 'tent city.'

A dangerous Rottweiler allegedly owned by the Skulls roamed the surrounding streets. Neighborhood watch groups reported a rash of home invasions.

A group of goody-two shoes threatened drug sales, by promoting a 12 step rehab option, were quickly shut down as drug clientele were protected by the Skulls.

WSFA-12 News was reporting a sensational connection between the Skull gang and murder after one man was found tortured and tied to a tree. Stoking the fire on an urban legend where junkies, easily lured by drugs had been abducted for ritual experiments. Possibly by the *klan*. Authorities turned a blind eye as there hadn't been witnesses and no one even came forward to identify the man's body.

Statistics on CNN suggested Alabama was the most oppressed state in the union. There was buzz of Anderson Cooper's TV producers scoping out broadcasting live from Montgomery, to shed light on the war on drugs, poverty, race and ghettos.

To top it off, city councilor Geoffrey Tanner was caught on audiotape making comments to school council, "Sure they want a person of color as principal. We all know any monkey could do the job!" thus sparking a local debate on whether his statement was intentionally racist or an innocent admission that the job was fairly easy!

Sam's interest was piqued, as he found research data Alabama had never had a person of color holding a position higher than entry level teacher.

Pike Road

"Gosh Sam, I can't believe the change in you!" Todd said. Sam was at Todd's place in Pike Road. Max was home, in and out of the room getting ready for a work function with his software company. Sam and Todd would head out for burgers downtown.

"You think I've changed? Well I know I have. I think I'm on the right path with activism," Sam said. "Did you hear Tanner's guffaw?"

"I did. Does it feel like it's your calling?" Todd asked.

"Of course it's his calling Todd. Look how he's lit up," Max said.

"Yes, thank you," Sam smiled at Max, "I absolutely do but not in some *asshole* way. Guys, I need to ask you something about Eunice."

"Okay, sure," Todd said.

"In my web research I came across a condition called *dissociative disorder*. It's amazing what you can find on there! It's when the brain saves the person from traumatic memories by blocking out feelings, good and bad. The brain erases entire sections of memory that would otherwise cause stress," Sam said.

"Not the internet again," Todd said, exasperated, "I told you to stop diagnosing your girlfriend on the web. You don't even know who posts those articles. So what is it? Like temporary amnesia?" Todd asked.

"Be careful about diagnosing. Todd does it to me all the time and he's *always* wrong. I just put my hand to his face like this and say, 'You can get any kind of validation online but I'm right here!'" Max said, joking but sincere.

"It can be temporary. The reasons cited most are child abuse and neglect," Sam said.

That part reminded Sam of something she told him at music camp but didn't let on to the boys. It also crossed his mind she might have a serious condition like her mother. If that were true he had behaved badly.

He wasn't sure if she was depressed before or she blamed him for it? It sounded like, *what came first the chicken or the egg?*

"The article advises the partner to sit tight and be understanding because the sufferer doesn't know any better. As if they're born missing a limb they never had," Sam said.

"Sounds legit because it's not blaming the victim," Todd said.

"That's what I thought. Top of the line *Psychology Today*! So I left her a copy of the article on the kitchen table, half expecting she'd think I was considerate," Sam said.

"Oh no, Sam," Max covered his mouth in surprise, "how did she react?"

"She didn't say a word for two weeks. I figured she hadn't taken it seriously. Eventually, she said leaving the article was equivalent to her, leaving me an anger management brochure," Sam said.

"I can't say I blame her. It's a classic case of you win some you lose some. I think you lost some, ha ha!" Max said.

"She came around later and said it was good info and she'd consider sharing it with a shrink one day. We might go," Sam said.

"Not a total loss then. Good work. I think," Todd said, "It sounds like you need some space. Spend the night here. Maybe call and tell her you need a breather to process things. It's not malicious. Guys are raised to be tough so they don't think in terms of self-respect. Do you think it's respectful for her to shut you out and save the good parts for her friends?"

"No," Sam thought for a moment. "You're right! Maybe I will stay over," he said.

"What does your heart tell you? And then what does your head say? Never mind pleasing everyone. I really think you need to take care of YOU. Make a decision you can live with. Life is more than treading water. It's about living with joy and dreams and acceptance from others," Todd said.

Max returned to the room in different clothes, "Not that I disagree but I hope you make it through your night of Todd's psychobabble," he smiled, "You boys behave. I gotta run. I hate these schmooze fests. My boss expects me to make all the sales. I'd rather be here solving your love life Sam!" Max said, then left.

Sam found it hard to believe he ever felt odd uncomfortable with Todd and Max. They felt like old friends. He used to gross himself out thinking about what they did in bed. Something he'd never consider about anyone else.

After Max left Sam turned to Todd, "What do you think of this amnesia concept coupled with her dating Terrence under my nose?" he asked.

"First check your imagination. I think you're doing an awful lot of problem solving for two. When there are three people in a relationship it's like constantly ignoring an elephant in the room. Don't settle for crumbs when you deserve the whole loaf!" Todd said.

"You think so?" Sam didn't expect his blunt response. *Asshole!*

"You already have the answer inside you. Maybe you're not listening to it," Todd said.

After dinner at the burger joint, on Bibb Street Todd clearly wanted to keep on partying. Sam had a good time goofing around but it was just after nine and enough for one night.

They had too many drinks for either to drive. "It's pretty safe around here, let's leave the car. Come stay over and we'll get it tomorrow," Todd said.

They caught a bus to the edge of town, to walked the rest of the way. The bus didn't go far enough so Todd suggested they get off at Taylor Road and take a shortcut through quiet streets, which would land them at Pike Road.

"It's not far Sam. Then at Troy, let's get a couple of six packs at the gas station," Todd said, as they got off the bus.

"Uh, okay. We'll call Max from there right?" Sam said, fed up with walking and Todd's sloppy drunkenness.

"Yep, sure thing. He's going to be pissed at me!" Todd pointed.

"Okay. You know where you're going," Sam gave up on guiding stubborn Todd. At least for the moment he wasn't troubled by Eunice and felt a dose of freedom trolling the back roads.

They walked Taylor Road in darkness. There was a quarter mile between each sterile-designed mansion and manicured lawn. Sam had no business being in this neck of Montgomery.

The only light came when a white pick-up truck drove by then they were in darkness again. It was so quiet the silence echoed sprinkled with frog bleats. Sam made out the north star and big dipper in the black chalkboard sky. He was uneasy. There'd be no warning if a bear jumped out from the woods.

How can Friday night at 10:00 be so quiet, "Rich people must be really boring. Where I live there'd be street lights, people walking and rollerblading, kids shooting hoops and car stereos playing. You know, living!" Sam said.

"I keep forgetting, you're not from around here. These are the roads I used to bike as a kid. They roll up the sidewalks and go to bed at dusk," Todd said, sounding less drunk.

"Wait a minute, is Max even home tonight, or did he go to Vegas again? Sam asked, still hoping they could get a lift.

"What? He's got so many work functions, I honestly can't remember. Too many shooters!" Todd said.

"Your eyes were like fireballs when we left!" Sam teased.

The revving sound of an engine approached from behind. Sam looked back and saw headlights getting larger and brighter. The vehicle was moving at a good clip, then slowed and stopped a half mile back.

"Must be casing houses along here," Todd said.

"Or good ole boys out joyriding!" Sam said.

The driver hit the gas and accelerated at top speed. The truck whipped past them too quick for Sam to get a look at the passengers. It was the same white F150, that had passed earlier. It must have circled around a second time. It squeaked to a stop 500 yards ahead of them.

Didn't every roadhouse horror movie have this very scene?

"What do those clowns want?" Sam said, feeling a pit of dread in his stomach, which killed any alcohol buzz he may have had.

"Probably just directions," Todd said, not sounding convinced.

The pick-ups red tail lights went white as it slowly reversed. Movement in the back cab indicated there looked to be four men in total.

Sam watched in disbelief as the driver and front passenger got out wearing white pointed masks with round eye holes. They walked toward them at a steady gait while the other pair got out from the back cab. They had the same hoods. One carried a hunting rifle.

Holy shit! What's happening?

Michael Donald had put up a valiant fight. He'd gotten away from his *klansmen* by knocking his gun away and trying to run into the woods but they caught him. His throat was slit three times to make sure he was dead.

Sam was paralyzed with fear.

"Stay cool. Remember they are cowards under there and this is a scare tactic," Todd's confidence waned to a whisper.

"Uhuh," Sam murmured. *Why didn't he run?*

The four *klansmen* stood a few feet in front of them.

He remembered learning about *lynching bees* and *racial terror* in grade nine history, where *klan* hunted and terrorized to enforce their supremacy. Justified in their intimidation, torture and murder of black men, as punishment for lust and rape of white women. *Klan* rituals served as warning shots showing others what would happen to them.

In 1916 *Jesse Washington* was dangled over a fire pit until his death. Children were permitted to watch as long as their school work and chores were done. Lynching photos were produced as postcards. *Here is the BBQ we had last night,* read one card. Hundreds of lynching's took place in Mississippi and Alabama into the 1950s.

Sam had been warned growing up, that *klan* members in numbers were dangerous but in recent years their activity was seen as a white boys rite of passage. Sam figured it was unlikely this would end well.

The one with the Winchester .22 lifted it and trained it on them while another spoke in a nasally voice, "You fellers looking for trouble around these rich *arsed* places?"

Sam and Todd remained quiet.

"Yo Jimmy, back the truck over yonder so no one'll spot it," nasal voice ordered.

A blinding flashlight shone into Sam's eyes.

"What do we have here. A black one and what looks like a queer one, or maybe it's two queers," one said.

"Heh, heh," one snorted, "the beginnings of a good poker hand!"

"Gentlemen. We aren't looking for any trouble," Todd said, in his most masculine professional voice, while ignoring the gay slurs.

"What d'ya say we have ourselves a midnight barbecue," said a younger sounding, more urban voice.

"Over there," rifle guy herded them to the forest opening with a sign that read, *Welcome to Park Crossing Trail.*

"No trouble, we were just looking to get home and we're a bit drunk!" Sam said, implying they were just a couple of regular guys.

"We gonna take ya'll on a wee detour o'er yonder," rifle guy gestured.

In single file, they started on the trail. Boots crunch, crunch, crunched over fresh laid mulch. In the lead one pointy hood bobbed followed by a quiet Todd, then another hood in front of Sam. He heard the other two following close behind.

Flashlight beams threw shadows between the marching legs, projecting silhouettes against the pine forest backdrop.

They hiked through a *ritz cracker* version of a forest with fancy picnic benches and horticultural landscaping. As the trail curved up ahead the first pointy hood and Todd were nearly out of sight

"Listen man it's me you want, leave him out of it," Sam aimed his voice at the *klansman,* in front of him.

"Shut the *fuck* up!" the voice behind him said.

They marched silent for several minutes.

"You just follow along *boy*! We ain't got business ta do witch ya," the voice ahead called back. Sam didn't know what he meant.

"Here Buck?"

"Ya here," a voice answered.

Sam heard a surge, of quick shuffling steps behind him and his ears filled up with sound until everything went dark.

Sam opened his eyes into darkness. He had throbbing pressure over his left brow. The earliest birds chirped and dawn light gave him an estimated time, of just before the rooster's crow. Either he was already dead or he'd never forget nearly being lynched by the *klan*. He must have blacked out.

Mulch, pine needles and dog *shit* filled his nostrils. His left eye wasn't open but jammed against cold steel, forcing pressure into his forehead.

He was at a downward angle, his face planted as if he'd been thrown nose first, like a paper airplane. Afraid to move a muscle his left arm was crushed, under his shoulder and chest. His lower body was at a higher elevation, so blood had rushed to his brain, which pulsed to the rhythm of his heartbeat.

What did they do to Todd?

He wiggled fingers and toes and brought a hand up to his eye to touch cold steel. For what seemed a long time he got his circulation reactivated with a tingling sensation of pins and needles. Pulling himself up to a seated position, he tried to differentiate his injuries, compared to his hang-over based on the liquor he tasted in his throat.

When he stood up he assessed he'd been hurled or pushed headlong into the wrought iron legs of a park bench.

Caucasian American

Todd Sheppard had been beaten, tortured and left to die in the woods south of Park Crossing, not too far from James W. Wilson Elementary. He was taken to Jackson Hospital where he spent six days in a coma due to his severe head injuries. He was found by a man out walking his dog.

Todd could have died but doctors said he was anesthetized by the amount of alcohol in his system. It seemed the excessive number of kamikaze shots had numbed and slowed his heart rate enough to keep him alive.

Sam had managed to hitch a ride to Marathon Gas and report the crime. He too was taken to Jackson hospital for stitches and observation regarding the possible concussion to his head. He was cleared a few hours later but obliged to answer police questions.

At that point, Todd had yet to be located.

Sam had called Sofia to explain what happened and ask her to pray for Todd.

Sam was escorted to the station by police cruiser. He gave police an eyewitness account of the events he could remember. The deputy sheriff went to great lengths trying to comprehend the connection between he and Todd. Police were dumbfounded how the *klan* attack left a black man relatively unharmed, while near killing an upstanding professional white male, albeit a homosexual man.

"Where is Todd?" Sam asked.

"He's been found barely alive. They've got him in ICU. We'll let you know," the officer said.

Sam's testimony included dialogue between him and the assailants, "Naw, we got lots of you before," and "We need to teach this fruit a lesson."

The deputy sheriff said, they had whacked Sam in the back of the head with a spade shovel, that was found lying on the trail next to the family picnic spot.

Sofia called back to report she had turned her ladies card game into a prayer circle, which may well have worked since Todd was found alive.

Later resting at home, with tea and a blanket Sam was calm instead of the blithering mess he'd been when Eunice first picked him up.

She sat with him watching TV coverage. The story quickly went national due to the nature of the crime. There had been gay bashings and there had been a history of lynching's past and present but never before had they been rolled into one. The questions raised put Alabama and the southern states on the defensive.

The media characterized the South as being backwards with countless examples pulled from its checkered past, thus stirring up memories of prior lynching's.

The status quo had thought crimes like these had been a thing of the past. Montgomery swiftly and fiercely became a poster child, for an America living in the dark ages regarding race discrimination.

What are you guys doing about your hate problem down there?

He watched how riled up Eunice got, "Sam you'll see. I'll get the posse gang on board pretty quick." She was near foaming at the mouth, as she watched the news.

Sam was too tired, to respond in detail but his love for her was set for life. Even though she was cold and neglectful, she was also this magical superwoman from another planet.

CNN's Anderson Cooper, showed up with his team to report live from the trail entrance on Taylor Road. Vans with satellite dishes, camera equipment and tons of crew milled around, juxtaposed against the wall of beautiful Longleaf Pines.

The spotlight on infamous lynching's, from the past generated necessary conversations. CNN started doing nightly segments linking Todd Sheppard's attack to a history of discrimination.

CNN News: History of Violence

"I'm Anderson Cooper, reporting live from Montgomery Alabama. Tonight Todd Sheppard, 27 years old from an affluent American family was purposely degraded, simply for being gay. Roll the tape."

Footage showed scenes of the hiking trail on Taylor Road, the field where Sheppard was found and Todd's mother Louise Sheppard saying, 'This simply cannot be. Not in Pike Road!'

"As we await details in the Sheppard case we delve into America's past. First to define lynching:

Lynching is not simply a hanging but a method of utter degradation. To hurt someone by capturing, torturing and executing in a public way aimed as a warning to those witness to it. [9]

"Of course this is not the first time. What can only be deemed the most notorious crime of this type was the 1955 lynching of Emmett Till a 14-year old visiting Mississippi from the North.

He was killed for allegedly having wolf-whistled at a white woman. Till was so badly beaten, one of his eyes was gouged out. He was shot in the head before being thrown into the Tallahatchie River. His body weighed down with a 70-pound cotton gin fan tied around his neck with barbed wire. [10]

"Till's mother courageously insisted her son have an open casket at his funeral, to show how badly his face and body had been disfigured. The images stunned the world reaching people through print and television in communities where they hadn't known about America's race problem."

Footage shows unidentified man's commentary.

"The south had a sportsman's penchant for it ever since slave days, mixed breeding, and accusations of seducing white women. It was the preferred lesson used by the sheet disguised *klan.*"

Blue Ridge Revisit

After her shift at Vespa's, Eunice hitched a ride with Gabrielle to Mike Watts' Blue Ridge cabin.

"Eunice girl, before we get into it, tell me what's really going on with Sam. Is he recuperating alright?" Gabrielle asked.

"Yes. He's getting better. I'm more worked up about this than he is, it's really gotten me crazy. We must retaliate with something fierce," Eunice said.

Gabrielle smacked her gum, as she drove while intermittently looking over at Eunice.

"I'm not too worried about Sam. He's sore all over but he'll be okay. We will focus on our original mission. I hope Mike has some information," Eunice said.

"You got it. Eunice please keep in mind you can have different passions, still be crazy and have a good man at home," Gabrielle interrupted, reassuring her.

The gang was all there, when they arrived. Eunice's instinct was to take charge, with strong opinions. It was imperative they take action with a single goal, rather than diluted demonstration messages.

Given the events of Todd and Sam, there was enough anger and unrest pent up all over town fueling Eunice's motivation to act now. She saw it as a perfect storm of real life tragedy and public outrage.

"It's incredibly important we make this count, for so many reasons ya'll know about. Let's do it for Todd who last I heard is still in a coma. Let's do it for all the victims of *klan* discrimination. We're gonna need something that scares people into action. Less demonstration and more, '*kill every motherfucker I see!*'" Eunice sang the lyrics to a *Nina Simone* protest song.

"Can you believe Principal Butler's folks got parents and teachers involved? Even your mom's involved Jax? How lame is that?" Patty ridiculed.

"Never mind, the entire First Street Baptist congregation. They have got the church ladies working overtime," Jaxon jeered.

"Now now, you guys, remember their intention is the same as ours. Think MLK vs. Malcolm X, two styles," Arisbel said.

"Not for long. I've got some feelers out, don't you worry Eunice! We'll have plenty of back up," Lil Red said.

"God love Sam's *gang of saints* but even they will appreciate our muscle. We'll avenge what happened," Eunice said.

"How about we let them do their thing and we do ours. Let's make a pact that anything discussed at Mike's cabin, stays at Mike's cabin," Arisbel said.

"The Mother Teresa route might not be cutting edge but they probably won't have WSFA-12 News, documenting every move they make like we will," Eunice said.

"CNN is already here. Don't you think we should just partner with Butler and Sam?" Gabrielle asked.

"No way man! We'll blow the lid off this thing. No offense to Sam's work but they'll fall for negotiations far too easily and it'll be over. Think of them as the opening act to *our* show," Terrence said.

"Trust me, Sam doesn't want militant vigilantes near him and we're okay with that," Eunice said.

"Keep it clean. It all blows up if we break the law and get ourselves arrested," Mike said.

"Mike's contacts say town officials have been aware of the Skull's drug operation for the past three months. Yet, for some god-awful reason they did nothing about it," Eunice said.

Over the weeks since the Skulls took over the area in Centennial Hill, there had been no police presence.

"We should call attention to the disgusting school grounds. Riff raff has taken over! Especially on weekends when staff and students aren't there," Eunice said.

"A guy I know says the Skulls paid off the cops. 'The drug money rolls in handsomely,' were his exact words," Mike said.

"Imagine cops getting paid to do less," Patty said.

"It works right into city councils reason for not funding Booker T. With students hooked on dope and gang bangers crawling everywhere. It makes the school easy to write off. Why throw good money after bad?" Mike said.

"It's another quid pro quo, amongst the powers that be!" Eunice said.

"My buddy says they make jokes at his office about the rate of overdose deaths. Spikes in O.D's are favorable to their budget spend and they can justify using the surplus, to educate younger kids before they get hooked," Mike said.

"Sounds noble on the surface," Gabrielle said.

"They don't patrol the place. It gives dealers free reign. It's a school for *Jesus sakes*! We're going to need artillery!" Terrence said.

"It'd be suicide if we started shooting. These guys are rough. We don't want to come between them and their drug money! Too dangerous!" Mike said.

"No guns, Terrence!" Eunice said.

"You have my word, *Babycakes!*" Terrence said, using the same pet name Sam used. Was it coincidence?

"Mike's right. This could be the break we've been waiting for but it'll be risky. We'll show the world the difference between right and wrong. They'll know who I am when we're done! We need something to take over the victim narrative. Ante up the stakes and raise awareness about Todd Sheppard's story," Eunice said.

"Until there is more evidence the media will forget the story," Jaxon said.

"And it'll go back to the way it's always been. Like through history where no one gives a *shit* about people," Terrence said.

"Eunice you are such a great person, to fight for justice," Jaxon said. His admiring smile was different, as if he regarded her as their leader.

"Thanks Jax. It's a team effort," she beamed feeling powerful, with a laser sharp focus. If she shut her eyes, she could see the scene playing out before her. This would blow the lid off of the *godamned klan. Those redneck idiots!* Fox, CNN and all the outlets would be there.

"Booker T is fast becoming another Vineyard. Did you hear? Neighbors signed a petition to have more police presence and someone burned that bungalow to the ground," Patty said.

"Okay, do I hear agreement? It's time to take a stand on drugs and the destruction of our high school right?" Eunice said.

"I don't know what's worse drugs or guns. You know I'm in Eunice," Patty said.

"The trouble is guns are integral, to the operation and flow of drugs," Lil Red said.

"We're in, right boys? Terrence asked.

"Lil Red stood up, "I'm willing to go the extra mile. I say we go Mach 10 on their *asses*. Skull dealers are making a base camp out of the place. It's gonna be a bloodbath," Lil Red said.

"Easy Red, don't forget they're hooked on drugs! No violence against the addicts. They literally don't know any better," Eunice said.

"Alright, alright I'm just messing around," Lil Red said.

"Red, I know what happened to Sara! I totally get you man. Juliet was like a sister to me," Gabrielle said.

"Red only meant wreak havoc on Manny's guys. If we don't get to the dealers this thing goes on and on," Terrence said, staring at Lil Red.

Eunice found the intensity between them curious. Red was related to Sara, the former student whose story had been a cautionary tale in high school.

"It sounds like a plan, let's huddle y'all. Red, you too, you mushy thing!" Arisbel said.

The meeting was over by 10:00 p.m.

"Eunice, would you mind hanging back a minute?" Mike asked, with a curious look on his face.

"Uh, yea sure but I got a ride with Gabrielle," she said.

"Not to worry, I'll make sure you get home ASAP! It won't take long," Mike said.

"You good Gab?" Eunice asked.

"Ya! see you tomorrow," Gabrielle waved at them, "or call me later if you want."

Eunice was alone with Mike.

"I just wanted to let you know how proud I am of you. It's like I've watched you grow up ever since our musicology days," Mike said.

"Thanks Mike, that's sweet. You didn't hold me back to say that. What's up?" she asked, becoming less comfortable. She sensed he was about to ask for her hand in marriage or try to kill her.

"Kooky beautiful girl. I asked you to hang back as a favor for a friend," he swung the door open and in walked her father.

She burst out laughing, "Daddy what are you doing here?"

Jackson Hospital

The day after Todd came out of the coma visiting was opened up to all visitors. Sam was relieved, Todd was going to make it. He'd had twisted thoughts like, what would he say about Todd if he had died? It really made him think. He loved his humanity and courage. There'd be less strife if the world was more open and free like Todd.

Sam also appreciated his encouragement on being more ambitious. He'd vowed to himself if they made it out, he'd submit his resume for the VP apprenticeship.

He waited in the hall outside the hospital room, while Todd's mother finished up. A passing nurse stopped by to reassure him Todd was on the road to recovery.

So much had happened since that night Sam was eager, to find out what Todd remembered. Replaying the story Sam was still puzzled. This wasn't the run of the mill muggings that happened in any city.

Signs pointed to something pre-planned or routine. Sam found it odd, that one of the assailants said, 'this isn't about you' to him. Why did they go after Todd instead of him? Was it Todd's comfort and openness about being gay? *Who do you think you are, mister confident faggot?*

Mrs. Sheppard came out of the room, "You are Sam right? I've heard so much about you from my son," she hugged him.

"Nice to meet you Mrs. Sheppard. How is he?" Sam asked, somewhat intimidated by her wealth.

"Call me Louise. Thanks to Jesus our Lord and Savior, he is going to pull through. Sam, formal invites will be sent out later today through my assistant but I wanted to invite you to a gathering for Todd, at the Golf Club next week. I hope you can attend," she handed him an enveloped invitation.

"Thank you Louise," he said, already dreading the crowd.

Inside the hospital room, Todd was propped up in an automatic bed smiling at him expectantly.

Sam was overcome with gratitude.

"Oh my gosh Sammy, look at your eye," Todd said, in a whisper.

"It's nothing man. How are you doing?" Sam asked, noticing he looked thinner.

"To be honest, I'm not sure how I feel yet. Not in my own skin, that's for sure. Tell me what happened," Todd said.

"They found you tied to a fence. The man walking his dog thought you were a scarecrow hanging on the fence. Lucky the dog, sniffed you out," Sam said, feeling more emotional than he expected.

"It's okay Sam. It's not your fault. They had hunting rifles for *God sakes*," Todd said.

"I told the cops where I thought you were but they said you were found somewhere else. What do you remember?" Sam asked.

"They marched me to a clearing. They argued about where they were going, then one of them put a sheet over my head. I didn't even know we were back at the same truck," tears welled up in Todd's eyes, "I thought you were dead because the four men were with me but you weren't. They had me laying in the flatbed of the truck. They drove some but not too far. Two of them were real *assholes*. At one point I thought they want me to do sex stuff but the other one stopped them. Thank *fuck!* He told them I probably had AIDs, which made them sort of panic. It was all very charming Sam," Todd's tone relaxed as he spoke.

"I'm sorry Todd. That should have been me. You are a tough man," Sam said. He could relate to his own experience, taking bully punches as a kid.

"What's a little degradation. They robbed me and pistol-whipped me which cut my eyebrow. I was blinded by my own blood. I don't remember being tied to a fence,"

"I won't repeat the curse words Sam but I listed them for the cops. No offense but the black one was the angriest," Todd said.

"Wait a minute. There was a black one?" Sam was stunned and confused.

"Yes. I saw his arm. I guess I didn't see the magnitude until right now seeing the look on your face. What does it mean Sam? Is this my white privilege right!" Todd tried to joke, triggering a coughing fit. he sipped from a juice box straw.

Should he feel betrayed by his own race?

"Well maybe you get a pass, for being in a coma for six days! Did your statement to the cops clearly explain there was a black man?" he asked.

"I must have mentioned it. I'm not sure. Funny if I did they didn't ask for details. They're coming back this afternoon. I'll make sure to restate it," Todd said.

"There can't be too many of us in the *klan*," Sam said, wondering what kind of black guy in his right mind, would associate with *klansmen*?

Cottonwood Golf Club

Sam had been to visit Todd a few times in hospital during the week. He would make a full recovery. Even though he was still recuperating Mrs. Sheppard proceeded with her event at the Cottonwood Golf Club.

Sam walked through the cocktail lounge of the gathering of relatives and friends, hearing people talk about the incident.

"Isn't he with that mulatto girl? Maybe the klan thought she was white, so he kind a had it coming..."

"That's just the way it is in the South..."

"That Eunice Johnston girl is here. My husband says he's got to do, extra Taskforce patrols around the wretched Vineyard, because of her..."

"I heard Anderson Cooper was staying at Renaissance la dee da! I do hope he's enjoying Montgomery. He's swell on the eyes though!"

"Why do they have to flaunt themselves like that? If Todd had just kept his mouth shut they would have got the black one!"

"My poor nephew. He just can't keep his flamboyance at bay..."

Sam found a discrete spot to sit.

Mrs. Sheppard kicked off the special function with a thank you toast, "I was hoping Todd would be able to attend today but he's improving every day over at Jackson. Given all the media attention this has attracted, I wanted to thank you all in private," she said, as if kicking off a run for office.

Eunice was meeting him there. She had asked if he could RSVP for her, Gabrielle and Terrence, so they could be 'eyes and ears looking for clues.' Sam wondered if her motive was justice or the glamor of the Cottonwood setting. "Sam, I've been there before. Gabrielle worked there last year remember? We're going to sniff out for leads," Eunice had said.

Eunice focused on catching and making an example of Todd's assailants. Her heart was in the right place but she seemed hell bent on revenge too. Perhaps that was the heart of a true vigilante. Did she forget Sam had also been a victim, now that he was fully recovered?

Eunice set her sights on being a bastion of justice and he had no doubt the cabin planning meetings had been about avenging Todd.

"Don't worry we're on it Sam! Those devils are going down," Eunice said. She could boil to the ranks of evil comic book villain with her ravenous drive.

Sam, you have to know your woman! Grandma Hood would say.

"How are you holding up Sam?" Sam turned his head and was relieved to see Max looking at him.

"Gosh man. I'm sorry Max," he said, giving him a hug.

"Me too. Onward and upward right? I'm mostly worried about getting through this soirée. Todd's mom is a bit of a show off. This shindig is a jab at his father, who barely acknowledges him," Max said, sipping a green highball with mint leaves stuck to the sides of the glass.

"Folks certainly chatter. I could hear them talking as I came through. They weren't even whispering," Sam said.

"Welcome to my world. I gather we share some of the same annoying judgments of people," Max said.

Sam wasn't in a great headspace to see Eunice's friends so, when he saw Gabrielle and Terrence standing around a bistro table at the back, he kept his eyes on Max. He wished he could've ducked away. He resented her friends for not liking him and blamed them for coming between them. He supposed it was Eunice's fault for allowing it. God only knew what she said about him.

Eunice arrived looking lovely in a black dress. She caught his eye, nodded then went to her friends table. He nodded back and finished his drink, "I best be heading to my girlfriend, Max," he said. He wondered why, they got to have an inside track of her attention.

"Hang in there Sam," Max said, patting his arm.

"Why do you share everything with them?" he remembered, asking her once. Her answer began with a kiss on the forehead.

"Don't be ridiculous Sam. I don't feel threatened, by prying questions from Gabrielle or Terrence. I can also cut them off if I need to, so I always have a way out," she said, so nonchalant as if disposing of longtime friends was normal.

He gave her friends credit, they were loyal to her.

A macabre thought came to him, if her eulogy were enacted it would be those friends who would have the most wonderful things to say about her. They knew her best.

Later at home after the event he and Eunice held hands, while watching *Big Brother* on TV. They were quiet and distant, perhaps each trying to let bygones be gone. He let go of saying too much. *Eunice, do you know what it's like to be constantly reminded, your friends are more worthy of your time and attention than I am?*

Instead he said, "Harboring anger is not good for me Eunice. It turns me into an ugly person, hence my outburst before the party Saturday. I'm embarrassed by my behavior. I'm sorry."

"Thank you Sam," she said.

They made love in silence. Sometimes words were *stupid* anyway. It all went away when she shared herself. It confused him how he might have been more accepting if he'd gotten lucky once in a while. He thought sex was withheld on purpose, her weapon being her headaches.

Post intimacy, the skies opened and springtime light shone off her smile. A day or maybe a week after the friction he'd fall for her invitation as if he'd been stunned by Cupid's Taser.

Resistance was pointless because immediately following a reconnection tryst he'd wished he'd abstained longer. Prove his animal instinct and good old fashioned sex drive weren't the culprit. He was no different than those girls held on strings in late night Elvis Presley flicks.

What was wrong with wanting someone to grow old with. He'd never thought of himself as needy but wanted a mate for life like apes, wolves, and coyotes.

CNN News: Deep Inside the *Klan*

"I'm Anderson Cooper. Tonight we bring you a story to help us understand what makes someone want to join the *klan.*"

"Anonymous accounts tell a story of how a person gets involved in the *klan*. What goes on inside the hate. Tonight we'll hear from 'Steve.' Since Steve was a teenager, he has been exposed to the America, South Chapter of the *klan*.

"At age 14, 'Steve' ran away from brutal parents. He says he got into petty crime and drugs with his black friends. He's been in and out of prison, where he learned he'd be welcomed in a biker gang.

Footage showing archival clips of various lynching scenes intercut with the 1915 film Birth of a Nation, often used to fortify organized racism. After the montage, the camera lands on the talking head of 'Steve' in silhouette sitting with a reporter.

"It's tied to power. It's got nothing to do with the victims," Steve says.

"Roaring around on large motorbikes with insignias and tattoos can be interpreted as an attempt at getting our attention and to frighten us. I felt the power in their fear. It's the only power the powerless have.

But we give them a false power with our fear. We must keep in mind deep down it's our love they yearn for. The love they missed out on in childhood.

Some bikers discover if they dress up in *klan* costumes and light up a cross out in the forest it gives them a feeling of power which catches our attention in a far more effective way. When they are incapable of getting our love, they settle for our hate. After all, that is better than being poor white trash and totally forgotten by the world.

It is the continuous feeling of being a loser. [11]

"I guess we know there really is a boogey man," Cooper said. "We did some research. Enslaved African-Americans told tales to their children of a Boogie Man who would abduct you, kill you or otherwise cause you harm if you were to leave the plantation. The Boogie man of which they spoke was in essence the white man. Quite possibly a connection to the ghost like appearance of the *klan* dress code."

Sam remembered, Grandma Hood telling him the story of the Boogie Man, "Ah Sam, be careful the Boogie Man don't get ya. He sure likes the velvet ebony ones baby boy."

Oil and Water

It didn't take long for Eunice to notice things were back to ice cold between them. She couldn't break free of the stoicism he sulked and resented her for.

"I don't like this black and white behavior. You DID this! I AM that! I'm a bully! You are selfish!" Sam shouted at her.

"Sam I don't react well to your all or nothing attitude," she said, looking right through him. She wondered if he knew how his body language changed, when he became adversarial.

"I'm sorry. Todd getting out of the hospital or the ongoing investigation is bothering me," Sam said.

"I'm not sure you understand, what your behavior does to my psyche. Maybe I do suffer undiagnosed depression," she said. It wasn't the first time she used her mother's mental illness as deflection. She wasn't sure if she'd ever been clinically depressed.

"Just because you aren't the jealous type, doesn't mean I shouldn't be jealous of Terrence? Not everyone is built the same way Eunice," he said.

"How come no one else thinks I'm a bad person Sam?" she asked. No one was going to tell her, who she couldn't see. *Silly fool!*

"They don't see you at home. Your talent is acting out another person for them," he said.

"Maybe you're right Sam. Maybe I lack empathy. What do you want me to do, fake real empathy?" she asked, avoiding eye contact. Empathy was her weakness. She hated the idea of being soft.

"Forget it! I'm going to Todd's, to play videogames," he said.

"Oh my God, you are so jealous of Terrence!" she said, knowing he hated it when she called him jealous.

"You choose to stay in your iceberg and busy yourself with friends. I care about people a little more. Let's not pretend we are EQUAL in that regard Eunice!" he shouted.

"Okay, Okay stop making such a big deal out of it," she said. He was right though. She did not care deeply about individual people.

"Like you said, Terrence and your friends have no issues with you. I honestly think your life would be rosy, if Terrence lived here with you!" Sam said, with a twisted expression of hurt.

"Don't you trust me? Your reactions tell me you don't," she bit her lower lip. He seemed to wince with desire. *Damn he was cute!*

Terrence loved who he thought she was. Sam loved her behind the scenes, the good and bad. That was special, she just couldn't bring herself to let him know it. That would expose her weakness and she would probably die.

"Eunice I just want to say it's taken a toll on me! I don't sleep well. My heart hasn't been interested in seeing movies or trying for sex," he said.

She heard the coldness in his voice, as if he were finally moving on. Maybe he'd learned a few self-preservation tricks from her.

"Oh come on Sam, you can't blame me for your lackluster motivation, or your life in shambles," she gave him a dead-eyed stare. She couldn't let him win.

"You cannot use 'not motivated' anymore. I've got lots going on. Remember when you told me to get a hobby, so I'd stop picking on you? Well I did!" he said.

She wasn't hell bent on being right for a change. It hurt her to be ugly and antagonize him but she had little control over it.

"Terrence doesn't make me feel bad about myself like you do," Eunice said quietly. "I forgive you for not understanding how you hurt me. I asked you to give me some time. If I must suddenly end my friendships, you need to give me space," Eunice said.

"I'm going to help Max at Home Depot now. Talk to you later Eunice!" he slammed the door on his way out.

Harpo's Lunch Box

In lieu of the school funding, city council granted Sam approval to pilot his Lunch Box idea at one school. It could be a huge win for the community and inspire confidence in philanthropy. The funding was minimal but he would be allotted extra wages for hired help.

Sam asked Curtis, if he had contacts from the Black Panther days to consult.

"I betcha I could rustle up a couple of guys from Kansas City but you're looking at one of em right here!" Curtis said, with both thumbs pointing to his chest.

"Wow really? You would help?" Sam was thrilled. "Tell me what it was really like Curtis?" he asked.

"Sure. I only know what I know. It was in Oakland 1969. Apparently some of 'em kids, had never had breakfast before the Panthers started serving. That was the sweet part. Justifiably the Panthers were always watching to see how the program could get them political inroads. They had the ulterior motive to fuel the Black Power revolution, so they weren't perfect saints," Curtis said.

Sam was on the fence about the second part of the Panther agenda. He didn't want to replicate the politics but if peaceful political action resulted, then fine. Sam's program would be sincere, without hidden agendas. He wasn't interested in risky stuff, like other vigilante groups might be.

He had approval to run the pilot, out of County Elementary on South Decatur Street. They used Curtis' Panther experience and a proactive attitude Sam gleaned from Tom Horsley. The intention of the Lunch Box was to generate excitement, in the children instead of focusing on poverty.

Sam managed the food logistics, straight out of his manufacturing textbook from grade 12. Flyers were printed and distributed to local black businesses, with Sofia and other church ladies helping. Volunteers requested food donations from grocery stores and prepared food free of charge.

To offset budget funds they passed the church basket around twice, once specifically for lunch donations.

With Sofia and Harpo on board, beloved hermit Martha stepped out of her tortoise shell, to participate in the daily soup menus! She had somehow been awoken, by the exhilaration of good deeds.

The biggest obstacle was daily deliveries, until his often crotchety father Harpo stepped up to the plate, with a freshly signed van, *Harpo's Lunch Box Truck*.

Students wound up referring to the lunch program, as Harpo's Lunch Box referring to the highly visible sign painted on his truck.

"Here comes *Harpo's Truck, Harpo's Truck.* Here comes *Harpo's Truck!*" they could be heard shouting at 11:00 a.m. sharp.

Sam was beyond touched by the program's initial success.

A Cat and a Dog

Sam arrived home in a fantastic mood, quite proud of having gotten the Lunch Box off the ground. He didn't want to be cocky but he couldn't stop thinking, about city counselor Tanner's controversial comments about the VP apprenticeship, "I challenge you to pick any monkey from a pool of applicants who apply in the next 48 hours."

Sam had chalked up Tanner's actual job posting, as PR damage control and an opportunity, that would never happen for real. The deadline was extended indefinitely, due to the controversy. Sam applied for it anyway. *You only live once!* He could say Todd made him do it!

Arguments with Eunice seemed laced with her resentment. It didn't make sense because his goals had always been for their future together. It's what spurned him forward.

Was he being an *asshole*? Had he taken on so much, he'd become arrogant? She had wanted them to have individual goals but he'd never heard of that before. How could a couple have separate dreams?

"Eunice can't we just agree, we are equally smart and have unique gifts? Neither of us needs to be better than the other and you will always be the prettiest girl!" he said, being lighthearted.

How hard was it to succumb to each other's needs, while keeping an eye on personal interests? Perhaps the *klan* trauma had been a test, to show him something about love. Maybe Frank was testing him.

It will take endurance, to make it to the other side.

"Eunice your mom has been all over, our Lunch Box soup planning. She seems really happy to be busy. The church ladies are in an uproar, over which is the most nutritious recipe," Sam said.

"It sounds like things are going really well Sam," Eunice said, sounding blasé.

He found her friendly comments open to interpretation. It seemed petty but the sardonic tone gave her away.

"It's kind of funny when our mothers, butt heads but I think they have bonded on disapproval of Marjorie!" Sam said.

"Very nice," she said, dryly as if she wasn't listening.

"Let me get something off my chest. When you said I was a *loser,* because I didn't care about my salary or making more money. I meant I preferred working on humanitarian stuff. I'm not naïve. I'm aware it doesn't pay well," he said.

"Let me get something off my chest too. When you mention Terrence, you say it in a sleazy way as if I'm doing something wrong. You obviously don't trust me. I feel like you're using something about my past against me. It makes me regret sharing stuff with you in the first place," Eunice said.

"Okay I get it, fast forward to now. I know you didn't mean it and I believe you, so can we please put it behind us? That's where my lashing out comes from. I'm not always *jonesing* for smoke or a drink you know," he said.

"What makes you come to the point of writing me emails, when we can just talk. Are you sober when you send them?" she asked.

"You never want to talk in person! You avoid reality," he said.

"That's because I'm discouraged, I can't say anything right so it's best I keep quiet," she said.

"Don't you see how being remote will never work with us?" Sam was exasperated.

"Stop saying there's something wrong with me," she said.

"Avoiding topics only makes them worse," he said.

"I need to pick myself back up but I can't figure out if it's supposed to be with you or not," she said.

"Ouch! What are you talking about? It seems like we're having a different conversation," he said. *Was she dumping him?*

He was going to lose it again.

Why did he seethe?

How could she always be right?

Why did she need to fight to the death to protect herself? Emotional games played to cover something up.

It made him nuts.

Take a deep breath Sam!

Yet his love for her never wavered. He'd eagerly anticipate seeing her but come the weekend, he'd already made plans without her, *Why waste weekends with a vacant person?*

His difficult choice was to stand on his own feet, or be disappointed with her crumbs. The obvious choice for him was to walk away but it never felt right in his gut.

He wished it didn't hurt like hell. God please send me a game changer!

The wacky part was in public, she supported him hitting all the technical elements to trick people and hide her *fembot* coldness. She was so good at the game, he wondered if she was counting beats as she made sure Sofia, Harpo, Todd and others liked her! *What are you talking about, she loves you Sam.*

Sam was like *McGruff,* the investigator dog who could never drop the case. He had to get to the why behind her behavior.

Maybe she has black outs or suffers from *missing time,* as described in those *Whitley Strieber* alien sci-fi novels, he used to read as a boy. True stories of huge-eyed aliens abducting him, in his bed. No good would come from alien paralysis, a good probing in their flying saucer and be left sore in your bed wondering what happened. It was too outlandish to be true but so was his *supernatural* relationship.

"Sam how did we slide so far off the rails this time?" she asked.

"I don't understand why you need to be a lawyer," Sam said. He had the ache in his belly, whenever things sank below civility.

"I'm not acting like a lawyer!" she said, like a cold prosecutor.

It was already too late and the days would drag out in silence. Sam's disappointment and sadness would turn to anger and he'd have no way to stop, until *Bruce Banner* became the raging *Hulk*.

"I don't like being controlled!" Eunice said.

"Here I was feeling guilty for hurting you. I'm *not* controlling you!" he said. His tone of voice reflected a monster. His reaction was different now, the Hulk was on the scene.

"Go have a smoke. You're agitated," she said, sounding superior.

"*Goddam* you! Always blaming my smokes! You think the root cause of our troubles are cigarettes? Always going down the rabbit hole of diversion, right Eunice! What the *fuck*!" he shouted.

"Stop using language!" she said.

"It's the way I speak, when I'm frustrated beyond reason!" he said.

"Controlling," she said.

"This is ridiculous. You don't give two *shits* about me or us!" he knew he'd just kicked off a fresh round of silent treatment and the *Hulk's* rant would extend the term. What the *Hulk* never realized, was the rope went out far enough to animate itself into a noose around his neck.

"And don't talk to me after your smoke. You're always apologetic afterwards," she said.

"I won't talk to you at all," he said.

Later Eunice would come home giddy after seeing Terrence, "*We* had such a great night. So much fun and good food. I told them you weren't feeling well. I hope that's alright," she said, as if they hadn't argued.

Sam was sickened, after her nights with Terrence but mainly angry at himself for losing his temper. Every time he wasn't true to himself, another layer was stripped away. He'd tear himself down with the guilt of poorly restrained *stupid* emotion.

If an olive branch had been forthright earlier, he could have gone to the dinner. He was a man for *godsakes*! Why couldn't he toughen up?

The cycle was such that for the next few days, his need for her accumulated. Friday he'd be desperate to be back on good terms again.

His buildup of anger began on long sweaty walks home from work, sometimes killing time running errands or helping his folks, to avoid going home. He'd be hungry and in a bad mood. The hot trek was the devil riding him, so he'd begin the diatribe in his head first. About how her fierce independence was to blame.

There was no relief until he sounded off or stated his feelings out loud. The second she started speaking pleasantries the poison jumped from him and attacked her. The outburst would let her know he was *pissed* at being treated like a dog.

Her non-reaction would make him so angry he wouldn't have a leg to stand on. He was already guilty of being the culprit. *How could he ever stop the train?*

He'd blown it with his tantrum this time. It bothered him to no end how she used the word *we* all the time. He'd be with her in a circle of people talking and slowly realize the *we* she was referring to was her and Terrence.

It silenced him and he was a bad actor. He imagined the crowd judging him and seeing his shame. What a double standard. If he'd inflicted such pain on her it would be bad, where hers was now justified.

Perhaps he was her mirror and she felt cornered by her exposed indiscretions. A darker thought was he purposely manipulated her into thinking, it was her clinical depression when in reality, his doppelganger had fed him stories.

Omission

In the sober light of day, when Sam wasn't overthinking the meaning behind everything, he had high hopes it would all work out between them. He knew part of problem was, he couldn't bend or accept her independence.

He'd seen it so many times on *Montel Williams,* you were an *idiot* if you thought you could change someone. Men were supposed to be tough. He knew he was a whipped *pussy man* who stayed out of his fear of being alone.

Harmony lay somewhere in the secret world of backing off and turning the other cheek. So why couldn't he let her be?

"Things are always as they should be Sam," Sofia told him but he didn't believe her. He *wasn't* wrong but the world pushed down on him as if he were. Making nice didn't work for him either. He could hear the lie in his own voice.

He went out for a walk, where they used to play by the pond but it had since been filled in and a strip mall built over top.

Oh Frank, I need you now!

He closed his eyes and conjured up the wolf image of Frank, hovering above him as large as an elephant with his snout close Sam's face. Frank's protective breath, wrapped around him like a force field.

Your emotions are too powerful. It's in your nature, its instinct and it's alright. No more being hard on yourself Sam.

Later while taking a shower, Frank's truth washed over him. For several minutes Sam understood the meaning of life and it's wonderful simplicity. *It is easy to follow your own path and let other opinions roll off.*

Then clarity slipped away and Frank's answer to the meaning of life was gone.

How do I keep that channel open Frank?

Defying Sofia's epithet, "headshrinkers are sent from the devil!" Sam and Eunice booked couples counseling.

"You don't need a high priced quack, living in sin is your root cause, Son!" Sofia had said.

The night before the first session Sam wrote:

I look forward to meeting you regarding how I have moved a serious issue. It relates to my jealousy of my girlfriend mentioning her past life too much. I was triggered bad Saturday. It had been a build-up of subtle feedback of how it bothered me. We managed to talk it through over the weekend. I was able to be brutally honest even at risk of it being over and done with.

It could have been the end and I would have handled it. Good to know I could have walked away. That I would have the strength for it, if required.

Eunice used to share more of herself. She kept people at arm's length, so they wouldn't hurt her. Sam was sad he'd become the exact person, she had described to him. He was now in the same container as the men, she'd been afraid of as a child.

"Even when you offered me ways out, at no time did I want you out of my life. I hope I'm just a fool for love and a sucker for your pretty face," he said, trying to lighten things up.

"Sam, I love you but I fear you. You have to engage in a level of civilized conversation. I can work on my distance, so don't assume I'm abandoning ship just yet!" she said.

"You have to admit, you don't love deep conversations!" he said.

"Are you saying I'm shallow? she asked.

"You talk in your sleep, so I've heard a lot!" he said.

"We have different needs and rather than voice them, we dig the hole deeper," she said.

"I think we need to stop assuming, what the other one is thinking. Something like, 'Hey, let's do something fun tonight rather than assuming the other doesn't want to do anything," he said, knowing he sounded frustrated.

"I get it. I get it. You are quite intense right now," she said.

He stopped talking.

"What do you mean?" he asked.

"I guess, I need to appreciate you more," she laughed.

"Why?" he asked, with appreciation.

"For trying for the both of us," she said.

"You get what I'm saying right? I think it would be good if we each tried," he said.

"We shall see Sam," she said.

No Ordinary Love

"Welcome Eunice. Welcome Sam," Dr. Lynch extended his hand to shake, "Now don't you kids go worrying, about tomorrow today. Some hurdles are difficult but moving through them can make life a little better, than it was before. Have you ever heard of the phrase, *the only way out it through!*" he said, making no effort to smile.

They both sat quiet.

"Sam tell me in a sentence or two, what you see as the issue between the two of you," Dr. Lynch said.

"I believe my fiancé," air quoting fiancé, "thinks herself superior. Don't get me wrong Eunice is definitely more intelligent than I am but I'm talking about sancti-mon-ious..." his voice trailed off realizing he'd forgotten, what the word he looked up meant.

His face felt flushed at sounding foolish. He hoped his use of a big word showed he was serious. He fantasized that Dr. Lynch would simply agree with him and provide instructions on how to make the trouble go away.

"Eunice I'll ask you the same question. Tell me in a sentence or two what you see as the issue between you and Sam," he looked at her as if to say; *ready, set, go!*

"Well. Um. How should I put it. Sam is definitely a jealous type. I'll admit, I see Terrence and Gabrielle because I need a break from his mood swings," her voice was assertive.

Her secretive ways made sense now. Sam started sweating. Out of the two of them, Sam appeared to be the *whack job!*

"Okay, let's pause for a moment. We are not trying to solve the world's problems but merely here to uncover issues," Lynch said.

They both stared at him.

Sam didn't see how that was going to help.

"Couples today find the world so fast paced, they begin to resent their partners for the smallest things," he said.

"But doctor we are total opposites," Eunice said.

"Yes, but opposites attract!" Sam said, hoping to cue Lynch to a magic solution, so they wouldn't have to see him again.

"Studies show true opposites are quite rare. What we discover is people are attracted to qualities, they recognize in themselves," Lynch said.

Sam was intrigued.

"Sorry. What do you mean?" Eunice asked.

"It's less complicated than you might think. It's simply different sides of the same coin," Lynch said.

He imagined Eunice already forming an argument, on how dumb she thought the session was for the walk home.

"Dr. Lynch I don't feel motivated, to make plans with her. I don't know what she tells her friends about me. I'm pretty sure, they think I'm the instigator," he said, knowing he sounded like a whiner.

"Sam! That's not true," she said.

"Oh really!" he said. His jealousy of Terrence bubbled to the surface. She was lying in front of the head shrinker! Cardinal Rule number one broken.

Didn't anyone else see what she was doing?

Eunice started to describe wrongdoings from her past; swearing at her mother, manipulating her father. She went on to explain gleefully, how those were juvenile behaviors and she wasn't like that anymore.

"Well once in a while, if I've had drinks I might be unkind but everyone is sometimes," she said. "With Sam I try my best. All I want is harmony," she said, blinking pretty eyelashes, like Clarisse from *Rudolph the Red Nosed Reindeer.*

Sam rocked back and forth in his seat, to keep from speaking out. He wasn't surprised by her slanted version. Of course this was how it would go. He finally got his revenge set up by making her see a shrink and here he was foiled again.

"Eunice's examples of drunk behavior, sound like sober Eunice's bad behavior to me Dr. Lynch. We aren't dealing with the root of the problem," he said.

"Let's face it Eunice, you have depression and that's okay. We'll get you help if that's the case. I've behaved awful," he looked to Dr. Lynch for back up but received blank eyes. Sam had reservations about Dr. Lynch. *Ma was right. What a quack!*

"You have no right…" Eunice glared at him in disbelief and began to cry.

"Sam, we do not diagnose, here?" Dr. Lynch interrupted gently.

That was rich! Eunice had never cried in front of him before. The tables were turning on him in a major way. *What a cow!*

"If I have depression, you have been the cause!" Eunice said, grandstanding in front of *Mr. Credentials*. She was acting out the movie clip, that played just before winning her Oscar.

"You really think, I cause your depression Eunice?" he asked. He felt out of control.

Dr. Lynch cut in, "Alright. Let's leave this for now."

A voice in Sam's head said, *Stop Talking.*

He listened.

Their words hung in the air.

His skepticism had him thinking, he'd played right into her hands. Was she manipulating him? Making him think he caused her depression? He couldn't guess how he was the cause of anything, prior to three years ago.

"Are you saying I trigger you? Sam asked.

"I'm saying, how do we know? It's like which came first the chicken or the egg, as you like to say!" she said.

"Our time is just about up," Dr. Lynch said, nodding to the large wall clock, with dollar signs for numbers.

"I thought communication was supposed to remove our misunderstandings," Sam said, back to his compassionate self.

"This is what is meant by, *Let sleeping dogs lie,*" Lynch said, handing each of them a pamphlet.

By the end of their first session of couples counseling, Sam felt betrayed. He imagined Dr. Lynch, would leave them with the assessment, 'The two of you are *FUCKED!*"

Practice Makes Perfect

Days later after enacting Dr. Lynch's pamphlet, *Ground Rules and Respecting Boundaries,* the tension between them cooled.

Eunice came home pleasant, cooperative and a little more interested in him. It took the tension away when she pranced playfully, flashing bare breasts and holding a mischievous smile. At least it contradicted his thinking she wasn't interested.

His downfall had been not reciprocating her playfulness. His mistrust assumed her sudden interest was fake and she had ulterior motives. He'd remained quiet carefully watching her.

She'd asked him what was wrong, which implied he was the problem. Pride kept him from being himself. It was a bad dream where fear left him mute.

"Nothing, just a lot on my mind, dealing with a situation at work," he said.

"Fine," she said annoyed.

"What? Now I'm the villain?" he said, regretting his pandering for pity.

"Sam are you playing mind games with me?" she asked.

He could have turned it around, by asking her to sit and watch an episode of *Friends* but he didn't. *Who was selfish now?*

"I'm off to bed. I've got to get up early," she said coldly. He got up early every day. *Oh well.* It was his own fault and his own stomach ulcer to live with.

The next morning, she still said, "Have a great day Sam!" chipper and smiling.

His jaw had stopped dropping in surprise, once he realized her congeniality was like putting a coin in a juke box. She was Miss Happy-go-lucky most of the time.

His thinking had changed since Dr. Lynch dissected their personalities and unearthed the ugly bits. Saving himself from regrettable interaction, he chose to stay away weekends to clear his mind. It inadvertently backfired, when it pushed her further into Terrence's arms.

He was afraid to let her go but suspected it was the only option. He didn't have the Teflon protection she had. He envied her. *Eunice, thank you for using your Teflon on our relationship.*

Was she ever hot for him? He was hot for her all the time! It seemed abnormal to spend the day at a family gathering and not be hot for each other. He had a right to know if she had eyes for Terrence.

He told her it wasn't about sex, "Baby, I just want to be with you like that, feel close and free like we used to," he said. That was true but he also felt like a horny teenager!

It was as if that *bastard* Lynch had unleashed evil by convincing them to remove their masks. With their raw flesh exposed, they were farther apart than ever.

What a great idea therapy was Sam! See! I was right all along, it could never work with a girl like her. She's too good for me!

Up and down the cycle with the highs came addictive lows that seemed like the end of the world. Sam had never been this lonely before. He wasn't sure if he lacked confidence or REALLY WAS being treated like *shit*. It would be great not to thrive on self-doubt but he couldn't imagine being without her.

Grandma Hood

Sam had flashbacks of being taunted for his dark complexion. The boys called him, *blue black, midnight oil* and *dark as night.*

It was no secret lighter people were considered more appealing, so of course Eunice would find Terrence more attractive.

He remembered Grandma Hood saying, "Sam there were all kinds of tales in our Hood family tree where men and women, would turn their own kin over to please the master. Not even thinking it whatn't right. In old time slavery days you lost who you were if you wasn't strong. It did damage to your head. Could you imagine denying your beliefs, no longer thinking for yourself. That's one scary business!" Grandma Hood said, while fanning her chest with a corn stalk woven fan. He listened to her thinking slavery still existed, with skin tone.

Internalized racism was an effect a of colonized people who lost their own identities valuing things the masters did. [12]

"When I was a girl, we wasn't slaves but the state of mind was as if we were. *Jim Crow* laws was almost worse as folks didn't know who they were supposed to hate. We learned we had to break some shackles inside our heads too.

"Your granddaddy grew up over yonder! He was a mighty spiritual chap. He was what you called a *Sambo*. I loved his eagerness to please but it was a strain on me being raised tough. He could smile graciously, as if he was dying to serve whites despite wanting to clock 'em senseless," she said.

"Sorry Grandma, what exactly is a *Sambo*? Is it like a tax man?" he asked.

"A *Sambo* was what we called our brothers, who were a little too eager to please the whites. When your granddaddy was a boy, he said there were house slaves who thought, they was high and mighty living up in the big house. Them were always lighter skinned not like you and me. You'd never find a deep skinned man working inside the big house, not before Louis Armstrong's day," she said.

"Where would they put me Gran? Field or big house?" he asked, already knowing the answer.

"Have mercy. With your lovely soft skin," she rubbed his arm and chuckled, "You sir'd be working them fields in the blazing sun. But listen no one spoke of the disadvantages of the big house. I heard the girls would never be left alone. They'd have to go with any white man who asked, master or visitor didn't matter. The house men were emasculated, while those outside grew stronger. Gratitude *chile*. It ain't great now but it ain't like back then. Be thankful for that," her harsh words were spoken gently.

"How'd the house folks treat the field folk?" Sam asked. He admired how she didn't mince words.

"Oh Lord! Terrible. Looked down their noses or avoiding eye contact with their own flesh and blood. If a poor *bastard* wasn't thick skinned, he'd melt with shame," she said.

"Do you think there was racism amongst black folks?" Sam wanted to know if she believed in internal racism.

"It was survival is what it was," Gran said, "but don't worry. There was a long tradition of paying special mind to those field men with special pies and treats smuggled out to them. All undercover of course," she said.

"That's sad Gran," Sam said.

"Fitting in was a bit like ladies fitting into the health and beauty regimes today. Ladies trying to be like the magazines. We all bleed the same the last I checked. Life can be snuffed out just as easy, no matter what you were born! I never understood why folks had to be like each other anyhow," Gran said.

"Maybe it won't last forever. As migration and intermarriage happen all over. Change is coming. It just might take ten generations," he said.

"Bless your heart Sam," she said.

Harpo

Sam considered Gran's words, in relation to his father's upbringing. He seemed meek in public but those who knew him saw how opinionated and self-righteous he could be. Especially with a bottle of beer in his hand.

On a rainy Sunday, Sam confided his feelings for Eunice to his father. He'd be out fiddling with the car engine, under the makeshift car port he'd built, maybe escaping the downpour or escaping mothers nagging inside.

"She's a fine gal but Sam ain'tcha askin' for trouble? Don't go changing,' into what she wants. You may feel encouraged to pluck parts of yourself she likes and present them as your whole but don't deny the real you," Harpo said.

It did seem ironic Sam loved the prettiest black girl in town, while figuring himself one of the least attractive.

"Son, it ain't right what happened to you out at Pike Road. Don't mix that business up with lady business. How do we know they wasn't after you, thinking you was takin' advantage of a white girl?" Harpo was perceptive before having too many *brewskies*.

"Pa! You know Curtis Johnston is black. It's not like she's a white girl. What if I was a gay guy, like Todd or a man changing into a woman!"

"Don't talk foolish boy!" Harpo said, instantly enraged.

"All I'm sayin' is there's always another thing to hate. The only way around is to let people be themselves!" Sam said.

With what he learned from Gran, Sam didn't need a degree to figure out opinions trickled-down the family tree like sap. Harpo probably learned self-deprecation, from his generation and that was passed from the one before.

After several *cold ones* Harpo shared openly about his day-to-day political views, the price of gas, stores opening on Sundays and his ball team the Atlanta Braves.

Sam didn't enjoy drinking with Harpo, when the evangelical preacher came out. That's when the window of civility closed without warning. The conversation inevitably turned scathing. Harpo would reach back into his temporal lobe, where the nasty stuff lived. Staunch views on religion, a woman's place, abortion, sex, wedlock, queers and what current unfairness he experienced.

Then he'd wind up ranting on how Sofia was the cause of his failures.

"Jeez Pa, why on earth did you marry her?" Sam said, laughing. He wouldn't have said that without alcohol.

"Don't you speak of your Ma like that or I'll tan your hide!" Harpo said, shifting to nostalgia.

"I'm sorry Papa. I got carried away," Sam said.

There were a few moments of locked eyes, until his father softened again.

"Sofia was a breath of fresh air from day one. What you first find cute and quirky in a gal, usually ends up being the thing, that makes you wanna clock her one. Yet it's still the thing that attracted you in the first place!" Harpo sounded melancholic.

Underneath, Harpo believed black folks opinions were of little use in today's world. He'd been down the road of hope too many times.

As their male bonding veered into nonsense, Sofia showed up. "I'll bet you boys are enjoying yourselves out here," Sofia stood smug, with hands on hips. "Gotta run over to the church. Marjorie called me in a tizzy. It seems the large fan in the sanctuary is broken. I'm like what'dya calling me for? She said the gals were as nervous, as long tailed cats in a room full of rocking chairs. The new ministers arriving anytime now so it's panic central."

"Isn't Marjorie wound tight most days? Where's Wes? He's still custodian right?" Harpo asked.

"I tried to direct her to the book, with all the numbers in it but sho 'nuff she won't have it. She needs me to come down and hold her hand," Sofia said.

"Ma, it's all on the computer in the secretary's office," Sam said.

"Ha! Of course it is! We *are* talking about Marjorie. Don't worry. I'll get down there and jerk a knot in her tail. 'Sides I wanna hear about this new minister. When I get back I'll make Po' Boys," Sofia said. She had her version of New Orleans sandwiches Sam loved.

"Ma, your ears musta been burning. We were talking about the old days," Sam said.

"Come over and sit a spell," Harpo said.

"What on earth?" her curiosity trumped her rush to leave. They rarely sat around shooting the breeze anymore. Ever since Rory and Otis had gone they didn't have family time.

"I'm working on bettering my education with the school board. What was life like in your teens compared to now?" Sam asked. He figured since Harpo never asked Sofia to join them, he'd try for a joint story to keep his father from finding another tangent.

"Which part Sam?" she asked.

"Being oppressed I guess. Siding with white society to get ahead," Sam asked, trying to figure out if his own way of thinking was internalized racism, like Grandma had described.

"Well I'll be damned. You know what we learned? How to serve without question!" Sofia said, her eyes lighting up.

Harpo grunted in agreement. His fingers greasy as he fiddled with the carburetor, he'd taken out of the engine.

"My brother Joe, what a little rascal. I was only knee high to a grasshopper. We kids loved Joe because he got into trouble for us. He was a fearless dickens. When he'd compliment Mamie, that's what we called our mother, he'd kiss her on the cheek and say, *'that meatloaf was slap yer Mamie good!'* then slap his own rump, while looking over at us to make us laugh. We did," Sofia let down her tough guarded persona and looked misty eyed at having a captive audience.

"What in tarnation does Joe gotta do with anything?" Harpo asked.

"Let me finish. If the men had all been like Joe, I believe we might have risen taller. Don't forget this was before the ghetto's came up in Atlanta and Jackson. Joe stood up for himself in a respectful amusing way. It seems to me the only way to get folks to see is through laughter!" Sofia said.

"Really Ma? You used to say *Richard Pryor* had a foul mouth! Comics do get away with the truth though," Sam said.

"I guess I got Joe on my mind. I watched this fellow on living colors the other night, who reminded me of Joe. He's that one with an elastic face and don't mind making a fool of himself," she said.

"Ha! Are you talkin' about *Jim Carey*?" Sam said. That guy turned stereotypes on their heads with white, black and Mexican characters. Sam wasn't sure if he was in on the joke or adding to the ridiculous.

"That boy's pretty funny!" Harpo said.

"I nearly peed my pants and I was already in bed," Sofia said, breathless at getting riled up.

If his parents subliminally got the message from a kooky white guy ridiculing prejudice, maybe those skit shows were really brilliant nuggets of education. Propaganda for peace.

"Now, gimme some sugar, I gotta run," Sofia said, tugging at Sam's golf shirt collar.

Peace Lily

"Sam when I look at your calendar it's filled with things I know nothing about. You're looking at applying for an apprentice Vice Principal? Going on trips by yourself. These aren't good signs at all," Eunice said.

"I told you about Little Rock," he said.

"It hurts me that I can't be the person that makes you smile. I seem to cause you grief, more than anything. I guess the reverse is true too," she said.

He felt a chill down his spine. Was she looking for him to console her? How had he misunderstood? She was turning the tables again, reciting his issues as her own.

"All I can do is pray we find a way back. I don't think either of us wants to continue like this much longer," she said.

She could live and die blaming everything on his anger and cursing. That's when he knew his *goose was cooked!*

"How about identifying your side of things, like Lynch suggested? I know he makes it sound, so *fuckin'* easy!" Sam said. He burst out laughing, at his own cursing.

Eunice cracked a *Mona Lisa* smile.

"Do you think that we can make each other happy? I don't know the answer anymore? Time apart when you are in Little Rock, will be good I guess. We've been walking a tightrope and the anxiety is debilitating," she said. She sounded as if her questions were answered and she was planning her future.

"I don't know. This is brutal!" he said, in a whisper while staring blankly at her. He was sapped of emotion and felt weak.

"How long will you be gone?" she asked.

"2-3 days as far as I know. Tom is a talker so it all depends. This is timely. I wrote you a poem. May I read it to you?" he asked. The only way was to forgive her, for what she didn't care to know.

"Anything but feelings Sam!" she laughed too.

You have not watered me lately
You feel guilty about not watering me
You try not to think about watering me because you know it's been too long
You know it's wrong
Lily leaves are brown and falling off
You see me looking awful but it seems too late to save me
You buy me a new planter to amend for not taking care of me
I just want water
I love watering your Peace Lily
Each week, I give you too much water
The Peace Lily doesn't say she's receiving too much water
She is afraid to tell me it's too much water
I'm getting angry the Lily doesn't appreciate my water
You are starting to revolt, your leaves over moist and falling off
You simply want less water
We only have two options
We can kill the Peace Lily and be done with it
We can blame each other and kill the Lily is nearly dead

Or we can collaborate lovingly, agreeing on the right amount of water

"You wrote that yourself? I think your poem is good. Maybe I'll understand you better," she said, looking awkward and embarrassed.

"I did," he beamed proudly. Sam had no clue, it was the last time he would see her.

Dead Reckoning

Mike Watts received an anonymous tip, that the Vineyard gang was about to amicably move drug dealers into Centennial Hill. Rival Skull's had allowed it simply based on supply and demand. The Vineyard haven was barren of customers, overly patrolled by cops and the clubhouse had been destroyed by fire.

Gangland accountants must have crunched the numbers and determined a significant take would be left on the table, without the extra sales push. Manny's dealers would show up on Skull turf to supply extra dope and take advantage of the *Candyland,* the schoolyard had become.

It might come as a shock to the layman but drug addicts used all day every day. Generally once addicts were good and hooked they needed reliable supply, to maintain their habit which gave drug sellers a built-in clientele.

The mid-month surplus would be like *goddamned* Christmas to addicts. There too was always the risk of losing a few customers, to overdose so dealers needed to keep sharp eyes on filling their pipelines. They needed to attract fresh young users at bus depots and shopping malls.

The posse and Terrence's crew, gathered late Sunday afternoon for their final huddle before the game plan would be executed. They had voted to proceed with a peace and love approach by inundating the grounds with food, 12 step information, condoms and clean syringes.

Eunice was dismayed but Mike promised her news outlets, were tipped off about their valiant efforts and crews would show up at dusk while activities were in full swing. Handing out condoms and syringes wasn't exactly the razzle-dazzle she had craved but it could lead to something bigger. Eunice compromised by keeping the big picture in mind. She could very well wind up as a guest on *60 Minutes* or *Both Sides Now,* with *Jesse Jackson.* Shows known for social interests and activism.

∽∽∽

When they arrived on location at the school, things looked pretty tame, which was a relief to the new guys. There was no sign of Skull squatters in the three abandoned houses on Grove Street either. Not that anyone would know if a world-class drug trip was playing out behind the shuttered windows.

Dealers often claimed, "I never touch the stuff," which was not altogether true. If they used and sold their existence was worse than just using because they weren't able to lose control. Riding the crest of a high without letting yourself *get off* was torture. Maintaining steady inebriation without ever reaching euphoric heights, was like settling for Tang when you had to have freshly squeezed.

Harpo parked the van at the side lot of the main building, so they could unload the donated supply of bagged sandwiches, carrots, apples, and canned tomato juice. They also unloaded condom and clean syringe dispensers.

The posse and Terrence's crew, had merged to make them a dozen or so, ran supplies out behind the school where the blue tarp shanty town had been erected.

To Eunice the wandering figures looked restless and discontent. Judging by the verbal cues she heard, their high must not last long, since most of them seemed caught in a limbo of wanting more. There were two states of being; this aimlessness moody one and the high itself.

The high was immediate lasting anywhere from 5 to 15 minutes but once the pleasurable effect wore off, the brain demanded more. Crack was cocaine cut with baking soda, so

214

much cheaper. Inhaling the smoke from a pipe gave users a high by flooding the brain's pleasure pathways with dopamine. The constant chore of maintaining the high was called a crack binge.

The posse crew did their best to navigate and interact with users but other than nonsensical speech and grunts addicts mostly stuck together ignoring their presence. They picked at sandwiches but in their heart of hearts, were motivated by crack and meth. Sadly it felt like walking through a safari theme park.

"Is Sam coming down here Eunice?" Gabrielle asked, in a private moment.

"Naw. I didn't mention any details. He worries too much about me. He wrote me a poem though," Eunice said.

"Really, a poem. That's so nice. Nobody ever wrote me anything, except a post-it note on the door asking me why I was ignoring them," Gabrielle said.

"It's about how he is a plant and I don't water him enough. I think when things settle down, I'm going to make a few changes and water him," Eunice said.

At the south west corner, were a thatch of trees beyond which a broken frost fence led down a path to the creek and ravine beyond. Eunice remembered sneaking to a spot by the creek to smoke Marlboro lights with Arisbel in high school.

The well-worn path was trampled down to cemented clay and decorated with bonfire remains, syringes, broken glass pipes, cigarette butts and other debris. This was where the hardcore addicts were. Many spent their days in various states of drugged inebriation, or sedation while others looked unconscious and dead.

Every so often the atmosphere changed amongst the crowd, caused by frenzied verbal sparring between two addicts. The ultraviolent sounds upset the quieter ones, making them cry like children. These guys were beyond being satisfied, by the prospect of a sandwich or a bag of carrot sticks.

"Oh dear," Gabrielle said, as she twist tied the condom and needle dispenser to a tree.

"That's probably not really an argument. In their minds. they might be best friends using together, or at least they used to," Mike said.

It was dusk.

"Eunice, you seem distracted," Mike said.

"It's near dark, are you sure the reporters got the message about what we are doing, for these people?" she asked.

"As far as I know yes," Mike said.

"I'm going up there to take a gander," Eunice said. She headed out front to where Harpo's truck was parked.

Eunice watched as a rented U-Haul van pull in to the lot.

Her first thought was the reporters had arrived, to do the story on them. *What the hell? Reporters in U-Haul's?*

As if they'd been waiting for the right time Lil Red and five of her own black clad camouflage geared army, got out of the van. They looked less like freedom fighting vigilantes and more like assassins, with yellow arm bands.

"Red, what's all this?" Eunice asked, alarmed.

She saw Lil Red's, *Napoleon* motivation through her hardened stare. She didn't seem allied with the posse crew anymore. This bunch didn't look intent on treating junkies like charity cases.

Lil Red had turned on them.

"Lil Red why? Where'd you get these guys? My God," Eunice said.

"Can't stop the train Eunice, can't stop progress," she said, waving her army forward.

The assassins quickly inhabited player positions straight out of a gamer's playbook and spread out around the perimeter.

This was a true ambush. The blindsided Skull gang members, dealers and Manny's Vineyard gangbangers wouldn't have time to retaliate.

The gangs must have been on watching, as they emerged from one of the Grove houses fully armed and ready to rumble. By the looks of things they had an arsenal of guns and ammo stockpiled inside.

Eunice thought the sky was going to fall down around her. She had no reference point, for what she had gotten herself into. She'd already surrendered in her mind.

She ran back to where most of the posse crew were still scouting beyond the thatch of trees and saw Terrence.

"Terrence, what the *fuck* is happening? Lil Red's got an army with real guns," Eunice yelled.

She saw two Skulls near the basketball courts.

She lost all sense of what they were doing there, shooting up their own high school in the first place. She wasn't drunk with power. This was not supposed to be happening. Some other plan was being enacted.

"FIRE!" she heard Lil Red call out.

"No! Oh God. Terrence?" Eunice screamed.

They shot random rounds, into the crowd of transient civilians and dealers alike. *Jonesing* addicts and vagabond carcasses, fell to the ground in tandem *fast, fast, bang, bang.*

The pace then quickened to *PlayStation Thrill Kill* proportions, in a real life video game with units firing on all cylinders, without discretion.

"You wanted to make a statement Eunice. It was your father. It was Curtis who got me those goons. They fought in Iraq okay so you all are *fucked*! Just remember I did it for Sara!" Lil Red said. Tears rolled down her cheeks, as shots popped from her rifle picking off junkies.

Sirens could be heard in the distance but no law were on site. Where the heck were her people? What happened to Jax, Gabrielle, Patty?

Terrence yanked Eunice toward him and managed to get her into a rough headlock, before she could react.

"What are we doing?" she asked, thinking it was all some phony role-play to deceive the police, who had begun to arrive.

"Shut the *fuck up*, I'm trying to think," he commanded.

"What the… no Terrence," she was alarmed, "You and Red planned this? It's sick!"

"Red's got her own *fucked up* issues," Terrence said. "Listen beautiful, I ain't going down because of you," he put the pistol to her temple, "think about it!"

Sirens, gunshots and walkie-talkies static gurgles, made for an eclectic soundtrack. Overhead stadium spotlights went on, flooding the grounds with light.

Of the shots fired, a policeman's bullet caught Lil Red in the clavicle, without much effort. The beautiful rabble rouser lay on the ground dead, along with several others. Her trademark cherry red hair extensions would make identification obvious.

Eunice realized Terrence was desperate, seeing himself as the fall guy and leader. They weren't going to pin this on Eunice, having been a bit of a town darling due to Vineyards last year.

Horrified, she felt tiny vibrations shooting through her nervous system. Being held tight under his arm opened up her adrenal valves, making her body rigid and strong.

"Weapons Terrence? When did we get into heavy artillery?" She didn't think he had the brains for planning this and must have been clouded by her goal of making the news.

"You thought you were better than the rest of us, with your daddy's connections. You're charm will only get you so far. Your white Eunice. This ain't about you anymore," he said.

"No Terrence don't say that," she said.

"I didn't want to do this, help me get us out of here. We'll go down to Mexico. Then I know guys in Argentina," Terrence said, rambling incoherent. His true colors on full display for her to see.

Eunice scanned the vicinity for her next move. Her eyes following the fence running along the walkway, that lead to the half-moon bus zone. In disbelief, she saw a *big ole* orange school bus swerve into the loopety-loop, squealing on two wheels. Eunice swore the vehicle was commandeered by a super-sized *Tina Turner* from *Mad Max*.

It was fight or flight. She was in shock as she tried reconciling her love for Terrence.

"Drop the weapon. Put your hands up!" the officer commanded, through megaphone. Three other cops had pistols trained on them, "I repeat. Drop the weapon and let the woman go."

Her head was still wedged under Terrence's arm as he took one step backward, closer to the path. Then another. She suspected his plan was to run down to the ravine but then what? She couldn't allow him to take her down there.

Officers stepped forward, mimicking his position.

Eunice made herself a dead weight.

"Terrence you gotta turn us in. They'll shoot us dead!" she pleaded.

"Can't do it," he said.

"What did you do?" she asked.

"Eunice you have to help me out here. Listen they want me to be the fall guy. Manny is my cousin. I'm a member of the Skulls. I'm the bridge between the rival gangs. I never agreed with Manny on pushing drugs on kids," he hissed the words in her ear.

"Terrence how can you say this to me?" she asked. With adrenalin charged, she became a generator ball of energy, concentrated in the center of her chest.

One, two, three. Kapow!

She broke free of his grip and hurled herself into midair, then threw her bodyweight backward into him, knocking him to the ground under her. She'd seen the move watching WWF wrestling with her dad. Free of Terrence, she rolled to one side just out of his reach and lay with the wind knocked out of her.

The police shooter got a clear shot at Terrence with a bullet striking his shoulder, precisely where her head had been.

She prayed for Aunt Angela's spitfire determination, as she rolled and rolled herself until her body halted at the gate post of the metal fence.

Terrence stood in silhouette, holding his injured shoulder about to attempt, a final dash for the ravine.

"You fucking *cunt*!" Terrence roared, his neck veins bulged.

Eunice ran toward the orange school bus, now parked in the dark lot on the quiet side, of the school. Police attention was on Terrence so they lost sight of her. Behind her gunshots went off but it was too late to think about Terrence now. He was a Skull. Manny was his cousin.

Where were the girls, the posse crew? Dead? She *fucked* this all up.

Sam I need you.

It was dark now.

She reached the bus lot and found the rogue school bus. She rushed to the door, "Tina are you in there? Help it's Eunice," she banged the door.

Her head swirled. She couldn't get arrested before finding out Daddy's involvement.

"Come on let's go! We've always got room for one more!" a voice said. She looked up recognizing Todd smiling.

He pulled her up the bus steps.

Todd and his supporters were unrecognizable in garish drag. They had created a diversion just as police arrived, responding to gunfire complaints in Centennial Hill.

"Honey, there's nothing like a gaggle of drag queens to create mischief. Come on *quick-sticks*," Todd said, trying to sound lighthearted, given the chaos outside.

Eunice couldn't believe her eyes. Inside the bus, amongst the painted men in drag were Gabrielle, Patty, Lindsay and Jaxon too! Relieved, she had instant proof miracles could happen, without her planning everything.

Thunderdome Tina drove the five or so miles, to the district school bus lot. They were still ahead of an area wide lockdown. The big orange school bus slid easily into its spot, like the final gold bar in the complete set. No one would be the wiser.

"Where to now?" Tina asked.

"Fuck me! I haven't thought that far ahead. Give me a minute to process," she said.

Daddy, why did you give me a way out?

"Can you get me a car?" Eunice asked.

Eunice had a bad feeling and sensed a frame up. Curtis had covertly shown up at Blue Ridge, the other night with a half-baked plan to get her out of town in case she ever needed to.

Curtis was convinced she'd need to sink below the eyes of the law. How was he so sure, unless he was a part of it? The betrayal had been too outlandish, so she hadn't questioned him.

"Baby if you're ever in trouble and have nowhere to turn heed my advice. You got to play it safe. Once a black man or black woman is in custody, the law gets real murky. Assumed innocence flies out the window," Curtis said, looking crushed.

"Daddy, you're scaring me. We're planning to make a splash but we changed our tune. We decided to bring food and aid, instead of making a bold statement. Blame the newbies in the crew. I won't need to run from the law?" she said.

"Back in my day, the law was back seat. You didn't snitch. *Goddammit* nobody snitched. Things have changed. Not gotten better but changed. If Sam or Terrence get arrested they're as good as gone," Curtis said.

"Oh my God Daddy, if I went underground I wouldn't be able to contact anyone and what about money?" she asked. She didn't know what else to say. He made her thinking irrational. Her head was throbbing with a headache. She had never seen her father looking sketchy. *Why was he saying this?*

"Baby it's okay. I've thought of all that. You'll see. Eunice everything will be okay with Doug…" Curtis said.

"I know you can't tell me what I really want to know. Let's simmer down. Give me specific instructions and I'll memorize them," she said, taking a breath. "If anything were to happen to me, what's my next move Dad?" Eunice asked, speaking slower.

"You'd get to Memphis. Just get there discrete somehow. Start out new. Where nobody knows you. The man is Dougie, Doug Barnes. He'll get you all set," Curtis said.

"I know the what and the why but this place ain't ready, may never be ready, for equal rights the way you kids are talkin.' And Eunice don't tell Sam a thing. He don't have the survival skills like you and me. Don't make him have to lie, the boy ain't a liar," Curtis said. He hugged her tight, like he used to when she was his princess.

"Daddy what are you saying? Me and Sam. Is Sam in danger? I kept him outta this," Eunice was flustered.

"You and Sam nothing. You think that *klan* attack was coincidence? Somebody going to lynch that boy, if he's anywhere near ya!" Curtis said, without sugarcoating.

Eunice was horrified. She was doing this for Sam and for the injustice. How could she think he wouldn't be a target by association.

Curtis handed her Dougie's address, "Memorize and destroy," he said.

"Alright Daddy," she said. A thought came to her, like a revelation. Her father had always been the voice of reason. His was the only voice she recognized as truth.

"Eunice we scored a car for you," Todd said, looking concerned.

"Oh thank you, Todd. There are literally no words in my brain to use right now. So I'll just say, 'you never saw me okay,'"

She got in the 1969 mini Austin Cooper.

What was left of the posse crew and several brave drag queens, crowded around the car. They watched and waved as Eunice drove away into pitch darkness.

Battle Lost

After leaving the library, Sam was hungry for a grilled cheese, so stopped at Vespa's where Eunice also worked and he knew most of the staff. Moments later Arisbel came out of the back with a club sandwich. Seeing him she quickly dropped it off in front of a gentleman at the counter.

"Sam have you seen the news?" she asked, pointing to the mounted TV with WSFA-12 News coverage, of the story unfolding live.

Images showed the recognizable darkened silhouette of Booker T. Washington high school surrounded, by a light show of blue and red police cruiser lights, *"After a delayed reaction by authorities, the Deputy Sherriff stated the crime scene and much of Centennial Hill is now under lock down with early counts of up to 36 killed or injured. Further information as it becomes available."*

"Holy shit! I gotta get over there," Sam said. As he said it he tried to remember what Eunice had on her schedule.

"Call me if I can help Sam!" Arisbel said.

Sam was out the door.

By the time he got through yellow caution tape, gunfire had ceased and things were breaking up into lifesaver stations with emergency crews. TV crews were on site trying to get the best background camera angle for reporters to broadcast live.

The red, blue and white lights were strobed flashed making the scene look like a tragic Christmas market, with bodies on the ground, people crying and rushing around. Three ambulances were at various stages of taking gurney's out behind the school.

Sam couldn't believe it was his high school.

He made his way to the active area where police and emergency response were on site. Uniformed personnel were crowded around an injured man on the ground. It was serious. *Oh fuck, it was Terrence!*

"Let them do their job now! Everyone move back," an ER said.

His bitter rival and mortal enemy Terrence lay dying. He had been unarmed and was riddled with seven bullets. Sam crouched down to his face. He had always been jealous of this *mutherfucker*. Was it Terrence's fault he had what Sam wished he had? Good looks and Eunice's heart.

Terrence was lucid, " Sam I'm done. I'm checking out. I loved her still. I tried to get with her. She blocked me at every turn. Told me… Listen to me Sam. Eunice only has eyes for you. Didn't want me. No way," Terrence said.

Sam didn't know what to say, so held Terrence's hand.

"Oh Lord, there you are Son, no, no…" a woman's shrill voice came from behind.

"Ma I hear you. Ma!" Terrence cried out like a little boy.

Sam stepped away. The sound stage of moving pieces swirled all around as if he were on a film set but invisible to all the action. He loved her. His stomach was in knots.

"Where is Eunice?" Sam asked.

No one heard him.

BOOK IV

1970-1980

Panther Security

In high school, Eunice noticed her friends interest was piqued whenever she told her father's stories. They were awed by events in 1970s New York, even more than she was. So when Eunice got the opportunity, she'd get her father talking.

Curtis showed her an old scrapbook, he kept from his heyday. He pointed at one of his cartoon doodles, with the caption; *Dear White Man: A part of the backlash of treating fellow humans as animals and slaves, even years passed slavery is running the risk of violent retaliation.*

In their *N.W.A., Public Enemy* obsessed school hip hop, rap and urban culture were huge. East Coast vs. West Coast rivals *Biggie* and *Tupac* reigned long past their respective lifetimes. Anything remotely related to urban New York or L.A. was of interest.

Once her father got talking about social activism, he looked and sounded different, "While the Civil Rights movement disagreed with racial segregation, many thought Malcolm X advocating separation of black people and white people controversial. When you use retaliation and negativity, you face the criticism of, *two wrongs don't make a right.* It was name calling, you know *pale face, blue-eyed devils,* but necessary back in my day. Communication clammed up between white and black. Instead of worrying about being offensive, people turned to *I'll just despise you from here and watch until you fuck up,*" Curtis said.

"If you think of ghettos as prisons, the inmates in Harlem were restless in their ghetto prisons. There was only so much one could take before boiling over and looking for revenge or recoiling into a netherworld of drugs.

"Wouldn't it have been safer, for you and mother to move away? Why didn't you go as soon as the interracial laws changed?" Eunice asked, so precious and hopeful.

"You're not wrong about the law changing but that didn't mean people's minds changed. It's a bit like what your

Ma thought too but I'd been getting letters, from my brother and sister back home. From Uncle Will and Aunt Louise about bad stuff going on in town. Killings and such. I steered Martha clear of any notion of moving south," Curtis said, never one to shield his daughter from facts.

"So laws didn't make a difference? I can believe that. It probably got worse because everything was secret," Eunice said.

"Malcolm X said something like, 'The white man will sick the dogs on us whether we're sucking up or not. It wasn't safe to mix outside your race until we got along with each other. He said the American Dream had been an American Nightmare.' Don't forget this man was a god to many of us. Later there were signs of corruption within the ranks. Power always eclipses morals," Curtis recounted.

"Then I moved to the big time. I was offered security detail for Malcolm X's Afro-American Unity organization whose motto was, 'If we have no rights, we may as well be separate from your status quo society.' Back then, gangs were recognized for making real and positive change," Curtis said.

In Eunice's opinion, black people had been freed on paper only. To this day they were wildly discriminated and resented maybe worse than before.

"If post Jim Crow whites were accepting, you had to be leery not to fall into being their pets. I think they called it being color-blind, where black people were considered half-witted children, who always needed white man advice.

"A color blind society sounds like equality Daddy. I don't see color," Eunice said.

"I don't know about you but as a person of color, I like who I am and I don't want any aspect of it to be unseen or invisible. The need for colorblindness, implies there is something wrong about me. Nowadays colorblindness has helped make race a taboo topic that people shy away from discussing but if you can't talk about it, you can't understand it," Curtis said.

"It's whacky to think you were a Black Panther," Eunice said.

"Well I was never a practicing Panther just hired for security at the Harlem Festival," Curtis said.

Harlem Cultural Festival

Eunice was fascinated by her mother's perspective of events. Her parents had been in the same place, at the same time but had such different experiences.

"Your father got a gig as a security cadet. He was committed for multiple Harlem festival concert dates, although I only was there for his last one. One of his favorite singers Nina Simone played live. By the next summer we knew we would move south and think about having you!" Martha said.

"When I really think about it, nearly everyone I met during that period in New York, wound up in the papers or on TV, for good or bad reasons. At one time or other I had met *Fred Hampton* a Chicago Panther leader and *Assata Shakur* Panther activist," Martha said.

"Tell me about that. The kids at school love these stories," Eunice said.

Martha and Angela attended the Festival together, since Curtis was on duty. The lineup included *Nina Simone, B.B. King, Stevie Wonder, Mahalia Jackson, Gladys Knight,* and *Sly and the Family Stone.*

The Harlem Cultural Festival stage, was at Mount Morris Park at the north end of Central Park. The estimated 100,000 concert-goers were celebrating youth, culture and black power. It became known as the *Black Woodstock.*

Due to an adversarial relationship between the cops and the black community, the NYPD refused to provide security. The Black Panthers stepped in with security cadet presence instead.

Martha was increasingly worried for Curtis' safety. Things had been tumultuous the past five days. There'd been riots, civil unrest and store lootings. It even spilled over to Bedford and Brooklyn, where two black boys were beaten. The city had deployed extra security, of which Curtis was one, everywhere especially the periphery surrounding the crowds attending the festival.

Martha moved her slender self through throngs of picnic blankets covered with people, coolers of liquor and the powerful scent of hotdogs and marijuana. Angela followed, carrying a small picnic basket, for the two of them.

Angela was in town on a break from teaching, to visit her family. She was a professor at UCLA but mostly known as a radical feminist.

"Geez Martha, finding a spot is as scarce as finding a hen's *arsehole!* How about here, or we'll be piddlin' around all day," Angela said.

"It's as good a place as any," Martha said.

"This is a big deal, way more crowded than I expected. Black politics with real artists is probably why. Instead of a bunch of lawyers and courtrooms. My brother was so jealous when I told him I was coming," Angela said, helping Martha undo her paisley scarf. Angela's brother was a well-known football player in Cleveland.

"I've got a hankering for a corndog! You want one?" Martha motioned toward a vendor row, along the edge under some trees.

"It's a little early for yet. I did see a gal over there with authentic barbecue ribs though," Angela said.

"Gee whiz, you're Alabama accent is back with a vengeance. I bet they won't let you back at UCLA now!" Martha said, teasing.

"I can't help it. When I'm with my folks, especially my brother, I give the Californian a rest. They tease me saying I sound like I'm faking a British accent," she said.

Martha admired Angela's *balls to the wall* attitude about life. She was no shrinking violet. If only women like her ran for government, all social trouble would melt away. Angela was a member of the Communist Party, which was affiliated with the Panthers. She met Curtis first at one of the club meetings two years ago.

Angela once told her when she was a teen, she'd organized mixed race study groups, so folks could intermingle and have a chance to discover they weren't so different. Be less afraid of what they saw on TV and perhaps less drawn to voluntary segregation, "Of course we were busted by the cops. Not the local police as anticipated but the Alabama state police," Angela said with a laugh.

"They busted student study groups! How could that be?" Martha asked.

"Oh please Martha, to authorities and FBI types we were all *Crips* and *Bloods,* trying to enlist whites!" Angela said.

Angela always had one cause or another on the go. She lived and breathed justice. Martha was curious about her opinion on Jane Jacobs' and city planning, she'd been volunteering for.

"Look at that one. He's as high as a kite," Martha said.

Angela looked over, "Sure looks like he's having fun!"

"Where's Chuck? Is he meeting us here?" Martha asked.

"He'll turn up. Getting agreement from those boys is like herding cats," Angela said.

The concert was about to begin, judging by the restlessness of the crowd, then the excited cheers.

Nina Simone walked to the piano, waved casually and sat down at the microphone, "Are you ready black people?" Ms. Simone said, "Are you ready? Are you ready, black man, black youth, black woman, black everybody? Are you really, really, really ready?"

"She's fired up, I can tell," Angela said.

Martha was giddy being at a show in Harlem, with Angela who knew everyone.

The air in the park was electric. Fittingly the park was later renamed Marcus Garvey who was known for saying maybe we black people should be heading back to Africa. *Fuck this America land of the free shit!*

[Nina Simone singing] *I'm here to tell you about destruction of all the evil, it will have to end.* She was militant but inspired pride and unity in the audience. Martha saw similarities in Angela.

Outside of academia, Angela had become a strong supporter of three prison inmates of Soledad Prison.

"I've been very interested in how this will play out," Angela told Martha. "The Soledad brothers are being blackballed into confessions and framed based on color and low income of course. It's California for *god's sake*. I thought we were a more civilized culture. If just one case is treated justly, it could set a precedent for others. At least we'd have a benchmark. It makes me nuts Martha, absolutely mental!" Angela said.

"What's wrong with asking for a fair trial and unbiased jury?" Martha asked.

"Oh right, because we've barely had enough voting years under our belt to warrant a smidgen of equality!" Angela said.

There would be bigger troubles for her. A year later, almost to the day, Angela would be a fugitive having fled California. Accused of supplying arms and being accomplice to kidnapping and murder in the Soledad brothers case.

She would hide at their house on Columbia Street for a few weeks and only moved around at night. FBI agents ended up finding her at a Motor Lodge in New York. The U.S. President would call her the dangerous terrorist, Angela Davis.

She was eventually incarcerated for 16 months which sparked the *Free Angela* movement. Many politicians and artists supported her.

Eunice found it oddly funny how Martha told stories, about such notable people in such a nonchalant way, "The day I met *Stokely Carmichael*, leader of a black power nonviolence committee at a coffee house in Greenwich Village. I didn't even know who he was, until your father and

Angela filled me in. I supposed I was quite a good listener and inoffensive so I probably heard, more than I should have. It was great. I felt like an insider! It was New York Eunice, and overlapping movements, made for a small world I guess," Martha said.

"Didn't you feel shy around people, who were on TV or wanted by police," Eunice asked.

"Actually New York helped me lose my self-consciousness, so I wasn't shy. Well maybe in the beginning but I got used to it. Your father worked peculiar shifts, so I became part the scene. I was old news and folks like Angela didn't seem to care. I related to women's issues over and above race issues. I could talk about women's lib all day. In my mind injustice was injustice so I didn't doubt myself," Martha said.

"What was the biggest secret, you knew about before anyone else?" Eunice asked.

"Mmmh, let me think. Oh. Did you know I was around at the time the *Black is Beautiful* slogan came to be. I bet you didn't know where it came from," Martha said.

"Where?" Eunice asked.

"Get Angela to confirm but legend had it *Diahann Carroll* came up with it when she was secretly dating Frank Sinatra. I am not sure if it's completely true but I like to think so because of they would have made for a lovely mixed couple," Martha said.

Lower East Side

Martha spent the first years of marriage living in America afraid of things. There were so many unpredictable unknowns for her to navigate and she was often too reliant on her husband. It wasn't until they moved from Harlem to the Lower East Side in the 1970's, that she let her hair down and started to believe in her own strength.

They rented a place on Broome and Clinton Street in the melting pot of the Lower East Side, where the Williamsburg Bridge to Brooklyn hung elevated in the air above them. It was a different world. Where Harlem had been homogenous, there were people from absolutely everywhere. Their mixed race wasn't unique and barely garnered attention.

How could New York be so large and so intimate at the same time? It seemed as if people had no choice but to interact. There were pockets of downtown, where mixed race couples didn't even stand out.

One morning newly invigorated, she made them coffee in the percolator, an omelet to share and accidentally burnt toast. They sat at the table and ate quietly.

"Why don't we just stay put Curtis. If we can make it work here, imagine how solid we'll be if we decide to move to Georgia," Martha said, looking at him, with passion lighting her eyes.

"Do you expect me to drive those old farts around forever?" Curtis laughed, "They talk my head off nonstop!" he said.

He'd taken the driving job after leaving security. Curtis was employed as a bus driver for the Stuyvesant Home for the elderly, on East 26th near Bellevue hospital not far from their apartment. He took seniors on day trips, to Coney Island to sun themselves and spend time interacting with others, in the same lonely predicament. It was sad the poor souls were wealthy but neglected by relatives and left alone in their *pissy* en-suite apartments.

"Maybe because you're handsome and such a good listener. Ha just kidding on the last part!" Martha teased.

He hugged her, "I know why I married you. You're here to teach me things I would never have learned. What a tough black woman, you've turned out to be!" he said.

It was too close for comfort, after the *New York 21* had been arrested for allegedly plotting bomb attacks on police stations. Curtis being a part-time security cadet had been questioned by police but with no information to provide, was released. After that he wanted out of New York, "Baby we need to get away. Have a family. Urban life is wearing us down," he said, after hints fell on her deaf ears.

"I've always been the one who wanted to leave but I'm fitting in now Curtis," Martha said. She wasn't going to argue with him again. She decided to maintain the best frame of mind and stick to the positives. She did not yet know leaving New York, would be the end of their loving relationship.

Curtis looked into her eyes, "Mrs. Johnston, I'd like to take you back to bed, for a quick trip to paradise," he pulled her slender arm toward him.

"Funny, I was thinking my stress levels have evened out in this apartment. Maybe it's because we don't have the Turner boy's playing basketball against our wall. We really should make this place more homey. Maybe you'll want to stay!" she said.

They crashed into a marvelous post-breakfast canoodling. Their body connection reminiscent of an earlier era, when intertwined arms and legs was the norm. They made love slowly laughing, while trying not to creak the rickety bed frame.

Afterward they lay in bed talking, "Curtis remember our love is different. It had to be. That's why most people don't attempt this or don't last. The spotlight is tough. Let's never forget the road we chose was a longer and tougher," she kissed his pink lips. His stubble tickled her chin.

"Whether we leave or not, just let me make the nest groovy okay? Come with me to the flea market," she said.

Martha tugged Curtis' arm, navigating the crowded streets toward the subway feeling as if after a decade of marriage she were on her honeymoon again.

They would finally check out the famous Sunday Flea market in Chelsea, she had always wanted. They hopped a D-train heading north toward Broadway.

By the end of the day, Martha was pleased with their finds; a scholarly looking wingback chair, two comfy beanbag chairs and a colorful *Grateful Dead,* tie-dye wall hanging for above the sofa.

Her goal was to cheer him up and make him want to stay but she knew, he was desperately unhappy with his driving job.

Once folks got to know and trust Curtis they let down their guard and preconceived notions about him. His clients were mostly, well-off and Jewish. A certain Mr. Saunders began confiding in him.

Curtis initially thought, he was a pain in the neck. He sat in the front seat of the mini coach bus so he could monitor and hen peck Curtis' driving. He seemed to get bored when there was nothing else to complain about, so talked Curtis' head off instead.

Mr. Saunders ended up glued to Curtis on break stops during Coney Island excursions. Most of the ladies sunned themselves at the quiet beach area, while Mr. Saunders and Curtis took to the shade.

"Never did like those *godamned* Ferris wheel rides, or that stomach churning greasy food that never agrees. I'm not a kid!" Mr. Saunders said.

One outing Curtis said, "My wife is a white woman." He didn't know why he told Saunders. Perhaps he was being a brat and wanted to get a rise out of the cranky bugger. Or maybe he wanted an honest critique from a new perspective. He expected to get a strip torn off him.

Mr. Saunders grunted slightly, indicating he'd heard. He often asked Curtis to repeat things, even though suspected Saunders wasn't all that deaf. The scent of sea salt and the light musk of dead birds wafted through the breeze, so Curtis figured it was a moot point.

"Well maybe it's wrong and maybe it's not. There are things in this life, I am opposed to like maybe polygamy but I do have a soft spot for love," Mr. Saunders said.

"How's that?" Curtis asked, surprised he hadn't bitten the lure.

"When I was a young man, I had a strong feeling for Jeremy my father's butler. I wanted to learn everything I could from him. He wasn't much older than me. Sometimes you don't understand your feelings and I didn't understand mine. I woke up each morning needing to know, where he was. So I understand different kinds of love you see," Mr. Saunders said.

"Thank you for sharing Sir," Curtis said.

"Love only hurts if you don't act on it," Saunders said, sounding introspective.

Curtis didn't take Mr. Saunders predilection for his father's butler personally. He didn't know if they were comparable. He got the impression Mr. Saunders was saying something more along the lines of forbidden love or that love has no boundary.

Whatever the case, the driving job wasn't so bad. He could hang on for a while longer, while Martha enjoyed fitting in.

The year Curtis was a bus driver, Martha had developed a keen interest in city planning. The city of New York would build more apartment towers by annexing large pieces of land deemed slums, this time century buildings in lower Manhattan including Greenwich Village were affected.

Martha stepped her toes in the water taking part in general interest meetings, led by *Jane Jacobs* at Washington Square Park in Greenwich Village.

It would mean more carving up of city blocks, to make way for monstrous St. Nick styled apartments, like in Harlem. The intention wasn't necessarily socio-economic purposefully displacing low income people.

It was the city hall boys club, led by Robert Moses whose ego superseded all else. Harnessing *avant garde* European architects like *Corbusier,* with stark cube designs, would be impressive on resumes. The designs were clean and uniform in shiny glass and metal but the consequence was the stripping away of diversity and color.

Robert Moses' opinion was the only salvation of cities was large-scale destruction of existing buildings. He catered to people living further away, in the suburbs wanting to effectively get them in and out of the city. Highways and automobiles to Coney Island or Long Island, was the way to connect nature, parks and beaches to city life.

He wanted to change the wild organic English garden into the sleek streamlined gloss of chic and clean.

At that point proposals included, a highway through midtown Manhattan. Jane Jacobs committee was up in arms and dead set against it. It was at that point, Martha started to grow tired. She thought perhaps a quieter life in a small town would be better for her and maybe a baby would take this time. She could blame city planners for proposing to Curtis they high tail it out of New York.

Gone South

Martha told Angela they planned to move, "How hard an adjustment can it be. I'm from provincial smaller towns in Canada," Martha said.

"You can't truly understand the nation unless you at least make a pilgrimage to the Deep South. As long as there has been oppression, people have resisted it. Living in the South has turned my attention to the countless women and men whose acts of defiance, broke down barriers and built new bridges," Angela said.

Martha thought she understood race relations from all those years living in New York but it had merely been the tip of the iceberg. When they got to Georgia, she realized the North had been a dress rehearsal.

In his Navy days, Curtis learned about the world and had broken away from his *lot in life,* of farmer but Martha's education was just about to begin, by moving south. Her experience would unfurl like a rich quilt tapestry, women of little means sew together from tattered fabric.

In the North, his having a white wife was of constant concern. In the South, her safety, her being a target of attack, her naively upsetting people would be of concern in different ways.

There were black men who found him crazy to get involved with her and some envied his gall. Black women were often disgusted he stepped outside his race. White men might be jealous, wanting to trade places, while white women found him handsome and could imagine how Martha have fallen for him. It wasn't easy finding a good man!

A story Martha always told Eunice growing up was about the first time she met Daddy's folks in Georgia. Martha told it so many times, she sounded like a late night radio host doing a soft spoken monologue.

I sat in the front room while your father and his folks discussed things on the porch. I could hear every word through the screen. I heard your grandma Cora say, "That wife of yours thinks her shit don't stink!"

"Mama you hush now! She's just nervous. She's never been South. We'll be fixin' to leave in a week or two so never you mind," your father said.

I could tell he was distraught, which made me feel guilty for sticking out like a sore thumb. Southerners white or black, seemed to be angered by my being in their community. It took its toll on me after a while. I'm still convinced the blistering heat can make folks unreasonable.

Grandma Cora said, "But don't you understand? Black and whites together just ain't right, not down here. She's a white woman for chrissakes! They'll kill you. Where's your head at Curtis?" she burst out sobbing.

"Hush woman, the boy is figurin' out his co-ordinates. 'Sides, I need help 'nussing this squirrel back to life. I nearabout ran over it on the road," your grandfather Ben said.

"I don't need the whole town chattering about this white woman you got mixed with, you is just asking for klan trouble boy!" Cora said, throwing her hands up in the air.

"Atlanta might be best for you Son. They don't mind folks doing whatever lifestyle they want nowadays," Ben said, sternly agreeing there would be trouble if we stayed.

"Alright Momma, enough of that rough talk," Curtis said.

Then your grandmother softened. "I reckon I can call on Sofia Hood over in Montgomery. That might be just the place for you given your choice to uh, marry one. It won't do here Curtis. I reckon you'll do what you want in the end," Cora said.

I wish I could have seen her face. I had come a long way though. I learned prejudice came in many forms; sometimes heart piercingly so.

Perhaps your father was distracted being under their influence. He seemed oblivious to what I went through. I felt completely ignored and alone. I was the only one who was different? I had never been south of New York state before. I was the only white person around and it was the first time I'd felt neglected by him. Didn't any of them understand?

Then I realized it was similar to what he must have gone through in Montreal and so I felt even closer to him. Grandma's health was on the decline and I chose to believe she had nothing personal against me. She just hated damned Yanks, never mind a damn Yankee cracker!

Martha could have done the international symbol for 'end scene' as she returned to her usual speaking voice.

Eunice had always wanted to understand her mother's battle with depression and its cause. Could it have been years of societal harassment at her audacity to marry a black man or something physiological in her brain.

She asked her to elaborate on those days. "Mother what was it *really* like being white with Daddy's family when you came south?" Eunice asked.

Cora and Ben Johnston

Curtis and Martha arrived after dark in the Dodge packed full of as many cherished belongings as would fit. They would send for the rest of their things, when they figured out where the heck they would live. Curtis wasn't certain how his folks would actually react to their arrival. In the meantime, remaining house belongings were stored in a friends warehouse locker.

Curtis' mother Cora Johnston, was the daughter of a Methodist minister. His father Ben Johnston a businessman who had owned a Laundromat and a farm until bouts of ill health forced him to slow down.

"Daddy, this is my wife Martha," Curtis said.

"Lovely to meet you Martha," Ben was cordial with no visible reaction. "That sure is a perty dress," he extended his hand to shake hers.

"Momma, Martha, Martha, Momma," Curtis said, with a sheepish smile.

To Martha this first impression was critical and the fork in the road, where she would be successful or fail miserably.

"Welcome Martha to our home," Cora said, "Now the first thing I gotta tell you is watch for the wasps. They're in season right about now. They'll surely pinch a plug right out of that lily white skin of yours," she said, speaking rapidly with alarm in her voice.

Martha found her intense. She couldn't decipher Cora's huge smile, which may have masked terror and heartache at what her baby boy had done to her.

Being a preachers daughter or perhaps warding off uncomfortable silences, Cora had no problem filling silence with opinions.

"You gotta watch the gnats too," Ben said. His demeanor was as Martha would have expected. She imagined him in an easy chair with pipe and slippers telling stories.

"Oh yes the gnats. There's an invisible line where the annoying *buggers* will get you for the summer months," Cora said.

"We ain't in the gnat line I keep saying," Ben snapped.

"People don't want to live in the gnat area if they can help it," Cora said, rolling her eyes at Martha.

"Gnats. Got it. I'll definitely watch for those. Curtis was saying the closest town is Washington?" Martha asked. She didn't see much except highways and road signs for the final two hour of their drive.

"Yes, Washington is a pristine place frozen in time. We were never in the way of any civil war battles if you can believe that. The armies fought all around us though. From Atlanta to the coast of the Atlantic. The coast down the Savannah River south was hit pretty hard. Lots of buildings got destroyed. Towns were either razed or have since gone to seed. Washington hasn't lost its past charms," Ben said.

"I don't go in too often. He have farmhands who do the shopping and supplies. Lots of farmers selling on the roadside too," Cora said.

"Oh that's so romantic. I'd love to have lived here back in those times," Martha said. She had always loved the rambling southern homes with pillars at the entrance she'd seen in old movies.

She didn't know why Curtis and his folks all looked at each other incredulous than began to giggle.

Curtis blushed bashful while looking at her. Martha was paranoid she had said something wrong but she probably hadn't.

"You would have loved the olden days. That's probably because you are white Dear," Cora said, with a dead-serious stare. There was silence until she couldn't keep up her straight face.

Then they all howled with laughter.

"I think its *Bedtime for Bonzo*…! Shall we Martha?" Curtis said.

Upstairs soaking in a bath she pondered the bad first impression she left with the Johnston's. Curtis' folks were probably not so different from her own parents, with their precious foibles and annoyances.

They stayed in a dusty old room near the bathroom.

"Do you think they were completely taken aback by me?" she asked Curtis.

"Baby, maybe you were trying too hard. It's very provincial here. Think of a village where everyone gossips. Remember they aren't modern and worldly. They couldn't get all the way to New York remember?" Curtis said.

He didn't mention the first four years of their marriage where he hadn't told them about her. Or during the following five years where he came down to see them without her.

"Just be yourself Martha," Curtis said.

Was she coming on too strong? She hadn't wanted to come across as a caricature asking those questions white people would ask. She had just read the book *Black Like Me* where a regular blue collar white guy goes undercover and scopes out the southern states in disguised in *realistic* blackface.

The next morning, Ben gave them a tour outside. When Eunice saw the house in daylight she was surprised it was so pretty, like a miniature Graceland. It had balance with extensions on either end and four grand antebellum pillars at the front. Adding to its mystique were years of overgrown wisteria and Spanish moss.

"I bet you never heard of rolled houses before, have you Martha?" Ben asked.

"The only rolling I could think of would be a log cabin. We have plenty of those in Canada," she said.

Curtis smiled at her, then at his father.

"In the old days Mr. Planter here lives in a modest house. Once he's wealthy he cannot leave his farm but needs a bigger house. He might buy up another house or two for cheap and get them there houses moved and tacked onto his original house," Ben said.

"How ingenious, like adding an extension by using another house. I've never heard of such a thing," Martha said.

"Nothing gets wasted around here," Curtis said.

"Why go through all the hassle?" Martha said.

"A few reasons. They could make a really grand home out of two or three rolled homes to make it larger as the family grew but also mainly to show status," Ben said.

"To prove how successful they were. How do you even move a house?" she asked.

"It took a lot of manpower to roll a house. They used logs, servants or slaves, mules and horses. The original footprint of this place is near two-hundred years old. This house here is made up of three. Those two west and east were additions. That was how the Johnston's did it anyhow," Ben said.

"Eunice, the funny thing is the two houses that were added have different ceiling heights and floor levels so upstairs you go up a few steps to Will's room and down a few to Ma and Pa's, because the floors don't line up," Curtis added.

Beating Cora to the punch, Ben took the reins on dinner conversation right out of the gate, "The thing down here is we don't mean to be unwelcomin' but nothing stands between us and our history. People don't remember Jim Crow and Civil Rights like they should, 'specially the young," Ben said, as if he'd told this one before.

After nearly a week in and Cora was more comfortable with Martha around too.

"But black folks up North cannot fathom living here. They think we're a bunch of old fashioned relics," Cora said.

"The blood is in the ground we walk on. For most old-timers round here, history lives in parallel to images of being beat down. There's nothing worse than being set free and then treated worse than before," Ben said.

"I just tell 'em they won't understand racism unless they spend some time here. You see, for black folk the South is our homeland. Most folks ain't dreamin' of Africa no more. We been long divorced from all that. This here is as close as they're gonna get to their roots," Cora said, on cue like a good old married couple.

"Sure, you can let it go but what's an easier way to brand the lower class, than by using skin color. To this day, dark skinned people are judged like book covers. The anger comes from a real place," Ben said.

"They was *playin' possum*," Cora said.

"That means pretending not to understand," Curtis translated.

Martha looked at Curtis.

"That's why we could never bring ourselves to venture visiting you in Harlem Son. It would have been something to see though," Cora added.

"You both make nostalgia seem beautiful. Let's talk about the good things. Make no mistake Martha, it is dangerous down here even today," Curtis said.

"Come now Curtis, your father isn't sugar coating anything. He knows all about the devil's rage full stop. They taught us in school, we wasn't as good as a white person. I can track down the text book," Cora said. She looked at Martha for the first time.

"Cora. Hold your horses, what'ya telling Martha all that for?" Ben asked.

"Quit yer bellyaching. She's got to know the truth if she's gonna take care of your son. This ain't the city," she said.

"Now don't be getting too big for yer britches. You have an audience now but it ain't Martha's fault," Ben said.

"That's okay Mr. Johnston, I want to know everything," Martha said.

"Mrs. Johnston, I would never claim to know what you've gone through but I do feel it in my gut hearing your stories," Martha said, feeling the words as she expressed them. "I want you to know how grateful I am to be here with you and with Curtis of course."

"Things are changing some," Curtis said.

"You're right Ben, I get carried away sometimes. Martha dear do forgive me," Cora said.

"Of course Cora," Martha said. She had to act fast and get in on the conversation, "I am haunted by an invisible affliction of fixing what I see wrong. Ask Curtis. In New York for example, we protested the city and their plan to carve an expressway right through Greenwich Village. It was a lot of trouble and took us several months but in the end it worked. Imagine a bunch of immigrant women banding together in protest," Martha said, bravely adding her two cents. She felt blessed for the opportunity to dip her toe into the conversation. Should she have stayed quiet?

"Sure, immigrants but were any of them black?" Cora asked, with a painted on smile.

Martha had it in herself to stand up to principles she believed in but for the first time a seed was planted. Was it worth spending all of her energy trying to convince Cora of anything. To convince anyone of anything? Letting people's opinions exist and wash over her was the seed that had been planted.

"Mama. I told you in my letters how Martha set up our home in Harlem. And then went hog wild with our apartment on the Lower East Side. I didn't even blink and it was done," Curtis said.

In her opinion he exaggerated a little but Martha was deeply touched that he noticed and acknowledged.

"Cora, there were plenty of black women native New Yorkers, from down here, Jamaica and Africa too. City hall knew they did wrong already, we ladies made them understand years of retaliation in protest would not be worth their investment," Martha said.

"Well I see we have a quiet but awfully stubborn woman here. I like that," Cora said. She looked at Martha and held her stare. A tenderness passed between them the men would never understand.

Early the next morning she went walking the grounds to gather her strength back. The swirling conversation and learning so many new things had left her spent.

They had opinions about everything inside and outside their household. *How was it that everyone was an armchair psychologist?*

Martha was disillusioned at gaining such wisdom from the likes of Jane Jacobs and Angela Davis yet felt like a stupid little girl with Cora's chatter and opinions.

Curtis joined her near the apple orchard.

She didn't say much to Curtis out of respect but of course with ten years of marriage he picked up on it, "Just think Martha. Ma was snipping at you just like she does all of us. You're now a part of the family, being nagged to death," he said, ribbing her.

She laughed.

"You are a mind reader. Are we really going to live here. I heard you all discussing things the other night. Maybe Atlanta is better suited for us," Martha said.

"Maybe it is. Let's sleep on it a few nights. I've got some feelers out. I'm going to call one of em right now. How about you take a drive on your own and see what you think of this country life," he said.

"Alright. Let your mama know I'll be back for lunch," Martha said.

It was the best advice she could get. From then onward when she felt overwhelmed she planned to step out of the swirl. When she got fed up with thinking about her race and his race, she found solace on those drives or walks.

If folks didn't know her she could hit pause on being married to a black man and simply blend into a crowd.

Martha had lived so many reincarnated lives already; a childhood with alcoholics and poverty, and a mixed union with three unique experiences in Montreal, Harlem and midtown Manhattan. She had jettisoned to the conservative south to do it all over again.

At first she questioned how she would ever fit in. Then decided she couldn't deny identifying as black inside, given the cultural influence of New York and the company she kept with Curtis and their circle of friends for over a decade.

The closest thing she experienced to racism herself, was when she was out in public with Curtis. The questionable stares and eye rolls saying, y*ou don't belong here white bitch!*

Hopelessness faded as her battery recharged. So what if she couldn't *pass* as a black imposter in Harlem and it was absurd to think she was *passing* for a white stranger in some Georgia town.

Thinking too hard messed up all she thought she knew.

She found those small towns too sterile and strange with the only people of color serving whites.

She had to be cautious not to perpetuate a stereotype that southern white folks were all *dumbass* rednecks. She also had to be careful, she didn't arrogantly preach to educate white people on how to behave.

Let it be, Martha.

ᏫᏫᏫ

They were seated on the front balcony. Curtis and Martha in rocking chairs, Ben on the wicker love seat while Cora came out with a tray of fixings for iced tea.

"Pa can you tell us the story about how you inherited this place outright?" Curtis asked.

Oh no. Martha wanted to disappear into the clapboard, still fearful and uncomfortable being present when personal topics were discussed.

"When the last Johnston passed, eleven years ago now, he had it in his will to us. The families had become so intertwined under the name Johnston that the parcel of land was left to us," Ben said.

"Penance alleluia," Cora said.

"That's a beautiful thing. Forgive my naiveté but my I ask how there were white Johnston's, then Afro-American Johnston's?" Martha asked.

"Oh that's a good one," Cora said, "it's the first question I asked Ben when I met him."

"Way back, when they were freed our ancestors hadn't planned a surname. It wasn't the norm but they took on the Johnston surname permanently. This probably appalled freed slaves of the time who knows. Most chose brand new names or names with meaning like Free-man or New-man or opted for Washington or Jefferson after a founding father," Ben explained.

"Thank you for telling me all your stories Ben, Cora. It truly is wonderful to have my eyes opened up to a whole other side of the world. We live so separately," Martha said, holding Curtis' hand as she spoke.

Alabama

They packed up the car and left one breezy Sunday after church. Martha could say she had acclimatized to the south but there was much relief in getting out of Cora and Ben's microcosm.

They drove over Georgia countryside to Atlanta bypassing the city center and continued on to Alabama.

At gas station fill up pit stops Martha noticed odd looks from people along the way. She found herself weak and vulnerable to the exposure. Naked to ridicule when she was tired or hungry. She struggled through bouts of self-doubt. To assume every look was disapproving their union seemed unlikely but what else could it be.

Martha sat by the motel pool outside Tuskegee, where the famous airmen trained, while Curtis napped in the room. She was an outsider. Her white skin was supposed to be supreme yet if she could change it she would. All she wanted was to disappear under a safe hide of mahogany so she could be a part of this real world.

Martha was afraid. She wasn't feeling herself at all. It crossed her mind to drown herself in the motel pool while he slept. It was so foreign to wish desperately to be someone else to feel more like yourself.

Later Martha would find out she was pregnant.

"As strange as I felt that day in Tuskegee, Eunice darling I'll never forget it. I can tell you now that you are a grown woman I cherish that memory for some reason. Being found in the pool would have caused a *helleva* ruckus so I keep it quiet from your father," Martha said.

"Thank you for telling me your story mother. I love you," Eunice said, with admiration hugging Martha.

Aside from mother being a pain in the *tits* sometimes, she was a damned good storyteller!

BOOK V

1998-2000

Memphis, Tennessee

Eunice had taken the Greyhound bus from Montgomery to Birmingham then up north to Memphis.

She wasn't disguised like someone on the lam but dressed purposely drab without makeup. She wore beat up sunglasses, a shapeless top and a sloppy ponytail.

Looking out the bus window Eunice felt like she'd been plunked into another world, the last one had been science fiction. A heat wave had finally ended so gardens and lawns were burnt yellow. It still looked like America with franchise chain stores and the same flag but it seemed foreign to her.

She had no idea what the outcome of the shootout was and didn't dare ask anyone. She would try and catch some news when she got to Memphis. A part of her wanted Memphis to be a fresh start, maybe a reason to never look back. However, the city was most famous for the musician Robert Johnson who made a deal with the Devil in exchange for his success. Was that what Eunice had to do for her freedom?

In the past she'd had the ability to erase bad things like arguments, mistakes or dropped friends. She waited for a sign to rid herself of hopeless thoughts of Montgomery.

The bus crossed into Memphis city limits by mid-morning. Along the highway she read the brightly colored posters and billboards advertising live soul, blues and jazz. How she wished she was arriving fresh out of Musicology Camp so she could erase what happened in-between.

Eunice was capable of doing just that.

She closed her eyes and concentrated so her mind wandered to her childhood dream of being a singer, allowing herself to pack away her current predicament. The bus rhythm helping her focus. The image of her on a dark stage except for a single spotlight and mic stand came to mind. She saw herself as a youthful *Edith Piaf* in a Paris theater.

A warm comfort came over her. Deep down she was already thinking forward. If she had the gumption to fight for justice and get on with things, certainly she could do it again and again. Justice for the hard done by and for Daddy would have to wait until she got her power back. Her ambition to succeed needed to revolve around herself right now. She had to put her own oxygen mask on before going back to save others.

CECECE

Eunice stepped off the bus and took in the fresh Memphis air realizing the bus had reeked like an afterhours canteen.

In the town center she found a transit map on a bus shelter wall and used the bus depot as reference.

"Excuse me Miss. Is this where they stone people?" a small bald man in an elegantly tailored tuxedo asked. He grinned warmly and pointed toward Beale street.

Eunice had never been good at impromptu conversations so was tongue tied. Lucky for her he didn't require a response, "My newspaper man told me the trains were down here. That's why I'm going bra less today actually," with his rhetorical statements she got away with a smile.

"I just love this city. There's a new story around every corner. Of course I've never been here before," he said. His childlike manner defied his senior appearance.

"It looks like it'll be beautiful today. Perhaps not so hot," she said.

"My name is Irrelevant, what's yours?" he extended a manicured hand, "Fear not young lady I'm always like this. It's something connected with my alien death," he said, with a pensive look on his face.

She couldn't help but laugh aloud at that one. She'd never heard such bizarre yet interesting phrases in such a short span of time. He could've been a stand-up comic. He was a welcome distraction.

"I certainly hope you find what you're looking for," she said.

"Thanks. I hope I figure out what that is," he said.

If he was an indication of what Memphis folk where like she was in for it.

Uncle Dougie

All Eunice knew about Dougie Barnes was he was a friend from Daddy's Harlem days and a one-time Black Panther, "Dougie is no stranger to helping folks not exist," Curtis had said, "but don't ask too many questions."

"Dougie's been living as a bachelor ever since Madeline passed away. He may seem eccentric but he's a good man," Curtis said.

"Why would he do this, does he get paid?" she asked her father.

"Never mind that, Dougie owes me one. He will be paying you!" Curtis said.

Dougie's house was two-level with peaked gables on either side of the attic, which she'd soon find out was her new hideaway apartment.

After cordial introductions, Dougie gave her a tour of the main floor, the kitchen and living room. When Curtis said Dougie was a bachelor, she envisioned a sloppy guy but she was relieved to see he was just eccentric, closer to a *neatfreak*. Eunice made up her mind he was kind-hearted. He also reminded her of *Lionel Richie*.

On the second floor he opened one door, "This room is a storage room for dear Madeline's clothes and mementoes, the things I can't bring myself to part with," he said.

"I'm sorry Dougie," Eunice said.

"Up here's all yours if you can muster the courage to head up them stairs," he said, pointing up a narrow staircase, "I'll never try 'em again unless I want to break another hip!" he snorted.

"I uh, really appreciate it," she didn't know what to say to the man, who was arranging her phony I.D.

"Take a look for yourself, nothin' to break up there," he said.

She climbed the uneven steps and opened the attic door. The central room was confined by the slanted angles of the roof. She hoped she'd remember to duck to avoid hitting her head in the low spots.

She had a twin bed with a patchwork quilt, a side table lamp and a dresser. If she had a bible and hung a crucifix above the bed, she'd have herself the perfect nun's room. The attic had charm, with its barn floors in need of a good scrubbing. At least she didn't have to share.

She sat on the bed, her heart sinking as the actuality of being on the run set in. Leaving Montgomery had completely shut off from the world. *And for what?* She hadn't actually killed anyone.

She fled to protect her father and maybe Sam she had fled to avoid police questioning. All she had to do was tell them Lil Red got the guns through Terrence's gangbanger cousin Manny and not her father but it wasn't as simple as that. She didn't know how Daddy knew those same men. If Curtis was already in custody, her testimony could unfairly implicate him and he'd been in trouble before.

Back downstairs with Dougie, "Girl, your Pappy tells me it's serious, 'bout what you got tied up in. Now go and think what your new name'll be and I'll get Harvey to get your I.D. in order," he said, making it seem simple as if she were signing up for a Costco membership.

"Really? Seems so easy," she said.

"Now some housekeeping, your daddy has a stipend set up which I will leave here weekly on Thursdays," he lifted the handle of a small roll top desk, which sat in the hallway next to the stairs up to her quarters, "No contact with anyone on the outside from before unless it comes through me first. It's for your own protection, *capiche*!?"

"Alright Dougie. If it's okay with you I need to rest a little," she said. It was the longest day, she'd ever had.

A few hours later Eunice lay on her bed trying to muster the will to get out to a grocery or CVS. Instead she rolled over and closed her eyes again. It was too much; Memphis, stipends, restrictions, fake ID's, crack heads, shootings.

She allowed herself to be mesmerized by the rattle of the old air conditioner, that was wedged into a square of the gabled window. Her thoughts floated in and around the soothing mechanical bleeps and farts, becoming some kind of melancholy rhythm. The lull eased her mind.

The sound turned into the first few bars of an electronic jazz version of, *Here Comes the Sun* sung by *Nina Simone. Little darling…it's been years…*

She decided her assumed name would be, Nina Wayman of North Carolina.

CBCBCB

Eunice had submitted necessary information for her I.D to Dougie, who said the turnaround time was just a few days. In the meantime, she took on the role of a housebound recluse but the waiting was a real test on her sanity.

The more time she spent in isolation, the more she wanted to protect her alone time. It gave her insight into her mother's affinity for locking herself away from the world. The few times she ventured out, she kept to off busy times and wore a floppy hat and glasses. Her shopping was preplanned and systematic, so she could race back to her room.

She was nervous about detection, too paranoid to be seen on the street after watching news snippets about her on TV.

Reports told of death, injuries and arrests. She scoured through the testimonials from those who were there, for any word about Sam and Terrence but no names had yet been released. Then she saw in the *Memphis Daily News.*

Gunfire breaks out at Montgomery school good will killing 16 injuring 20. An armed vigilante group intercepted community efforts to feed the homeless at a Montgomery school Saturday. A dozen members of an unidentified gang opened fire onto the crowd of over 50 people, many known drug addicts who had formed a 'tent city' on school grounds. Neighborhood bystanders were also injured, Alabama officials said.

The Montgomery Police Department said in a news release one man, Terrence Battle was killed and one woman Eunice Johnston fled and is wanted for questioning by the FBI. Both had been involved in a previous altercation with police during an anti-drug activist effort at The Vineyard one year ago.

"We are extremely grateful the incident was contained to one property. Our teams quickly surrounded the school, likely saving even more lives," Deputy Chief Ted Atkins said in a statement. "This suspect opened fire at a crowded public park. This could have been so much worse."

The shooting took place Saturday at Booker T. Washington High School. (Montgomery Police)

She put down the newspaper and closed her eyes. There was no specific news of Sam, so it was a blessing she kept her posse plans secret from him. Maybe he hadn't been at the scene, the day of the massacre.

Eunice's synthesized assessment of public perception, was something along the lines of her journal entry.

In a lawless town like Montgomery, the bad guys are all working together. Eunice, Lil Red and Terrence planned the violence. Or possibly the ladies craftily piggybacked on Terrence's evil plan, knowing he was a member of the Skull gang and cousin of Manny of the Vineyard gang. Terrence and Lil Red were likely in cahoots, with her father Curtis Johnston a former Black Panther.

Eunice Johnston had been torn between justice and vigilante revenge. She had supported the Skull gang, because she and Terrence were likely lovers. Lil Red's insane idea of full force vigilantism, in massacring drug dealers and junkies was of nefarious intention, planned by all three from the start.

Eunice still didn't know what their true objective had been, so figured some of the story was factual. It was an embarrassment of deceit and by no means what she had intended.

Lil Red dying upset her but the notion that Terrence was dead, took her breathe away. He had been someone who met her match, understood her best and the one person she felt at ease with. Be a nerd around and share her fascination with minutia, intricate details and useless facts without fear his ridicule. She trusted him to keep things she shared secret.

How would life be the same without Terrence. She even had compassion for his attempt to kidnap her and save himself. Somehow she regretted never being intimate with him.

She must've gotten a naughty thrill out of Sam's jealousy of Terrence. It gave her proof Sam adored her, which felt good. Sam never understood he had to earn a place in her heart, it didn't just come that easy.

In any case, she preferred solving intricate problems, with like-minded people like Terrence. She didn't have disagreements and altercations with him, the way she did with Sam. He put up so many roadblocks in her plans, with his nonsensical bleeding heart. She wasn't going to be stopped and definitely wasn't going to be blamed for having ambition.

That night she had a feverish erotic dream of rough lovemaking, with a man pressing a pistol into her cheek. It was Terrence worshipping her, as they made passionate love. Or was it sexual assault. It was a dream so the lines were blurred, like the heiress Patty Hearst who supposedly fell for her kidnapper.

When she shuddered awake in a hot sweat, she was relieved it had only been a dream. The unfamiliar attic bedroom gave her little comfort.

Evenings she made it her goal to enter the house with feline stealth, so Dougie didn't hear and feel obligated to holler up the stairs and check on her. The last time it happened she'd been stuck chatting with him for twenty minutes, with American Idol blaring from his TV, each of them pretending the volume wasn't distracting.

Dougie's attic had become her self-imposed exile but it was a safe harbor, where she could breathe easy. *No one knows you're here.*

The first week inspired a depression, even worse than the one she had back at the R.V. To help her feel safe, she wore headphones with or without sound, to try and silence her thoughts.

She was grateful for the white noise of the oscillating fan but it only blew hot air. Dougie hadn't mentioned the attic temperature could rise to 100 degrees of dry sauna heat and she suspected the window air conditioners days were numbered.

The downside of the lonesome attic was, she got weaker as sloth laziness sapped her energy. There had to be a silver lining to this or she would simply be discovered, expired in her bed. *So now what Eunice?*

At night exhausted from doing nothing she'd be sleepy by 7:00 p.m. paralyzed with an inner monologue that offered no escape. Time went slower without a definitive goal and she missed her personal belongings. Here she had a clock radio, a small TV and a few books she would never read.

She imagined Sam pacing the R.V. worried sick about her but brushed it away as too emotional. She dared not overanalyze the fact, she'd recently found him lacking motivation. As his girlfriend she *should have* felt remorse for disappearing and leaving him distraught but she really didn't.

On restless night number four, she started writing her first songs which would become a cache of morose hopelessness to put into rhyming verse. Something she hadn't touched since her juvenile music camp ramblings.

Songwriting was the only thing that seemed to plant the seeds of hope.

Nina Wayman

In the morning Eunice heard the front door slam closed, so came down to greet Dougie. He stood smiling proudly, as he motioned to her I.D. cards laying on the kitchen table.

"Don't be afraid little Darlin'," this may not matter in a year or two. Okay, maybe five years from now. You just never know where life is going to take you," Dougie said.

She inspected the two cards. In her hand they felt exactly like her real ones. How on earth was she supposed to function. She had no idea who this Nina person was.

"I must admit it's a little shocking," Eunice said, groggy from being housebound like an over medicated asylum patient. What happened to her drive to do errands, try restaurants or go to movies. *Oh yeah, you joined an amateur vigilante group and got in a lot of trouble!*

"It's only shocking the first time. The next go round you'll be a pro!" he said, laughing.

"Dougie. It's not funny," she said, stifling a naughty giggle.

"*Lighten up Francis!* I want you to get yourself out there and buy Nina some new threads. Enough hiding in the attic. I put a little extra together for you," he slid over a short stack of twenty dollar bills.

"I'm sure you're right, thank you Dougie. You've been awfully good to me," she said, feeling uneasy.

CRCRCR

Eunice took Dougie's advice and ventured through the streets of Memphis, farther then she had gone before. She noticed something looser and freer than the oppressed vibe in Montgomery. Locals and tourists of all ilk's and ethnicities intermingled, without the usual sand drawn line separating ghettos. The same went for homeless panhandlers, who were a diverse mixture.

Memphis was on Highway 61, an important north and south connector, especially before the interstate highways were built. Many southerners traveled north along 61, heading for St. Louis or Saint Paul. Daddy said Memphis was also a place people came to for anonymity.

She walked the neighborhoods, without care for a map or directions figuring if she got lost maybe the feds wouldn't find her either. Somewhere along the way she ended up on a street of trendy second hand boutiques and saw a funky dress in a window. She went inside.

For the next half hour she tried on skirts, dresses, shorts and hats. They could have played a *Brown Eyed Girl* montage like in a *Julia Roberts* movie, as she spun around modeling for store clerks, who didn't know her from the news. She left the store delighted by her purchases feeling the familiar precocious glee, she got from shopping so headed over to Beale Street instead of going home.

She found an open air patio to sit and people watch, while sipping fruity sangria. The alcohol eased her troubles away. There were people visiting Memphis, from all over; Miami, Dallas and Vancouver, judging by their t-shirt markings. Her anonymity was more secure due to her new *Jackie O* large framed sunglasses.

A woman caught her eye coming toward her from a ways down the street. She had wavy sand-colored hair and a salmon body hugging dress. Her eyes sparkled supernaturally, perhaps she had colored contact lenses. As she got closer Eunice noticed her androgynous face and ethnic background ambiguous, yet she was striking. An aura projected out of how she carried herself with self-assured expression. Only an expert aura reader could read her colors.

Maybe she is Nina. The thought gave Eunice an excited tingle up her spine. This woman had a style Nina could adopt.

Eunice poured the last of her sangria, the blood stained citrus slices mushed together at the bottom. With newfound gusto, she thought things were looking up. If there had been a checklist, she'd accomplished a lot today.

On the way back to Dougie's, she stopped at CVS for L'Oreal hair dye, a straightening iron, colored contact lenses and a bottle of Vodka.

The cocktails filled an empty void allowing her to identify new parts of herself. Eunice was Nina. Nina had the unabashed strength and courage Eunice lacked. Perhaps she became Nina when she drank, as if alcohol were a magic potion.

Karaoke Queen

After a while Eunice left the past behind. It wasn't Nina's baggage to deal with. *No regrets, no resentment, no hurt, no pain and no death. Let it go.* Instead of relying on precise thinking as she always had, she followed the Memphis current. Whatever new thought or idea popped in her head, she accepted and went with.

She got into the habit of baking, she dabbled in cookies or muffins and a cake once but it didn't rise, no matter how many times she opened the oven to see. She left care packages of muffins and scones for Dougie, with personalized notes on how she was faring and wishing him well. They had opposite schedules, with him away days and some overnights, while she had turned into a night owl. He started leaving replies for her, with kooky stick figure drawings.

Eunice would be up till all hours writing songs, or listening to music in her room. Ads in Memphis Magazine piqued her curiosity, she thought of venturing into the array of musical nightlife, jam sessions, recording space offers and the live music venues. Karaoke offered a safe environment.

With a few vodka Fanta cocktails, she got her courage primed to and went to a place called Dru's Bar on Madison street. With her hair lighter, in Nina clothes with contacts she was amazed how easy it was to blend in.

She enjoyed watching karaoke singers, from a quiet stool at the back. Some sang to make their friends laugh, while others looked to be taken seriously. It was only a matter of time and drinks, before she would be up there showing off. Maybe one night she'd have the courage, to sing one of her own songs. Dru's instantly became a favorite, with its low frills and nice pizza.

She would start practicing two songs in her attic 'studio' during the week, then trek to Dru's Thursday nights for karaoke. After a third cocktail, she usually had enough nerve to hit the stage. Her song and performances were forgettable but she didn't care. She was breaking down barriers and gaining the courage to try out her alternate persona.

Being female on her own, she didn't feel targeted aside from the odd man, trying to strike up conversation which had been flattering over sinister. She found Nina attracted different attention. Without focusing Eunice carried herself different, held her hands different and flirted different as Nina.

In the past, she'd been told she was quite a good singer so it was less a shock and more validation when the DJ said, "although you're not technically the best, your voice is the most recognizable."

"Why thank you," she said, flirting with the goofy wannabe record producer, in case he could do something for her.

"Have you seen the poster at the back? There's a karaoke contest next week that pays pretty well. I'd like to see you win it!" he said, a twinkle bouncing off his white teeth.

"Mmmh, maybe I will," Eunice said, with more confidence based on the night's performance. She had settled into a routine and felt safe going out in Memphis.

Memphis had its share of drug use but it was tame compared to the destructive behavior back home. She'd seen enough disturbing episodes first hand, so had zero temptation to experiment.

Alcohol mixed well with being Nina and she seemed to handle her liquor better than Eunice. Nina was less interested in saving the world and more focused on herself, so when she got attention she wanted more of it. Eunice kept hearing herself mentally tell Nina, to 'tone it down' so she didn't call attention to 'them.' *We're still on the lam you know!* She was definitely more of a selfish *bitch,* than Eunice had ever been but it was easier to go with Nina's flow.

Nina hungered for a singing career and was constantly on the lookout, for men who could make that happen. Nashville and Memphis were still places to get connected and discovered and there were plenty of predatory star makers, hunting for that special *it* factor. The scene was a breeding ground for musical yin's in search of yang's.

One night she went down to the locally owned Memphis Sounds Lounge, a jazz and blues joint on Island Drive. The hotspot took karaoke seriously, calling it *audition night*. It was frequented by performer types and a sprinkling of wealthier tourists, who often bragged arrogantly once they got tipsy.

Since her first win of $300 at Dru's, Eunice didn't think karaoke was worthwhile and not as corny. It helped her get comfortable in front of live audiences and winning competitions helped her gain more experience. Regardless of her chances of blowing away audiences with epic power ballads, she kept rehearsing two new songs a week, using skills she'd learned from Mike Watts a few years earlier.

It was at Memphis Sounds Lounge, after winning a another top prize for her rousing rendition of *Black Velvet* by *Alannah Myles,* she first met Matthew Roswell.

"Congratulations Nina! Fantastic song. Drink?" Matthew offered. He had blond loosely curled hair and a sun kissed surfers glow. His dimples more pronounced as his mouth moved in a curved smile.

"Thank you. Where are you from? You remind me of the curly haired guy from that *Brooke Shields* movie *Blue Lagoon*," she said. *Damn*, Matthew was an aspiring musician, songwriter and explained he was starting to produce other artists. She took it with a grain of salt, since that's what they all said.

Every second *regular* on the Memphis bar scene, seemed to be an A&R guy or a music mogul. It was like the cliché that every waitress in L.A, has a 5x7 headshot tucked in her he was easy on the eyes!

uniform to hand out to movie directors, "Why yes Sir, I happen to have my portfolio, right here in my blouse."

"You called it but I'm the *Creature From the Black Lagoon*. I'm from Galveston. That was quite a song choice. Have you ever thought of doing C&W?" he asked.

"C and… oh Western. I don't think I could pull it off. I know the lyrics to *Jolene* though. Why do you ask?" she asked.

"Well I could hear a serious artiste in your delivery. You know how country songs are epic love songs right? Even the rollicking ones," he said.

"Yes," she said.

"I know a country top 40 band looking for a singer. They have a rotation of singers and need another female on their roster. They have a regular gig at the Green Beetle on Main," he said.

"Really? How cool. I suppose I could think of the country option. I like blues so I could probably improvise to country. Wait. Are you serious?" she asked. As Nina she was bolder, plus a few drinks never seemed to hurt her forwardness.

"If you're into coming down to rehearsal sometime I can set that up," he said.

Some things sound so good at the time!

After her third singing contest win, Eunice had confidence to spare. Matthew was cool to hang out with but highly competitive. He wanted to impress her at every turn, which inspired her to try to outwit him. Nina excelled where Eunice dared not. She ended up getting an audition call back and securing the gig, with her soft but unique take on *I Love Rock and Roll*.

Eunice also sang with the Green Beetle bar band, two nights a week. The regular gig gave her a schedule, that allowed her to quit her karaoke nights.

The Green Beetle band called themselves, *The Fix* but Cindy Lewis informed her they'd had many names and incarnations, so *who knew how long this one will last!* Cindy was a backup singer, who took Christine's part when they covered *Fleetwood Mac.*

Like many true musicians the Fix guys were somewhat disorganized and had no leadership, so it wasn't hard to convince them to learn one of her songs.

"Play it for us before we agree Nina. You might be trying to turn us into your backing band! It's happened before," drummer Keenan said.

"Very true. Good observation boys!" Cindy teased.

Not wanting to come on too strong, Eunice purposely downplayed singing her own compositions boosted her confidence. She hoped the boys liked the song, so she could introduce a few more later.

With some reservation, they agreed and over time they consented to doing one of her songs per gig.

Demo Recording

It had been nearly six months since the shooting, so things had died off the news, almost as if it had never happened. She stayed driven, wrapped in music gigs to ward off the paranoia about Montgomery. Why had she never been located and detained for questioning? How good was the FBI if they couldn't find her? She guessed she wasn't top priority and began to doubt they were even looking for her anymore.

When she couldn't fight thoughts of Montgomery, vodka usually did the trick. Or she would try to write her songs. She would never admit the songs were deeply personal, inspired by living in exile and missing Terrence and Sam.

Matthew Roswell had gotten her access to a week-long recording space at Royal Studios, an historic sound stage open 24 hours.

"What do you mean make a demo record. Just like that?" she asked, with delight, hoping beyond hope that he wasn't full of *shit.*

"Nina anyone can make a CD it's the recording equipment rental that matters but we're in luck. An artist owes me money, so gave me his space for the week," Matthew said.

She had a picture in her mind of a glassed-in soundproof booth, with a large jazz age microphone and those large headphones you had to hold onto, with both hands as you sang with your eyes closed.

The studio on Willie Mitchell Street had orange walls and purple shag carpet. Eunice, Matthew and two other loaned musicians worked on nine tracks she had written. *It was surreal.*

"Okay track four was great. Let's do it one more time a beat slower," the one guy said, into his microphone from outside the booth.

"Maybe you don't have enough confidence to sing songs you wrote yourself," Matthew said, the *prick.*

She was insulted. She heard Mike Watts' voice in her mind, "Come on beautiful, you already know how to do this. Sing from your core!"

"Come down to the beach. Feel the salt on your skin, the sun on your face..."

After the first song was *in the can* as they say, Matthew kissed her on the mouth. It was the first time he had made a move on her which she'd found refreshing.

"I'm changing the key," Matthew said.

"Are you saying I don't have range?" she demanded. Nina was forthright. She hadn't grasped the fine line between assertive and aggressive.

"You want the truth? You don't have range but you can hit high notes cold. When you sing low your voice cracks. Most singers can't get up to the high notes like you. Don't worry we'll choose songs for your range," Matthew said.

"But Matt I want to do my own songs," Eunice said.

The cliché *too good to be true* crept its way into the studio. One night Matthew seemed uncharacteristically insecure or paranoid like a boy who'd lost his puppy. She overheard him on his phone begging for a drop off or pick up or something. He was frantic.

She clued in it was a drug thing. He must have been high the entire time she'd known him since he was extremely agitated now. It was like the expression, *I didn't know you drank until I saw you sober*, her mother would say.

Within less than an hour he was back to his usual arrogance making her think he must have scored when she wasn't looking.

After that Eunice started to notice Memphis music types, had a penchant for cocaine. Snorting coke was a status symbol, like an elite badge of honor. Back home heroin was high-end over crack or meth but anything smoked from glass pipe or needle to vein was derelict street junk.

Knowing Matthew was all over the place and not always in the best frame of mind, she soldiered on with her demo. She always kept her eye on her own prize.

On what should have been their final session, she and Matthew stayed well past studio time having drinks. The session musicians had gone, so she allowed Matthew to tinker with one of her songs. It was regrettable, as she watched him destroy the song with his drunken mixing.

He started to make moves on her but with her relative sobriety she easily foresaw his sneaky inebriated behavior, so kept two steps ahead of him. Thankfully she had the wherewithal to lock herself in a little hostel room, available to musicians for rest between long recording sessions.

She had been careless in managing his expectations of her staying late, so wasn't too upset he came on to her. She had only agreed to stay, so she could get her hot little hands on the demo tape. Of course she was also attractive enough that anyone would want to seduce her, so that aspect also fed her.

When the musicians returned the next morning, the song was recorded. She remembered how sickly hung-over she was, "Can you boys see an axe sticking out of my head? Trust me it's there. What did we do? I taste scotch but I don't remember drinking it," Eunice said. She was hung-over but played it up a little to stay on Matthew's good side. *Still don't have my demo tape!*

Over the course of a week, Matthew didn't let up making moves on her. She neither wanted to lead him on nor make him angry. She responded to his kiss but jumped like a spooked colt every time he laid one on her. She wasn't overly concerned he'd figure it out since she pegged him high most of the time anyways.

"Matthew, what does a girl have to do, to get a copy of her own demo recording?" Eunice asked.

"It's still getting equalized," he said.

After the umpteenth time, she decided to leave it alone. She hated pestering anyone for anything.

Matthew's communication became sporadic then dried up altogether, so she suspected personal drug problems had gotten the best of him. Those who knew him said he'd gone AWOL and was likely on a bender that could go for months. Too bad, she had lost a good contact.

Losing faith in the music business, Eunice shelved her recording ambitions for the time being. She felt foolish about the entire thing. Waves of embarrassment would pass over whenever she thought about the recording sessions and how bad the demo tapes likely were. She never did find out how many of her demo songs were actually recorded. *Who are you kidding Eunice?*

Luckily she had kept her singing gig with the bar band.

After Matthew had kissed her at Royal Studio, she'd had trouble blocking Montgomery memories out of her mind. Perhaps Matthew's cold kiss broke the seal, unlocked the door that kept Sam out of her mind. Sam's kisses were warm and tender. She had known him from his awkward teens up to the mastermind behind more than one orgasm.

Sam inadvertently taught her never again to ask, "What is an orgasm?"

Purple Haze

One night Eunice and Cindy Lewis, her band mate went out for drinks at Lafayette's Music Room on Madison. Any night could be a surprise jam session, with out of town musicians dropping in to show off their talents.

Cindy was from Wisconsin and had wanted something more than her small scale life. "Nina, you're so pretty. I'd bet money you're gonna hit the big time. You've got this special thing, that's smart and also sexy," she said.

"Oh gosh. Thanks Cindy. What do you want out of this town?" Eunice asked, changing the subject.

"I dunno. I had to get out of Nekoosa, so running from gramps was the reason. I like Memphis because every day starts fresh!" she said, sipping through a red straw. She was every guys wet dream; blond hair, a little girl voice and fake boobs.

Eunice discovered Cindy was the greatest gal pal, until there were men around. That's when she'd turn into a needy coquette and drop you like a rock. The last time they hung out, two guys from Kansas City slid into a jam session with the locals and Cindy fell in love. By the end of jam, she had become a full blown groupie, leaving with him. It was fine as long as you knew that about her. Eunice wasn't interested in being best friends anyway!

"Say, I got some coke in here somewhere. I swear I can never find anything in this purse. Oh here it is. Go into the can," she said, handing her a small compact.

Eunice's resolve had recently worn down with a lot of aimless socializing. Everyone was on high-end drugs in Memphis, so it's perfectly normal. It's not like they looked like the sick zombies from the Vineyard. She reasoned it out determining it was a good idea.

"Sure. Why not! Thanks Cindy. I might get a kick out of it!" Eunice said. She got up and went to the ladies room. She took a snort of cocaine already deciding, she wasn't a drug type person. After mere seconds, her first thought was how her breathing and nasal passage felt all open and clear, as if she'd inhaled high altitude mountain air.

Returning to the table, Cindy excitedly said, "Eunice guess what? I've got VIP tickets for Purple Haze later!" by 'later' she meant the after party because the club only did private functions. "You're coming. We'll find that *asshole* Matthew and get your demo tapes!"

Eunice was all for fighting justice but less so when it came to her own personal art.

"Alright then. I best get myself back home for a beauty nap!" Eunice said, newly excited at possibly meeting record label executives. She would really dress the part.

"Honey, you won't be napping. Enjoy the mania! I'm going home to reorganize my kitchen. See you at midnight," Cindy said.

Cindy was right, Eunice was wide awake and felt the best she'd felt in a very long time.

Later that night, she met Cindy outside Purple Haze, a block south of Beale across from the famous Gibson Guitar factory. The afterhours club was VIP only, nearly impossible to get into since there were no tickets, only guest lists and referrals. *When you gonna learn, it's all about who you know.*

Local celebs from TV and the usual Memphis, Nashville crowd. It also didn't hurt that famous people remembered, Purple Haze was a club once owned by *Joe Pesci.* Rumors that LA types would be there because *Prince* was in town for a concert and was known for throwing intimate late night pop up shows.

Inside the hopping club she followed Cindy to the washrooms, passing beautiful people of all shapes and sizes. "Just one line Nina," Cindy said, "we don't want to get sloppy if *Prince* shows up do we?" Cindy took a few belts from her flask of liquor.

Eunice followed orders doing only one line. Moderation was the key to anything in life.

Time was irrelevant on the dance floor. All Eunice knew was Purple Haze was probably *the* best experience of her entire life. The coke and whatever else she had made her float divinely. She'd never felt so present but with zero sense of time. Nobody on the dance floor seemed to care about anything.

The DJ revved up the crowd with teasing announcements, "Now the moment you've all been waiting for..." he sang the words like a circus emcee. The crowd roared anticipating he'd introduce *Prince*. "*Morris Day and the Time!*"

The crowd went mental anyway, since the Minneapolis sound was in the house. After the set the DJ spun records again.

Later Eunice's absolute dream came true but she was too drunk and high to fully enjoy it. She was dancing near *Alfonso Ribeiro,* the guy from *Fresh Prince of Bel Air*. A song she didn't recognize started playing but somehow she mouthed the lyrics to it anyway. She subliminally knew the words. It was oddly thrilling because the words were close to her journal entries.

Oh my God! Amazing!

The Purple Haze DJ was playing a song she wrote.

Prince will surely hear it.

Wait. How was it possible? She hadn't seen *hair nor hide* of Matthew Roswell for six weeks. That song hadn't even been completed. In fact she had only heard snippets of chorus vocals.

"But that's *my* song?" she said. Eunice was enraged.

"Yeah, I love this song too," Alfonso said, he'd gotten closer to her the more he danced.

"No! That's a song I wrote! They stole my song!" Eunice shouted. She was *pissed*. That little *asshole* Matthew must have stole her song for drugs.

"HAHA! Surprise Nina!" Matthew Roswell appeared before her. He had rushed onto the dance floor, "I sold your song Nina! Your vocals were mixed out. It's going to be huge! Country dance. Sort of a new genre I invented!" he was screaming in her ear and had foul breath. He must have been waiting to swoop down from his broomstick to gloat. DJ buddy had played it.

The night at Purple Haze marked the end of the road of Nina Wayman's music career. All she wanted was to see Prince now. *Where the fuck is Prince?*

Missing You

Ever since Eunice fled Montgomery the night of the mass shooting, Sam had been on an excruciatingly emotional seesaw. The police said the case was under FBI jurisdiction, so information would only be forthcoming, if it didn't affect any related cases. Grief counselors were assigned to those who wanted them and that was all.

"You don't really understand things like, cancer treatment, learning to walk again or having a loved one go missing. Mr. Hood do you have anyone you can talk to?" Sam's first counselor had asked.

Sam was blank. He had to do something. He didn't want to hear, *I'm sorry for your loss,* or, *I can only imagine how painful this must be for you,* for the rest of his life.

According to the nightly news someone went missing every day; young, old, rich or poor. They rarely reported the person ever turning up alive again. Loved ones were left on their own, obsessing over updates from authorities or signs from heaven. Sam had given up hope.

Sam was alone and without closure his challenge was living with longing, anger and guilt over the ambiguity of losing her. He still expected her to walk in the door any day.

He sought help from the only person he could think of Dr. Lynch.

"My first certification was in grief counseling," Lynch said. He was hell-bent on running Sam through the *levels of grief.* He held up an image of colored circles with the words *denial, anger, bargaining, depression* and *acceptance* written on them.

"I don't get it. That's a lot of bubbles," Sam said, somewhat frustrated with Lynch, for expecting his pain to go away with a model.

"Dr. Lynch, have you ever lost someone like this? Until it happens I don't think you can know what it's like. No one tells you it hits you all at once," Sam said.

"I know Sam. Keep working at it okay?" Lynch's expression was sincere. "The science behind the model is not to remove the pain but to help you move through obstacles over time and accept then what is."

"I'm primarily angry all the time. Then thinking of Eunice, breaks me into tears, so I get frustrated that I have no control over the anger," Sam said, remembering how he broke down and threw her clothes all over the bedroom.

Montgomery had grieved publically over the deaths with memorial ceremonies and time faded people's memories but not his. He believed Eunice was alive since evidence suggested her escape was by her own initiative.

People around him didn't understand why his grief took so long and presumed he was over it. When a person doesn't move on, people steer clear. He couldn't relay how he felt to anyone so didn't talk about it.

"Dr. Lynch, I resent the fact nothing more can be done by the FBI," Sam said.

"You said yourself, they won't provide updates due to confidentiality. In all likelihood they are working on it. The case is still open, right?" Lynch asked.

"Yes," Sam said.

"So logically, you know it's out of your control. Let's keep practicing the letting go piece. Are you still exercising?" he asked.

"Not really. I try to focus on my work at the school. I'm grateful for your suggestions. I guess your help is better than no help," Sam said, picking up the page of colored circles. "I think I'm in anger now. Not knowing where she is. I'm angry because not knowing is worse than if she had died," he said.

"Good. Admitting the emotion is progress. Keep that in mind. Tomorrow is a new day. Do you pray Sam?" Dr. Lynch asked.

"Naw. Well I talk to Frank," he said. Sam would have lost his grip if he didn't have his imaginary friend. *Frank, I know she is alive, please protect her from suffering, being homeless or wandering the streets.*

That night before bed, he pulled out a story he wrote about his hot and cold romance, with Eunice called *Cat and Dog.*

A cat is a creature who doesn't need anyone, doesn't show affection or loving kindness. Unlike a dog who runs goofily chasing anything that seems delicious, a cat prefers the safety of pride and arrogance, even though she is starving. The cat instead, tends to watch and judge the comings and goings of everyone else; dogs, raccoons and birds, reveling in snide remarks on their amusing creature habits.

If a dog is around, he is usually dying to be pals with the cat, until his nose has been bat and receives at least one scratch from her sharp claw. He is the underdog.

Mostly, the cat doesn't accept the love-greedy dog for what he is. Instead, the cat looks for the dogs faults, formulates material for stand-up routines to entertain like-minded felines or for no one in particular, since the cat is often a solo artist.

Over time, the silly dog gets exhausted trying to please the cat. Every dog has his day! When there is no room left in his heart, he snaps! He is the one to push the cat away, even at the risk of appearing intimidating or aggressive. Sometimes the cat is the absolute worst thing for the dog's self-esteem!

"I don't understand. What is this?" the dog asks.

"You hit all my annoyance triggers," the cat says.

"You are never there for me," he says.

"I can't help it if you cannot accept my feline ways" she says, completely bored.

"Why don't I let you go?" the dog asks himself, "It's not cute anymore. The fun of the chase is gone. I don't have capacity to take care of you with nothing in return," but the dog will be long dead before he utters those words allowed, for it is in-his-nature to give love.

The dog is sad.

When the cat is alone, she wonders why she never has any loving kindness to spare. She never thinks of the answer because it has never existed for her. No harm no foul!

"It makes me so sad!" the cat says to herself, alone. Why does she have to accept the dog BUT the he doesn't accept her?

Curtis Lock Down

Sam woke up in the morning with the same void in his belly, every day for the past six months since she'd been gone. He usually felt better after his shower, the water washing the worst of it down drain. Some days were better than others.

When self-pity crept in, he kept Eunice's parents in mind knowing whatever he experienced, they likely suffered even more. He stopped in on Martha regularly. His mother had assured him, Marjorie and the church ladies took turns making rounds to check on her too. She didn't go a day without a visitor with home cooking.

Sam drove out to Kilby Correctional, to visit Curtis who sat in jail awaiting trial after his plea deal refusal.

Curtis smiled wanly at Sam through the glass between them.

"Eunice has got herself into a heap of trouble. I believe someone knows where she is," Sam said, flustered.

"Son, we need to keep the faith she is in good hands," Curtis said.

"I should have stopped her from getting close to Terrence. My jealousy got in the way. I chose to ignore her comings and goings. I put my head in the clouds because I didn't want to find out bad stuff, like she was with someone else. I knew some of her other friends were troublemakers too, especially Lil Red. I never trusted her. She didn't look me in the eye ever. I got the impression she had a chip on her shoulder. Curtis you know when you can read someone because they remind you of yourself? I knew what made Lil Red tick because it was familiar to my own thinking," Sam said, trusting Curtis, who'd been a father figure to him.

"You knew Lil Red was involved with guns?" Curtis asked. He gave Sam a piercing stare fluorescent reflection bouncing off his eyeglasses.

"I predicted it but kept it to myself and never went after proof. I've got to trust myself more," Sam said.

He wondered how Curtis knew Lil Red but didn't probe further, as the facility recorded conversations.

"Eunice was close to Gabrielle and Terrence. Lil Red was lurking somewhere behind the scenes," Sam said.

"Did they offer you a straight up plea deal?" Sam asked. "My friend Jose's cousin took a 5-7, deal instead of risking 15-20 at trial," Sam said.

"*Goddamnit* no! They bargain with your life. It's only plea deals there's trials. 98% of cases. If you don't take one you sit in jail for years awaiting trial. Bargains happen behind closed doors without a judge, so you can imagine they mostly go in favor of the wrong side. Those guys have plenty of ways to get their hands on police reports. You know, forged documentation. Lawyers want it quick and done. What are you going to do wait years for a trial, when you'll surely be proven guilty or take the 3-5 instead? Most are bullied and broken before trial." Curtis said, slobbering as he spit out the words.

"Did your lawyer have a game plan?" Sam asked.

"You see the thing is Sam, he says I have two priors, one in the Navy and one from New York. Did community service for one but the other was in 1969, when 21 Panthers were arrested. I was never a member but did a small job in the Bronx. I didn't have the info they wanted but the lawyer says I have a letter in my file. Tell you 'bout that some other day.

Now I'm trapped in what the smug lawyer calls, 'three strikes you're out,'" Curtis said.

"I'm familiar with three strikes. That's why a lot of guys I know don't have fathers. Some deterrent that rule is," Sam said.

"Lawyer says I coulda had it easier given my history of good deeds and community service but since the massacre is tied to thugs, drugs and killing I can kiss leniency goodbye," Curtis said.

"It makes it seem like the government keeps minorities down. They'd argue it's the same law for all ex-convicts minority or not," Sam said.

"They're *shit scared,* there will be a revolution so they lock us up every chance they get," Curtis said.

"Afraid of a reckoning that will come one day. Back when I was a lad, we ate possum pies so we killed 'em. After the deed, I swear I felt I was being watched by God or that possum's family. I had bad dreams they would kill me for a long while. I wonder if these lawyers sleep with one eye open," Curtis said.

"I've been trying to understand criminality around drug charges, for my project with Principal Butler. Did you know crack and cocaine are the same substance? Crack is cocaine cut with baking soda and smoked, yet the criminal charges are completely different," Sam said.

"Yeah. Ever hear of bread pudding? It's like taking day old bread crusts, that's the cocaine. Smashing it together with cream and sugar or baking soda as is with crack. It gets turned to crystalized rocks and sold to *poor ass* ghetto kids," Curtis said.

"The law treats them different but I can't find out why. They say crack is a black drug and cocaine is white but costs a *helleva* lot more," Sam said.

"The war on drugs is a war on black folks. You'll never see a SWAT team raiding, a university of white cokehead students," Curtis said.

"What's your lawyer telling you? What's next?" Sam asked. He'd read that prosecutors have more power than anyone else.

"Sam, lawyers are all the same. Even your own lawyer. He says at least taking the plea, starts the clock on doing the time," Curtis said.

"It's the lesser of two evils. They're using fear to con people into taking the plea," Sam said, sickened by the hopelessness of it.

"It's a colossal injustice. That's what it is!" Curtis said.

It was time for Sam to leave so he stood up.

Curtis got up.

"Just one thing I gotta ask Curtis. You ever hear from Eunice?" Sam said. His words sounded like a trap and perhaps subliminally it was.

"Ach. Course not. How can you ask me, Son?," he said.

How could he not ask?

"I know. I suppose you couldn't say so. I'll stop. Curtis you know I love your daughter. I don't wanna live in a world without her," Sam said, getting choked up.

"I know Son. I know. It's called coping. Sometimes we got no choice. You give my Martha a hug for me," Curtis said. "And Sam, you got *no* choice but to hang onto the *good* things."

Was Curtis saying, Eunice was fine and to hang tight?

"Yessir I'll bring Martha with me next time, if she's up for it. Take care of yourself Curtis," Sam said.

On his drive back, Sam thought about the nonsense of justice. He admired Curtis for choosing trial over plea deal but if only 3 percent of cases went to trial, how was America the land of the free? It was as if the constitution didn't matter.

Thomas Jefferson had implemented, *I consider trial by jury as the only anchor ever yet imagined by man, by which a government can be held to the principles of its constitution.*

The Sixth Amendment guaranteed, *the accused shall enjoy the right to a speedy and public trial by an impartial jury.*

Little Rock, Arkansas

Sam kept sane by moving forward. He still saw Todd and Max for videogame and beer nights at their place. Todd didn't like shoot 'em up games, so preferred *Crash Team Racing* while Max and Sam were partial, to the escapist violence of *Grand Theft Auto* and *Resident Evil*.

Gaming was a great way to be together, while not getting into deep topics of discussion. He and Todd vented, about work at IBEW call center. Each sounding boards for each other.

Sam shied away from the painful topic of Curtis at Kilby or missing Eunice. The one time he and Todd spoke about it, felt odd. Sam got a sense Todd may have lied about being in New Orleans, at the time of the massacre.

Sam proceeded with his trip to Little Rock, that had to be rescheduled after the incident. He looked forward to a few days away. Tom Horsley had him staying at a Motel 6, off of I-30 at Baseline Road, just a mile from the school.

Since Sam last saw Tom Horsley at his awareness rally in Montgomery, Tom had won the Arkansas Teacher of the Year award and been promoted to principal. Now he could be Sam's mentor and groom him for his VP interview.

Horsley was known by those in the public school system, as the *Turnaround Principal* since he'd done several special interest interviews for local Little Rock news. His school had previously been the lowest performing, until Horsley recruited and trained 22 new teachers in two months. He was kind and decent looking, which may have added to his local celebrity appeal.

After a day auditing classes, Sam had dinner with Horsley a Kelsey's near the motel.

"Sam, I started as a middle school teacher. I joined the *Teach for America* program and signed up for a two-year stint, in a public school in Little Rock. At first I hated it. This tiny rural town felt more remote than an island. It seemed detached from time and reality. I couldn't even describe it to my friends back home. It's very *real* down here, was the best I could come up with," Tom Horsley said.

"Look at the numbers coming out. No one is looking at the lowest scoring schools. The numbers are being touted as, *See, I told you so!* We can't afford to play victim Sam. If nothing is done, it'll go on for generations. Tell me what you thought? What was the most noticeable difference, to what you're used to?" he asked.

"I saw the kids relating to the teacher, as a coach supporting them with pointers instead of as an army sarge. The kids got along with each other, there wasn't the usual bullying and fighting. I don't know how to describe it. More camaraderie I'd say," Sam said.

"The concept is, we coach to our core values of family, leadership, empowerment, progress and the student. If we make decisions that don't align with these five, we know we're making a bad decision and the students will suffer," Horsley said.

"I can see us using this back home," Sam said, feeling overwhelmed by Principal Butler's expectation of him. How was he going to remember all of this?

"The reason no attempts have been made is we wait for the government to solve our problems. The difference is a bottom up approach," Horsley said.

"It sounds new but we really are just going back to basics. The new part, is not waiting for permission. People are afraid to act without permission," Sam said, afraid of the risk he'd be taking at home.

"Exactly. Take the elements of your activism and the *just do it* Nike slogan," Tom said.

"One challenge is getting more diversity in the teacher pool. For years, the trend has been for people of color to leave the South. Why stay in a place reminiscent of humiliation and second class treatment. Along with reminders like confederate flags and slave owner statues all over the place," Tom said.

"I can see that it'll take a ton of luck, for this to work back home. Say a prayer for the stars to align. I'll definitely take what I've learned to Butler," Sam said.

"I bet the teachers at your school are done and you'll need buy-in from the existing staff. If this type of change isn't taken well it can be an auto fail!" Horsley said.

"Yes true, it could end before it begins," Sam said.

"I'll make you a deal. I'll get permission from the Arkansas board, to help you get your ducks in a row. Maybe we'll lend you teachers on temporary assignment, who can lead by example and help get your staff up to speed. They will pay it forward, to make up for our questionable history of education," Tom said.

"By that time we're done, it won't matter who runs the show because it'll be a team effort!" Sam said, more convinced of the concept than before.

Forgotten Amnesia

Sam had a nightmare he was at a bar along the famous Highway 61, searching for Eunice. He imagined her hanging around shady characters, who wanted to possess her. Zombie crack addicts chased him away. In the dream, he discovered that Terrence Battle was the zombie leader and Eunice had already been taken over.

He jerked awake in bed at home in the R.V. He often woke from nightmares, that left him filled with remorse and missing her. Instead of his usual pity party, he'd been using Dr. Lynch's coping exercises. The wolf photo on his bedside table with a post-it that read, *Leave these things to the wolf Sam,* helped a little.

Maybe Frank used the dream as an allegory to test him. *Sam, you haven't learned yet. Let's do another basketball drill.* He remembered dribbling practice in coach Stan's class. Terrence was the ultimate basketball test. If he got another chance and Eunice came back, he promised to listen to the drill.

"Come back and give me another shot Eunice!" Sam said, out loud.

If he passed the test, they would live happily ever after! So why be afraid of her coming back?

The more confident he felt inside his mind, the more fearful he was it could be undone.

In all Sam's attempts to fix the relationship and smooth things over he should've felt relief she was gone but he wasn't. He never fathomed the emptiness in his life without her. It was like the cliché *if only we had more time.* If he had her back today, he wouldn't be so maniacal about trying to fix the relationship.

You don't know what you got till it's gone.

At his Dr. Lynch appointment, Sam was discussing the bargaining bubble, from the *levels of grief* model, "She must have forgotten me altogether," Sam said.

He relayed the story of how he discovered, on a drive back from Atlanta she vaguely remembered him visiting her at Music Camp. They'd been hungry and decided to stop at Waffle House in LaGrange, on the way to Montgomery. He drove while Eunice lolled sleepy and quiet.

"Wow, I haven't heard this song in ages," Sam said. He turned up the volume trying to perk her up before they stopped for dinner, "Eunice do you remember this was our song?" he asked, referring to the first few months they dated.

"Huh, our song? I know this song, is this our song?" she looked at him, as if trying to figure out how, *Space Between* by *Dave Matthews Band* was their song. "I think Waffle House is just off the next exit. I don't remember," her response was slurred and childlike.

A ways through dinner with some subtle probing conversation, he confirmed she didn't remember large chunks of their courtship. Intimate moments during the first weeks, where they discovered each other's histories and bodies. Things he cherished like the first kiss, first intimate sexual activity and the intense philosophical conversations of budding love.

All along Sam had clung to those memories, hoping they would find them again. Many a night on his drives home from that camp, he'd thought their bond was too perfect to be real. *Intuition is a powerful thing.*

He wasn't angry. He was baffled.

There's nothing you can do about amnesia Sam.

He couldn't decipher between his disappointment and his sadness. He felt like laughing at not knowing anything. How could she have forgotten what they shared?

He suspected Eunice disassociated him out of her life. If it was truly amnesia she couldn't be blamed. *She remembered so many other things in detail.* He guessed it was selective.

Seeds of resentment were planted, on that ride from Atlanta. After that he couldn't help notice every nuance backing up, her lack of interest in him.

"Dr. Lynch, it killed me that I was so used to picking on her, when I witnessed her self-centeredness. It caused us more problems," Sam said.

Lynch did one of his listening nods, instead of providing answers.

"She banked on my weakness saying, 'I just want someone who doesn't have a microscope on me like you do,'" Sam said.

Another thought came to him. Often when they argued she could recite every curse word he had ever uttered but rarely could she remember speaking basely herself. She denied her participation in fights.

Men weren't supposed to call women names, so Sam was ashamed. Yet she labeled him all kinds of psychological afflictions, *Sam you are so insecure, needy, weak, dumb, violent or angry*, Dr. Lynch what would you call those words? They hurt me much more than *fucking asshole* ever could," Sam said.

Her defense mechanism during scuffles, was to play on his weakest link and bring up a taboo about his family, as if to imply she came from blue blooded lineage.

She might start in on his brother Rory, by asking provocative questions that could only have pitiful answers. "I know Eunice, Rory shouldn't have swindled the family out of money like that," he had said, with growing defensiveness.

"Sam don't be silly, it must be one of your mood swings. I was only judging Rory, from afar. Don't take it so personally. I guess I'm hungry and *bitchy*," she said, proving she could push his buttons, with the wave of her finger.

"Did you ever ask where the defensiveness might have come from?" Lynch asked.

Sam remembered, Eunice told him about being ridiculed, in Mr. Osborne's class but he hadn't seen it as traumatic as her description.

"Yes. She told me about an episode in high school. The teacher called her out for being unprepared for the year end oral exam, after she bombed in front of everyone. She's such a *brainiac* she was embarrassed. It was a huge source of shame for her," Sam said.

"I don't want to pry into her side of things but you could say it is a gift she shared with you right?" Lynch said.

"I felt close to her because she trusted me enough to share. I told her so. I didn't think she'd resent me, for knowing something embarrassing about her. I got this feeling she regretted telling me. I could see it in her poker face afterward," Sam said.

He hadn't yet learned it was foolish to look for reasons behind someone's sensitivity, even if it was well intentioned. "Can I ask you something personal? This is the part I find leads us into the woods," he said.

"Us? You mean you!" she snapped back, defensively owning no part of it, instead turning the tables on him. She was crafty in her self-protection.

He never claimed to be innocent. He had slipped up many times, trying to resolve issues but now even his own words sounded like attacks. He failed miserably at letting sleeping dogs lie. *Love is blind!*

CℰCℰCℰ

The morning of the school massacre and the last time he saw Eunice, he'd been infuriated by her admission she would rather give up instead of try. He was angry because it was ludicrous and inauthentic for a couple to live in a false state of agreeability. How would he ever know if she was being agreeable or it was a true opinion?

"Listen Sam I'll agree to disagree to keep the peace," she said.

He popped an anger vein in his head. *God dammit!*

"Gotta be honest Sam, my recollection of yesterday is a little different," Eunice said, "I don't want to get into the weeds now. I'm going to assume full responsibility for keeping the peace."

With her newfound agreeability she took everything on as her fault like a martyr. He wondered why she would own something, she didn't remember?

His mom suggested he needed a *date with God,* by taking some time to himself, "Let Him whisper the answers. If you keep still you will receive messages in your mind. It might be God speaking. Don't ignore Him!" Sofia said.

She also advised him to pray for Eunice's happiness, if not for his own. In her way Sofia was advising him to tell her good riddance. He was crushed thinking of that, *Merle Haggard* song; *I thought I finally won a hand, then everything I planned fell through.*

"It's not like you are married anyway," Sofia said.

Instead of listening to his mother, he kept to himself and moped. He surrendered to being unhappy ever after, like his father before him, *"Shit* trickles down hill, Son," Harpo said.

Sitting all these months later in Lynch's office, Sam couldn't think of anything specific he'd done wrong. He hadn't explained or over explained, or even upset her. His head swirled with bits of recent conversations. There was a big difference between sharing your knowledge and being an arrogant *prick.*

"Think of a time back at school, when you weren't motivated to learn. Did you learn anything?" Lynch asked.

"Probably not. At least I don't know or don't remember learning anything," Sam laughed.

"You probably didn't. We need to be willing to learn, otherwise nothing sticks. When we are hell-bent on teaching our lessons, we aren't listening to others or any of the signs around us," Lynch said.

Why had he tried to educate her to the point of harassment and intimidation? Why had he called her a *stuck-up white privileged bitch*, selfish *asshole*, ingrate and so many other reviled adjectives? How could Sam, the abuser and victim co-exist?

There was no rest for the wicked. He was ashamed, broken hearted and resentful. She had been here and now she wasn't. It was as if she had died. There was nothing left to ask or say; just an R.V. of her things and an echo of silence.

Goddess Arpita

At Saint Francis Hospital, Eunice wandered in and out of sedative induced sleep. Fuzzy drive-in movie images passed before her eyes, every time she woke up. The hospital bed with its protective guardrails, should have been cause for alarm but the Ativan protected her from anxiety. She was grateful for soft cotton linens and the cool room temperature, easing illicit toxins from her body.

Drugs are like making a deal with the devil!

She didn't remember how she got there. Disturbing thoughts kept flashing in front of her, each a horrifying snapshot of her bad behavior. She pushed the thoughts out.

She had no memory of what substances she might have ingested, over the past 24 hours. Just snippets of memory, followed by hot and cold sweats. The sweats were the worst part of detoxing.

Eunice had been star struck in the ladies room, when one of *Prince's* ex-girlfriends came out of a stall and over to the vanity sink next to her. She began fixing her hair then pulled out a tiny make-up case from a cue card sized purple purse.

"Hey honey, you want some?" she said, in a sultry whisper. She proceeded to snort powder from a beautiful antique mortar and spoon set.

"Sure. Thank you Uh, Denise..." she said. Eunice couldn't remember what had happened next.

"You sweet thing, you know my name. Only angels call me Denise these days. It's rare indeed," she said.

The DJ played *Let's Go Crazy* outside.

Stop it Nina, I'll go insane!

She took a sip of water from the bedside table and noticed a Uncle Dougie's business card, indicating he'd been there.

Another memory capsule was of the doctor speaking to her, "Ms. Wayman initial tests have found alcohol, secobarbital and cocaine in your system. You will make a full recovery but consider yourself very lucky. These combinations can be deadly. Ms. Wayman you are young so I'm referring you to a twelve step program. We can have someone take you to a meeting. Also, the nurse tells me you weren't covered under any health insurance policy in our system. It's a good thing your uncle paid your invoice in full," the doctor said.

The memory of the doctor's message, spooked her enough to stay awake. She sat up in bed. Out the window she could see the stars in the sky.

She sensed something just outside the curtain, which wrapped around two sides of her bed, then heard a light cough sound. The stainless steel rings squeaked open.

A woman stood before her, with short bobbed black hair and dark eyes wearing a colorful teal garment. She was about thirty and had similar skin coloring to Eunice, except maybe Mexican by the look of her thick straight hair.

"Hallo Nina, how are you feeling?" she said. She had a soft motherly voice and her tone implied, Eunice should recognize her. Eunice scanned her memory for other fragments.

She had memories of Purple Haze. Her pulling a wig off a girl's head and throwing it on the dance floor. She remembered beautiful Denise in washroom and that was about it. She had a feeling she wouldn't be welcomed back to Purple Haze anytime soon. *Fuck* em. Those elitist Hollywood types weren't her scene anyway.

"Hello, do I know you? My memory is a bit foggy at the moment," she said.

"My name is Arpita, we met last night," she said, coming closer to the bed. "We need to get you out of here. This sandalwood will ease you out of your sedation," Arpita gently pat two fingers of ointment under her nose. It was like Vicks vapor rub except had an aroma that conjured up white tailed deer and apple blossoms.

"Are you my angel Arpeeeeta?" Eunice asked.

"Well I just might be," she said.

Eunice accepted the voice of her angel unconditionally following her instruction, "Yes. Okay Arpita. We can go," she said.

"Let me tidy you up," Arpita said, gently taking a warm washcloth to Eunice's face and fluffing up her matted hair. "You've been through a lot. Nina, it's urgent we make haste and leave here immediately," Arpita said.

She helped Eunice out of bed and into the waiting wheelchair. Arpita threw a colorful pink pashmina, over her lap, "Now take a deep breathe Nina. I'll have you here, as soon as you know it," she held a postcard with the words Krishna Ashram, across the top and a scene of a rocky waterfall, with sunlight sparkling off the water. "I have a car and driver waiting for us out front," she said.

Eunice admired Arpita's serenity, regardless of finding it strange the woman was here to escort her to the recommended rehab.

As she took in the scent of sandalwood, Eunice got a feeling her past was about to catch up to her.

Hospital observers might have thought the image of Arpita, pushing a patient to the awaiting Town Car, was a brochure for the hospital's exceptional out patient program. True, if it were not four in the morning.

Cuba, Tennessee

Eunice and Arpita rode the highway in the chauffeur driven Town Car in silence, until the pink sunrise began to break the horizon up ahead.

"Allow me to give you a little information, about where you're going," the driver said, making eye contact with Eunice through the rearview mirror. "The retreat sits on an acreage of beautiful flatland and big open sky, just outside Cuba, Tennessee. Over yonder if you squint, you can see Arkansas across the Mississippi river," he said, in a pleasant sing song tone, that had Eunice thinking, she was on a hop on, hop off bus tour.

"Thank you. You're awfully perky this morning," she returned his smile.

"I pride myself on being an early bird, that's for sure. Up ahead is Merman Shelby State Park," he said.

"It's not far now Nina," Arpita said, patting her arm.

He pulled the Town Car up a circular driveway and stopped in front of the main entrance, "Namaste. Here we are at the Krishna Ashram. The main building is shaped like the letter H, if you ever happen to fly over it!" he said, as he waved goodbye.

Eunice followed Arpita inside the dimly lit lobby, down a long hallway to a door, "First let's drop your bag in your room and you can freshen up," Arpita said.

Her room was simple with a small window, a futon style cot and washroom with a pedestal sink.

Eunice was grateful to Dougie, who had left a small valise of items he'd picked up at Walmart. She was also relieved she'd not been awake, to face him in her shameful state.

Arpita plunked herself on the bed and motioned for Eunice to sit down, "Allow me to properly introduce myself. I'm Arpita. A servant of Krishna Ashram and a follower of

Lakshmi, the Hindu goddess of fortune and well-being. I am a part of the wonderful group of volunteers here. I'm going to help you adjust back into the real world," Arpita said.

Maybe it was her drug addled brain but she could swear Arpita's lips barely moved as she spoke.

"Who is Krishna?" she asked.

"He's the Hindu god who represents love," Arpita said. "Let's go, I want to show you around," she stood and led her out the door.

Arpita took her to a large central room, with cherry red walls, a vaulted ceiling and a very large aqua blue fireplace. Soft instrumental harpsichord played in the background.

Eunice was surprised to see people up and ready to take on the day so early. A group of performers sat as if discussing musical arrangements, on a vibrant tapestried rug at the center of the sprawling room. They had foreign looking instruments resembling bongo drums, flutes and what looked like an accordion.

A beautiful young woman in a canary yellow sari, sat cross-legged in lotus position. Another was gorgeous in fuchsia, quietly humming her own chant with her eyes closed.

The men were bald-as-eggs, clean shaven wearing orange one-piece linen tunics. They lolled on the ornate rug posing al fresco, as if they should be fed grapes.

Followers in colorful outfits, were grouped in various circles sitting cross legged on the floor. Others seemed camouflaged by decor and clothing were hidden in corners and recesses along the walls. If not for their movement she wouldn't have noticed them.

Eunice had never been anywhere like it before. Everyone seemed calm and committed. It was a comfortable environment but she didn't know what they were doing there.

Arpita motioned her to an empty cushion on the floor near the aqua blue hearth. She poured her a cup of lemon ginger tea, from the refreshment cart and handed it to her, "Try this," she said.

"Thank you," Eunice said. The sweet and sour tea popped sublimely in her mouth, followed by an evergreen tree medicinal taste.

"It will surely chase any toxic chemicals, out of your body," Arpita said.

For once, Eunice promised herself to sit tight and stay quiet. On the long drive she told herself to surrender, to whatever Arpita's direction would be. She had run out of options and was too exhausted to question anything. She could have been sitting in police custody.

"Here at Krishna Ashram, we look inside. Don't be afraid. Part of the ritual of being still, is to listen to what is going on inside ourselves," Arpita said.

"Okay Arpita. I'll try but if I burst out laughing blame my nerves. This is a little weird for me," Eunice said.

The room was lit with amber glowing candles and a forlorn Middle Eastern soundtrack of flute and mournful vocals intensified things. Eunice's nose tickled as if she'd cry. She rarely ever cried. The ceremony was about to begin.

"I look forward to seeing you on the other side Nina!" Arpita said, as she moved through the room greeting others along the way.

"What? Wait you're leaving?" Eunice asked. "Oh wow. You're the leader," she said, hoping to sit this round out or be a fly on the wall. The hypnotic scent of Sandalwood had her gripped so she would give meditation a try.

Arpita was center stage with a headset and microphone.

"Namaste everyone. Now let's start with our breathe. Take a deep breathe in ...then out. Close your eyes. Deep breathes, inhale, exhale. Now imagine yourself a piece of seaweed in the ocean near a coral beach. You look up and see the beams of sunlight coming down through the water. As the waves come and go you gently sway. As you inhale, you see the waves moving you. The sound going in and out with your breath is the sound of waves going in and out. Seeing yourself moving with the flow helps relax your whole body as you imagine the sensations of 'going with the flow.' Listen to your breath. Feel yourself letting go," Arpita said in a seductive voice.

Eunice thought the ceremony was lovely but it would never work on her. Thank God, no one knew her here. She wouldn't tell Arpita she thought meditation was pretty silly.

Arpita must have read her mind as she toured the room checking in with each follower.

"If your thoughts wander, bring yourself back to the sound of your breathing and the waves. Match the motion of the waves to the sound of your breath," she continued.

With her eyes closed, Eunice focused on the sound of Arpita's voice, as it got closer than farther away. She got to Eunice and put two fingers of ointment on her forehead, like she had done at the hospital. The scent was closer to eucalyptus and lavender this time.

Eunice focused on identifying the potent aroma, until the line between awake and dreaming blurred.

Eunice was light and hollow, as if floating inside the boundaries of her own body.

"There is no place you need to go right now," Arpita cooed, her suggestion becoming the truth.

Eunice lay on her back, in a pre-historic cave with her eyes open. Fire light above reflected burnt umber, raw sienna and cadmium yellow. Light danced and illuminated row upon row, of stick figure drawings, an illustrated comic strip etched onto the cave ceiling. She had been transported somewhere in time.

Deep inside herself, she knew she was in pre-civilization, before the continents separated, as appearing on the world atlas today. Pre-historic thoughts were of the invention of fire, fur pelts and a hunt for food. Hypnotic flutes, the mournful wail and foghorns lured her to tears in a restful fantasy, straight out of *Clan of the Cave Bear*.

A large jaguar floated overhead, neither male or female. She inhaled its musky lavender scent, as strong as ammonia to her nostrils. The jaguar's soaring body caressed her as if she were its protected cub. Even though her parents had conceived and raised her, it was the jaguar who created her.

The jaguar would protect her into the next life and the one after that.

Her heart was ecstatic as she received psychic messages. She had clarity of her placement in the world. She might have the power to levitate or even fly. No earthly drug could top this euphoria. *I must tell someone about this miracle.*

She understood how people were hooked on religions, cults, gurus or heroin. *I'll have another glass of that raspberry Kool-Aid!*

Eunice was spent.

"Get some rest, Eunice. I will introduce you to the Guru, this evening," Arpita said.

She could do little else but lie in solitude on her buckwheat cot. A few auras had been stripped off her, like Acetone bubbled layers off an antique chest. She didn't believe in the occult but she didn't know what else to call it.

Hours later, Eunice rose refreshed for once instead of obsessively planning her next move. She was thrilled to have actually meditated. She had really been in a trance. Of one thing she was clear on, she would make things right with Sam.

After the *seaweed* experience, Arpita had announced their upcoming practice would be transcendental meditation and ecstatic dance but Eunice couldn't imagine anything akin to what she had just experienced.

The ashram rituals had elements taken from Hindu and Jain mysticism along with a splash of Hare Krishna. Eunice remembered old movies that mocked the orange clad, Hare Krishna's as weirdo's who smiled a lot as they handed out daisy's at airports. Now she was one of them!

That evening Eunice sat with Arpita, for ginger tea in one of the many vestibules of the great room, "I've been meaning to ask you Arpita. What exactly is an ashram?"

"You are funny. You ask after spending many days in an ashram! In India it's a place to get away when life takes a toll.

The ashram offers peace and spiritual guidance," Arpita said looking radiant.

"What's the guru like?" Eunice asked.

"He is a true devotee of several Hindu gods. He's full of life and energy yet able to meditate for hours on end," she said.

Eunice was sure Arpita was blushing.

"He sounds interesting," Eunice said.

Arpita smiled.

"You said we met before the hospital. Was it at Purple Haze?" Eunice asked.

"I saw you at both places," she said.

Eunice's stomach did a somersault. *Both places?* She didn't remember another place or anything after Purple Haze. It broke her comfort zone of denial. She felt flushed on her forehead as memory fragments came through.

"Nina you are one crazy *bitch*!" it was Cindy Lewis from the band, "What the *fuck*? Picking fights with a bunch of Arizona bridesmaids! I had to pull you off one of em," Cindy shouted at her.

An image of her slapping a girl across the face, pulling off her wig and tossing it clear across the room came to mind.

"*Bitch*! I'm going to finish you off!" said the mascara streaked cowgirl. Then bouncer involvement. Then her screaming at a doorman to let her back in the club.

"Nina, where did you go just now?" Arpita asked. "I came to find you after the club. You were at the Regency on Federal Drive, with some Nashville people," Arpita said, without judgment.

"How do you really know me? It's more than Purple Haze. How is it you seem to know all about me?" Eunice was more curious than afraid.

"I was waiting for the right moment. Doug Barnes is a friend of the ashram. When he calls we hear him. He has been very good to us over the past few years," Arpita said.

Eunice was stunned silent. She absolutely could not picture Dougie sitting in a lotus position chanting or meditating. What a great way to absolve himself from illegally procuring falsified government documents.

"Oh my! Wait a minute, does Dougie come here Thursday to Saturday every week?" Eunice asked.

"Yes he does. You must have wondered where he was," Arpita said.

"He told me he visits his mother in the mountains," Eunice said.

"That was true enough for several years. His mother spent her final year as our guest. He came to visit her each week. When she passed a few winters ago, he continued coming to get away. He mostly volunteers as a custodian now, he remains dedicated," Arpita said.

"Did Dougie ask you to find me at the Regency?" Eunice asked. He had her tailed? He betrayed her trust. Eunice was angry for a split second then was okay. Nothing in Memphis had been based on trust anyway and who better to be tailed by, than peace and meditation gurus?

A suave, formally dressed man with a beard strolled by. He could only have been Guru Kavi, proven when Arpita jumped up to introduce him, "Kavi, this is the young woman I spoke with you about," Arpita said. She was more prim and proper in front of her guru.

Kavi didn't smile but his face looked kind enough. He bowed to Eunice in that funny prayer hands greeting from yoga. *So why is a guru bowing to a girl who just had her stomach pumped?*

He was of medium build, with dark brown eyes and a perfectly manicured King of Clubs beard. Eunice wanted to touch it but abstained. She guessed he was Indian. Her first impression was of a wise owl who seemed legit but she wasn't the best judge of character.

"Uh. Oh. Hello," Eunice said. She probably had never been addressed this formally, nor expected it to happen in back water Tennessee.

"Nina will meet you tomorrow at 8:00 a.m Kavi," Arpita said.

"Nice to meet you Nina. Namaste!" Kavi said. He bowed again! He left the room.

"Well that was interesting. He seems pretty intense," Eunice said, doubting Arpita had never fallen for him.

The way Kavi presented himself, Eunice assumed he had grown up on the streets of Calcutta but Arpita told her his heritage was a mix of Italian and Afro-American, "but he claims to have direct ancestral lineage to Hindu gods," Arpita said.

Eunice started laughing, "I'll bet he does. You know what's hilarious? While he was speaking I was thinking he was familiar or related to me somehow. I guess it was a recognition of our shared ethnicity. I was mistaken for Indian once in elementary school," Eunice said.

Kavi's Teachings

In the morning, Eunice met up with Kavi at the opposite end of the compound. She sat where he ushered her, while he stepped out for a moment. The small sitting room had wall to wall banquet style sofa's and a soothing water feature. The décor was of similarly exciting colors, as she'd seen throughout the ashram.

The thought of small talk with him rattled her nerves. How does one shoot the breeze with a guru? She led with a hard hitting question, to hopefully get him to do all the talking.

"Kavi, I'd like to know more about *spiritual healing for the sick, tired and oppressed*. I saw it on a plaque in my room. I think minorities in the U.S. feel ignored and shunned don't you?" Eunice said, hoping to show off a well-versed intelligence.

"Nina, pain of the heart is the worst kind of pain. It takes over all other thought. Why do you hold onto things?" Kavi asked, rhetorically yet the way he asked it, startled her. He seemed to have no doubt, she was harboring things.

"Wow! You are smooth. A hard hitting question right out of the gate!" she smiled bashfully. It felt like flirting but she suspected it was one-sided.

"What do the things you hold onto ever do for you? Have you ever tried to see where they came from?" he asked.

"What a great question. I'd have to think about it!" Eunice said. *Gotcha!*

Eunice had never thought about it. She despised people who analyzed themselves to death. She never found the *why* to be that important, it was the *how* that mattered.

"Have you had dreams or premonitions since your arrival?" Kavi asked.

"You're asking about the jaguar aren't you?" she said, with a blank look. She purposely tried to show no expression, so he didn't pick up on her clues. She'd heard fortune tellers were scam artists, expert at reading people then fleecing money out of them.

"Let me first say, I'm no apostle. I'm just a guy who's been awakened and wants to share what that means for me, with others," his accent was indecipherable maybe the Midwest, Canadian or even British. She liked him but she still thought he was full of *shit!*

"I'm listening," she said.

"Even though it's important to have feelings, it's equally important not to be dramatic. Taking care of yourself, doesn't mean total self-absorption," Kavi said.

"So you're saying my anxieties will be gone if I breathe, meditate and exercise like they tell me here?" she asked.

"Yes, it's that simple. The antidote to fear is being present. You remind me of myself. I rarely shared myself with people, even those I loved most. If we are committed to evolving we must be more open with each other. Will you allow me to lead you in a meditation?"

"Sure," she said. She would have been hesitant prior to the seaweed experience but that jaguar was really cool!

"Close your eyes. Nina think of yourself as the perfect woman you are at this moment!" he spoke like a hypnotist *Oh dear!* "Allow your mind to wander back through the years. Go through school, grade by grade," he said.

She didn't find it too difficult to go backwards through her years of high school then to Nixon elementary.

"Where are you now?" he gently asked.

"I'm six years old," she sank deeper in her chair.

"What tells you you're six?" he asked.

"My mother and I are baking and Daddy's gone to work," she whispered.

"What images come to you. Real or imagined. A picture or photograph," he said.

"A picture of me," she said.

"Can you describe it for me?" he said.

"I'm in a white cradle or car seat. My skin is dark against a white background," she said. She got a warm feeling in inside. *I'm not mixed.*

Her body was immovable in its relaxed state and she noticed her breaths were deep. She didn't have precise thoughts of her own, only images in her mind like a canvas. She was conscious of crossing into unknown territory. Could it be a sign of his spiritual possession.

Her thoughts were amazement in having no thoughts. She searched her lifelong list of responsibilities but couldn't put the items into words. Impossible. They were items that drove her ambition. If ignored they always bit her in the *ass.*

Confused she felt like curling into a ball. *Please send the jaguar back to protect me.* Rejection was her aphrodisiac. She had found a similarly obsessive personality to what she despised in Sam. She could see Sam's motivation.

"Love isn't just about gazing into each other's eyes but looking out toward a horizon in the same direction. In India we have the saying, *love comes later.* Falling in love with yourself always comes first," Kavi said, after several minutes of silence.

Fleeting realizations floated in her mind. It was true, she was tired of thriving on chaos. She opened her eyes to find Kavi pleasantly looking at her.

"Guru Kavi have you ever worked in greeting cards?" she asked, dryly.

With a pen Kavi drew a straight line on a piece of paper in front of her, "Nina here you see the easy road. The path of least resistance that can take you far. How far is if from your destination?"

She watched him.

He then drew a zigzag line, "An easy trek in the wrong direction can be more exhausting than an uphill climb to euphoria. Mistakes are wisdom. Now is the time to look at trouble as a road map by asking *why is it trouble*. When we ask ourselves where the tender spot is, we can troubleshoot. Instead of looking to others we look within," he said.

"So what you're saying is problems are always my fault? I don't buy it Kavi! Pardon my French but there are a lot of *assholes* out there," she said.

"If your life is your movie. Other people's lives are their movies. No two movies are the same. Neither do we react the same to all movies. Do you see what I'm saying in concept?" he asked.

"I understand the movie," she said.

"Your movie is your perspective in life. Why else do we sometimes connect with strangers. We connect with those who accept our perspective and vice versa. Those are often the ones who would do anything to see us smile," he said.

"It sounds wonderful but I'm no doormat to someone's perspective!" she said, irritated by his idealism.

"We live until we die, while our minds are constantly working. Even while we sleep, our brains are running without an *off* switch. Naturally some thoughts are based on assumptions based on the facts we have. I call them filler thoughts without value they may not be true. It all this is going on in our heads and we don't know the access filler thoughts in others. So assuming other people's thoughts is unwise," Kavi said.

"Sam used to say his anger came from being disappointed in unrealistic expectations. Is that it?" she asked.

"Yes, it sounds like the train station story where a delay is announced. Passengers get into an uproar about what it'll do to their day. Five minutes later a new announcement says the delay is clear. So if we wait five minutes sometimes our problem is no longer there," he said.

"Ashram practice sounds an awful lot like self-help. I swear there should be a section in book stores called *Self-blame*. What about people or things that are plain annoying," she said.

Kavi's expression remained neutral.

"Using our anger or annoyance can drive our good intentions without causing harm," Kavi said.

"Anger used for good?" Eunice asked.

She didn't know what he was getting at.

"History repeats itself. I'm afraid of making mistakes because I'll get angry with myself. If I don't ask myself why I get angry I'm ignoring it. When history repeats my anger does too," Kavi said.

"I'll be honest I don't know what you mean. I never used to make mistakes but now I do. Nobody knows me here so I feel lost. I guess I don't mind if a stranger sees a mistake I made," she said.

"There is no such thing as lost. You are here at this moment. You are where you're at. Think about walking on a street and finding a growling dog standing in front of a cardboard box. You might be afraid of the dog right?" he paused.

"I guess," she said, zoning out a little.

"Someone else walking from the opposite direction would see the dogs litter of puppies she'd been nursing in the box and it's growling to protect them. Two perspectives," he said.

Eunice understood. It made sense in her ridiculous disagreements with Sam. They were always at odds over the smallest things and it came down to *there are two sides to every story*.

"How can we make a judgment on what someone's mother taught them? Their view is perfectly acceptable to them," he added.

"I'm so confused. It's no wonder people go postal and blow things up! I won't but this is crazy making!" she said, hoping her time with him was nearly up. She was exhausted.

Eunice got more out of Kavi than she had with Dr. Lynch at couples counseling but it was eerily familiar. Kavi was a know-it-all like Sam but he spoke to her in a voice, she recognized so it didn't bother her.

She thought about her folks, the posse crew and Sam. They would have a field day ridiculing Kavi's advice but maybe they wouldn't understand. If she ever made it back to Montgomery she wouldn't share intimate things she learned about herself with them.

Maybe Mother, Daddy and Sam were her allies all along. Like a mystery, where the answer is right in front of you.

"We never make the same mistake twice. The second time, the mistake is a choice," Kavi said.

This guy has an answer for everything!

Tea Leaves

Later she and Arpita were having ginger lemon tea, "Do you understand every concept Kavi talks about?" Eunice asked.

"Kavi says enlightenment, is noticing our behavior as if we are seeing a play and we are the actor," Arpita said.

"Well said. I get the part where, *your movie is different than my movie* but it's a lot to take in. Arpita I think you're trying to break my brain!" Eunice said, laughing while taking a sip of tea. "All I know is, Nina is a selfish drunken *slut,* who would do anything for a record deal but I'm really not like her…" Eunice stopped. She hadn't meant to reveal she wasn't Nina but she felt open enough with her to say it.

"It's an evolution. Don't think about it all at once," Arpita said, without questioning anything about identity.

Arpita would not know if Dougie dabbled in crime, or maybe wouldn't care.

"Amongst my friends, if I suspect my tendency is to sound harsh or abrupt, I'll look at myself from an outside perspective and ask myself, *Will they feel good, bad or indifferent?*" Arpita said.

"I'll never remember to do that. You know so much," Eunice said, feeling down about her inability to evolve.

"I hit a point where my true self began shining through. She isn't afraid of what others think. On good days I remember tapping into her qualities. On bad days I don't. It's liberating to admit you feel envy for example. I now know I can be envious without it being a surprise or shameful," Arpita said.

"That's incredible," Eunice said.

"Bitter feelings drain my energy. The miracle is I've become more comfortable in my own skin knowing I'm growing," Arpita smiled.

"I like how Kavi knew how to challenge me without my knowing it. I was telling him I find Sam talks too much. Then he asked me what the opposite of that was. I said, 'What? I talk too much or I don't talk enough.' How have you not fallen for him again?" Eunice asked.

"Surely you get intimate feelings with someone who knows inside your mind. You can call it love. It's a devotion to a common belief," Arpita said.

If that were the case Eunice felt love for both Arpita and Kavi. She might not have connected any dots yet but she forgave herself for the mess she had made.

In the Sunshine

The day her thinking shifted from concept to practical, was when Kavi took her on a picnic by the Mississippi river. She rode on the back of his motorcycle, holding him around the waist. Most memories become cherished long after the fact but this one would already last a lifetime.

The Krishna Ashram penchant for delving inside yourself, good or bad, was not what she'd known growing up. It was more like, *to each his own* and *fend for yourself.*

Watching her back, on those days her mother was too ill to straighten her hair. Or reveling in adoration popular girls get in high school. She would never think to ask herself *why* something made her feel bad or good.

Was this what Sam had called empathy? She despised the word she'd been accused of lacking. It stung worse than being called a selfish *bitch*.

The ashram changed her thinking. Similar to how algebra went from complex to simple, like a light bulb illuminating above her head. She probably couldn't do algebra, now that fact and feeling existed together.

Sam is a good person, was a logical absolute. *Sam is a soul mate,* was not provable but only a feeling. His love wrapped around her and protected her like a jaguar.

Before bed Eunice closed her eyes and tried the seaweed meditation on her own. It was surprisingly easy to get to the ocean floor, by imagining her hands, moving above in sync to the waves but it didn't work. As if accepting being awake during insomnia, she meditated on Sam instead.

Sam obsessed on how she froze him out. *Why was it so easy to discard him?* She didn't trust his love for her. *Why?* She didn't trust anybody's love. He wouldn't care if she removed her love. *What if he did care?* His being crushed by her lack of connection never occurred to her. Perhaps he now despised her for the ultimate discard.

Kavi spoke of boundaries. She remembered blinking and staring as she waited for him to get to the point.

"Nina, to be cognizant of where we end and someone else begins is the magic spot you need to find," Kavi said.

The thought of confession made her uneasy.

"I'll be honest. I can't imagine thinking where I end and Sam begins," she said.

"Wonderful. Tell me more about Sam? What's important to him?" he asked.

"Sam looks at me like no one else can," she said.

Lying in bed, the seaweed ocean long gone, Eunice felt hot tears falling to her pillow as the answer came to her. She had no choice but to stop ignoring Sam's love.

I'm sorry Sam, I never knew what love was.

Person of Interest

Eunice woke up and looked at the journal lying beside her. The words on paper were written by a scared little girl.

What now?

The last news update called her a *Person of Interest,* wanted by the FBI just like Aunt Angela had been 1970. Right or wrong, living this way was insane. She played out the possible outcomes of staying underground. Be a fugitive forever, do nothing to help her father in jail and never see Sam again. They all led to dead ends.

What would Angela do?

"Why Eunice, the last time I saw you, I swear you were knee-high to a grasshopper. Look how grown-up you are!" Angela said, "Come here and give me some sugar!"

It was high school maybe grade 11.

"I've missed you," Eunice said, hugging her.

Eunice was old enough to appreciate having this *ass* kicking freedom fighter woman in her life. She bragged about the cool factor and used Angela to give her street cred. She loved when school mates asked if they could meet her.

"Ahem Eunice, I looked it up at the library. Angela Davis was only associated with the Panthers for a short time," Gabrielle said, staring at her with hands on hips.

"Sure *naysayer,* but she's been accused of being a Panther so many times she may as well have been one," Eunice responded, half-joking, half-pissed that Gabrielle called her out.

The Panther code was, *enough with laying down and waiting for the world to be fair.* It had worked to inspire and get Eunice fired up.

"To take back Black Power, one needs to act with militant boldness, which sometimes includes violence," Angela said.

Eventually, Eunice granted her friends permission to meet Angela. One of her favorite stories was the one about Huey P. Newton. She asked Angela to tell it.

"A man got pulled over by police. The Panthers had been patrolling for police brutality. Lord knows they were brutes with weapons and acid sharp tongues. The police were none too pleased with recent infringements on their procedures while the Panthers had read up on their constitutional right to not only bear arms but the right to observe police operations. Huey riled them up when he acted on his right to witness arrests. Of course police threats and nonsense were immediate but Huey stood firm. He let them know he'd studied the law, which he recited line by line as they searched the man they'd stopped. He stood with his law book in one hand and a gun in the other reciting his constitutional right to carry an unconcealed weapon. Folks crowded around flabbergasted at his gall," Angela said.

"What happened? Did they arrest him later for something he never did?" Arisbel asked.

"Surprisingly no. That's what most of us thought would happen. The flustered cop was so confused, he got the hell out of there," Angela said.

"That was way back in the 1960s, we need to pick up that revolution!" Terrence said.

"True. First of all, if you're gonna talk about a revolution, you have to have people who are brave and physically able to stand up. People who are able to do what is needed. You all have a positive attitude and change is still most effective through organized activism," Angela said.

Whenever Angela told Huey's story, an internal fire burned in Eunice's chest. She imagined the sensation as true Panther energy, a genetic blueprint she had birthright to and permission to use for justifiable revenge.

How brave the Panthers were, to stand twenty paces watching police arrests, while reciting civil rights. The difference was the Panthers had enough facts to take risks, while Eunice had none. Depending on which avenue she took it would be a shell game. She had one chance to guess which option had the pea under it.

With that *power* in mind, Eunice had come up with the plan for their involvement at Booker T. She *had* been the ring leader all along but was guilty for not thinking through all the possible outcomes. She had been a coward to flee the scene of the crime? *Angela would tap into that power.*

Her internal power had nowhere to go, like *Carrie White* in Chamberlain, Maine eventually it would escape restraint.

"But Angela how do you get to equal rights without the violence?" Terrence asked.

"Oh, is that the question you were asking?" Angela asked, "When you talk about fighting for civil rights, you might think violence without realizing the real content of any kind of confrontation lies in the goals you are striving for not how you get there."

Visiting Curtis

Sam went to Kilby Correctional to visit Curtis. Besides checking on him, Sam hoped to confirm some information he heard about a possible Todd assailant.

He didn't expect the gift Curtis had waiting for him.

"Good to see you. It was a rough night with old *peckerhead* in the next cell. He had panic attacks and was screaming all night long," Curtis said, looking through the cubicle glass. He was in customary orange, had a fresh buzzed haircut and black framed glasses.

"How you holding up?" Sam asked.

"We been having cake. A bit of a celebration. First white on black killer to get the chair," Curtis said.

"Yeah, I read that this morning. It was down in Atmore. It was the only time a *klan* member was executed for the murder of a black man in the 20th century. My mother knew Michael Donald's mother back in the 70s" Sam said.

"Small mercies," Curtis said.

"Curtis, remember a while back before all this, I'd asked if I could interview you? Do you mind if I ask you a few questions?"

Curtis nodded affirmative.

"We are ready to deliver an updated black history curriculum for teachers," Sam said. He purposely held Curtis' stare for an inordinate amount of time. His hope was Curtis would remember, years ago how they agreed on a way to communicate if he ever got arrested.

When Sam was a teenager, Curtis taught the neighborhood boys a trick he'd learned in his Navy days. By communicating using *double entendre* or something that could have more than one meaning.

Sam would ask Curtis about his work, hopefully in a way Curtis would understand the hidden question and provide the *real* answer. This way, if they were overheard the transcript of the recording would be vague.

"We want to train our teachers our history in practical terms. Give them more information than what is generally known. Does that sound alright?" Sam asked.

"Sure thing. Whatever you need kid," Curtis said.

"When you were a lad, had you ever heard of black folks saying anything positive about the *klan*?" Sam asked.

"Jeezus Sam, what kind of question is that?" Curtis looked genuinely surprised.

"I apologize. Allow me to read a short piece from the curriculum to give some context. These historical quotes speak for themselves," Sam said.

> No, I think the Ku Klux was a good thing at that time. The darkies got sassy (saucy), trifling, lazy. They was notorious. They got mean. The men wouldn't work.

> At fu'st I though dat dey was ghosties and den I wuz afeered of 'em, but atter I found out dat Massa Bennett wuz one of dem things, I wuz always proud of 'em." Leroy Day thought the Klan initially served a good purpose.

"Got it," Curtis nodded, with recognition, "there were some, who I wouldn't say supported the *klan* but rode with them, looking to snitch on lazy slaves. So I guess you could say they didn't think the worst of them. They were probably out for any perks they might get in return. Don't forget it was the wild west. The *klan* were like vigilante police," Curtis said.

Sam's opinion of them now was all hate and bullying.

"So how about a black man joining them? *As if!* Right?" Sam said, in an effort to sound casual.

"There was a police sergeant in Colorado Springs who went undercover as a black member a bunch of years ago. He did all his stuff over the phone, so the *klan* never seen him. He sent in a white cop partner in person to pose as him," Curtis said.

"How did he keep *that* under wraps? Is it possible to have a black *klansman* and not hear about it?" Sam asked.

"Naw. Around here if a guy was to pull that, he wouldn't get past state round-up, where they initiate all new members," Curtis said. He closed both eyes tight but kept talking, "I swear I got me some allergies today. To answer your question, I don't see how there'd be interest in that. Times are a changin' for state round... up." he said.

"I might have tired you out! I will leave you to it," Sam said. He wasn't sure if he got actual answers using *double entendre*.

Curtis chuckled, "You know Sam, if you get out to that Texaco on Sprott Road, before Martha's dinner time, the gas'll still be cheap," he spoke quietly. "Now go on, you don't have much time," Curtis abruptly signaled for the guard to escort him back.

In the parking lot, Sam was jittery with excitement shaking as he got the keys out. If he understood correctly, Curtis had something waiting for him at thc Texaco at 3:45. Martha's dinner time was always fifteen minutes before *The Young and the Restless*.

Eunice has come back.

Fifteen minutes later Sam pulled into the Texaco parking lot. Dougie Barnes was standing by his vehicle. *Bingo!*

"You Sammy boy?"

"Yessir," Sam said. He might have met him before but wasn't sure.

"Dougie here, she's ok is all I'm saying to you. She done forgot all about y'all back in Alabama. You might want to move on with your life. Forget about her Sam," Dougie said.

Sam's mouth hung open. He felt a mixture of relief and confusion. It didn't sound right.

"You know the song, *Under the Bridge* or *Over the Bridge* or something?" Dougie asked.

"I think so …Uh, *one more turn at the rodeo…*" Sam said.

Dougie looked at him funny.

Sam felt stupid like it was a practical joke.

"Anyhow, it's a big country hit on Memphis radio. When I went to get her outta the hospital a few months back she told me she wrote and recorded that song. I gotta believe her. All she did was sing and carry on most nights till the wee hours. Good singer though!" Dougie said.

"You mean you know where she is now? She's alright? How can I get to her?" Sam had so many questions. After all his therapy, he knew this was not a healthy way to be letting go.

"Listen Son, I dunno what's in this envelope but our friend asked I get it to you. I gotta get back before dark," he said, putting the letter in Sam's hand.

Dougie got into his Aerostar minivan and drove off.

Sam, You and I make quite the pair. I have a big broken hole inside of me and you fill a lot of it but not all. Even though I don't have a lot to give in return I loved receiving what you had. At least until I woke up to it.

I was selfish. I didn't know I was selfish, I was just really unhappy with my life and I was looking for that exact right thing that would fill the hole.

When I first met you, well later at musicology, I knew you were a gentle and loving person. You gave me a great lift and made me feel wonderful. I just didn't have it in me to return the favor, even though I actually did want to. Eventually the emptiness in me returned and I questioned the value of our love. I started looking for a new lift with the posse crew activism. I didn't do it consciously but I did do it to you.

I thought I was justified when I was angry but it was abusive. I left you when I wasn't getting what I needed from you anymore. I know you hate me now and that's your right.

It wasn't until my experience in Memphis and the people I met here, did I realize I was self absorbed. I'm sorry that I took your light to feed myself and didn't give anything back. I'm sorry that I confused you and made you vulnerable. I realize I can't go through life using people without it catching up to me.

The thing is I didn't mean to hurt you. I never actually realized that I was. I was just trying to get through the world in a way that made it bearable for me to manage the emptiness inside.

Wake up Nina

Eunice woke from an erotic dream. She was back in her attic room at Dougie's place. In the dream a man held her down as she reached the top of ecstasy. It seemed like Terrence. He'd been a player but she'd been his wing man like *Top Gun* from the start. The scent of Legend cologne was on her mind.

Legend was Sam's cologne!

Holy fuck!

It was Sam in her dream. She had never had a dirty dream about him before! Her heart skipped a beat thinking about what he'd been doing to her. *Nasty girl!*

Passion turned to fear at the thought of losing him. Sam had always been more dangerous than the others because he could read her like nobody else. She was afraid he knew too much about her. It was uncomfortable much like facing a fear is. However, if your ready to face a fear you want someone who knows you. If you're not, the last person you want near is the one who knows all your excuses.

Sam knew her mental ups and downs. He tried to find ways to help her even forcing her to see Dr. Lynch. Maybe she avoided hearing ugly things about herself because she knew they were true.

She felt brave.

How often does someone come along, who will fight to be with you even after seeing the grotesque?

The ashram gave her courage to admit, "I don't know how to navigate feelings. I built a case against you Sam," she said.

When Sam said she was in denial, she took it as a cheap shot because he was calling her a liar. What if denial was lying and lying was denial? Interchangeable. Ignorance as protection.

She wouldn't mention Terrence's name because it upset him. Did denying the subject of Terrence make her a liar? Maybe it had but she never thought so.

"It's okay to be real with me in private," Sam always said.

"I'm am being *me* Sam. You want to call it real or fake that's your business," she said.

"Are you threatened I'm going to tell everyone about your phony side?" he asked.

"There's nothing you could tell anyone would believe you," she said confidently.

"Your friends think I'm a total nerd. They'll think I'm lying? They'd believe you more?" he asked.

"I know so," she said.

"I think you struggle to admit when you're wrong. You are a good person. What's your struggle with truth?" he asked.

Ouch but it was a good point.

He was right. She spent a lot of time wriggling out of her true feelings.

Later at out shopping, Eunice caught the scent of Legend a second time. She looked around but saw no sign of who was wearing the cologne. She'd never been a believer in signs but that was twice in a day. A scent was more a concrete fact than a feeling was. It was a sign.

She was cold from her insides out. She started to panic at the thought of his being hurt. She had knots in her stomach. She'd been a virgin to feeling for people. Something started to shift in her brain where she thought she could lose her mind.

CNN News: Lynching in Texas

"I'm Anderson Cooper, Tonight we report the disturbing details around the unimaginable murder of James Byrd Jr. Not since the most notorious Lynching of Emmett Till and following the timeline all the way to Rodney King in 1992 have we seen such an atrocity.

James Byrd Jr. an African-American man murdered by three white supremacists in Jasper, Texas on June 7, 1998. dragged Byrd for three miles behind a pick-up truck along an asphalt road. Byrd, who remained conscious throughout most of his ordeal, was killed about halfway through the dragging when his body hit the edge of a culvert, severing his right arm and head. The murderers drove on for another mile and a half before dumping his torso in front of an African-American cemetery in Jasper.

Sightlines of Trouble

Dougie told Eunice the annual *klan* meeting was called a round-up and the location had been determined. He had found out via word of mouth. He explained how the round-up was always the Saturday nearest the new moon and the location kept secret to ward off any meddling authorities.

Once the location was known, the *night rides* would commence, where hateful propaganda was distributed door to door and tossed from pick-up trucks like grocery store flyers. The ads promoted round-up attendance, recruitment and included a self-congratulatory newsletter, with plenty of stories to excite the base. Folks new to the neighborhood might wake up to a special surprise on their lawn.

They were sitting in Dougie's kitchen drinking Sanka instant coffee, "Come on, tell me Dougie, where's it going to be?" she asked, pretending to beg but she really needed to know. She planned to go with or without anyone.

"The back woods over near Huntsville," he said.

"Is that Alabama?" Eunice asked.

Her eyes must have danced with eagerness because Dougie said, "You aren't going there little girl. You just got yourself mended up. You're in hiding remember?" he said.

"Dougie, I just know Sam will be there. I've been having premonitions since the ashram," she said.

"He might well be there. Your daddy seems to think Sam's pretty close to finding what he's looking for. All the same, this thing is bigger than you," Dougie said.

"Well *I'm* going!" she said, aware of her manipulation that he join her.

He looked conflicted between a man who should represent a responsible father figure blended with the tone of someone who wouldn't stop her.

"Golly, you remind me of Madeline. She was determined to kick her disease," he said, pointing to a picture of her near the window. She looked motherly and reminded Eunice of a nurse.

"So what do you say, Doug?" she asked.

"I'll be damned. You have such fire in you," he said.

"I'm sorry. I learned from the guru you sent after me," she pat him on the arm, "My trouble is connected to foolhardy courage. I never cared about kicking and screaming my way around. But Dougie when I think of James Byrd, that beautiful soul dragged to death for miles, I'm absolutely sickened. Look at the trouble we can clear away for Daddy. Sam isn't street smart like we are. If he gets caught they'll murder him. I'll risk dying for it," she said.

Dougie stared out the window for several moments.

"Alright. I suppose the time has come. I'll call Cal. We'll need help," Dougie said, relinquishing his paternal authority.

"Listen to me. You'll need to get into Huntsville during daylight so you can find your way around. You'll hide out until nightfall. I don't imagine hiding will be a big deal for you," Dougie said.

"Thanks for not stopping me Doug," she said.

Eunice took some time alone in her room to think things through. This time when her *save the world* mentality kicked in it wasn't solely to feed her ego. Instead her selfish desire was to show Sam Hood, she was ready to love and accept his love. The thought of losing him gave her a peculiar lump in her throat.

"They do the ritual stuff near midnight," Dougie had said. "The ceremonies have evolved, to staged horror spectacles. It takes more to scare folks into membership than it used to. Skepticism makes people dismiss the *klan* as archaic and farcical. It's become a sick circus," he said.

Isolation in Memphis and meditation with Kavi had messed with Eunice's heart and short circuited her thinking. Things she'd been fearless of before, felt nerve-wracking like being brazen. Yet, she also felt brave in areas that previously eluded her, like running to tell Sam she loved him.

The legacy of *klan* attacks and the inhumanity of dragging a human beings three miles behind a truck proved to her lynching's were not a thing of the past.

An image of Angela standing firm, with intelligence and passion came to her. She had been determined to show the world women were capable of enforcing right from wrong.

Eunice wasn't afraid to go home to Montgomery, even if it meant prison or body bag. Living a lie wasn't working for her anymore. She wasn't about to hide behind a fictitious name like the *klan* hiding behind masks.

Her love for Sam was do or die!

ෲෲෲ

As per Dougie's plan, Eunice set off from Memphis to Huntsville driving Madeline's Aerostar beater. He had gone ahead with Cal and a few other *riggers,* he called them. She arrived in late afternoon without trouble and parked in a mall lot to wait it out. Her stomach was upset with anticipation.

"Do you know how to make fresh water into salt water?" Dougie had asked her, after agreeing to the mission,

She nodded no.

"By adding table salt!" he said.

"Really table salt, where'd you hear that?" she said.

"I never told you I used to work in fisheries, in South Carolina. I worked with this guy Cal on the docks. Helped hoist these big ole fish from the fishing boats and hoisting them onto trucks using pulley systems."

"Okay I'll bite. What's a pulley system," she laughed at her own joke.

"It's really a primitive machine. If you want to lift a really heavy weight there's only so much force a man's muscles can supply. By using a simple machine, like a pulley you can effectively multiply the force your body produces," he said.

"Dougie I know you're speaking in code. Who do we need to hoist Sam?" she asked.

"Pulley systems are also used by acrobats. We called it *flying fox* in Carolina but folks also call it a *zip line*.

It made her think about circus trapezes.

"Ah now I see. Can you get me a harness and pulley?" Eunice asked.

"Now slow down. They got shotguns Eunice and they is all hunters with good aim. A wee girl like you or a ten-point buck is all the same to them. They shoot to kill," Dougie said.

Her eyes narrowed and locked onto his. Right from wrong had never been more clear to her.

Sitting in the parking lot waiting, Eunice had a few hours before heading to the location in Dougie's instructions. She decided to try relaxing, with the seaweed meditation again. Arpita said it was for these very situations.

With her eyes closed and head against the backrest she inhaled and exhaled. The images flew by her mind quicker than the last time; her mother alone at home, her father in a cell, and an image of a Cabbage Patch doll.

The doll named Cleon looked as if he could have been her own daughter with similar skin tone. It was one of a kind signed by Xavier the leader himself. Cleon came with a birth certificate and adoption papers.

It was Uncle Vic who flashed the doll to her. She caught a quick glimpse of it tucked inside his doctor-style travel bag. She'd already told herself she would do anything for it. She pushed away her gut feeling Cleon was connected to something very bad. She denied the thought.

It was Uncle Vic, so friendly and sweet. He kept promising such wonderful things like dollar bills or McDonald's pies but she'd never been interested in those things.

She heard Kavi's calming voice, *"Keep going Nina keep searching where are you now? What happened next?"*

Uncle Vic did the worst thing to her. Perhaps the thing that changed everything. He said he would give Cleon to his niece Lucy instead so the offer was time sensitive and had consequence. It was the exact moment she felt colossal unfairness.

"Yes, Uncle Vic, whatever, yes, I want..." she said.

"Come sit on my lap and you can hold the doll," he said, holding Cleon on his knee as he pat the other.

Eunice's sights zoomed in on his lap near his groin. Something didn't look right. Shapes, sizes and colors weren't usual. Some kind of vibrating went through her limbs like the time she put her finger in the wall socket sending a current down to her foot. He pat, pat, pat his knee. Eunice took two large runway strides and kicked Uncle Vic's shin as hard as she could with her glossy black Mary Jane's.

"What the *christ* girl?" he howled. The doll fell to the floor crumbled face first.

At that moment Aunt Angela's distressed voice hit within earshot and broke Eunice's spell.

"Oh my God EUNICE! Is he at you?" Angela shrieked, as she hurled herself like a quarterback into his chest with her hands and full body weight.

"I'm sorry, I'm sorry," Eunice cried out. She had fallen to cradle Cleon in her arms, "I'm sorry, I wanted the doll!"

"It's not your fault, go to your room," Angela shouted. Her arm extending pointing to the door.

Eunice never heard her voice raised like that except when the adults were all laughing and telling loud stories. She went to her room as commanded.

She sat on her bed feeling a burning all over her face and cheeks, afraid and ashamed of herself. *You asked for it.* She wanted to please Uncle Vic for the doll.

"I wanted the dolleeee!" Eunice cried uncontrollably in her bedroom mirror. She was about to do whatever was required to have the doll. She had no idea what that was but assumed by Aunt Angela's reaction it was bad.

Eunice had only just remembered. No wonder she'd always had an invisible umbilical cord attached to Angela.

In nightmares the dimensions were messed up. The doors and windows too tall and too skinny. Her mother checking in on her stood in silhouette in her doorway, squished into a three inch crevice.

Dressed like a cat thief in black tights, a snug black jacket and gloves she was to wait patiently for nightfall until she could get behind enemy lines.

At sundown she started making her move to the suggested location. Driving she spotted the neon orange ribbon on the guardrail right where Dougie said it would be. She pulled onto the gravel shoulder, then parked on a private road of someone Dougie knew.

Eunice got out of the car and proceeded on foot to a path over rocky terrain. The sky had a deep purple veneer and the air smelled of fire smoke. The pines and sycamores were dense and it already seemed dark in the forest.

When she got closer, she veered off the path so no one could creep up behind her. She walked a few hundred more feet, until she caught a glimpse through the trees of a gathering.

Thirty or so men, women and children in the distance, some costumed in *klan* gear, some with masks and some without. The kaftan robes were mostly white but some had color-strips embroidered into the trim delineating rank perhaps.

She found a hiding place between a boulder and low brush to wait for the next part to unfold. Minutes later a couple of women having a private conversation came nearby.

"We are very discreet you know. You might have a next-door neighbor in the *klan* and you'd never know it," the woman in a white sheet said.

The other woman in jeans and a blouse listened. She held a white robe over her arm as if still unsure whether this was for her.

"Right here, at the round-up we're just regular housewives holding bake sales, raising money for white children and elderly," she said.

"Now *that* is important. Taking care of our own and all," the civilian woman said, putting on the robe evidently convinced.

In the distance over and above their conversation, Eunice heard voices on a loud speaker. Possibly the grand wizard rehearsing a speech.

The women moved toward the action. Eunice carefully followed doing her best to evade detection. She found a spot to hide behind a tree. The clearing was lit by a huge bonfire at the center.

The congregation were in full costume with hoods. The sight of mask after pointy mask made gave her a chill. It looked like mother's First Baptist Choir rehearsal from a twisted episode of the *Twilight Zone*.

She could hear the speaker clearly. The event had begun.

"… in California where they let the zoo animals roam free… See what happens?" He bellowed, "You can take the n* out of the jungle but you can't take the jungle out of the n*," The grand wizard said. The crowd applauded.

Eunice felt bulletproof to the grand wizards obscenities. If only the serenity of Arpita was with her. Or even the jaguar she'd visualized. She counted to twenty in her head envisioning the jaguar.

"If I said I hated fags because it's forbidden by God's law, praise God for AIDS, they'll be the first ones to hang for their sins…" the cloaked grand wizard droned on.

Eunice's blood boiled at his instigation of violence. Freedom of speech was one thing, but to sell ignorance and influence through brainwashing with hate was evil.

The sky was pitch black with no help from the moon, which was covered by unseen clouds. The fire had been stoked so burned bigger and brighter. Crowds had grown, accumulating beyond the shadowed periphery into the forest. Some homemade masks were ghoulish Jack-o-lanterns with crooked eye holes. She estimated there were a few hundred in attendance.

The plan instruction was for her to get closer to the podium at the time of the sacrifice. When she'd asked Dougie how she'd know what the sacrifice was, he said, *it'll require no explanation* and she'd know it when she saw it.

The grand wizard continued his program amid intermittent roars of approval, erupting after each pointed exclamation.

"No *klan* faction has ever been as successful as our South Dixie! We have recruited Marines! We have joiners from the U.S. Army. Just think of it folks we'll need army trained soldiers for the upcoming battle," he said. The inflection in his voice and raised alleluia arms inspired cries of anger and glee. Their goal was to incite a race war using politics. Eunice's heart sank.

Three huge crosses were lit by way of pyrotechnics as they *whooshed* into instant flames. The crowd was ballistic. The setting must have been staged after *Gone with the Wind* crossed with *Wizard of Oz* in glorious Technicolor.

"We can affect change legitimately through the political system by voting our *klan* members into office! We no longer need loose radicals, committing rogue terrorist acts to scare voters off the undesirable voting bloc," the grand wizard, now yelling with his neck engorged.

This guy is fuckin' nuts!

The pitch black sky and dense forest were united into one black hole. *She'd hit the mutherfuckers where it hurt. Burning crosses were nothing compared to what they were gonna get!*

With a changing of the guard on the podium the grand wizard stepped aside. Eunice figured her time had come.

Burlap Sack

Sam was intent on finding out which *klan* chapter had an African American member, so he had sent his connection feelers out. He spoke to Eunice's pal, Mike Watts to see if he or his network had leads, on finding where a cross state *klan* rally location might be.

Most folks in Montgomery got their news from WSFA-12 or the *Montgomery Advertiser* but they each had a spotty track record of censorship, so weren't always considered trustworthy in the black community.

He could have gone to police but trust in authority, with them was also low. Traditionally news travelled better by word of mouth. In the 1950s the black press *Chicago Defender* and *Pittsburgh Courier* had proven reliable, often running completely different perspectives on mainstream reporting. Though gossip accuracy was risky news travelled faster and often more credible.

Sam had dropped hints over the past several weeks with friends, his parent's, Eunice's mother and select townsfolk for an ear to the ground.

"Do y'all supposed the good old *klan* boys have a more fearful presence nowadays?" he asked. If there really was a black *klansman* it was a juicy story, that would surely be talked about. Interactions at bake sales, barber shops and church choir could be more reliable than Reuters.

"You want to be careful sniffing around too much Sam. You're being watched closely by the *klan* and the feds. Things could get dangerous. Let's get this in front of the sheriff," Mike said.

Sam looked at him in disbelief, "Mike you know the cops won't rush on this. Don't they still get paid off by the *klan?*" he asked.

"I'm sorry. I'll ask around and let you know what I find out," Mike Watts had said.

Sam had heard gossip through his folks he had a target on his back. The *klan* was *pissed* a young black man had the gall to buck tradition and pursue them with his identification of the black *klansman* to FBI.

Them fuckers are so lazy. No wonder they ain't looking for Eunice Johnston no more.

He was frustrated there wasn't one solid lead and it was difficult to know who or what the *klan* were up to. There membership was wider than any census could count and there was no all access TV channel showcasing their day to day affairs. Not yet, at least.

೫೫೫

A day later just after 6:00 p.m., Sam left the law office along historic Commerce Street and headed for his car in the adjacent parking lot. He'd been trying to glean more information on how plea deals worked, puzzled by how there were so many. Maybe Curtis was right, "your own lawyer could be a crooked bloodsucker." Were lawyers afraid of losing cases or were they too much work?

As soon he heard the crunching shoe scuff on pavement sound behind him he scolded himself for knowing better but he'd been so deep in thought. Always be vigilantly aware of your surroundings. You never knew who could creep up.

He was immediately surrounded by several masked men, looking almost comical wearing ladies dark nylon stalking's over their faces, squashed their noses into pig snouts.

"Alright fellas, what are we playing at here. Now come on, I'm just minding my own business," Sam said, less able to contain his frustration at whatever this was, would interfere with the plea bargain research.

There was no cajoling or *fucking* around this time. The assailants swiftly and had him to his knees overpowered to the ground and preceded to tie him with rope and coil him into a sheet of landscaper burlap cloth.

"We're shutting you down Hood. You've been chosen to be made a token example," one said.

Sam wasn't sure they were *klan* and if they were, they didn't seem to be on a joyriding expedition like the time with Todd but had specific instructions about what to do with him.

"D'yeah an example of what not to be," another said, laughing at his own joke.

Assuming they were *klan,* Sam noticed they were less confident without their full regalia to hide behind, seeming almost erratic and rushed. He tried defending himself but assessed by their nervousness, too much aggression on his part might be like setting off a hairpin trigger.

"Once we get rid of *driving ambition* here there'll be no one to take his place. Look at those other big mouths. They got snuffed out and it took twenty years for another one to come along. We're putting a muzzle on your squawking," another said.

"Where the *fuck* we gotta take him? All the way to Huntsville?" one said.

"Shut your pie hole *idgit!*" another scolded.

"Duh, sorry. We need to get him outta town for a few days," he said.

Huntsville? *Shit that's way the hell up state.* Although captive Sam got a cherry blossom of excitement in his belly signaling potential. *Could this be your escort to the klan rally?* As far as he could tell, the men were all white under nylon masks but maybe he'd find the black *klansman* after all.

"This is here is called Rohypnol. It won't hurt you none. It'll just paralyze you," the bumbling one said. Sam didn't even feel the prick in his arm with all the itching burlap on him. The anesthetic took effect as fast as a dental freezing.

In the blink of an eye Sam was embroiled in one of his philosophical 'solve the world' conversations with Todd.

"So you didn't study *klan* in your privileged history class? Black history without the *klan*? I guess some history book pages got glued together," Sam said.

"Not to the point of knowing all that. I'm actually going to apologize on behalf of all Caucasians. Seriously, it's disgusting," Todd said, looking embarrassed.

"Go figure, with that private school education! I don't take your apology lightly. Thank you Todd," Sam said. He'd never been able to talk race with a white guy before. Speaking freely without fear of reprisal was rare.

"Too bad the *klan* boys didn't skip those pages," Todd said.

"Yes I agree. I'm not even going to joke, they're too dumb so they wouldn't know, because the *klan* hide at all levels of education. Did you know it all started as a game?" Sam said.

"How so?" Todd asked.

"Allegedly supremacists began in a small town in Tennessee in like 18 something. They were goofing around on horseback dressed as dead Confederate soldiers. They had sheets with eye holes cut out playing ghosts," Sam said.

"The beginning of heinous crime as innocent *Cowboys and Indians,* racist for other reasons," Todd said.

"Boys will be boys. Back in the day they clowned around in good fun but who would they target in their except for a black boy? Sound familiar?" Sam asked.

"It sounds like hazing in University, supposedly meant to be a fun tradition," Todd said.

"Until the game turns deadly, even if unintentionally. Then murder turns to 'he had it coming' or 'too late to turn back now,'" Sam said.

Three hours later Sam's burlap head covering was pulled off, leaving him looking headlong into a forest yet again. *Fuck!*

It was nearly dark out.

This time he'd been between awake and paralysis for the near two-hundred mile drive presumably to Huntsville. He guessed it to be their turf, their lair, the *klan* factory for torture and grinding humans into hamburger meat.

He was securely fastened to a ten foot birch log, propped up against other logs, presumably stockpile firewood for the pit. He was bound with thick rope, that cut into his hands and feet. His muzzle tasted rubbery in his mouth, secured by a kerosene stinking strip of canvas.

"You sit tight here. You will meet the grand wizard shortly," a *klan* member said.

Sam pointed at his own mouth, making a gurgling sound with a mimed request to have it removed. He was ignored. His previous escorts were nowhere to be seen presumably working their next assignment.

He had a bird's-eye view of folks readying the expanse of forest rally space. Members paid no mind to him while they focused like roadies setting up for the next act at Lollapalooza.

The teepee style wood fire pit was being lit by an experienced team. The *klan* thrived among the lawless pines with members looking at ease in their natural habitat. It wasn't as if they got the chance to walk around town sporting white sheets. Except maybe for an annual parade appearance or one-off talk show guest spot, they didn't have opportunities for pomp and circumstance.

From the center, he scanned the periphery like a protractor. The moon was clouded over, so he couldn't see stars above the tree tops. The fire pit glowed, rippling out to the forest edge, a circumference halted by the dark velvet theater curtain of majestic pines.

Maybe fifty pointy masked, white-robed ghosts made their way in single file past the burning cross toward the fire and formed a circle around it.

Surely the black *klansman* was among them.

A hundred or more *peasants* in garish homemade masks surrounded the rim outside the first one. Their masks were less pristine in grays and browns. The common element being the horrific amateur sewn eye holes. Even farther beyond them were layers and layers of supporters making a ring of Saturn bleeding beyond the woods infinitum.

From his standpoint the entire scene looked like a large white cake for the devil's birthday with the flaming bonfire as the candle. The symmetry made for a picture perfect demonic postcard.

It was only fair to expect the hate-filled followers to exact revenge on meddling in their ways. Sam wasn't frightened anymore, accepting his fate as the unwelcome troublemaker. The *klan* has despised the cockiness of black men since the first ship arrived from Africa.

What they didn't know was he'd already planned ahead with Tom Horsley's guidance. Like the underground railroad, the school program was not one person but a team. Good triumphs over evil.

He brushed thoughts of Eunice Johnston away. *Maybe next lifetime Babycakes!*

The grand wizard appeared under a stadium spotlight, stepping in front of the microphone. His robe was whiter and crisper than the others with a double stripe trim at the hem. The crowd noise faded to hushed whispers out of respect or curiosity.

The last few bars of acoustic banjo playing *Like a Prayer* petered out as the maladjusted microphone squealed, "Hear ye, hear ye! These insults to white supremacy are the very image of self-hatred. Let us pray," the grand wizard said.

Out from under, every pointy mask the gleefully berserk crowd prayed along with the grand wizard then cheered in soprano, tenor and alto. There were men women and children under *klan* sheets. Boisterous, loud but surreal without a view of lips and mouths moving.

"Now to begin the sacrifice ceremony. As annually we have three human sacrifices to prove our faith in what is right and just," the grand wizard said. "I give you the sacrificial lambs. Praise the Lord!" he wowed the crowd yet again. They mob roared turning to each other excitedly as if in Times Square when the New Year's ball ascends.

Three large crosses spontaneously burst alight as flames raced from base to tip. High above the frenzy, three figures had been strung along like birds on a wire, in direct line to the raging bonfire. Three emaciated bodies dangled beyond human from extensive meth and crack use. The poor bastards were likely addicts picked up from a drug infested urban ghetto.

Regardless of race, religion or other orientation the souls had long been abandoned be family due to an abhorrent lifestyle of addiction. The *klan* being mindful not to lynch productive members of society just junk no one cared for.

Sam was stunned. He was witness to the unimaginable hell that was *Dante's Wood of Suicide,* the last stop ritual performed annually by *klan* who used drug addicts as human sacrifice.

Their last moments taunted and tortured by *harpie monsters who tormented wrongdoers and carried their souls to a netherworld.* Only the *klan* Harpies were white sheet wearing *mutherfucking* psychos who reveled in sacrifice for the sake of their white supremacy.

The final stage addicts had gone missing, abducted from parks or crack dens. Their poor unclear minds perhaps surprised the last hit didn't do the trick.

Their souls transitioned to gnarled, sunken cheeked, thorny trees on a courageous road to meth suicide. The vegetable minded trees refusing life remained fixed in drug-dead sterility no longer recognized as human beings.

Sam planned out his last words, "We are connected as humans inside our hearts. Killing me doesn't change that!" He winced when they exploded.

Pulleys moved the bodies along the tightrope wire. Once they got close to the heat they combusted with a quiet *woof* sound turning them into slow burning roasted marshmallows.

It hadn't been clear to spectators if they had been alive until the rodent-like screams escaped from their mouths. The crowd erupted into cheers or horrified screams depending on whether it was your first round-up. The snap crackle and pop of the raging bonfire burned on.

The grand wizard was back on the microphone as if nothing out of the ordinary had occurred, "Hear yee. Tonight we have a special occasion. We have chosen one of our living breathing enemies of the people to make an example of. This man is a demon to us. Sam Hood has tried to undermine and silence us on numerous occasions in his young live but we won't be silenced.

Sam's post had been lifted to standing position with the aid of [well-known farm machine company] to hoist and position post in a pre-dug hole at left of center of the podium.

"This Neanderthal is sneaky. He tried to tear our legacy of the past fifty years in equality down in our unrivaled Montgomery center. Sam Hood is the *number one black blemish of the year*. But first we'll hear from … " the grand wizard sounded more educated than blind followers knew.

"*String him up! String him up!*" the lemmings chanted.

"You been lookin' for me Sam Hood?" a *klan* 'pall bearer' whispered in his ear while purposely stepped forward to reveal skin under his white sleeve. His arm skin matching Sam's own.

It was the black *klansman.*

His brethren did nothing to intercede.

The grand wizard kept things lively with rousing story of why hate is so important before introducing the sopranos choirgirls.

The black *klansman* then jerked his mask off from above. His face was nose to nose in front of Sam's snot dripping from his nose and drooling mouth. He didn't look to be in charge of his faculties. He was either inebriated or insane maybe both.

"String him up! String him up!" the lemmings chanted.

Sam's brain cleared away the snot and drool and he froze in the realization. It was a mic drop moment. Full stop.

What? What Sam pieced together didn't add up. How could he be the *klansman?*

But I certainly have missed you brother!

It was Sam's little brother Rory Hood.

"But why?" Sam said into his deranged looking face.

"String him up! String him up!" the lemmings chanted.

"Why? You wanna know why?" Rory was millimeters from Sam's face stinking of *shit* and *piss*, "All that pussy-whipping you done took. You whiney little *bitch!* Making your race ashamed of you! *Klan* see you as a bunch of whining ingrates who hide behind history. Hide the fact you is as lazy as *fuck!*"

Sam's life really did flash before his eyes. Rory had been gone since he was 14…

"String him up! String him up!" the lemmings chanted.

"It's with pride I ask our fine soprano trio to take us through the original national anthem instilled by the forefathers. And then the moment you've all been waiting for to STRING HIM UP!" the grand wizard said. He stepped off the podium to sit with the *klan* elders.

The soprano trio began singing the *Dixie National Anthem.*

> Oh, I wish I was in the land of cotton
> Old times there are not forgotten
> Look away! Look away! Look away! Dixie Land
> In Dixie Land where I was born
> Early on one frosty morn'
> Look away! Look away! Look away! Dixie Land

Flying Fox

Eunice wasn't mentally prepared for what she had just seen. Three murders by lynching over a fire with an exuberant crowd going mental. This in America.

"Praise the Lord," the crowd chanted in unison.

"The moment of reckoning is coming for us. Our troublemaking sacrifice is what you've all heard about!" The grand wizard said, stepping aside to sit with others on portable camping chairs. He waved his robed arm to his side as six white robed 'pall bearers' surrounding the ultimate sacrifice. In a tight circle they stepped away so the crowd had a clear view of Sam Hood, the large black man tied to a birch log.

"Holy *fuck* Sam!" Eunice instantly *freaked* at the gravity of the situation and how she hadn't made her next move in time. Perhaps meditative influence had made her easily mesmerized by the twisted spectacle.

She moved from her hiding place behind a tree to the coordinates provided roughly 45 degrees due east of the grand wizard's microphone stand.

She quickly found the lift harness marked with florescent orange.

Oh Sam I'm coming. Eunice prayed, *God help me. God if you get me out of this I will never drink or do drugs again. I will love and take care of Sam.*

She figured out how to strap on the harness belt as rehearsed.

She yanked the wire twice in quick succession. An invisible weight offset hers and she soared up into the treetops. A few pine branches whipped her face on the way up.

The instructions had been incredibly risky so she was using blind faith. There were no guarantees and the plan was not foolproof. It was a one-way ticket without a breadcrumb trail back to safety. She'd need *Spider-Man* and *Wonder Woman* skills combined to make this happen.

At the top she grabbed onto a thick branch, searched and miraculously found the second orange marking. This time she attached herself to the other zip wire.

Using a similar pulley system as the *klan* torture contraption Dougie's riggers had innumerable tricks of the trade set up or so Eunice told herself.

Marching band drums, twangy guitars and a trio of covered figures were partway through the *Dixie National Anthem* in unison.

Old Missus marry "Will the weaver"
William was a gay deceiver
Look away! Look away! Look away! Dixie Land

In a nutshell the plan was for her to make physical contact with Sam by swooping down the zip line from above. The odds of her getting to him and having enough time to count to ten was yet to be seen.

She hoped *Cirque du soleil* had come to Huntsville and they were on the good side.

She grabbed the wire.

Unclipped. Clipped.

But when he put his arm around her
He smiled as fierce as a forty pounder
Look away! Look away! Look away! Dixie Land

She was taken by surprise how quickly she shot down the lubricated wire. There was no time for fear. She careened feet first toward the huge bonfire. Then skirted toward the six pall bearers who surrounded Sam's post.

I wish I was in Dixie, Hooray! Hooray!
In Dixie Land, I'll take my stand

The element of surprise could not have worked better as she landed hard as nails knocking two of the six robed *klansmen* out of the way with her feet. The other four scattered confused as if a grenade had gone off or sasquatch had attacked them from woods.

The nearby sopranos at the microphone looked at each other, shrugged and kept singing as it was there first round-up none of them knowing if acrobatic cat burglars were part of the was pomp or circumstance.

To live and die in Dixie

Partially unbound Sam fell to the ground with a thud then looked up at her eyes wide in surprise.

Look Away, away, away down south in Dixie

"Holy mackerel Eunice!" He shouted.

Away, away, away down...

"Listen Sam, I'll be nicer to you when we're out of here okay? Turning you over NOW!" she had full control of her faculties and there was no time to explain.

She rolled him on his side slicing through a thick rope with four scores of her cat burglar exacto blade. She had robot efficiency focused on her mission to save Sam and get them the *fuck* out of there.

One Mississippi; two Mississippi; three Mississippi... Eunice counted in her head.

The banjos kept twanging along as the singers kept singing. The crowd was chaotic with boos and shouts of obscenity while others appeared intoxicated by the excitement. Most watchers hadn't noticed cat burglar Eunice flying down her fox zip and hotly anticipated Sam's lynching finale.

Six Mississippi; seven Mississippi...

The grand wizard sat frozen faced at the unexpected turn of events, "Wallace, Wallace boy..." he turned and barked, grabbing hold of another members attention, "Did you pay Sheriff Griffiths his fee like you were as told?" he demanded pointing at the captured Sam Hood untethered on the ground along with others.

"Yessir, I did to. *Holy Christ,*" Wallace said, standing up at the sight of events on the podium.

Eunice was *gobsmacked* to see the elusive black *klansman* at Sam's side. Faith told her to stay on point. Could be a game-changing distraction. She kept to the countdown.

Eight Mississippi;

For all she knew nothing would happen at the count of ten but Dougie had made it imperative she count this way, "Eunice we *must* be synchronized. When you've made physical contact with Sam the riggers will adjust their zips. You need to count with Mississippi's in between. Eunice it is critical okay?" Dougie said, in earnest then demonstrating with his firm voice.

nine Mississippi; ten Mississippi…

On second eleven she heard the sound of metal skidding down from above as Dougie barreled down on a fresh zip line. The riggers had fashioned a massive shark net set with springs to spread out and encompass the grand wizard and those within range of the web.

At the same time, two of Dougie's men in masks with *fucked-up* eyeholes snuck to the gold spectator seats from the woods. Audible gasps were heard from stunned as the masks of high ranking leaders were yanked up and off revealing their identities. Eunice wouldn't recognize them but imagined it would be quite a shock or delight to find out a judge, teacher or real estate agent was high ranking member *klan*.

You just never know who is klan!

She found out the *Mississippi countdown* meant a lot for Dougie's plan to work. He had gotten a rough copy of the round-up site coordinates so could estimate where the Dixie South leaders would be seated. His men on the ground had been given detailed instructions, "You boys do your best to put as many of 'em leaders into the net. It's easy, they got colored stripes!"

Like a choreographed tango Dougie unhitched his zip line clip, sidestepped the shark net and yanked twice on his line. The signal triggered the net to enclose around the still masked grand wizard and three unmasked *klansmen*.

The huge net sprung and closed so the grand wizard and *klan* leaders were trapped in such fine netting; the more they struggled to escape the more tangled they became.

The four captives were hoisted half-way up and left dangling in the air like a disco ball over an afterhours rave.

The singers stopped singing. The banjo kept playing.

Without sound system announcements to direct the crowd they didn't know which way to turn. Some ran around hysterical feeling trapped within the area around the fire pit as if pine forest was an invisible force field. While others grew weary and many had dispersed.

Without the *spectacle* folks began questioning why they were there or if they even hated African, Hispanic, European, Asian, Caucasian, homosexual, or trans people at all. Later all would agree never before had an audience witnessed such a show.

Eventually Eunice grabbed the microphone, "My name is Eunice Johnston. I am a fugitive wanted by the FBI. You might have heard of me from Montgomery's school shooting massacre last year. I am here to turn myself in to authorities. I stayed in hiding so my daddy would get out of prison. My daddy is African American. My mother is white…I can't change your mind but take it from me, living a lie for other people or hiding a secret is a slow death. I will never do it again. You all know this here is wrong. I suggest you make your confessions when the police arrive or you scram right now," her voice was hoarse from exhaustion.

Sirens grew louder and a hint of blue and red glow could be seen coming through the forests curtain of darkness. The dwindling fire made for mood light on the held captives dangling in the *Aliens* pod.

By the time authorities arrived there were no signs of Dougie or his men, only nets and pulleys in the trees that could very well have been used by *klan*.

Eunice looked to the spectator area where Sam chatted with a hoodless white-robed black man. She had no idea what that was about but was sure she'd find out from him later.

You've been gone a long time Eunice.

CNN News: Lone Wolf Vigilantism

[show opens with quote on screen]

A rioter with a Molotov cocktail in his hands is not fighting for civil rights any more than a *klansman* with a sheet on his back and mask on his face. They are both more or less what the law declares them: lawbreakers, destroyers of constitutional rights and liberties and ultimately destroyers of a free America. (13)

- Lyndon B Johnson

"I'm Anderson Cooper. Tonight we take a look at lone wolf vigilantes. These criminals, yet superheroes to many, illegally plan and execute justice on behalf of everyday Americans. From what we know Eunice Johnston either acted alone or had help through a network of like-minded individuals who may or may not have known or been complicit with aiding and abetting a felony."

"With 18 charges now laid against her including coercion, conspiracy, drug trafficking, aiding-abetting and disorderly conduct, we take a look at how it all started. Roll the tape."

[A Documentary-style film shows highlights with photos, news clips and home movies from Curtis and Martha Johnston's time in Harlem; associating with Black Panthers and radicals including Malcolm X, circa 1970.

Highlights of Montgomery affiliations with the First Baptist church and Angela Davis in the 1980s.

A 19 year old Eunice Johnston at large wanted by the FBI for the better part of a year.

Clips of her in court wearing an orange jumpsuit like her father. Photographs from her cell where she stands trial on 18 charges.]

Martha Johnston Scrapbook files: News Clippings

"Eunice Johnston has just about singlehandedly infiltrated and shut down South Dixie, a major *klan* rally and top secret location only known to the upper echelons of the organization." - ABC News reporter.

[Video clip]

"Sure I'm a racist but mainly because them folk are always playing victim, taking our jobs and an all-around nuisance. I ain't never wanted to hurt a living soul. What I saw that night I will never forget. They were burning bodies alive on a trapeze thing."

– Admitted racist former *klan* member

"It's jaw dropping how this kid from a *shithole* in Montgomery has ripped the lid off the never-before-known *klan* rituals including kidnapping and murdering transient drug addicts. You can't even say simply murder. This is modern lynching!" - Birmingham resident.

[Video clip]

You know I can live and let live now as long as none of that is ever done to another American. I'll never forget those screams. They weren't real.

– Admitted racist former *klan* member

"With speculation that jury deliberations will be quick, the Eunice Johnston trial has captured the worlds attention for months. For once it seems humanity could take precedent and public opinion seems to have shifted from."

- WSFA-12 News reporter.

[Video clip]

"To have a more compassionate understanding of walking in someone else's shoes is what I want for my kids.

– Crying, white privileged woman

Courthouse Drama

Eunice Johnston's court case played out with unexpected public sympathy, perhaps in part due to her being the key player, in uncovering the Huntsville atrocities. Thousands of mobilized high school students swarmed Montgomery to await the verdict.

Local media and major national outlets supplied glamorous reporters, news crews and satellite dishes, which dotted Lawrence street in front of the courthouse. Media had been covering the Johnston story ever since the massacre even during the months she had been a fugitive. Being first to publish a detailed report showcasing the smart, beautiful Eunice Johnston, along with the sense of closure to the story with the verdict would be considered a huge 'get.' Surely, she would have her pick of book and movie deals.

As a show of support the newly formed activist group, *Montgomery Together,* had set up audio of an Angela Davis' interview which emitted gently from loudspeakers on a continuous loop.

[Angela Davis heard over loudspeaker]

I grew up in Birmingham, Alabama. Some very, very good friends of mine were killed by bombs, bombs that were planted by racists. I remember, from the time I was very small, I remember the sounds of bombs exploding across the street. Our house shaking. I remember my father having to have guns at his disposal at all times, because of the fact that, at any moment, somewhere in --- we might expect to be attacked... [14]

Todd Sheppard had rounded up a fine collection of gay activists and drag queens who descended from Miami and New Orleans. Whatever the verdict, resistors were bound to enjoy a groundswell of positive press for weeks to come. The vibe was like a big old fashioned coming out party for those who had ever felt persecuted!

Verdict predictions ran wild. The case against Eunice Johnston had been mostly circumstantial, except for one surprise, eyewitness testimony. Audiotape was discovered putting Eunice at the Vineyard commiserating with Manny G, the 7 foot tall, blond gang leader with gold teeth. This was also Terrence Battle's cousin. Rumors circulated that Eunice could be unduly punished for the sins of her who was still awaiting his own trial.

[Angela Davis heard over loudspeaker]

...and then, after that, in my neighborhood, all the men organized themselves into armed patrol. They had to take their guns and patrol our community every night because they did not want that to happen again. And that's why, when someone asks me about violence, I just find it incredible, because what it means is that the person who's asking that question has absolutely no idea what black people have gone through. [14]

The unspeakable acts of the *klan* even silenced their own membership, which manifested in a surprising reversal.

The media picked up on a former *klan* member's costume that caused a sensation. The Georgia woman's white costume was spray painted with a large red "no" symbol *a la* smoking, whilst holding a blood-stained *klan* mask at her side appearing as if beheaded.

By the next afternoon, there were dozens of unmasked *klanfolk* dressed just like her. Hour by hour people arrived dressed in homemade bed sheet costumes with red "no" symbols mimicking the look.

It caused a media frenzy. Video footage flashed around the world putting Montgomery, Alabama on the map with it's motley crew of anti-*klan* black folk, white folk, Indian folk, gay folk, trans, young, old, disabled. Red and black paint symbols made their way to foreheads as dots and smudges symbolic of Hindu chakra or Christian Ash Wednesday. There was nothing like seeing garish drag versions of *Mariah* and *Whitney* wearing anti-*klan* garb to make a statement.

In anticipation of the verdict, organizers had secured Montgomery's Riverfront Park for a celebration concert. The event was made possible by the newly formed *Montgomery Together,* the unity group aimed at making equal and civil rights top priority. It aimed to be the biggest such event since the Harlem Festival.

Rock icon *Prince* sent word his *Jam of Year World Tour* would make a special stop at Riverfront Park, along with an entourage of his famous Minneapolis musicians. In solidarity with *Free Eunice,* Prince protégé's were set to perform together.

"This is not only black power, this is equal rights in America. Enough is enough," read the statement from Prince's camp.

ೞೞೞ

Meanwhile at First Baptist Choir rehearsal, ladies separated fact from fiction just as they had done every week for decades:

"That Eunice'll go to hell in a hand basket. You know how rough them gals get in prison! Lawd have mercy on her," Allison said.

"Jesus, Mary and Joseph! She's very light skinned, so I doubt that very much. She'll probably be made a hero, a white girl saves the day again!" Charlotte said.

"She always identified with her black side. I guess a criminal record will give her street cred now," Mavis said.

"Sure thing Miss triple cream, light sugar. I do swear I picked her getting off Scott free, due to that pretty smile of hers," Peggy Ann said.

"First of all, I don't think facts had anything to do with it. I think it was her color. She is white so that's how she'll get off..." Charlotte said.

"They say it's because her daddy is well connected..." Charlotte said.

"Well that's pure nonsense. Curtis wouldn't hurt a fly...." Mavis said.

"Now ladies that's enough. We sound like a bunch of chatterboxes," Sofia said, looking guilt-ridden for adding to the swirl of gossip. "I betcha Curtis'll be fit to be tied, if he don't get a chance to testify at trial. He had two strikes against him already, which is why they're holding him in prison..." Sofia said.

"I'm worried about ole Martha, she ain't well ya know..." Marjorie said.

"Marjorie I'm sitting right here, aren't I?" Martha said.

"Oh Dear, I didn't see you slip in the door dear. You're as light as a feather," Marjorie said, ignoring the slight.

"Sam says he now knows first-hand, what meth and crack can do to someone," Sofia said, changing the subject.

"Was he talking about Rory? I don't even get what these kids are on. Back in my day, we called it reefer madness," Margaret said.

"Yes, it was Rory," Sofia hung her head. "He says Rory don't ever want to come back home. That he's as good as lost," Sofia said.

Sam walked into the First Baptist rehearsal, carrying a bankers box, "What was that I said Mama?" he asked.

"Son. What on earth are you doing in here? I'm so happy to see you," Sofia said.

"A few errands for the minister," Sam said. "I heard some singing going on in here but now I can hear some hens chattering too. Tell me what real news!" he smiled wide.

"We were just talking about Rory and those terrible drugs. The poor thing. But I still don't get how one of our sons woke up and joined the *klan*. High as a kite or not," Marjorie said.

"I'm not sure either Marjorie. Rory told me when he put on the historical robe he felt magical, instantly surrounded by attention and fellowship. Maybe like being part of the choir," Sam said.

"Sam! That's no comparison and you know it. We ain't high on anything 'cept life!" Marjorie said.

"I asked him how he could spend time hunting and fishing with them. He said there was no difference between them and all the other whites around here?" Sam said.

"Sam, don't they lay that stuff on pretty thick like brainwashing. I hear there's more *klan* meetings and rehearsals, than a southern white wedding," Charlotte said.

"Rory said it's not as crazy as it seems. They only lay it on thick, when they have reporters or the public's attention. He says they just stand around socializing in between. He says some of them are just there for the free stuff," Sam said.

"And you believed him?" Marjorie asked.

"I dunno. The way he described them as coming from broken homes, I guess it sounded plausible. In other words, the *klan* acts as their family to compensate for the love they never got at home," Sam said.

"It makes me sick to my stomach," Charlotte said.

"Rory saved Sam's life, didn't he Son?" Sofia told the others.

"What do you mean?" Marjorie asked.

"You think them boys really wanted to go after a white guy more than a black guy? They would have lynched me, if Rory hadn't suggested they go after Todd. He warned them Todd could have AIDs. That's wrong of course. He doesn't but that made them stop their attack," Sam said.

"Alright ladies, I've got to run. It was a pleasure catching up on the day's real news with you all," he kissed Sofia on the forehead. "Try not to worry. We got Rory checked into Meadhaven rehab for a full week which is a good start," Sam said.

 C3 C3 C3

By trial decision day the celebratory unification up to that point had grown restless for a verdict. As fatigue grew faith in justice waned. Protestors became confused about what was true amid the sensationalized stories.

Finally it was announced, the resolution verdict would come at 4:00 p.m.

"Would the defendant please rise? The court will now hear the verdict," the judge said.

There was silence on the courthouse steps as viewers and media alike watched the televised broadcast on four monitors.

"Yes, your honor, we have," the jury foreperson said.

"Will the defendant, Eunice Johnston please rise? Will the foreperson please stand and read the jury's verdict?" the judge asked.

"We will your honor," the jury foreperson said.

"Please proceed," he said.

"On the count of coercion and conspiracy we the jury find the defendant, Eunice Johnston guilty as charged," the jury foreperson proceeded to reading the verdict on the eighteen counts.

The crowd outside were unified in a disappointed groan, followed by audible reactions of anger.

"On the count of drug trafficking we the jury find the defendant Eunice Johnston guilty as charged," the jury foreperson said.

Outside the crowd had become increasingly unruly.

"On the count of voluntary manslaughter we the jury find the defendant, Eunice Johnston guil…" The monitor connection cut off. All monitors turned to static for several moments and faded to black.

With the lost feed, the crowd went absolutely berserk. People screamed obscenities at the screens, cell phones rang for no reason, car alarms sounded and car horns beeped. There was the sound of possible gunshots police sirens in the distance.

They had heard three out of eighteen guilty decisions so far. Reporters looked just as confused as the supporters.

Seventeen minutes passed until the television monitors fluttered back on. The crowd in the immediate vicinity were silent, so they didn't miss anything. The judge's close up talking head appeared on screen.

"Ladies and gentlemen. As per the jury, Eunice Johnston has been found guilty on all counts," the judge turned to Eunice seated in the court, "However, Ms. Johnston the court of Alabama state has been informed by the highest authority, The President of the United States that based on the fact you and Sam Hood have, in effect, and I quote the president, 'taken down the South Dixie arm of the *klan,*' you have been granted clemency," the judge said.

The camera remained on Eunice who had tears welled up in her eyes and quivering lips.

The crowd outside remained surprisingly quiet and reflective, perhaps shocked that justice had been served in the end

Eunice Johnston took a dozen key members of the South Dixie *klan* down, some literally by way of shark net and others by way of their fear and resignation from the organization. Losing the most powerful faction of South Dixie was enough to topple the entire North American branch of the *klan* forever.

Give it to Me

Sam and Eunice lay in bed chatting. The friction, anger and resentment between them seemed to be gone. "I'm not good at reading between the lines or interpreting meanings from non-verbal stuff. I can be a big dummy Eunice but I'd like to be your big dummy if you'll let me," Sam said.

"Being away has really opened my eyes. There were times I felt these funky vibrations all over my body. Physical ones that made me feel outside myself! It's hard to explain right now but I'll share them with you one day. I guess my point is I've been having sensations and feelings I've never had before," Eunice said.

"I've already noticed," he said.

"I didn't think of home while I was away. Well not that much anyway. I was a complete woman living each day as a regular Memphis citizen. I will say I am sorry I didn't tell you I was having memory gaps. I understand them better now. It's not really memory, it's more like a preference for horse blinders. Purposeful distraction or something," she said, holding his gaze as she spoke.

"Eunice I understand why you didn't tell me you were having memory gaps. I did a lot of things anyone would want to forget. I'm guilty of treating you terribly. By denying your memory gaps I assumed you were purposely lying and pushing me away," he said.

When she held his hand she got a mild stomach cramp. She figured it was a physical symptom of loving him, "I learned from Kavi, that guru in Tennessee that I had to think in baby steps. Put the training wheels on to ride my bike. I'll always need to work on staying in the present moment with you and facing uncomfortable things head on," she said. She marveled in her ability to feel but also put them into words.

"Okay. Maybe I seemed more upset than I was. I'm so relieved you are here beside me. I never once thought you were dead. I didn't know how it would play out but I knew you'd come back to me," he said.

It hadn't crossed her mind being gone hurt him so much. She thought no one could really love her.

"You must find it funny I don't show a wide range of emotion. At least now I'll recognize when I go numb. The *when* is something I can work on. The *why* may never be solved," she said.

"Eunice I never wanted someone with wide ranging emotions so there's no pressure. I just wanted to know how to communicate and understand how you feel sometimes. I won't push for feelings but I ask you to remember one thing. I want to get to know you," he said.

"I swear I've been through a portal to my insides. Maybe it's true what every self-help book says, we all carry childhood baggage. The bottom line is I'm no angel and I took you for granted. I've been a cold uncaring person on the outside but I've discovered I'm more sensitive than I thought inside. All this rambling to say, I do love you Sam. You're the sweetest guy I've ever known!" Eunice said.

"Okay then believe that I love you too. It's only fair you should believe it. You are worth all of my love. Connection is love," Sam said.

Reunited she felt confident they would find common ground in similarities, rather than differences this time around. Maybe they were soul mates each with a protective fortress around them. It was high time to amalgamate the house. It was time to roll one house up the hill and tether it to the other house. It was time connect the floors and ceilings without perfection even if they weren't aligned. They could build mini staircases to bridge the house together.

This is no ordinary love.
This house is extraordinary.
Sam and Eunice together forever.

EPILOGUE

Internet Diagnosis

When Sam and Eunice made a couple's counseling appointment Dr. Lynch suggested they each see him separately, to check in with him before seeing him together.

"You have no idea where I've been Dr. Lynch. It was glorious and terrible at the same time!" Eunice said.

"Well I have some idea Eunice, I do own a TV," he smiled.

"It sounds like you've learned a lot about yourself," Lynch said.

"What can I tell you? There's so much. I feel alive. I can feel things I've never felt before," Eunice said. She felt her eyes welling up. She couldn't remember what she felt like back then but knew she'd been an entirely different person. Was that her or was that Nina? Had Nina been with her all along and taken a backseat? If so, where was she now?

Nina was a wild girl but she had some enviable qualities and the best of Nina was accessible when Eunice needed her. Either way, Eunice felt like a survivor, beautiful inside and out. *It's okay to let them see you sweat and ask for help!*

Later Sam joined them in Lynch's office. He reeked of Legend cologne. She'd never forget that scent for as long as she lived.

"Eunice, you may have found it scary to go to couples counseling so I asked Dr. Lynch to meet us without his psychologist badge," Sam said.

"What do you mean? It's okay Sam. I can handle it," she said. She hadn't felt the usual anxiety in coming to his office.

"Eunice I'm going to share a compatibility profile in a general sense. As Sam said, it's off the record. We can call it a casual intake session, where I first meet the couple and determine if I'm the best fit. Are you alright if we indulge in Sam's request?" he asked.

"Eunice I wanted to keep the session light so Dr. Lynch will walk us through a compatibility profile for our animal protectors. It's from the internet," Sam said.

"Sure, it sounds wacky but it'll be fun," she said. She rolled with it but her red flags of mistrust went up. It was sweet he wanted to surprise her.

Lynch began reading a report from his computer screen, "The two of you are more or less at an equal level of similarity and difference. You both prefer a routine way of life and have a strong sense of responsibility. And you each differ in your emotion and personal impulses. You may be compatible if each of you can learn to adjust and adapt," Dr. Lynch said.

Eunice agreed with it. She was at ease in Dr. Lynch's office. Her mind wandered to her instinctual inner critic who would cloud her head in skepticism. Maybe that was Nina or maybe that was Eunice. It didn't matter anymore.

"Your compatibility lies in being responsible people. That's your best chance for survival. Eunice, for all your perfectionism you are motivated by a strong sense of commitment to your goals…"

Sam distracted her by fiddling with something in his pocket as if he had an itch or something. She pat his arm so he wouldn't distract Dr. Lynch from what had turned out to be an overlong monologue. *These friggin' shrinks!*

"and Sam, in a similar vein you feel deeply responsible for people under your care. Together you have the strongest protective instincts among all the animal signs. In fact Sam would go so far as sacrificing his dreams when motivated by love.

"Animal signs, as in horoscopes? That's funny when I was away I used a jaguar to help me through some sticky situations. Then Sam told me about his wolf, you named it Frank right? I guess the jag and the wolf are together now!" Eunice said.

"That's such a romantic way to look at it," Sam said, poking her shoulder laughing.

She laughed too. As if she had ever thought about cute animals being in love before. Like those grade school anonymous valentine's cards the kids left on each other's desks. "Will you be my valentine, Sam?" she asked.

"Maybe I will," he said.

Dr. Lynch stared through them, perhaps wondering if he should have chicken or fish for dinner. He continued reading from his compatibility report, "Since both of you are conscious about the value of responsibility, the relationship you forge will be grounded in a strong sense of commitment. There I'm done over analyzing you," Dr. Lynch said, amused by his own joke.

Sam had dropped to one knee right beside her.

"What the heck are you doing?" Eunice asked.

"Eunice will you do me the honor of being my wife?" he asked. His expression perfectly neutral and still.

She burst out laughing, so hard and deep she thought she wouldn't be able to stop. Tears began streaming down her face as she laughed and felt so happy inside. She didn't see any this coming.

Sam and Dr. Lynch each had their mouths hanging open in surprise.

"Sam I never thought you'd ask! YES I will. I can't wait for you to be my husband," she pulled him close for a hug and inhaled his cologne.

Sam and Eunice left Dr. Lynch's office hand in hand, "Now that's one crazy couple of kids!" David said to himself.

October 25, 2018

REFERENCES

1. https://www.washingtonpost.com/news/the-fix/wp/2015/02/09/alabama-was-a-final-holdout-on-desegregation-and-interracial-marriage-it-could-happen-again-on-gay-marriage/?utm_term=.5ceea82ad4ed
2. https://www.washingtonpost.com/local/social-issues/after-40-years-priest-who-used-to-be-in-the-kkk-finally-apologized-to-couple-he-targeted-in-cross-burning/2017/12/08/b2a90f1a-dc3c-11e7-b1a8-62589434a581_story.html?utm_term=.8c97b8f0b4d1
3. https://en.wikipedia.org/wiki/Earl_Warren
4. https://en.wikipedia.org/wiki/Loving_v._Virginia
5. https://littlenine.weebly.com/2468-we-aint-gonna-integrate.html
6. https://www.nps.gov/malu/learn/education/jim_crow_laws.htm
7. https://books.google.com/books?hl=en&lr=&id=1jfAhghdH7MC&oi=fnd&pg=PR9&dq=Inner+city+desperation+has+forced+groups+&ots=u-CqU1wqeX&sig=CVI8mF1huwXhUt_9EuIXhzSNqwM#v=onepage&q&f=false
8. https://www.fbi.gov/investigate/violent-crime/gangs/violent-gang-task-forces
9. https://en.wikipedia.org/wiki/Lynching
10. https://en.wikipedia.org/wiki/Emmett_Till
11. http://www.american-pictures.com/english/racism/kkk-us-2.htm
12. https://en.wikipedia.org/wiki/Internalized_oppression
13. https://www.quotes.net/quote/226
14. https://search.alexanderstreet.com/preview/work/bibliographic_entity%7Cvideo_work%7C2787221?ssotoken=anonymous
15. http://www.pbs.org/wnet/need-to-know/environment/the-legacy-of-robert-moses/16018/

Father William Aitcheson; Martin Luther King Jr.; Chief Justice Warren; Alabama: Neil Young; Sweet Home Alabama Songwriters: Edward C. King / Gary Robert Rossington / Ronnie Van Zant; Musicology camp, Mike Watts, @musicology_smithtown; Alice Walker for Harpo and Sofia; David Lynch

22070811R00212

Made in the USA
San Bernardino, CA
14 January 2019